CURSES! FOILED AGAIN

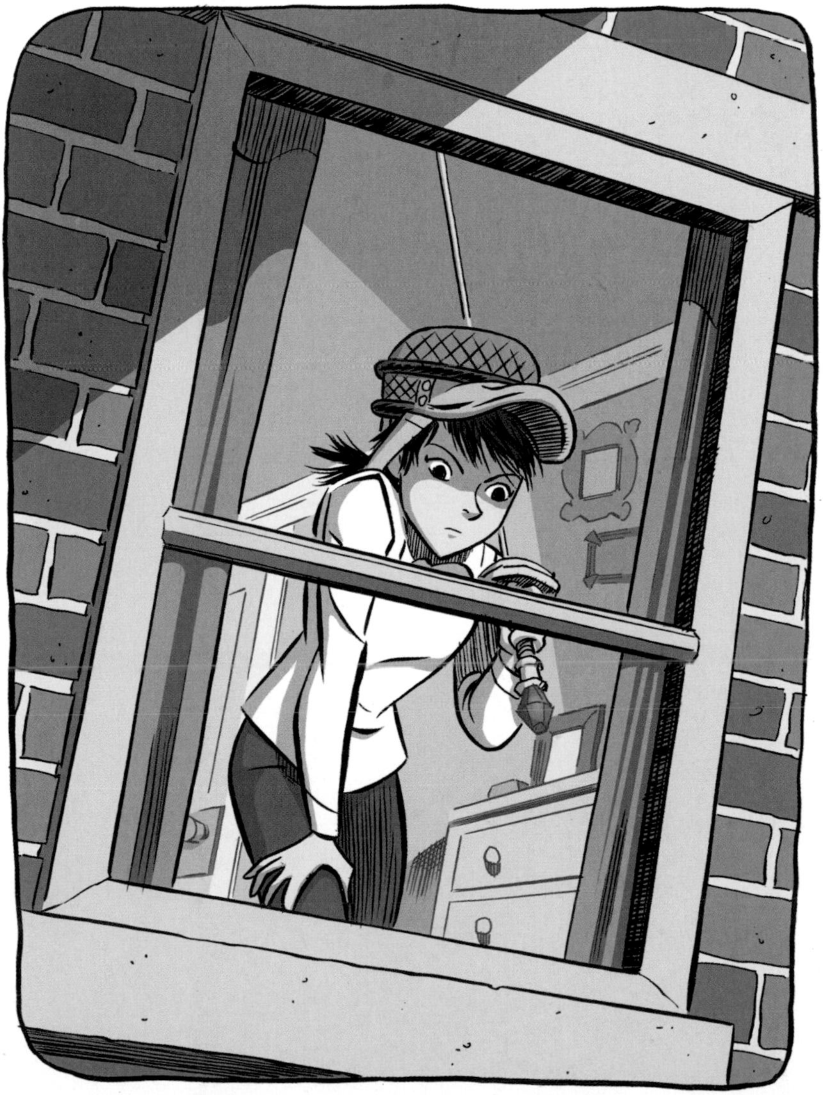

CURSES!
FOILED
AGAIN

Written by
JANE YOLEN

Art by
MIKE CAVALLARO

:01
First Second
NEW YORK

PREVIOUSLY . . .

Aliera Carstairs thought she had it all figured out.

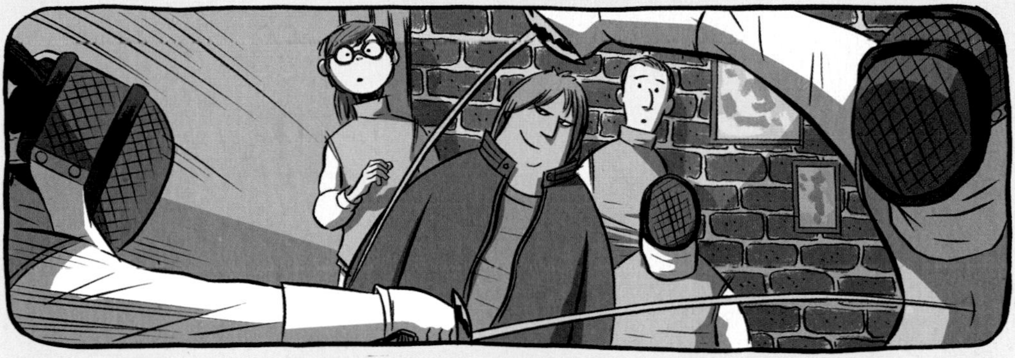

She didn't fit in at high school or in the fencing studio.
But she knew who she was.
A smart, lonely girl with a singular talent for swordplay.

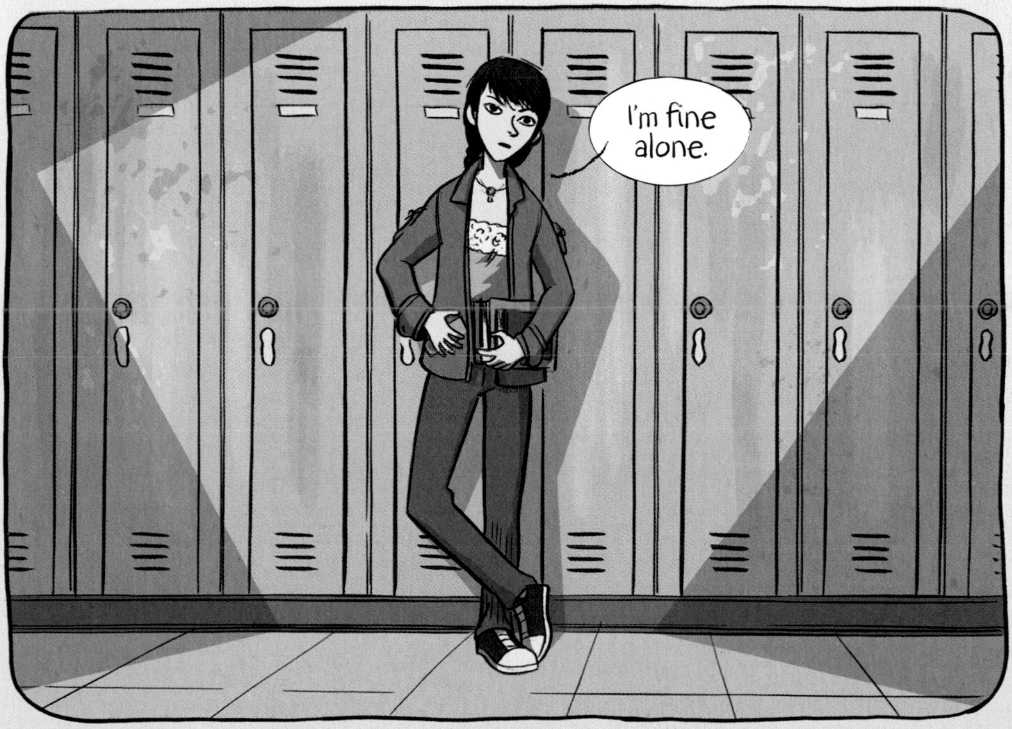
I'm fine alone.

Aliera knew who Avery Castle was, too.
A handsome, popular jock
with a twisted sense of humor.

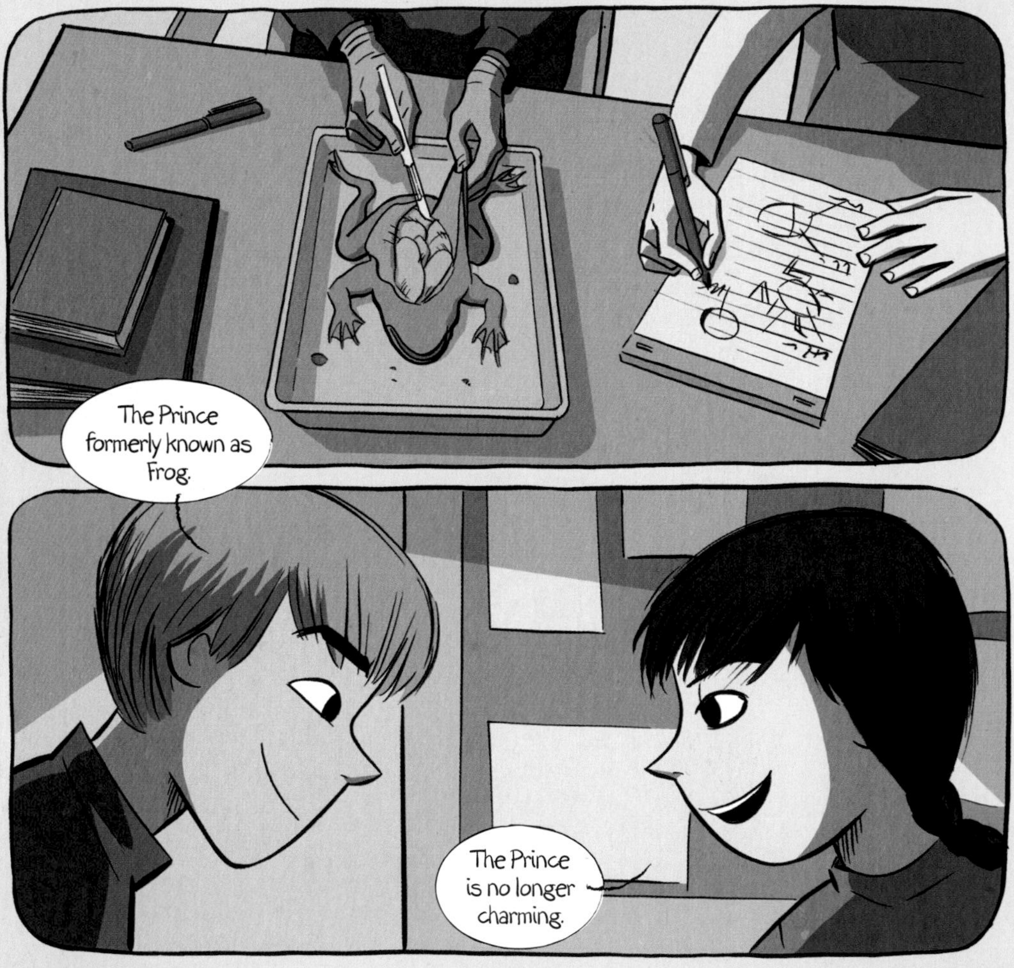
The Prince formerly known as Frog.
The Prince is no longer charming.

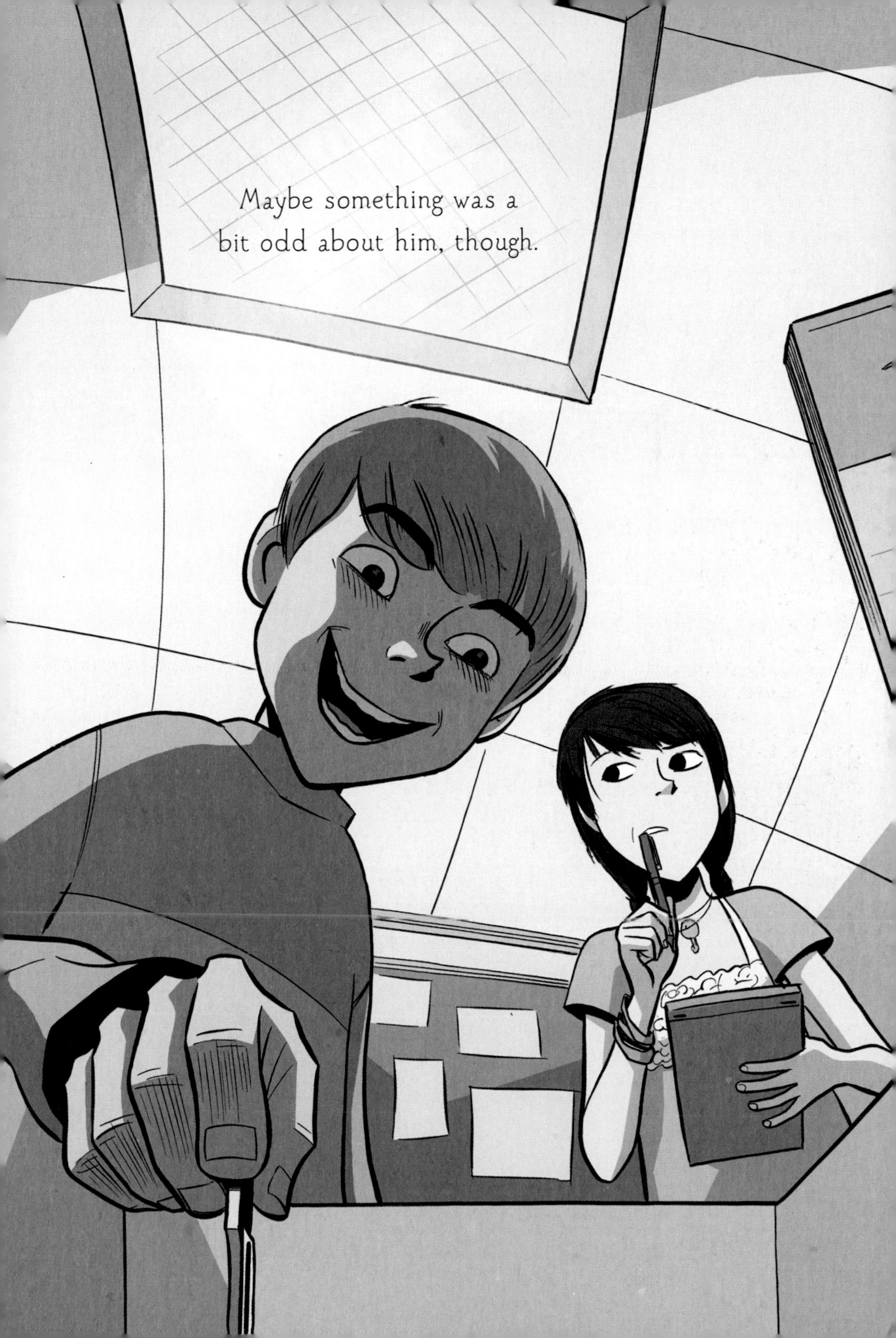
Maybe something was a bit odd about him, though.

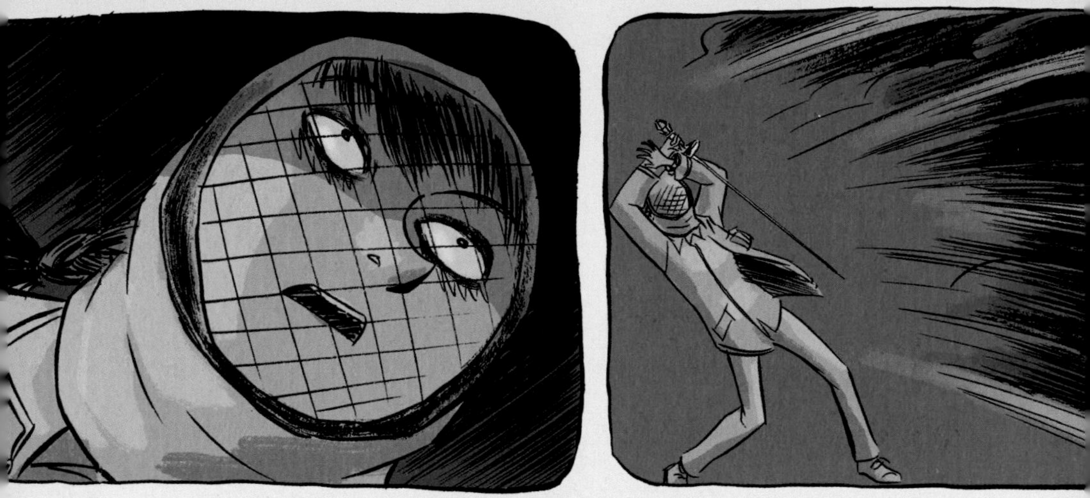

Maybe everything Aliera thought she knew . . . was wrong.

She wasn't just a talented fencer.

Avery wasn't just a pretty boy.

And the world was not a safe place.

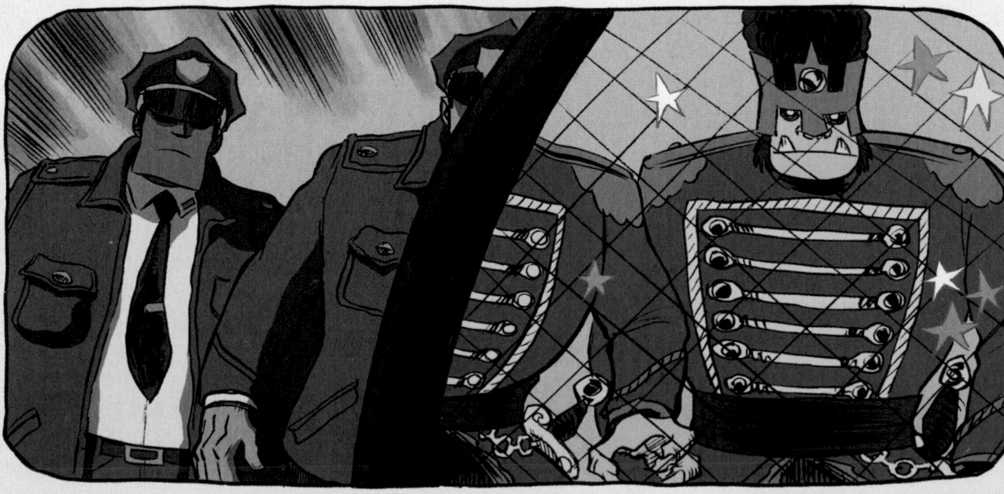

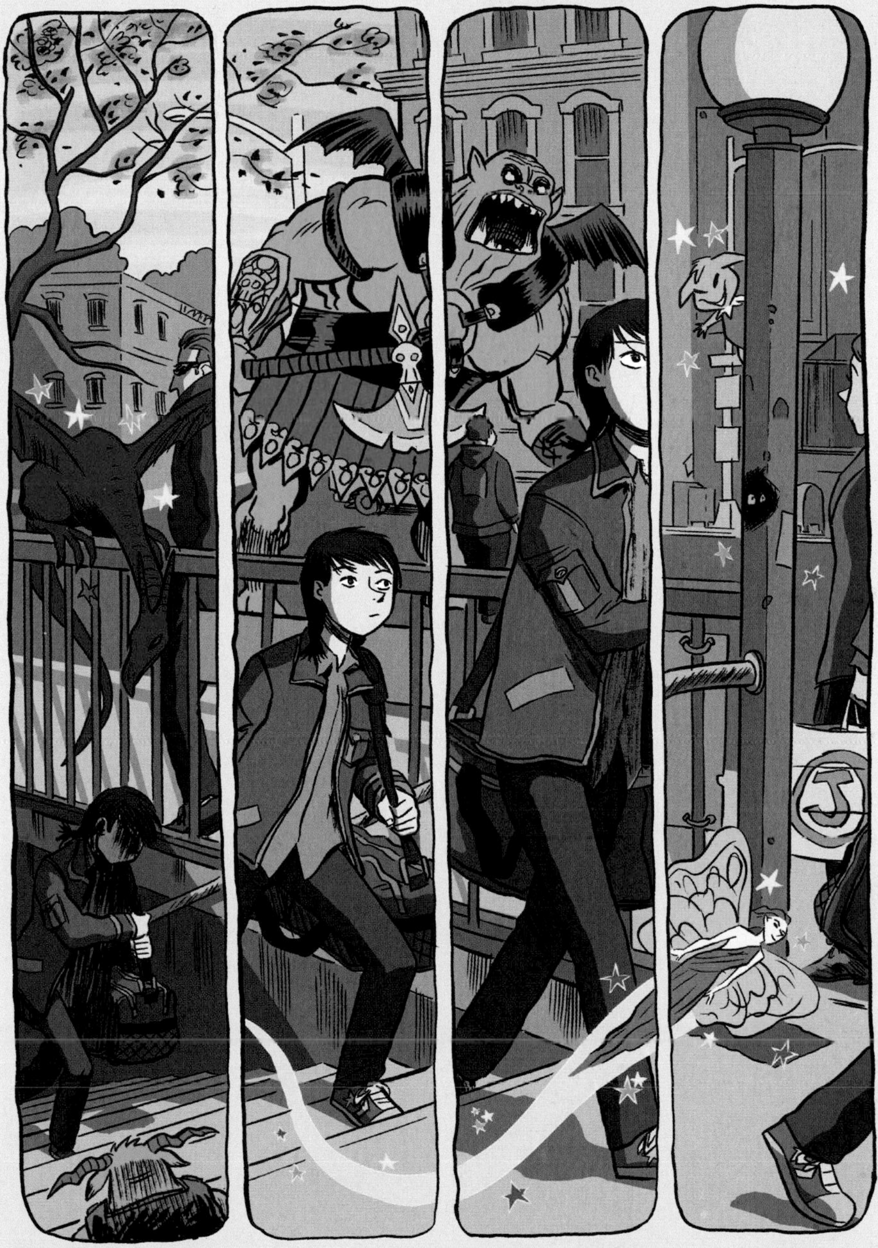

Today, Aliera's had a little time to get used to being the Defender of Faerie. To having a troll pledged to defend her life. To balancing the mundane world with the mystical.

But she's about to have the carpet
yanked out from under her feet again . . .

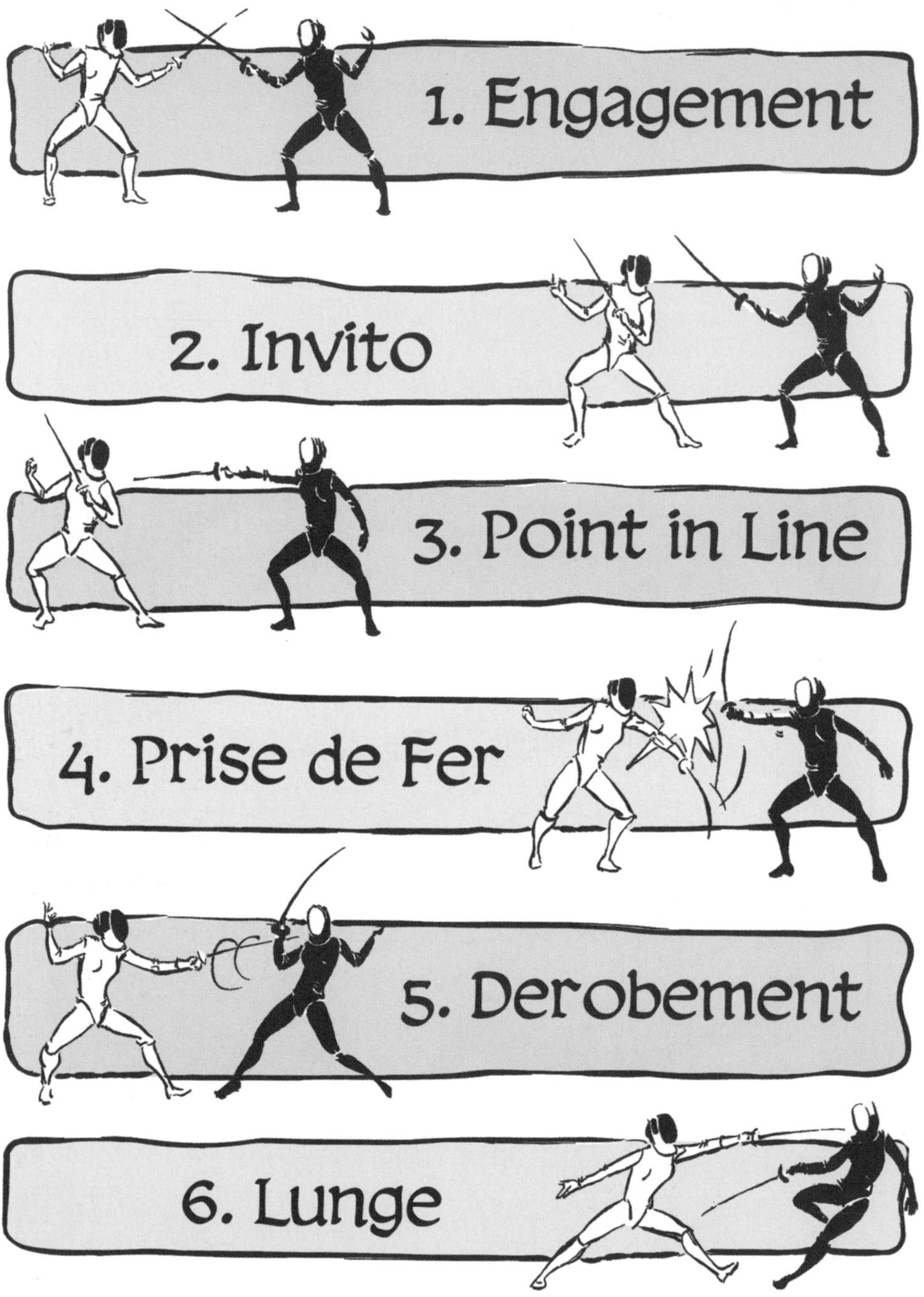
1. Engagement
2. Invito
3. Point in Line
4. Prise de Fer
5. Derobement
6. Lunge

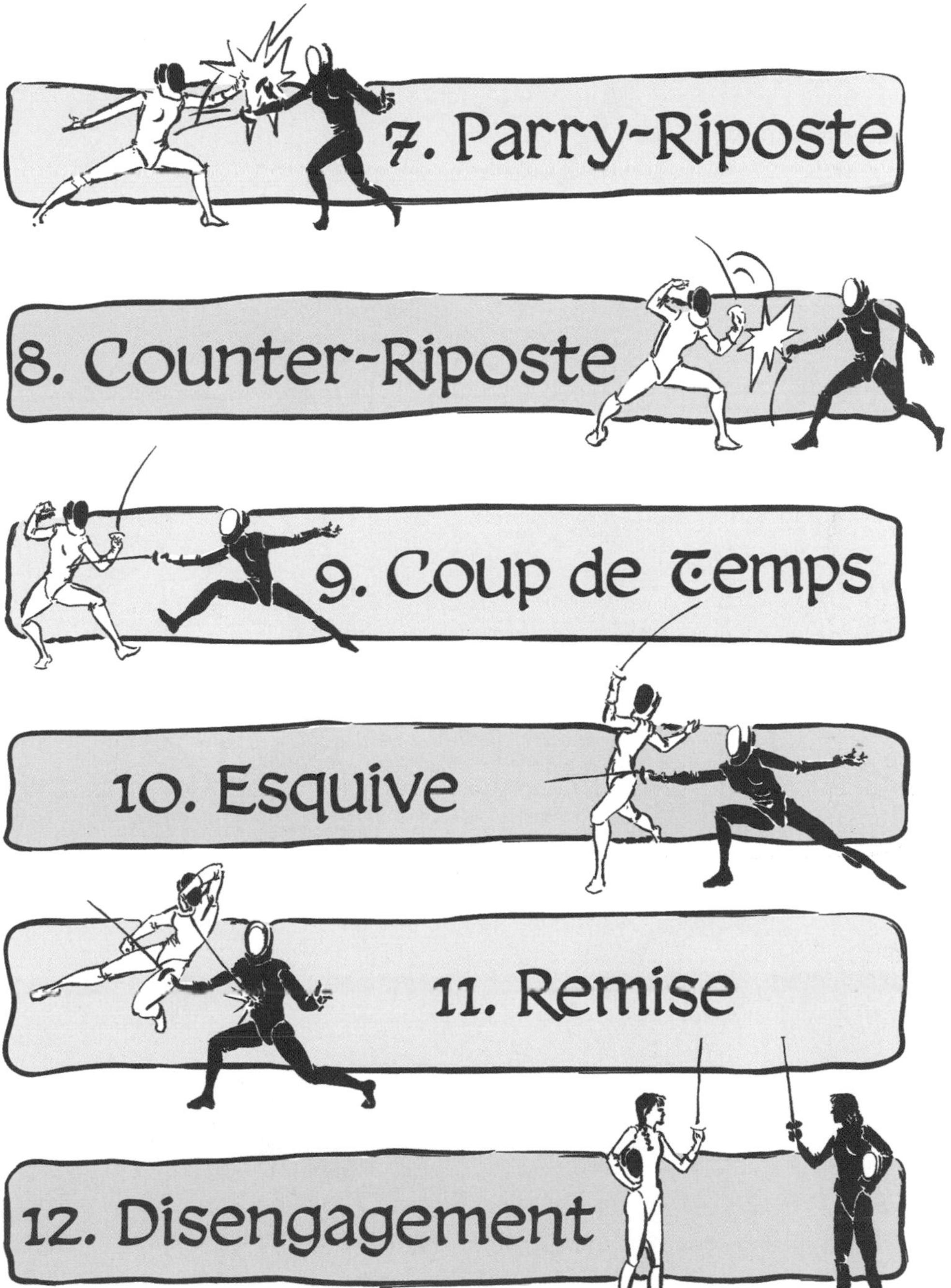
7. Parry-Riposte
8. Counter-Riposte
9. Coup de Temps
10. Esquive
11. Remise
12. Disengagement

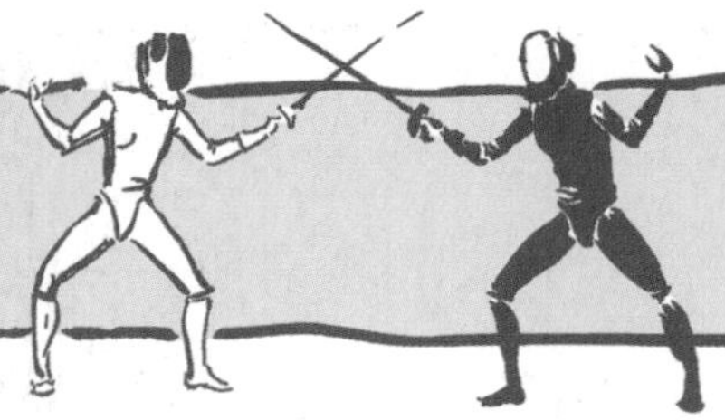

1. Engagement

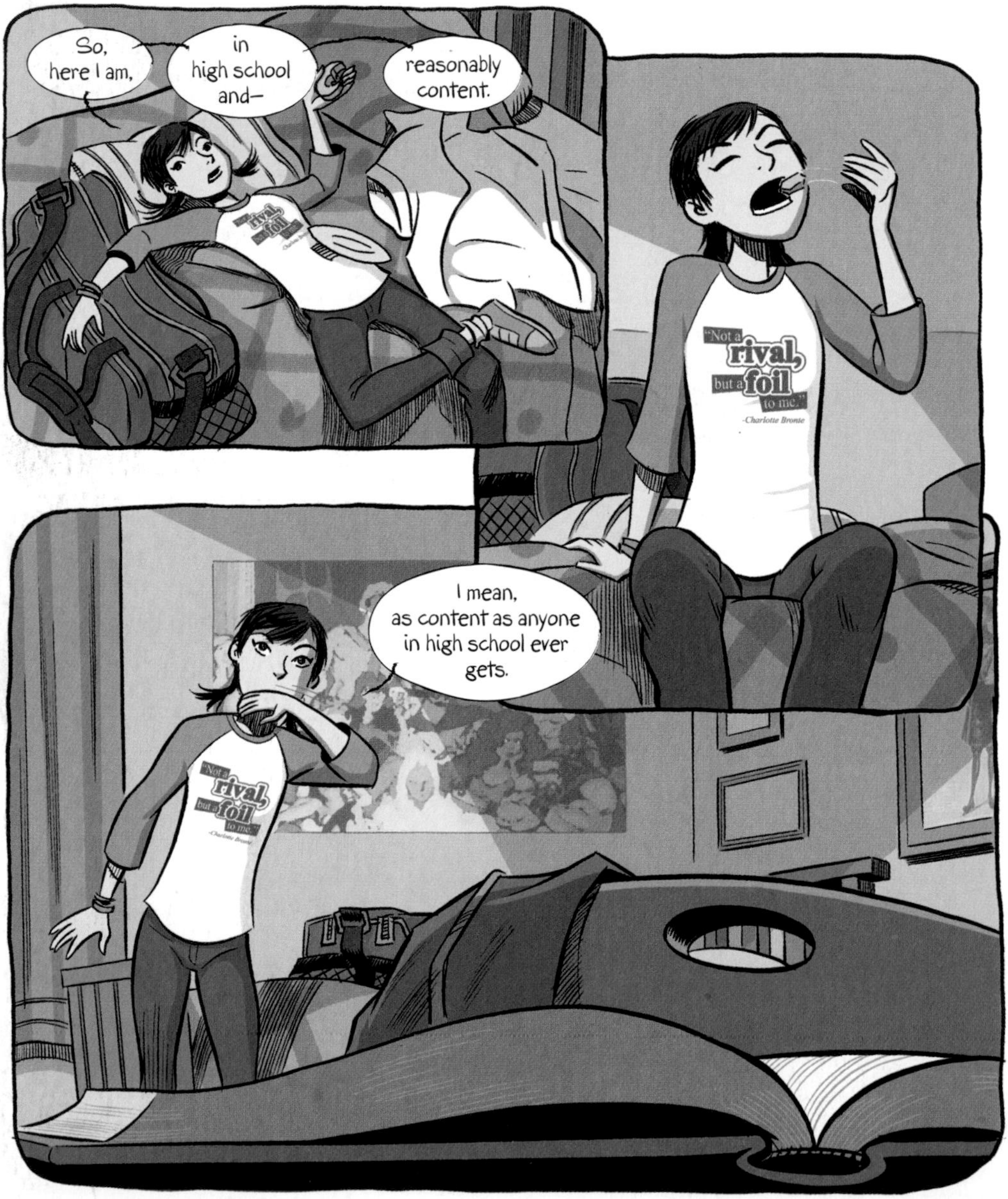
So, here I am,
in high school and–
reasonably content.
"Not a rival, but a foil to me."
-Charlotte Bronte
I mean, as content as anyone in high school ever gets.

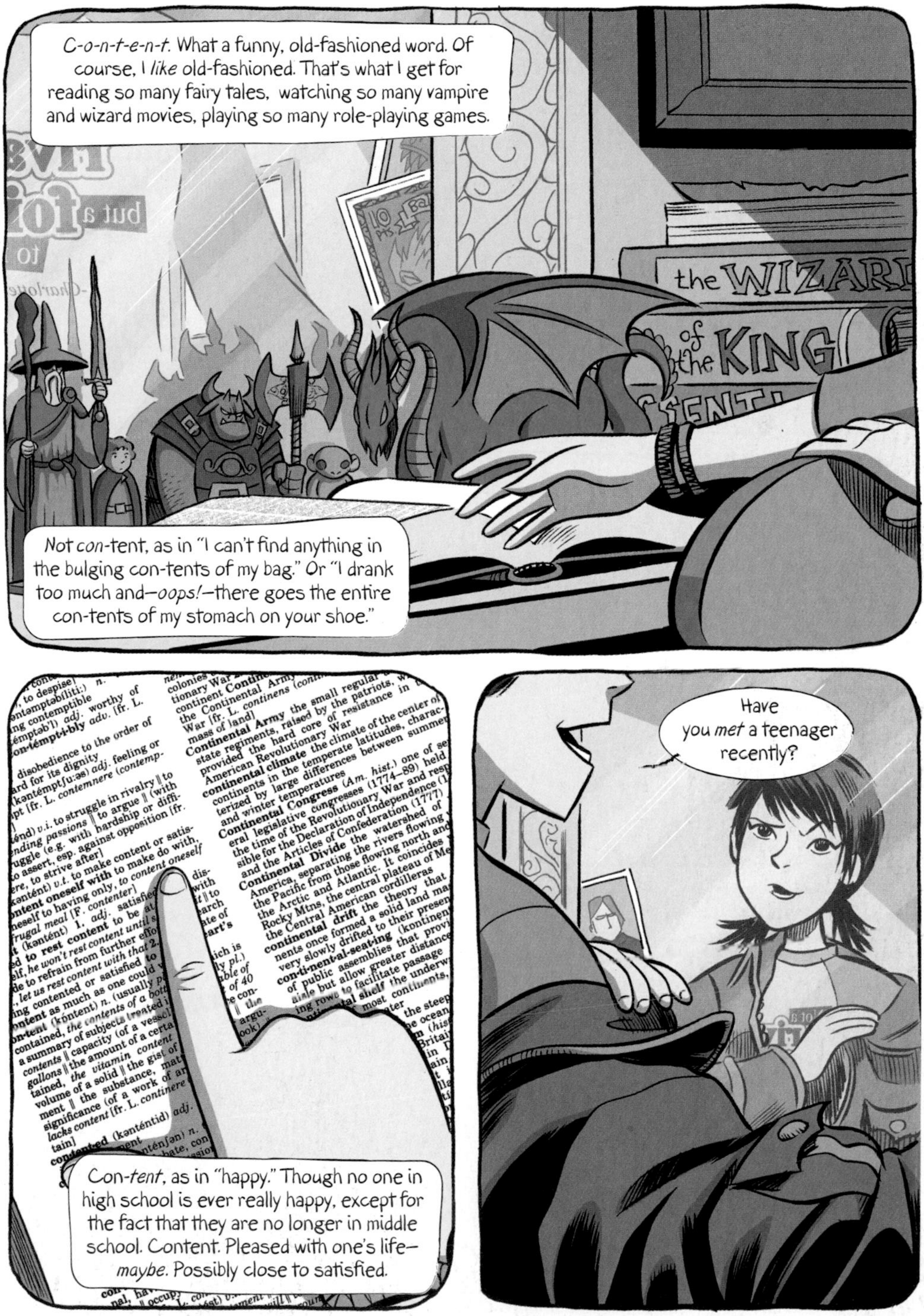
C-o-n-t-e-n-t. What a funny, old-fashioned word. Of course, I *like* old-fashioned. That's what I get for reading so many fairy tales, watching so many vampire and wizard movies, playing so many role-playing games.
Not *con*-tent, as in "I can't find anything in the bulging con-tents of my bag." Or "I drank too much and—*oops!*—there goes the entire con-tents of my stomach on your shoe."
Con-*tent*, as in "happy." Though no one in high school is ever really happy, except for the fact that they are no longer in middle school. Content. Pleased with one's life—*maybe*. Possibly close to satisfied.
Have you *met* a teenager recently?

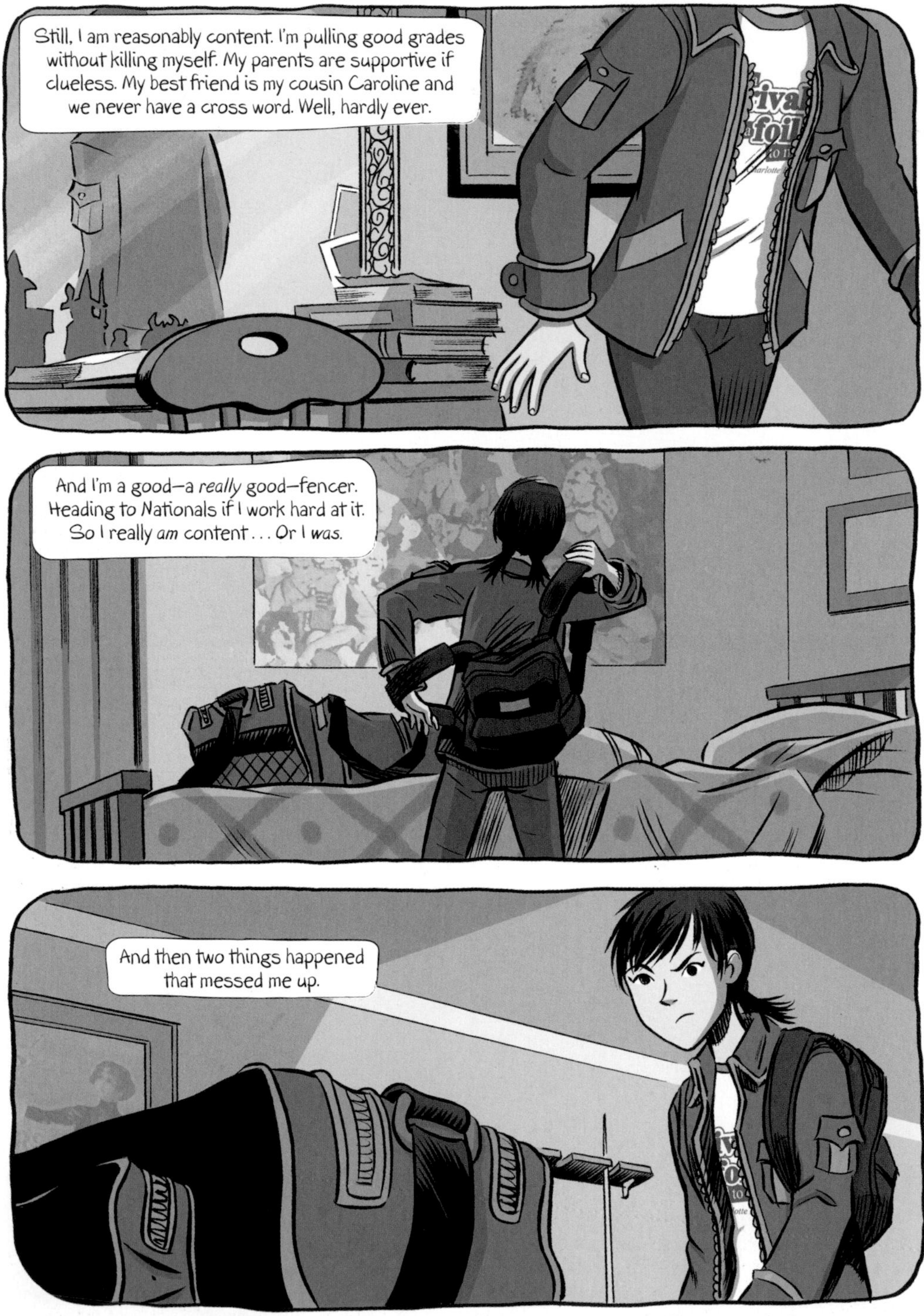
Still, I am reasonably content. I'm pulling good grades without killing myself. My parents are supportive if clueless. My best friend is my cousin Caroline and we never have a cross word. Well, hardly ever.
And I'm a good—a *really* good—fencer. Heading to Nationals if I work hard at it. So I really *am* content . . . Or I *was.*
And then two things happened that messed me up.

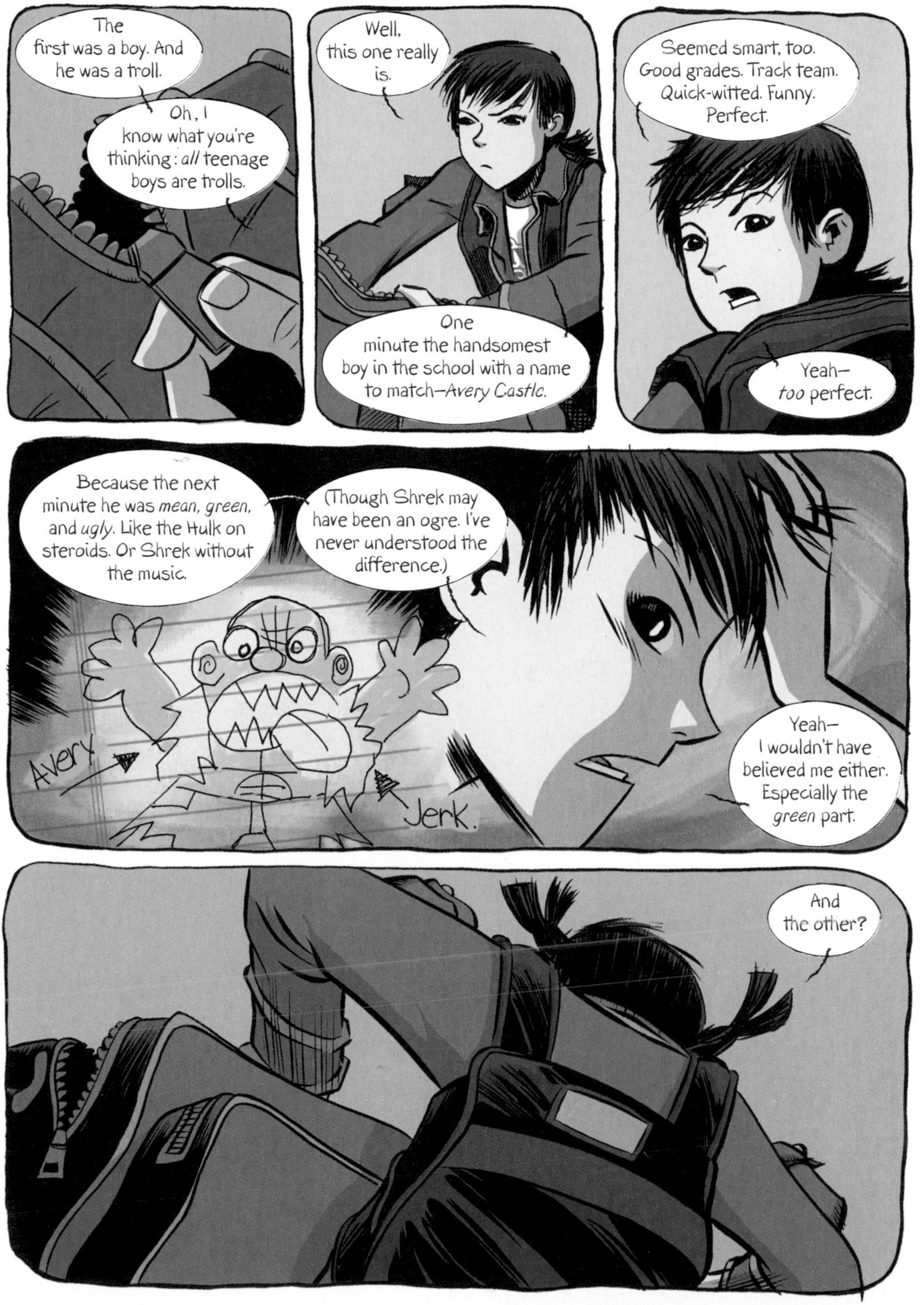
The first was a boy. And he was a troll.
Oh, I know what you're thinking: *all* teenage boys are trolls.
Well, this one really is.
One minute the handsomest boy in the school with a name to match—*Avery Castle.*
Seemed smart, too. Good grades. Track team. Quick-witted. Funny. Perfect.
Yeah— *too* perfect.
Because the next minute he was *mean, green,* and *ugly.* Like the Hulk on steroids. Or Shrek without the music.
(Though Shrek may have been an ogre. I've never understood the difference.)
Avery
Jerk.
Yeah— I wouldn't have believed me either. Especially the *green* part.
And the other?

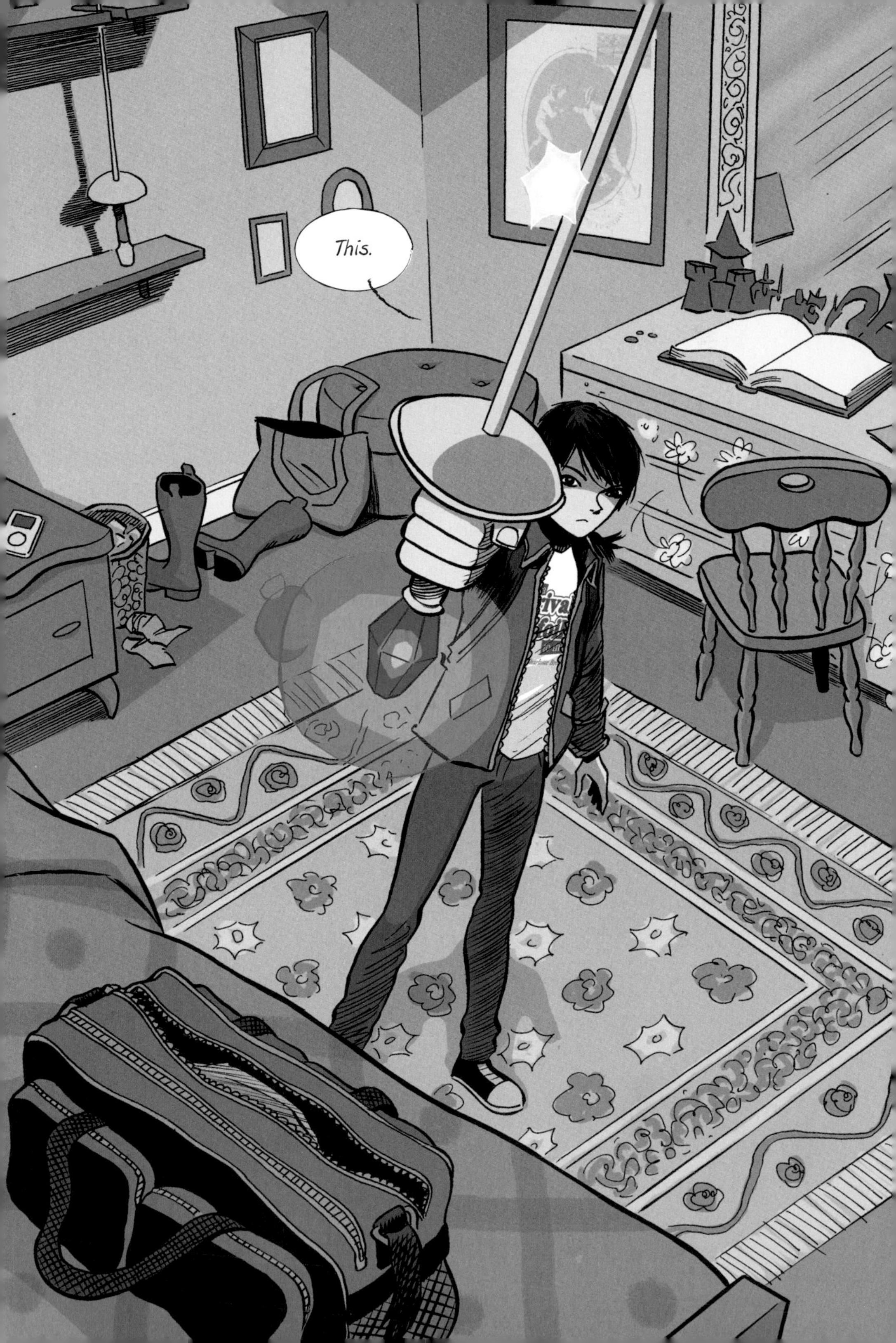
This.

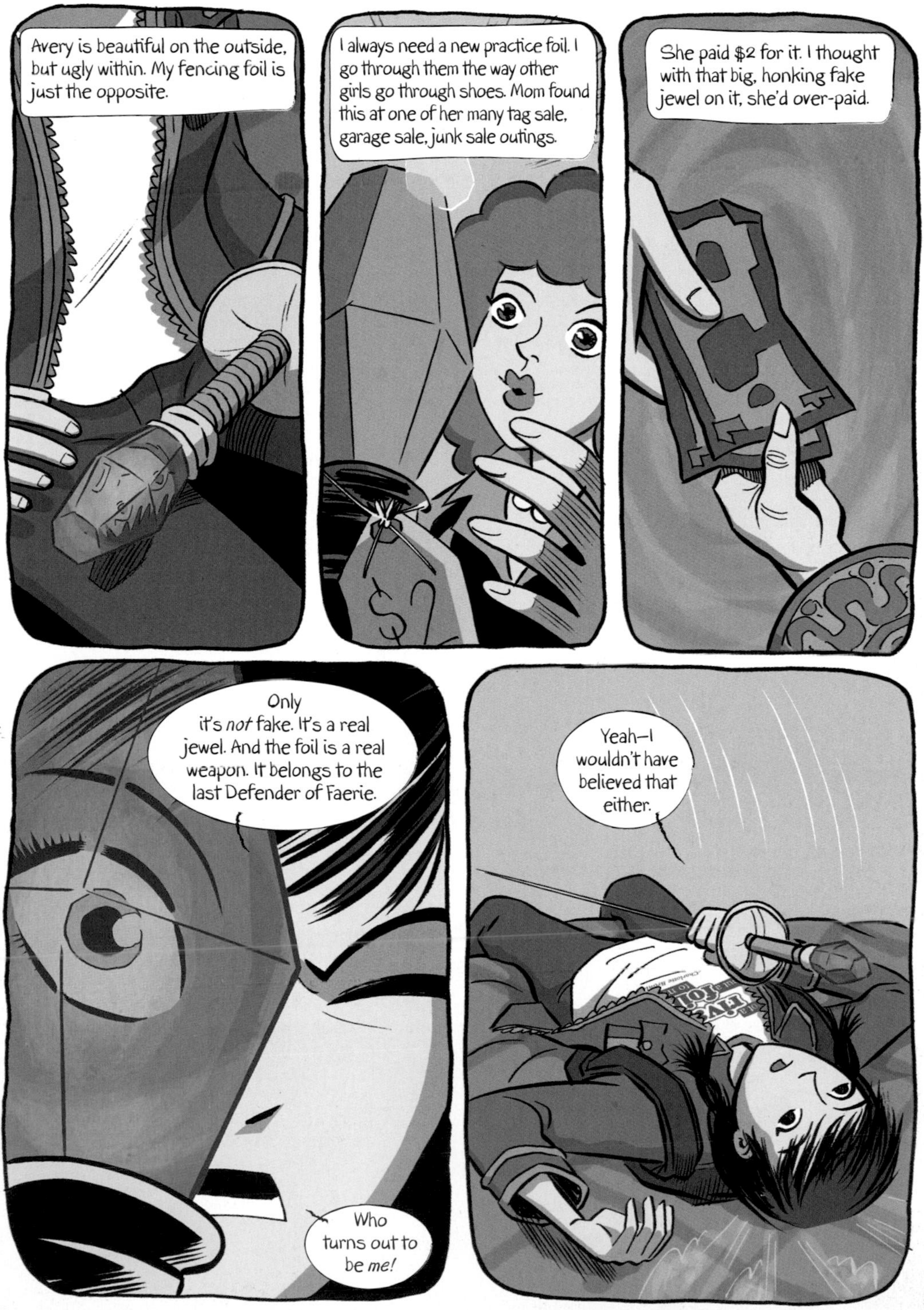
Avery is beautiful on the outside, but ugly within. My fencing foil is just the opposite.
I always need a new practice foil. I go through them the way other girls go through shoes. Mom found this at one of her many tag sale, garage sale, junk sale outings.
She paid $2 for it. I thought with that big, honking fake jewel on it, she'd over-paid.
Only it's *not* fake. It's a real jewel. And the foil is a real weapon. It belongs to the last Defender of Faerie.
Who turns out to be *me!*
Yeah—I wouldn't have believed that either.

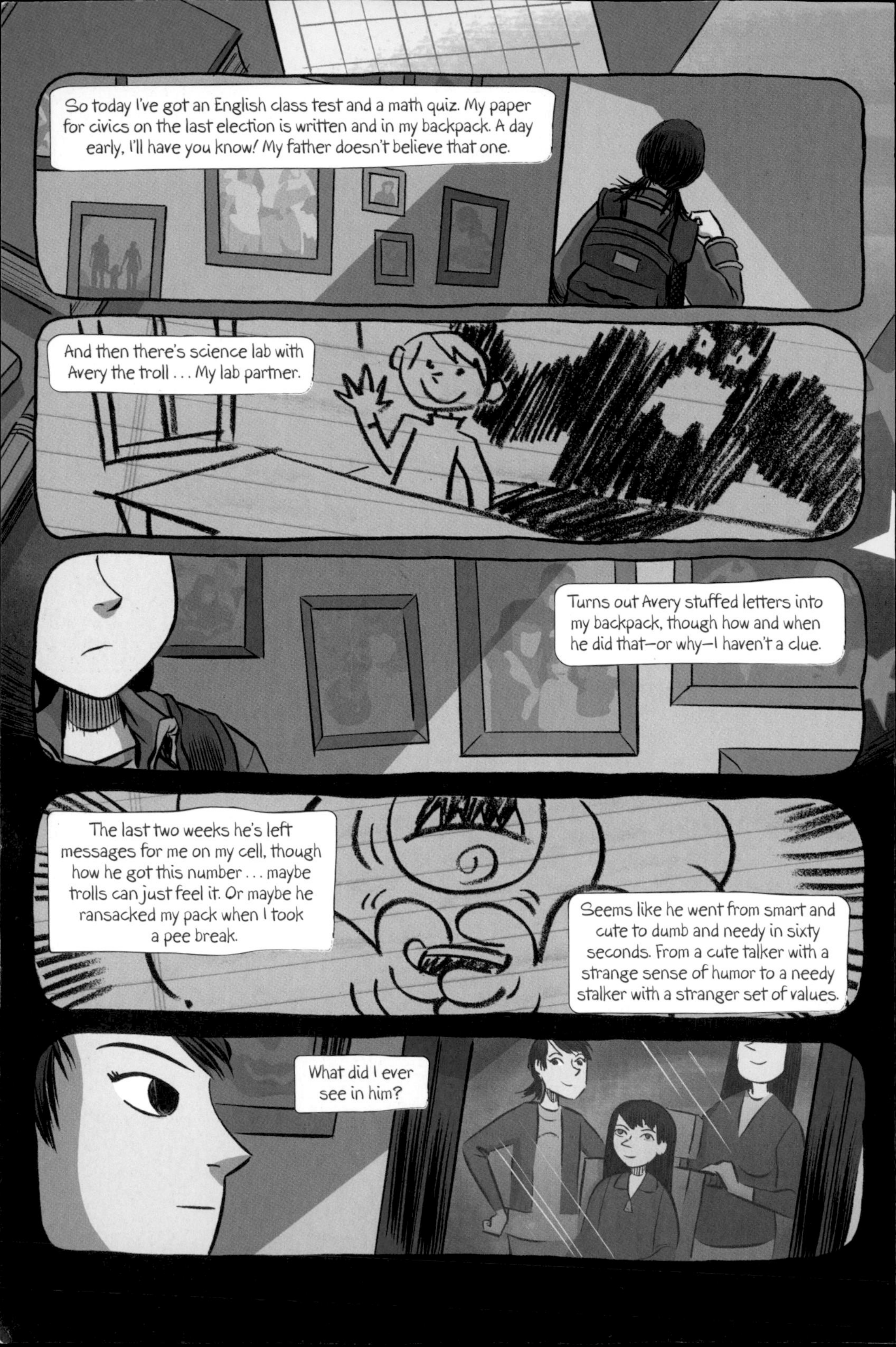
So today I've got an English class test and a math quiz. My paper for civics on the last election is written and in my backpack. A day early, I'll have you know! My father doesn't believe that one.
And then there's science lab with Avery the troll . . . My lab partner.
Turns out Avery stuffed letters into my backpack, though how and when he did that—or why—I haven't a clue.
The last two weeks he's left messages for me on my cell, though how he got this number . . . maybe trolls can just feel it. Or maybe he ransacked my pack when I took a pee break.
Seems like he went from smart and cute to dumb and needy in sixty seconds. From a cute talker with a strange sense of humor to a needy stalker with a stranger set of values.
What did I ever see in him?

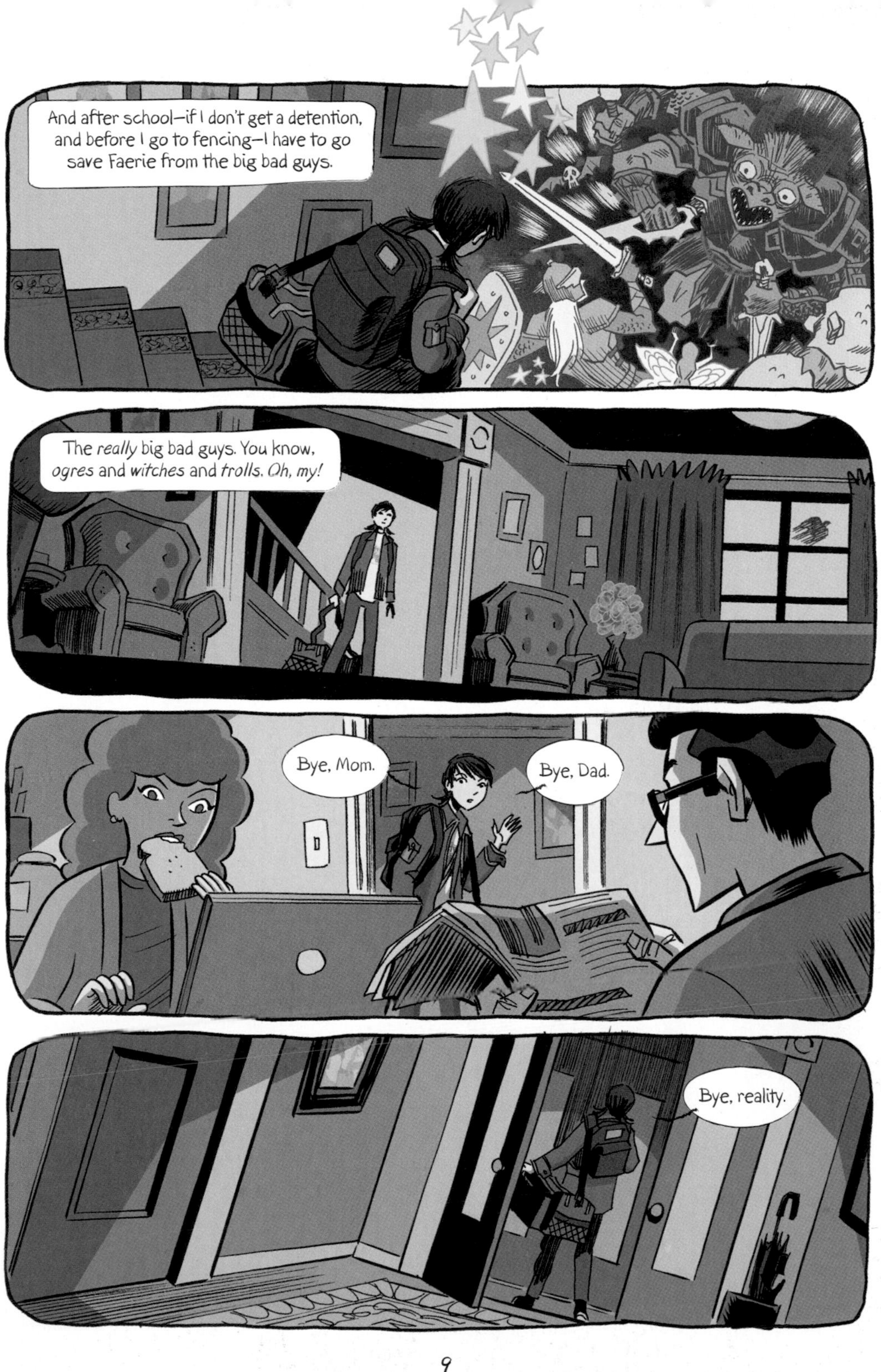
And after school—if I don't get a detention, and before I go to fencing—I have to go save Faerie from the big bad guys.
The *really* big bad guys. You know, *ogres* and *witches* and *trolls*. *Oh, my!*
Bye, Mom.
Bye, Dad.
Bye, reality.

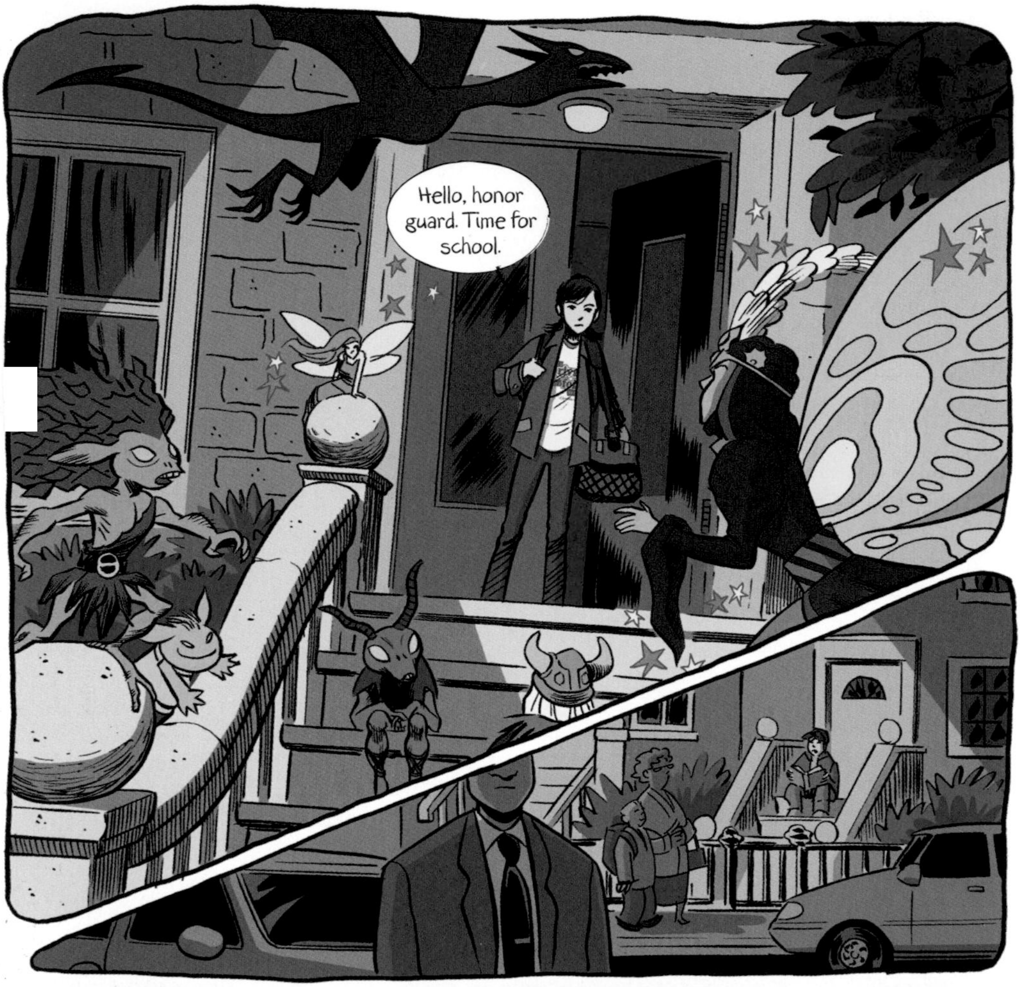
Hello, honor guard. Time for school.

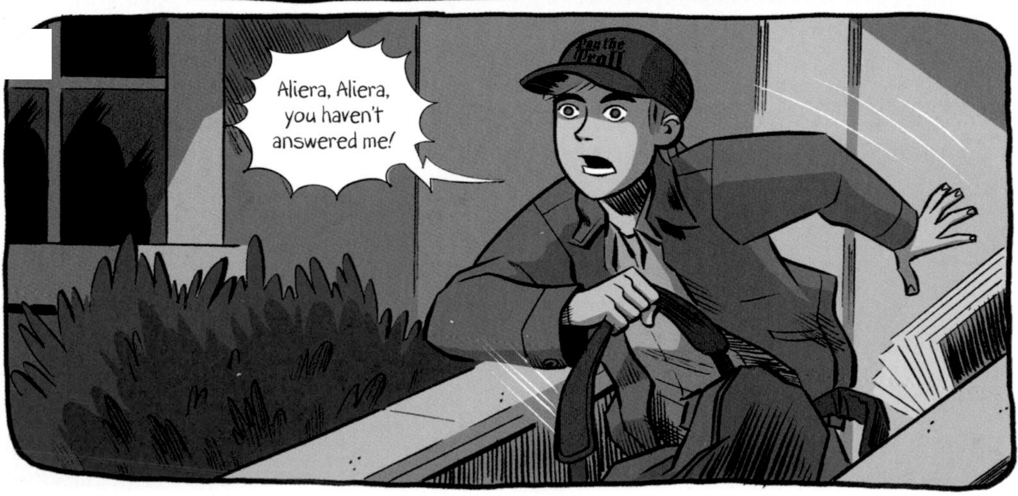
Aliera, Aliera, you haven't answered me!

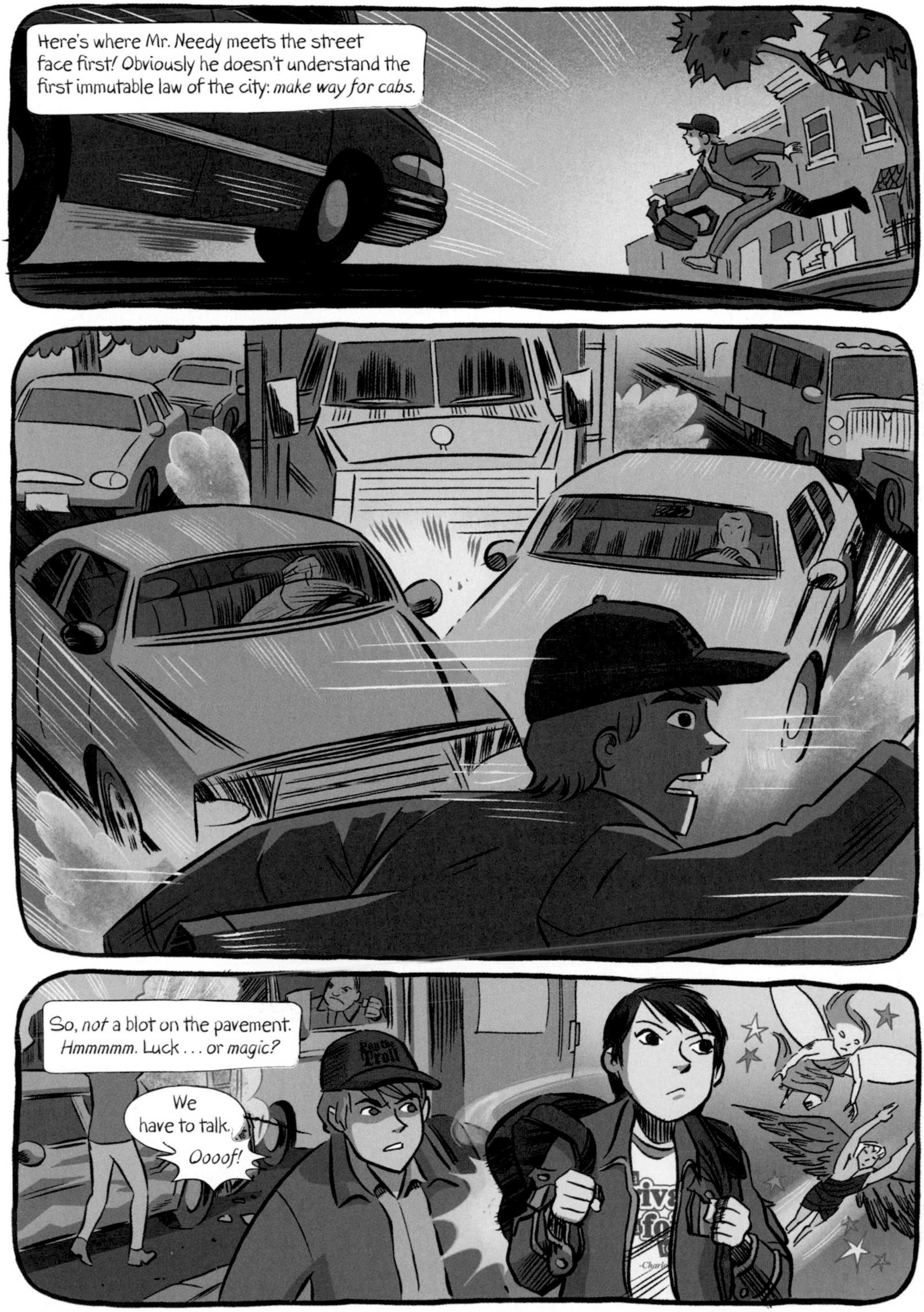
Here's where Mr. Needy meets the street face first! Obviously he doesn't understand the first immutable law of the city: *make way for cabs.*
So, *not* a blot on the pavement. *Hmmmmm.* Luck . . . or *magic?*
We have to talk.
Oooof!

Aliera, I have things to tell you, things you need to know.

I already know plenty about you, Mister Troll.

No, no, you don't understand. By finding the sword, holding it, taking on your role as Defender, you have unleashed . . . certain . . . certain . . . *creatures* who . . .

Get it through your thick troll skull: *I* have unleashed nothing. *You* came to my school and set all this in motion. I'm just picking up your trash. I *so* don't want to do any of this.

I already *have a life.* I do my homework, get A's, go to fencing. My parental units are *as good as they get.* My fencing teacher is *attentive* . . .

And it's not a *sword*, it's a *weapon*, get it? So use its proper . . . um . . . name.

Okay, Aliera.

You are my *liege lord.* You *command* me. I am *bound* to you,

like it or not.

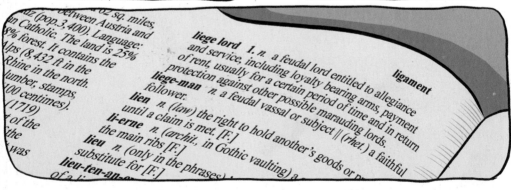

between Austria and
. . . (pop. 3,400). Language:
. . . Catholic. The land is 25%
. . .% forest. It contains the
Alps (8,432 ft in the
Rhine in the north.
. . . lumber, stamps,
. . . centimes).
(1719)
. . . of the
. . . the
. . . was

liege lord **1.** *n.* a feudal lord entitled to allegiance and service, including loyalty bearing arms, payment of rent, usually for a certain period of time and in return protection against other possible marauding lords.
liege-man *n.* a feudal vassal or subject || *(rhet.)* a faithful follower.
lien *n. (law)* the right to hold another's goods or p. . . until a claim is met. [F.]
li-erne *n. (archit.,* in Gothic vaulting) a . . . the main ribs [F.]
lieu *n.* (only in the phrases) . . . substitute for [F.]
lieu-ten-an. . . of a li. . .

ligament

12

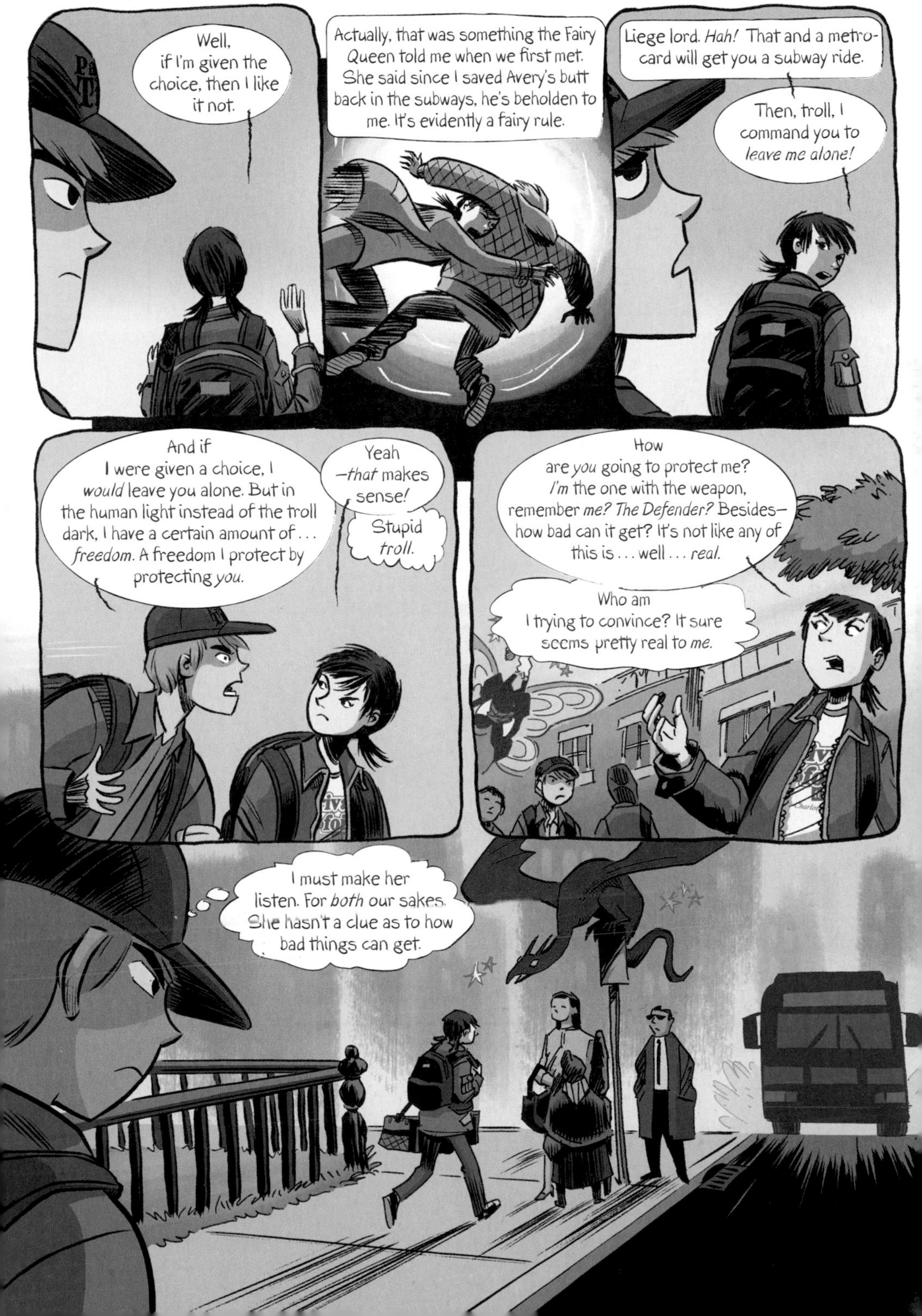
Well, if I'm given the choice, then I like it not.
Actually, that was something the Fairy Queen told me when we first met. She said since I saved Avery's butt back in the subways, he's beholden to me. It's evidently a fairy rule.
Liege lord. *Hah!* That and a metro-card will get you a subway ride.
Then, troll, I command you to *leave me alone!*
And if I were given a choice, I *would* leave you alone. But in the human light instead of the troll dark, I have a certain amount of . . . *freedom.* A freedom I protect by protecting *you.*
Yeah —*that* makes sense!
Stupid *troll.*
How are *you* going to protect me? *I'm* the one with the weapon, remember *me? The Defender?* Besides— how bad can it get? It's not like any of this is . . . well . . . *real.*
Who am I trying to convince? It sure seems pretty real to *me.*
I must make her listen. For *both* our sakes. She hasn't a clue as to how bad things can get.

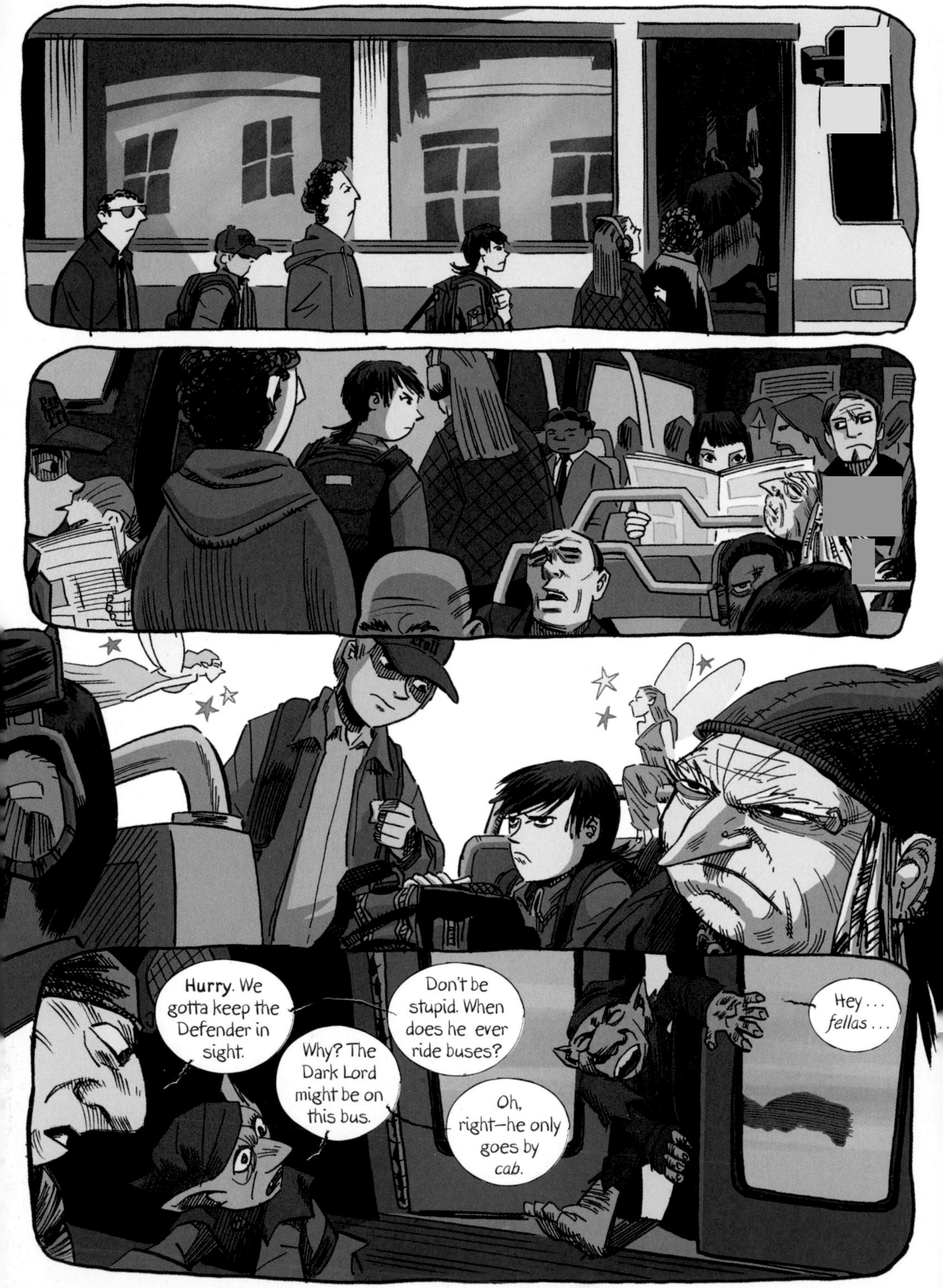

Hurry. We gotta keep the Defender in sight.
Why? The Dark Lord might be on this bus.
Don't be stupid. When does he ever ride buses?
Oh, right—he only goes by cab.
Hey . . . fellas . . .

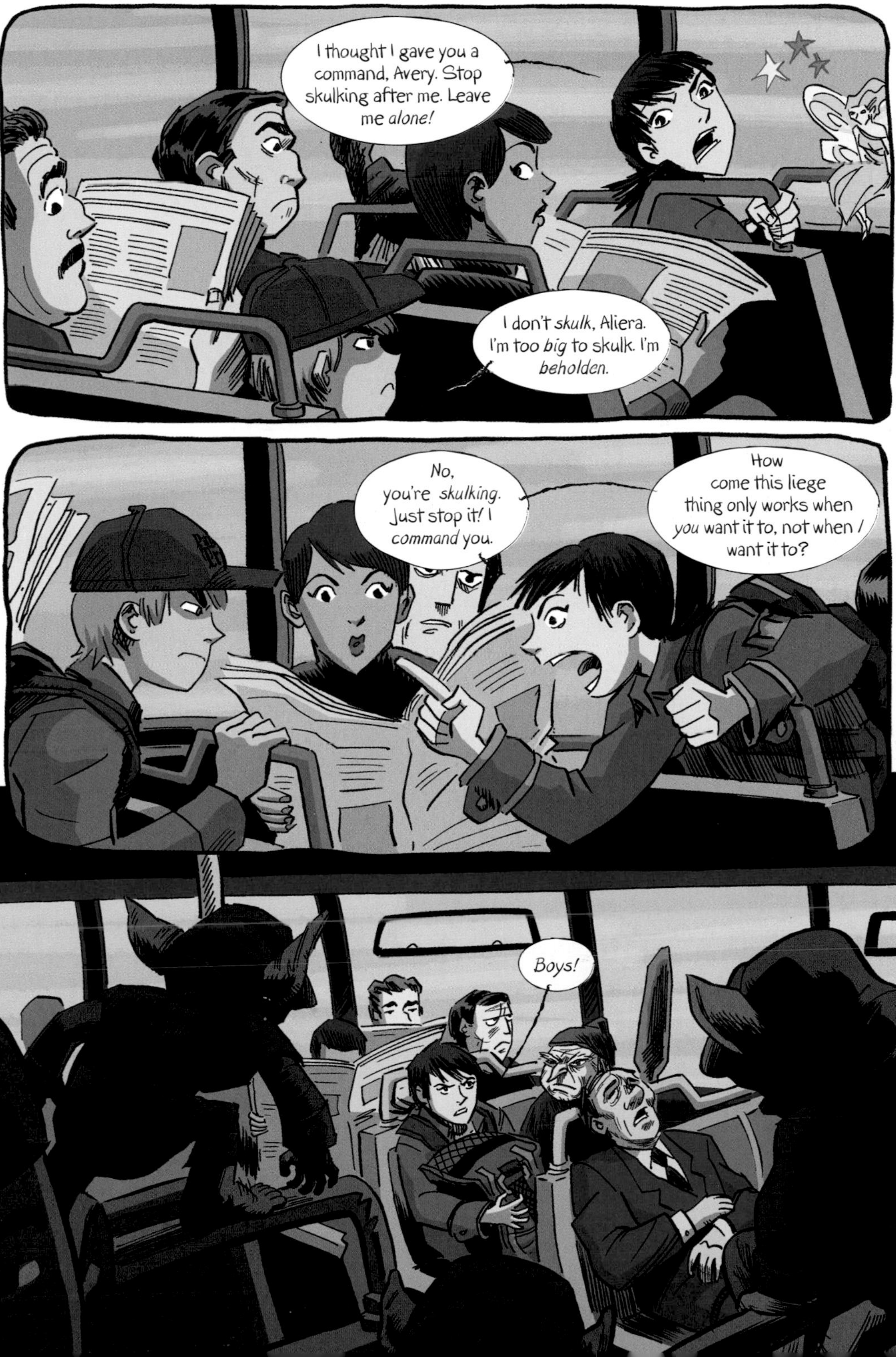
I thought I gave you a command, Avery. Stop skulking after me. Leave me *alone!*
I don't *skulk*, Aliera. I'm too *big* to skulk. I'm *beholden*.
No, you're *skulking*. Just stop it! I *command* you.
How come this liege thing only works when *you* want it to, not when *I* want it to?
Boys!

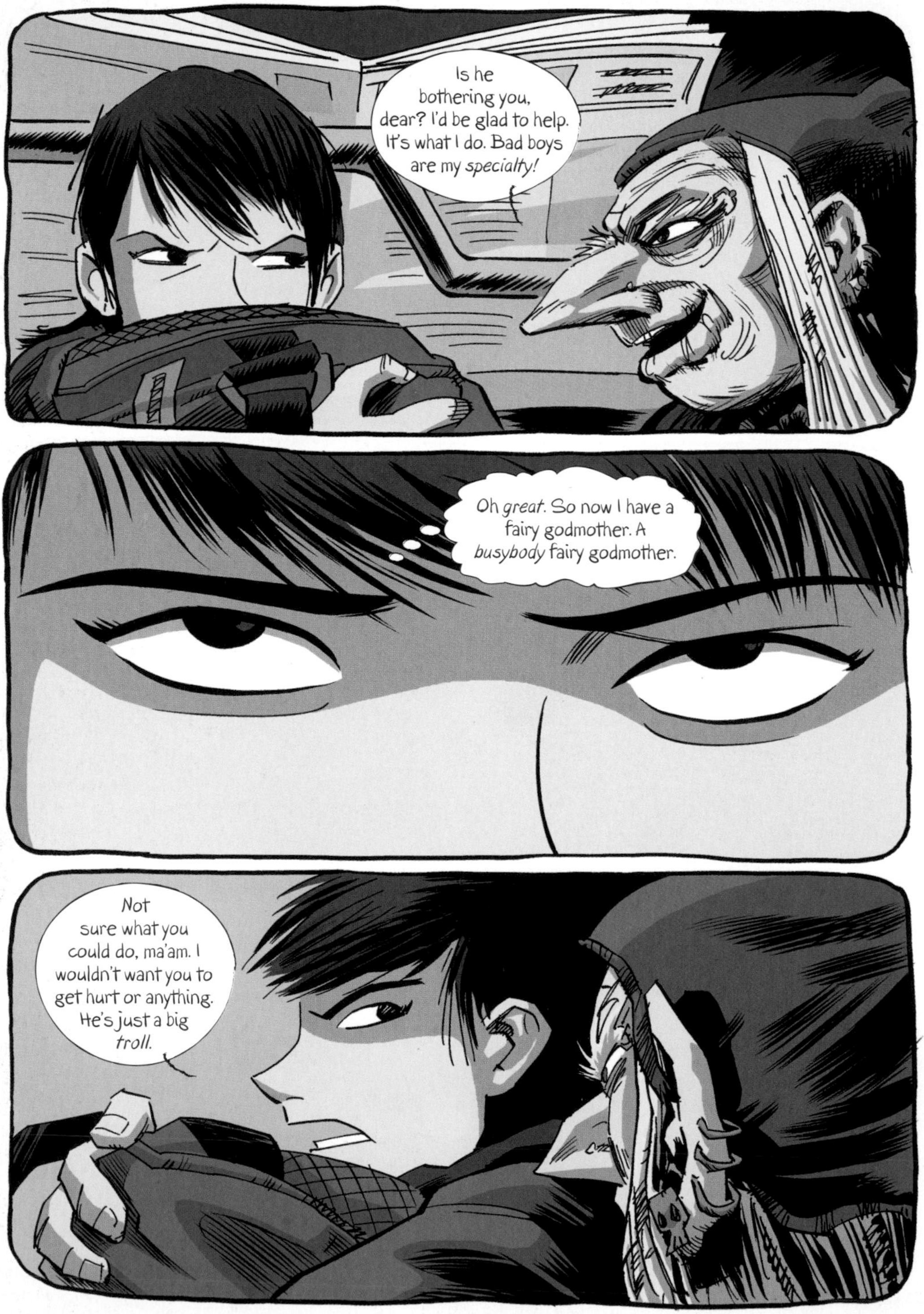
Is he bothering you, dear? I'd be glad to help. It's what I do. Bad boys are my *specialty!*
Oh *great.* So now I have a fairy godmother. A *busybody* fairy godmother.
Not sure what you could do, ma'am. I wouldn't want you to get hurt or anything. He's just a big *troll.*

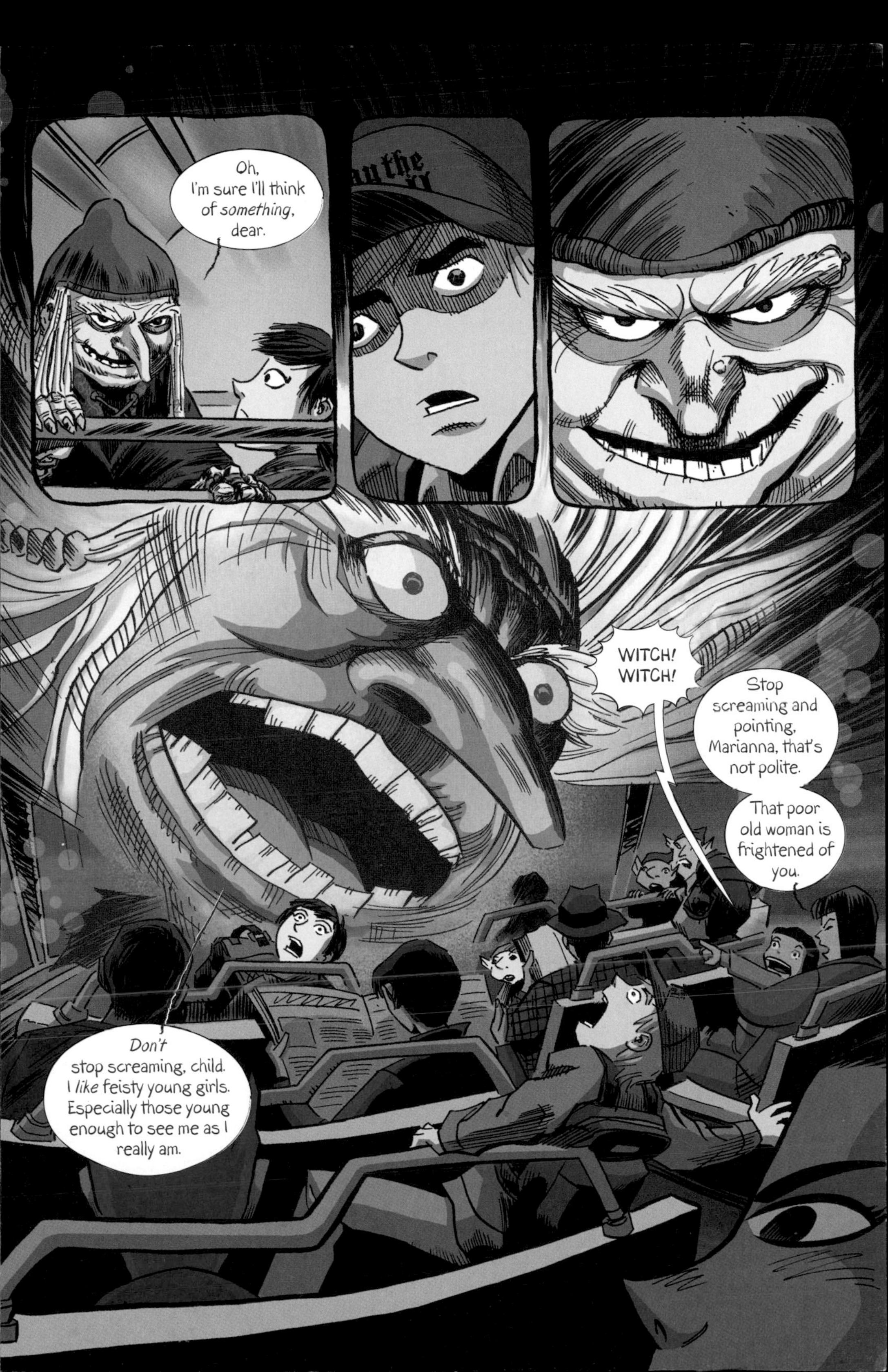
Oh, I'm sure I'll think of *something*, dear.
WITCH! WITCH!
Stop screaming and pointing, Marianna, that's not polite.
That poor old woman is frightened of you.
Don't stop screaming, child. I *like* feisty young girls. Especially those young enough to see me as I really am.

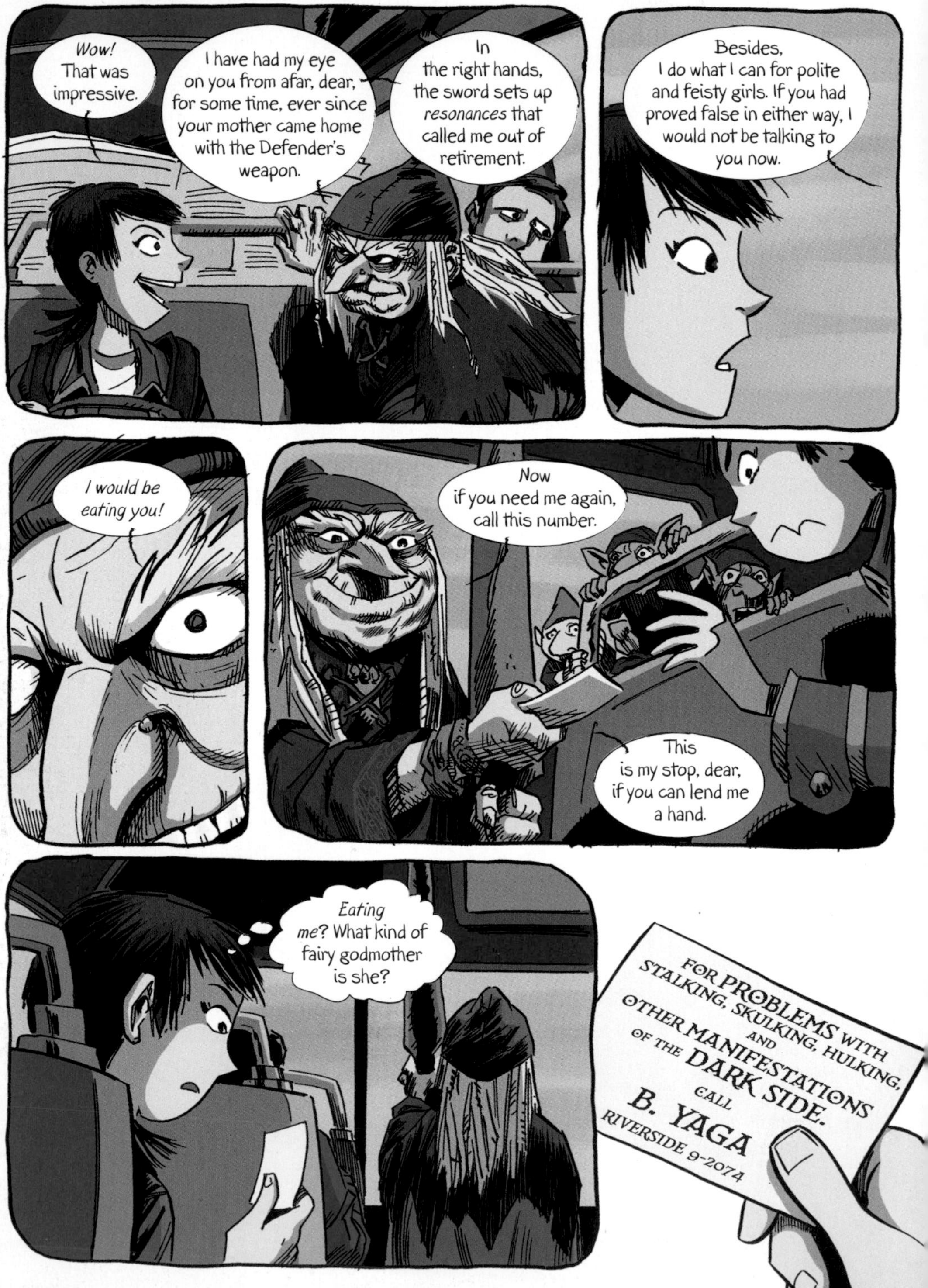
Wow! That was impressive.
I have had my eye on you from afar, dear, for some time, ever since your mother came home with the Defender's weapon.
In the right hands, the sword sets up resonances that called me out of retirement.
Besides, I do what I can for polite and feisty girls. If you had proved false in either way, I would not be talking to you now.
I would be eating you!
Now if you need me again, call this number.
This is my stop, dear, if you can lend me a hand.
Eating me? What kind of fairy godmother is she?
FOR PROBLEMS WITH STALKING, SKULKING, HULKING, AND OTHER MANIFESTATIONS OF THE DARK SIDE.
CALL
B. YAGA
RIVERSIDE 9-2074

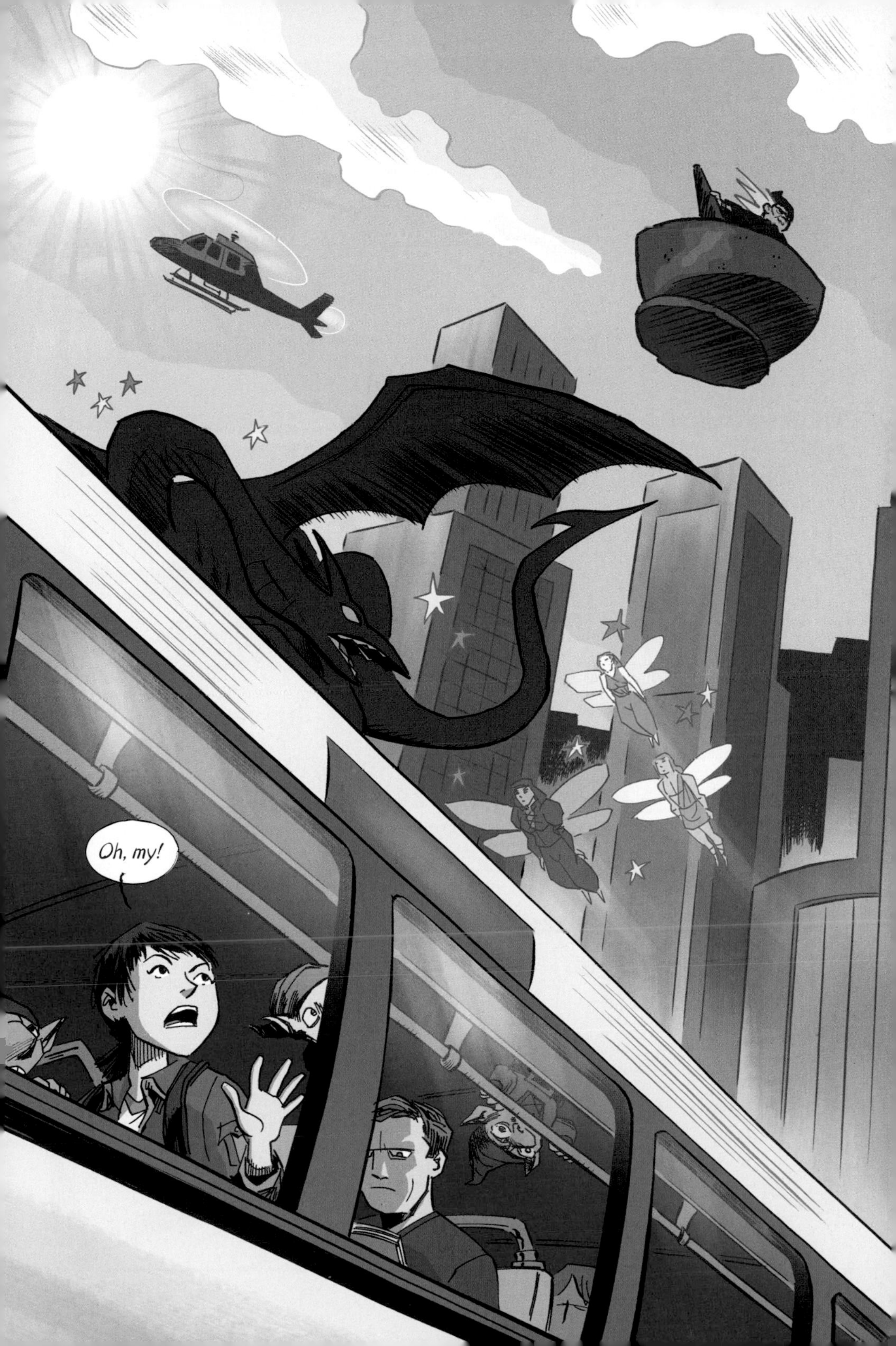
Oh, my!

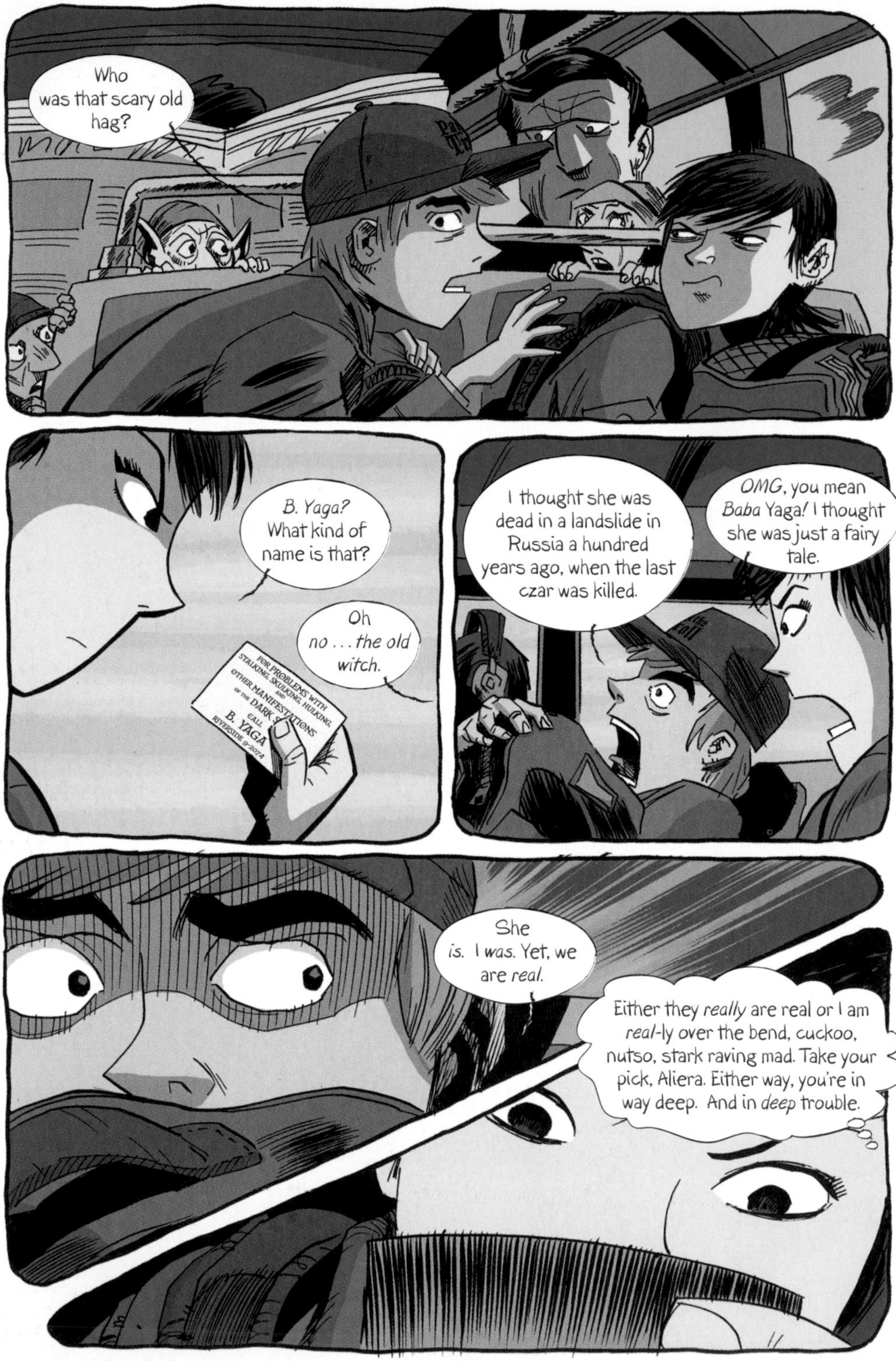
Who was that scary old hag?
B. Yaga? What kind of name is that?
Oh no . . . the old witch.
FOR PROBLEMS WITH STALKING, SKULKING, HULKING, AND OTHER MANIFESTATIONS OF THE DARK
CALL
B. YAGA
RIVERSIDE 9-2074
I thought she was dead in a landslide in Russia a hundred years ago, when the last czar was killed.
OMG, you mean *Baba* Yaga! I thought she was just a fairy tale.
She *is*. I *was*. Yet, we are *real*.
Either they *really* are real or I am *real*-ly over the bend, cuckoo, nutso, stark raving mad. Take your pick, Aliera. Either way, you're in way deep. And in *deep* trouble.

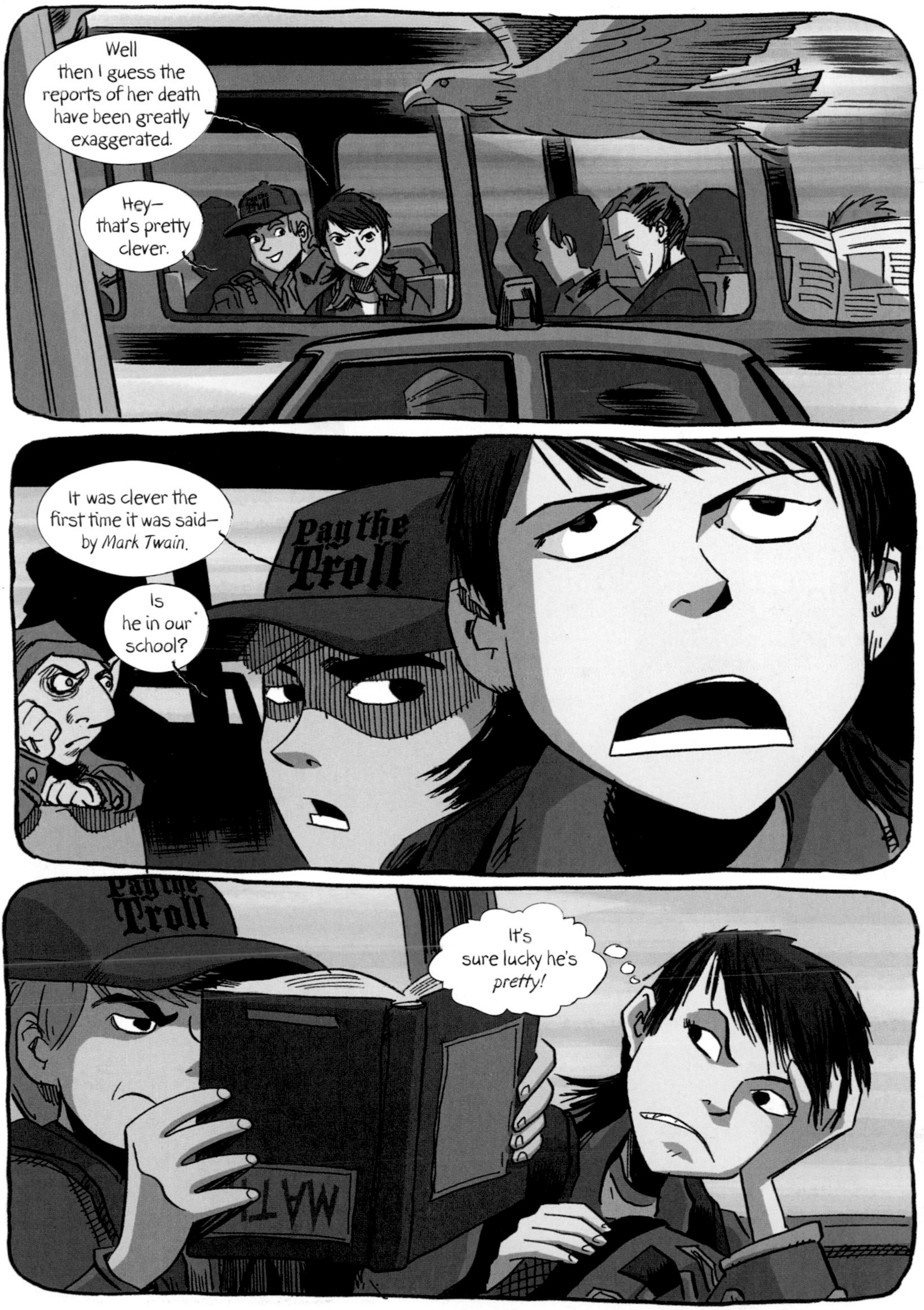
Well then I guess the reports of her death have been greatly exaggerated.
Hey— that's pretty clever.
Pay the Troll
It was clever the first time it was said— by *Mark Twain*.
Is he in our school?
Pay the Troll
Pay the Troll
It's sure lucky he's *pretty!*

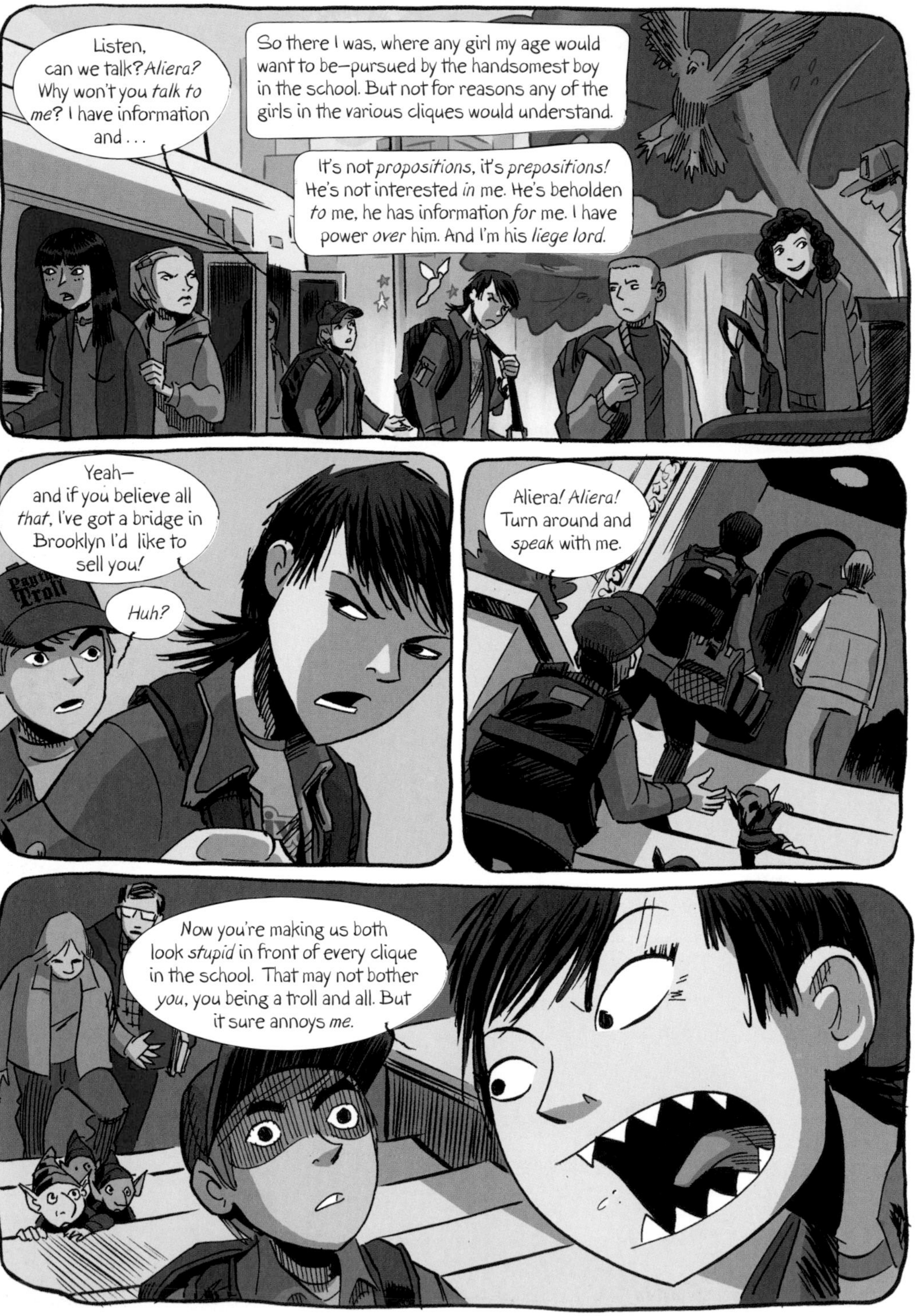
Listen, can we talk? *Aliera?* Why won't you *talk to me*? I have information and . . .
So there I was, where any girl my age would want to be—pursued by the handsomest boy in the school. But not for reasons any of the girls in the various cliques would understand.
It's not *propositions*, it's *prepositions!* He's not interested *in* me. He's beholden *to* me, he has information *for* me. I have power *over* him. And I'm his *liege lord*.
Yeah— and if you believe all *that*, I've got a bridge in Brooklyn I'd like to sell you!
Huh?
Aliera! *Aliera!* Turn around and *speak* with me.
Now you're making us both look *stupid* in front of every clique in the school. That may not bother *you*, you being a troll and all. But it sure annoys *me*.

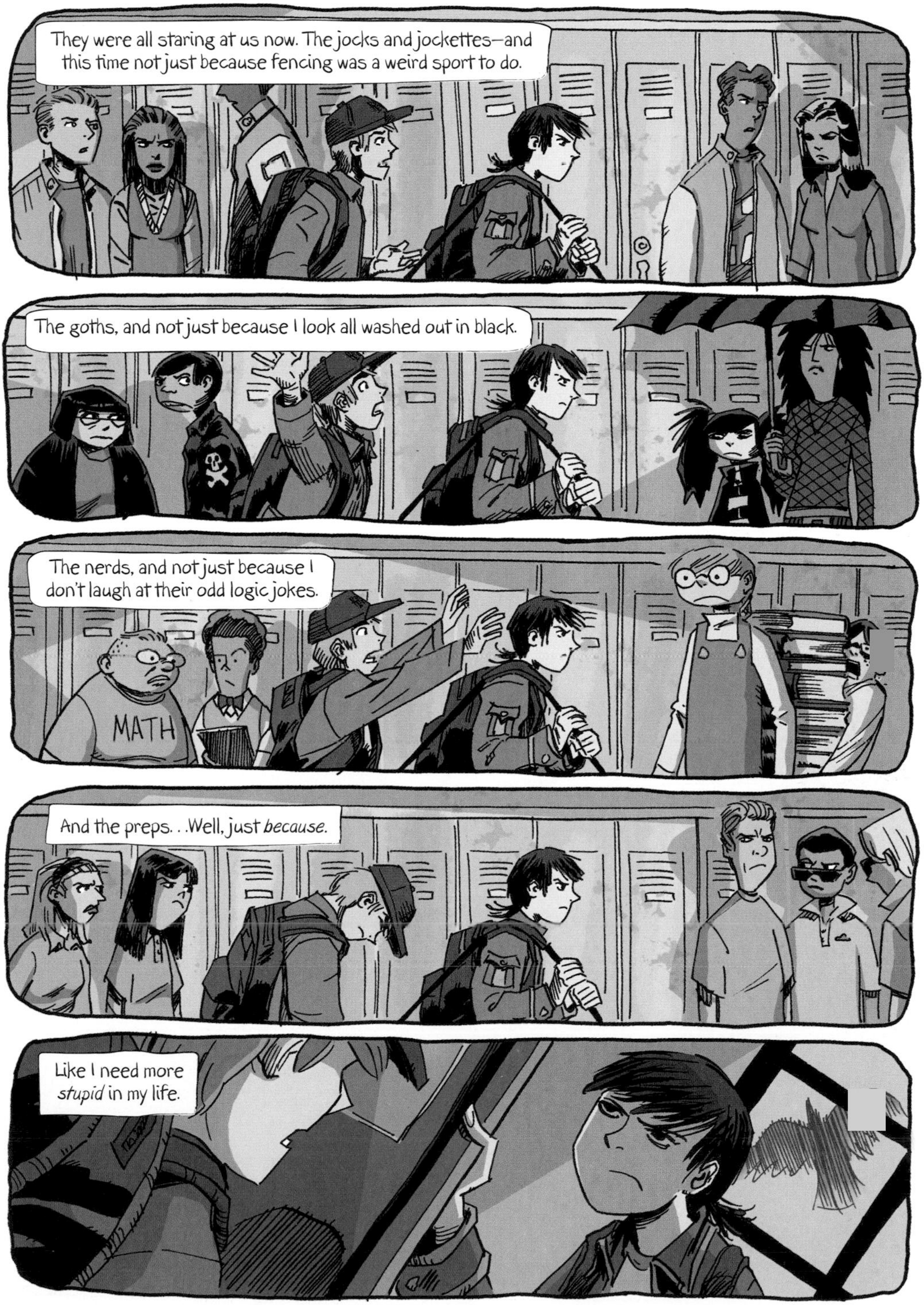
They were all staring at us now. The jocks and jockettes—and this time not just because fencing was a weird sport to do.
The goths, and not just because I look all washed out in black.
The nerds, and not just because I don't laugh at their odd logic jokes.
MATH
And the preps. . .Well, just *because.*
Like I need more *stupid* in my life.

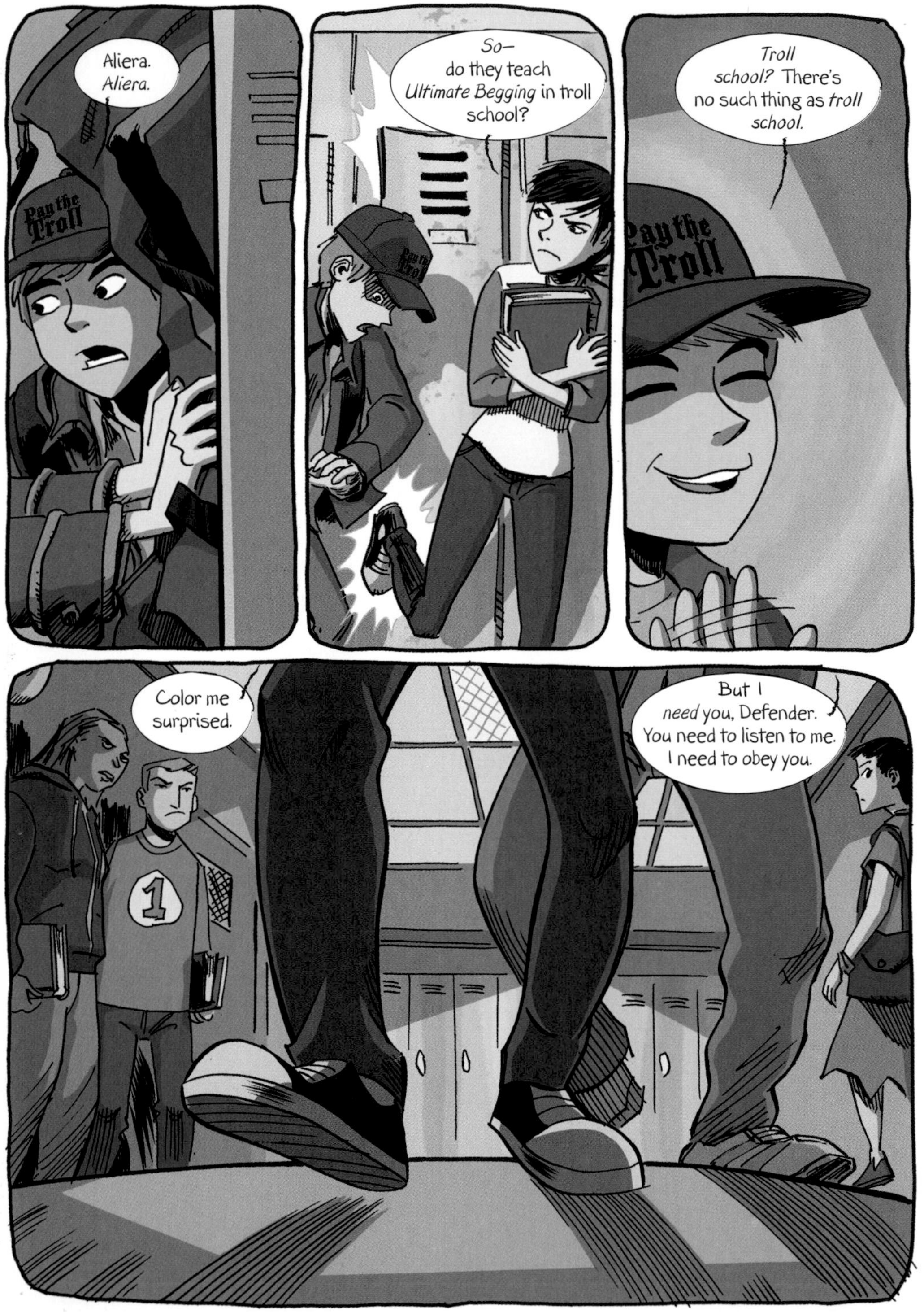
Aliera. Aliera.
So— do they teach *Ultimate Begging* in troll school?
Troll school? There's no such thing as *troll school.*
Pay the Troll
Color me surprised.
But I *need* you, Defender. You need to listen to me. I need to obey you.

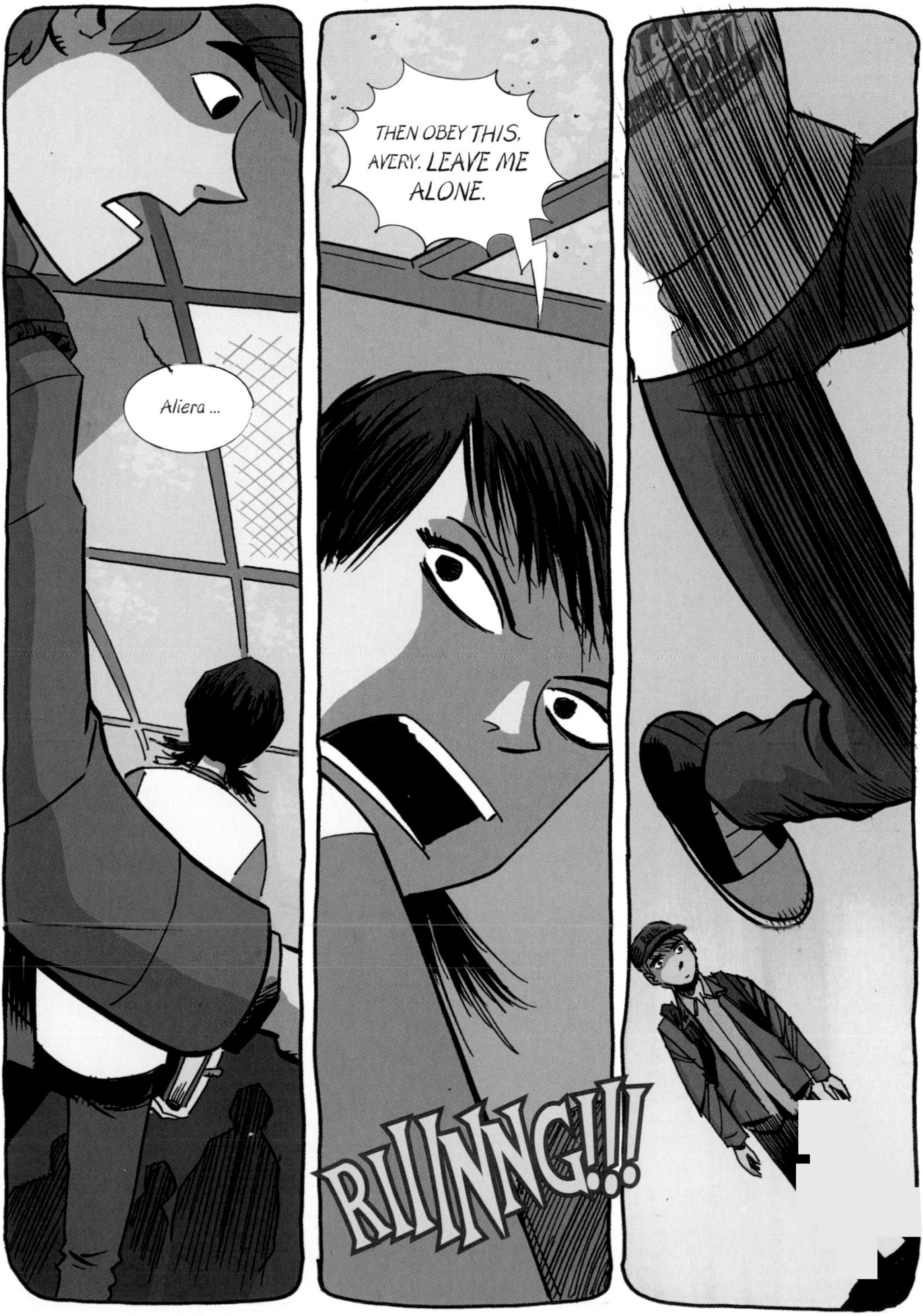
Aliera ...
THEN OBEY THIS, AVERY. LEAVE ME ALONE.
RIIINNG!!!

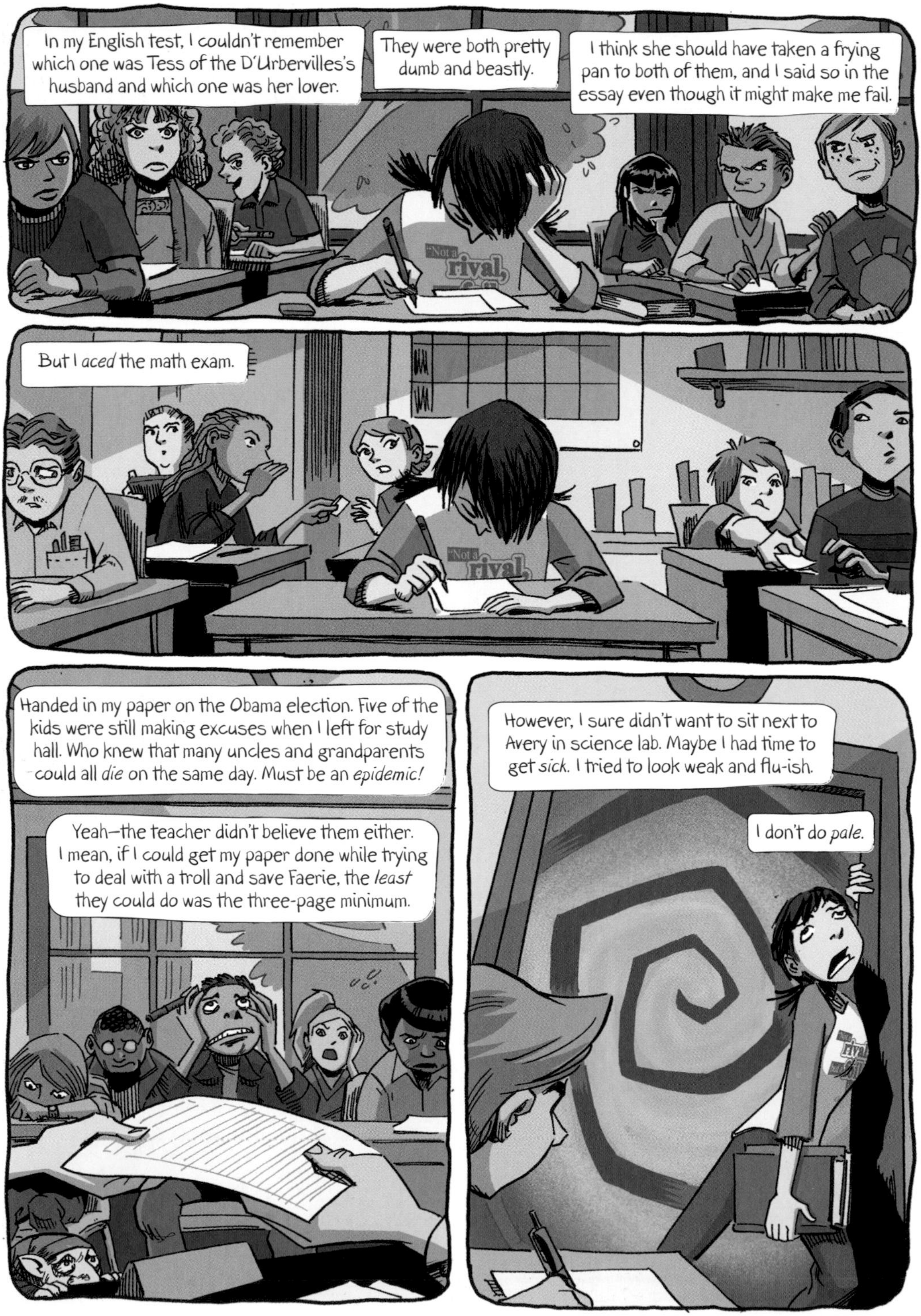
In my English test, I couldn't remember which one was Tess of the D'Urbervilles's husband and which one was her lover.
They were both pretty dumb and beastly.
I think she should have taken a frying pan to both of them, and I said so in the essay even though it might make me fail.
But I *aced* the math exam.
Handed in my paper on the Obama election. Five of the kids were still making excuses when I left for study hall. Who knew that many uncles and grandparents could all *die* on the same day. Must be an *epidemic!*
Yeah—the teacher didn't believe them either. I mean, if I could get my paper done while trying to deal with a troll and save Faerie, the *least* they could do was the three-page minimum.
However, I sure didn't want to sit next to Avery in science lab. Maybe I had time to get *sick*. I tried to look weak and flu-ish.
I don't do *pale*.

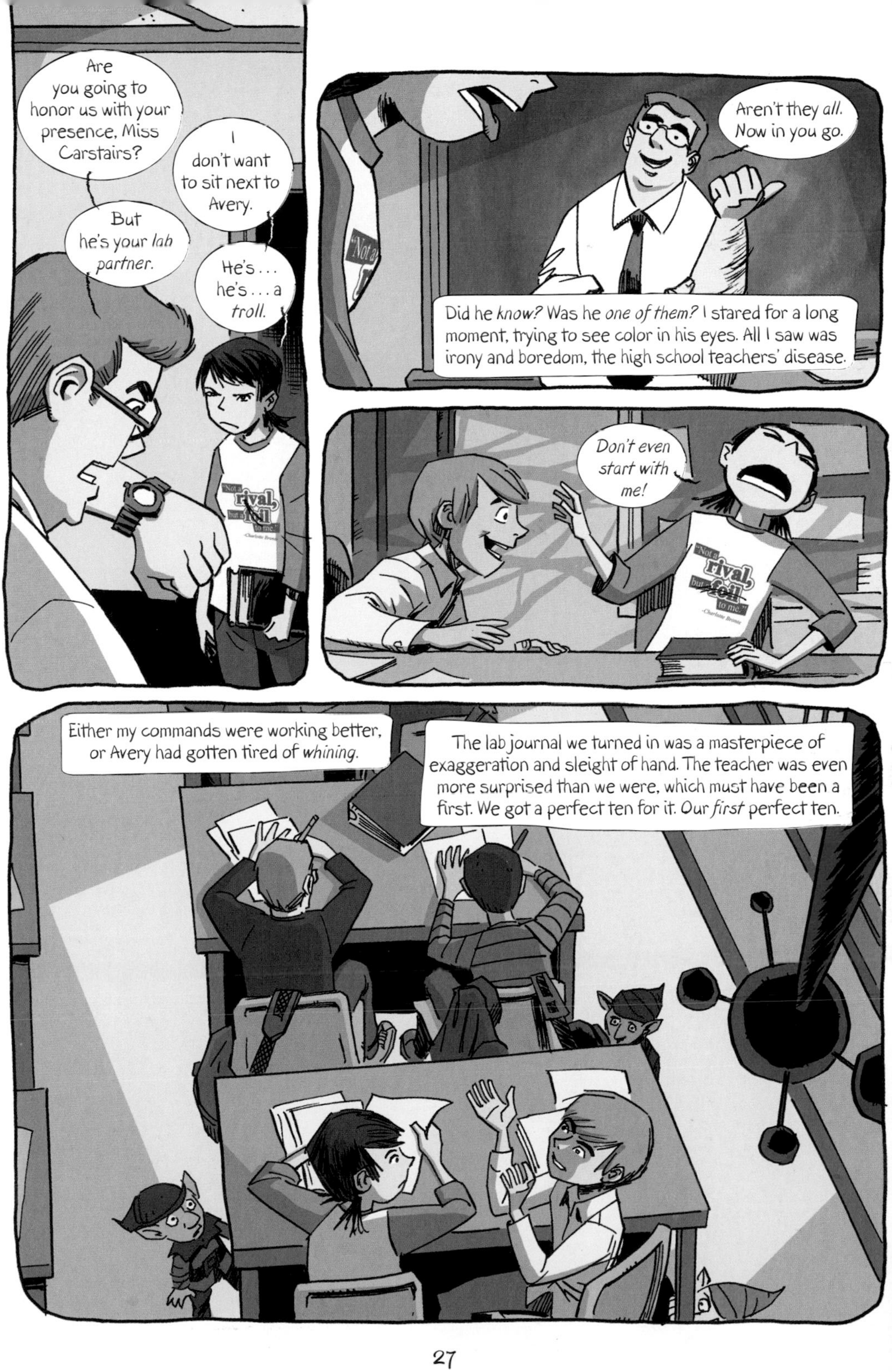
Are you going to honor us with your presence, Miss Carstairs?
I don't want to sit next to Avery.
But he's your *lab partner*.
He's . . . he's . . . a *troll*.
Aren't they *all*. Now in you go.
Did he *know?* Was he *one of them?* I stared for a long moment, trying to see color in his eyes. All I saw was irony and boredom, the high school teachers' disease.
Don't even start with me!
Either my commands were working better, or Avery had gotten tired of *whining*.
The lab journal we turned in was a masterpiece of exaggeration and sleight of hand. The teacher was even more surprised than we were, which must have been a first. We got a perfect ten for it. Our *first* perfect ten.

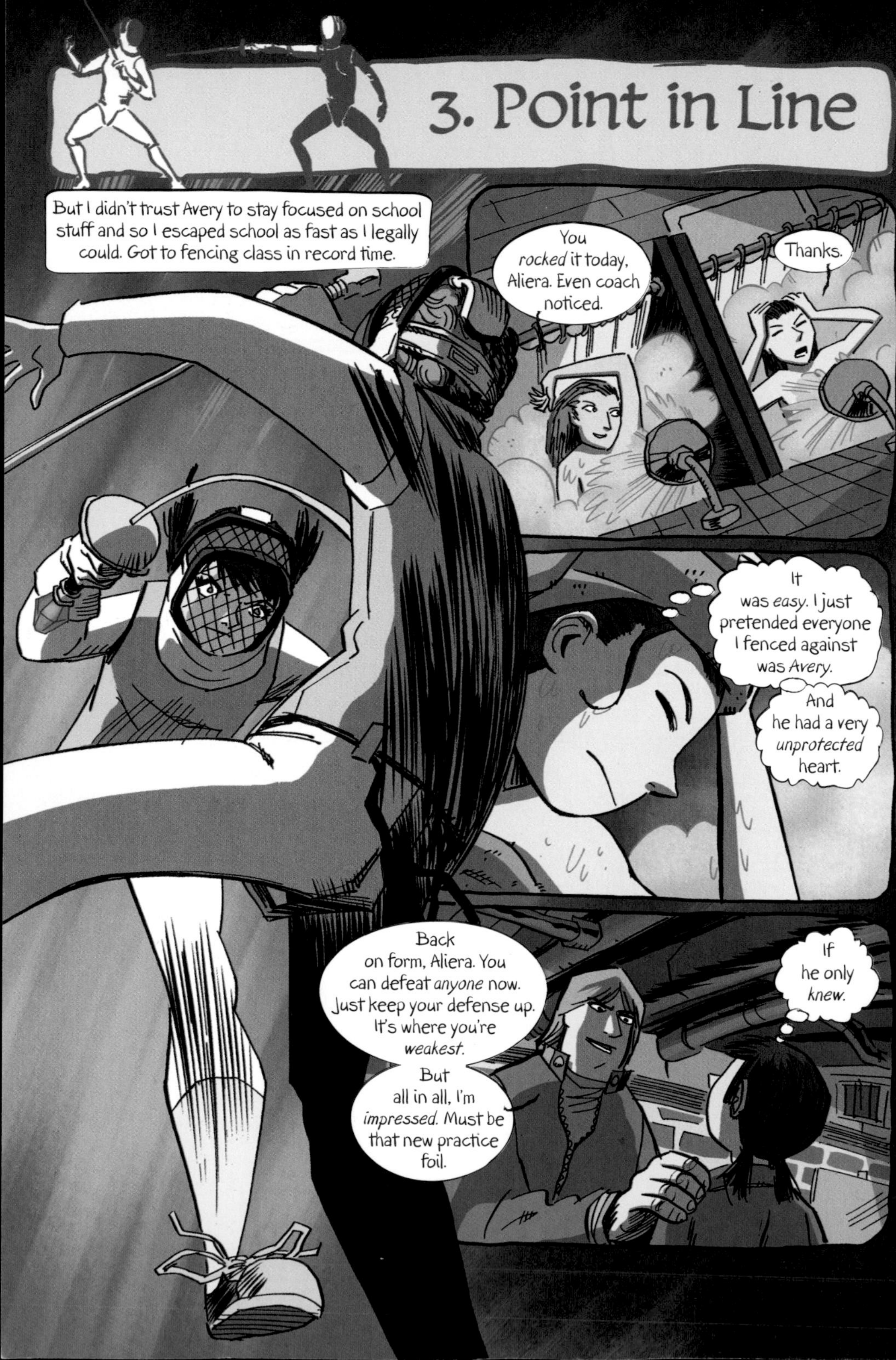
3. Point in Line
But I didn't trust Avery to stay focused on school stuff and so I escaped school as fast as I legally could. Got to fencing class in record time.
You *rocked* it today, Aliera. Even coach noticed.
Thanks.
It was *easy*. I just pretended everyone I fenced against was *Avery*.
And he had a very *unprotected* heart.
Back on form, Aliera. You can defeat *anyone* now. Just keep your defense up. It's where you're *weakest*.
But all in all, I'm *impressed*. Must be that new practice foil.
If he only *knew*.

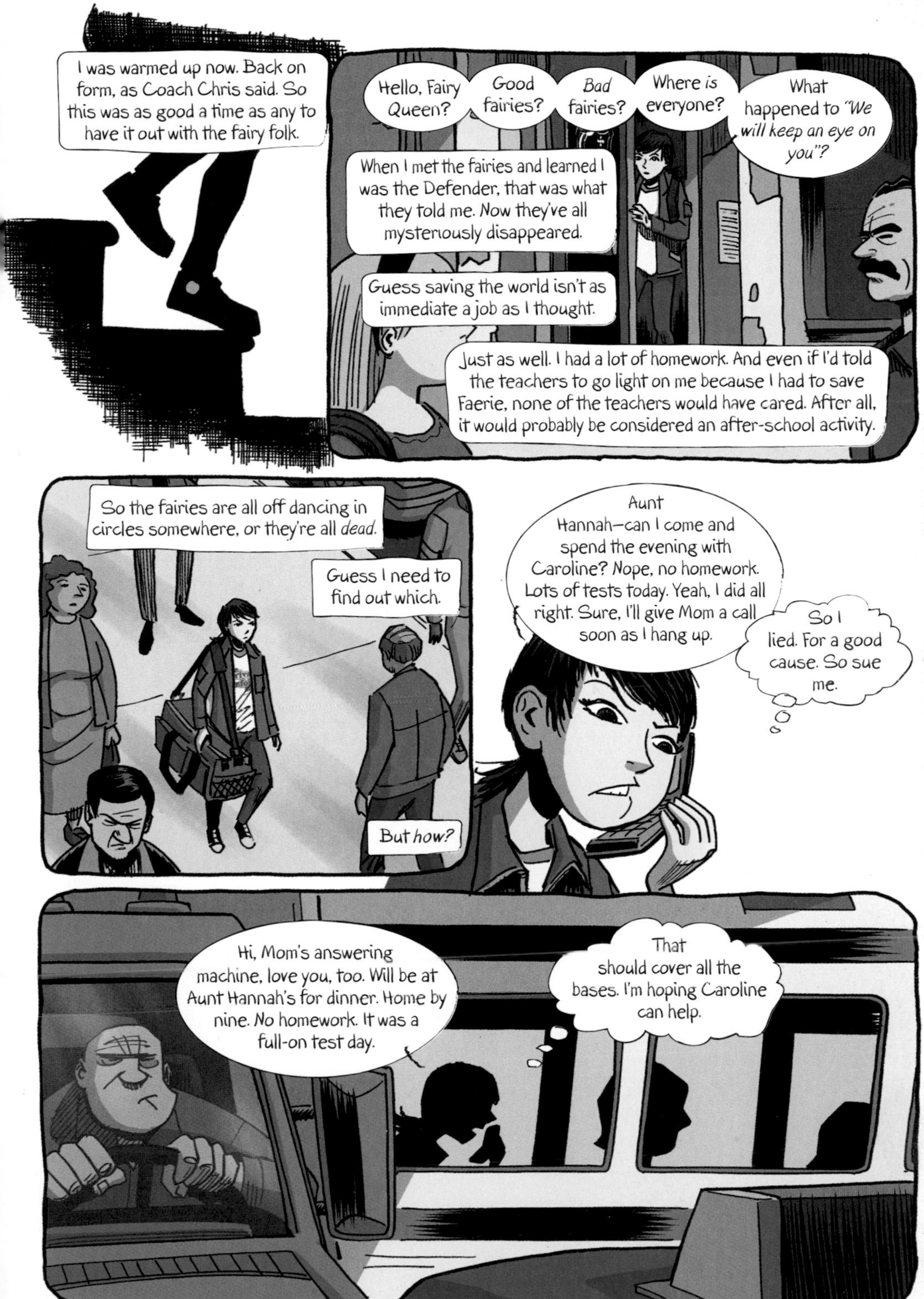
I was warmed up now. Back on form, as Coach Chris said. So this was as good a time as any to have it out with the fairy folk.
Hello, Fairy Queen?
Good fairies?
Bad fairies?
Where *is* everyone?
What happened to *"We will keep an eye on you"*?
When I met the fairies and learned I was the Defender, that was what they told me. Now they've all mysteriously disappeared.
Guess saving the world isn't as immediate a job as I thought.
Just as well. I had a lot of homework. And even if I'd told the teachers to go light on me because I had to save Faerie, none of the teachers would have cared. After all, it would probably be considered an after-school activity.
So the fairies are all off dancing in circles somewhere, or they're all *dead*.
Guess I need to find out which.
But *how?*
Aunt Hannah—can I come and spend the evening with Caroline? Nope, no homework. Lots of tests today. Yeah, I did all right. Sure, I'll give Mom a call soon as I hang up.
So I lied. For a good cause. So sue me.
Hi, Mom's answering machine, love you, too. Will be at Aunt Hannah's for dinner. Home by nine. No homework. It was a full-on test day.
That should cover all the bases. I'm hoping Caroline can help.

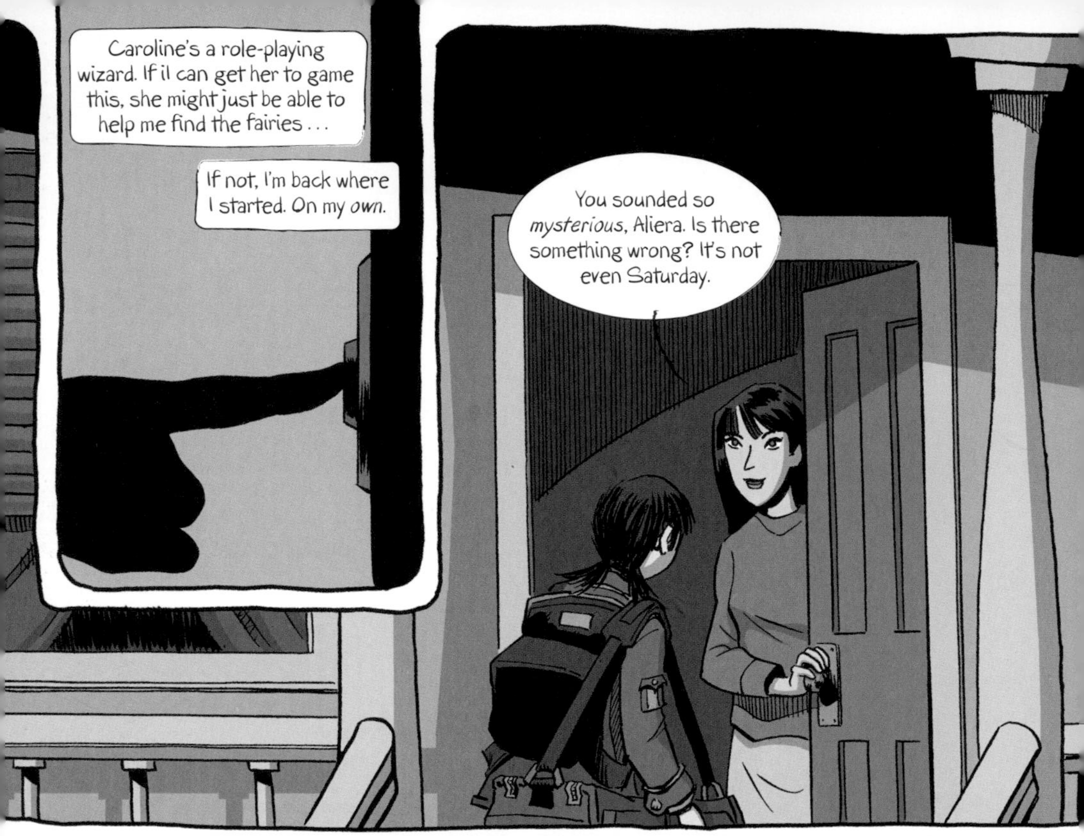
Caroline's a role-playing wizard. If il can get her to game this, she might just be able to help me find the fairies . . .
If not, I'm back where I started. On my *own.*
You sounded so *mysterious*, Aliera. Is there something wrong? It's not even Saturday.

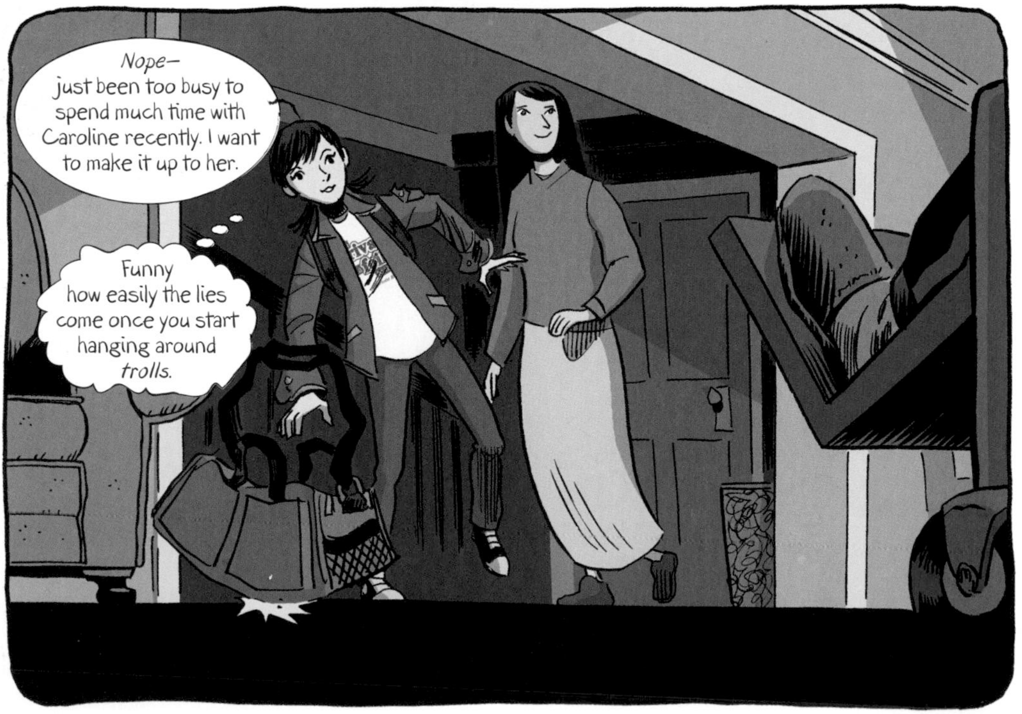
Nope— just been too busy to spend much time with Caroline recently. I want to make it up to her.
Funny how easily the lies come once you start hanging around *trolls*.

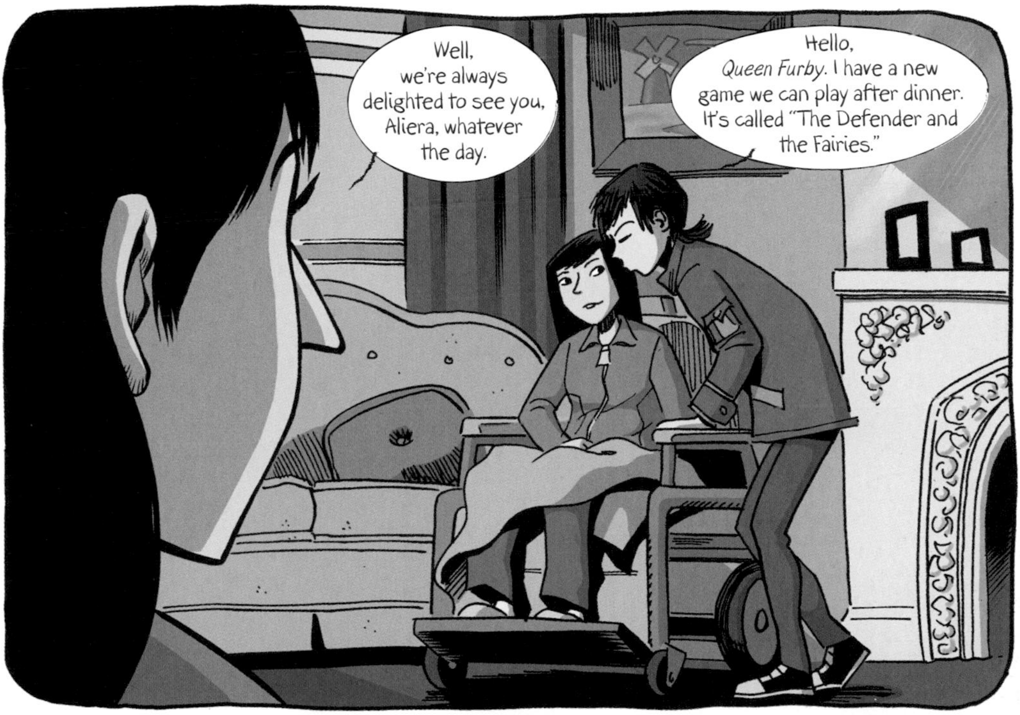
Well, we're always delighted to see you, Aliera, whatever the day.
Hello, *Queen Furby*. I have a new game we can play after dinner. It's called "The Defender and the Fairies."

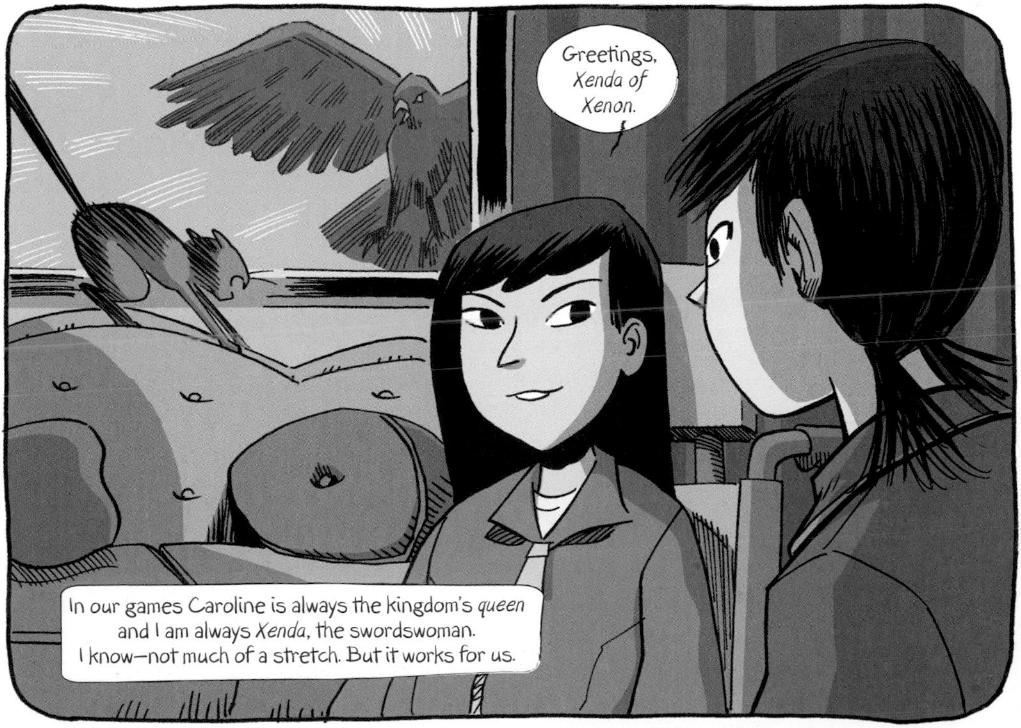
Greetings, *Xenda of Xenon.*
In our games Caroline is always the kingdom's *queen* and I am always *Xenda*, the swordswoman. I know—not much of a stretch. But it works for us.

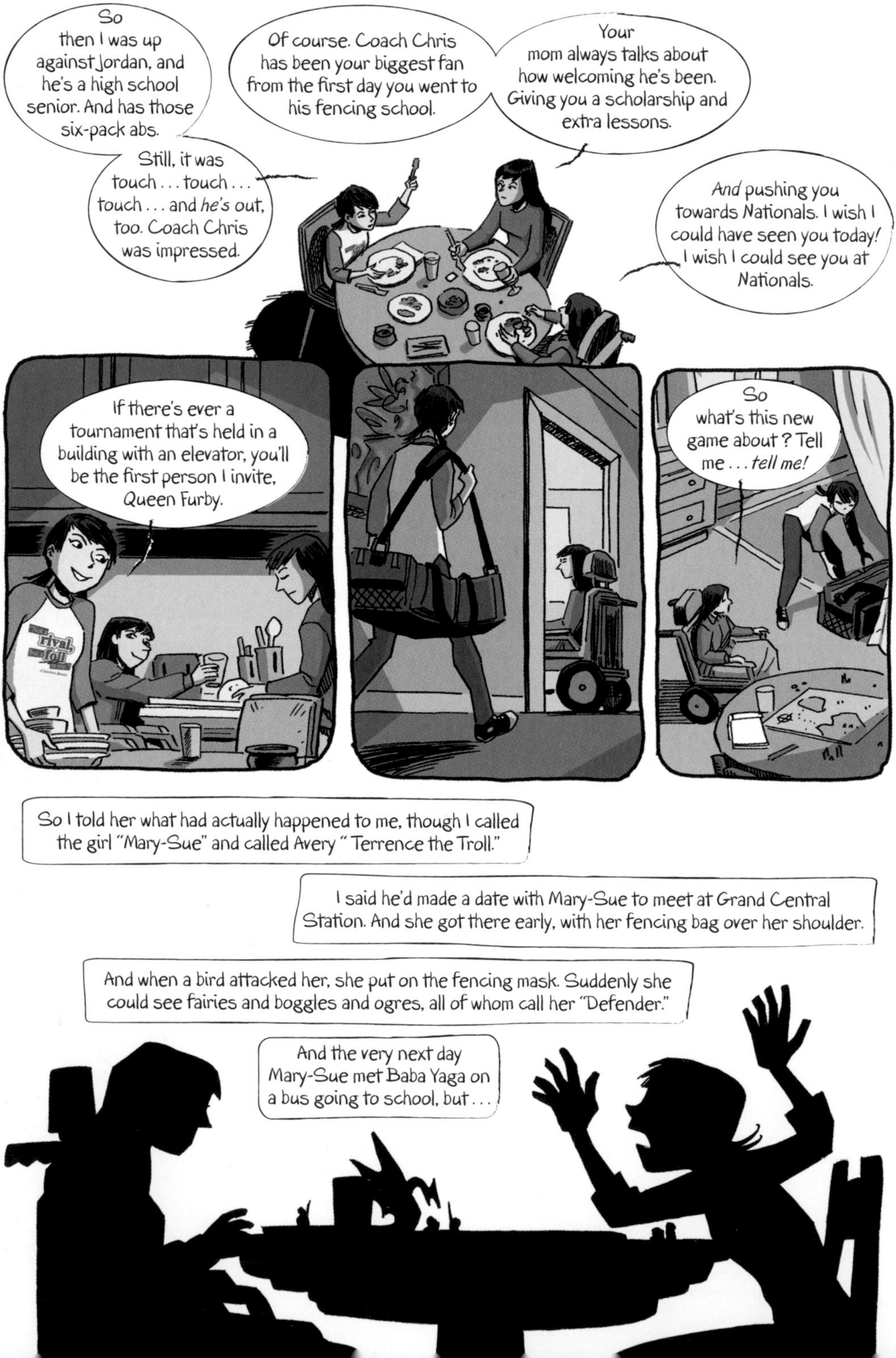

So then I was up against Jordan, and he's a high school senior. And has those six-pack abs.
Of course. Coach Chris has been your biggest fan from the first day you went to his fencing school.
Your mom always talks about how welcoming he's been. Giving you a scholarship and extra lessons.
Still, it was touch . . . touch . . . touch . . . and *he's* out, too. Coach Chris was impressed.
And pushing you towards Nationals. I wish I could have seen you today! I wish I could see you at Nationals.
If there's ever a tournament that's held in a building with an elevator, you'll be the first person I invite, Queen Furby.
So what's this new game about? Tell me . . . *tell me!*
So I told her what had actually happened to me, though I called the girl "Mary-Sue" and called Avery " Terrence the Troll."
I said he'd made a date with Mary-Sue to meet at Grand Central Station. And she got there early, with her fencing bag over her shoulder.
And when a bird attacked her, she put on the fencing mask. Suddenly she could see fairies and boggles and ogres, all of whom call her "Defender."
And the very next day Mary-Sue met Baba Yaga on a bus going to school, but . . .

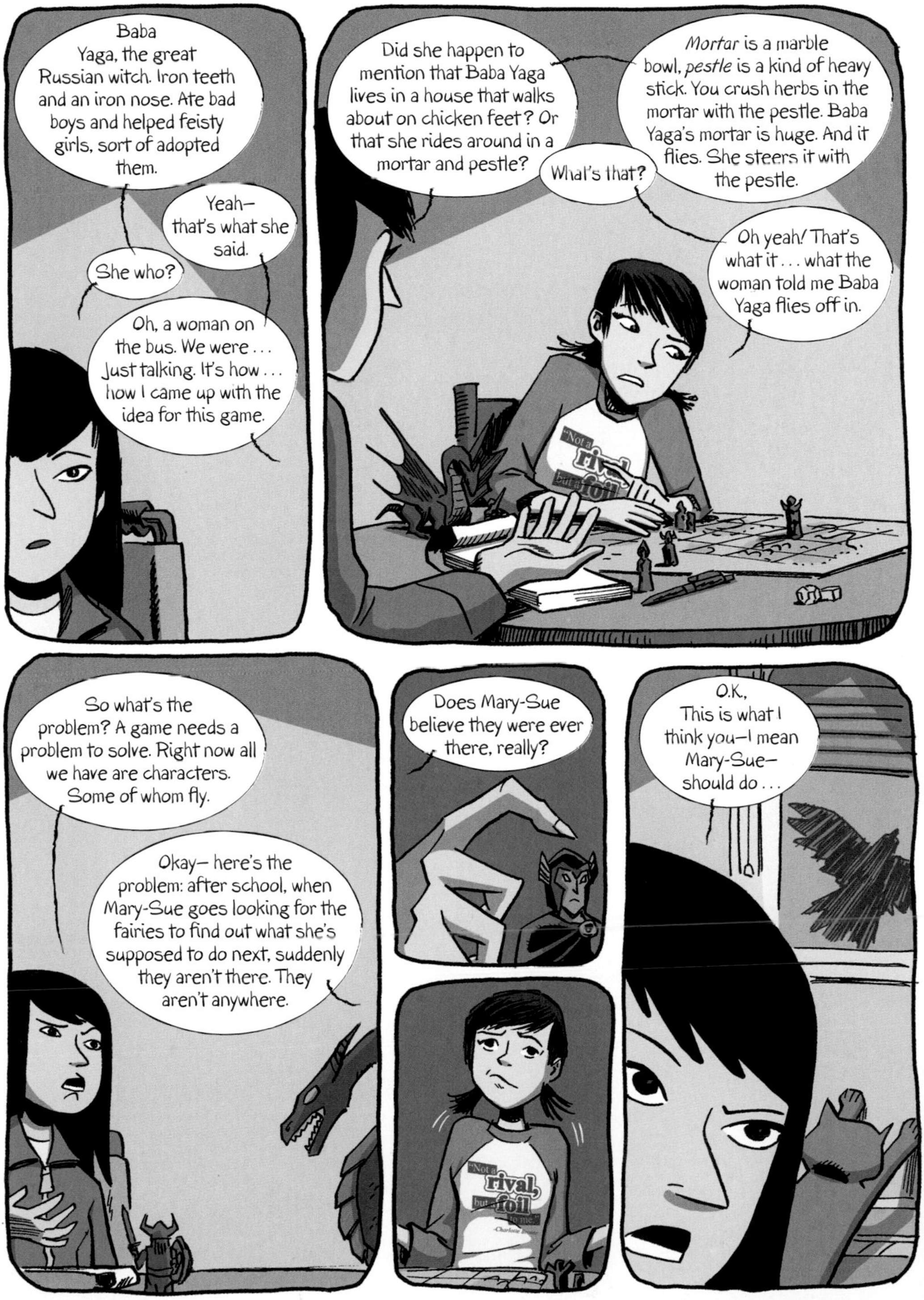
Baba Yaga, the great Russian witch. Iron teeth and an iron nose. Ate bad boys and helped feisty girls, sort of adopted them.
She who?
Yeah— that's what she said.
Oh, a woman on the bus. We were . . . Just talking. It's how . . . how I came up with the idea for this game.
Did she happen to mention that Baba Yaga lives in a house that walks about on chicken feet? Or that she rides around in a mortar and pestle?
What's that?
Mortar is a marble bowl, *pestle* is a kind of heavy stick. You crush herbs in the mortar with the pestle. Baba Yaga's mortar is huge. And it flies. She steers it with the pestle.
Oh yeah! That's what it . . . what the woman told me Baba Yaga flies off in.
So what's the problem? A game needs a problem to solve. Right now all we have are characters. Some of whom fly.
Okay— here's the problem: after school, when Mary-Sue goes looking for the fairies to find out what she's supposed to do next, suddenly they aren't there. They aren't anywhere.
Does Mary-Sue believe they were ever there, really?
O.K., This is what I think you—I mean Mary-Sue— should do . . .

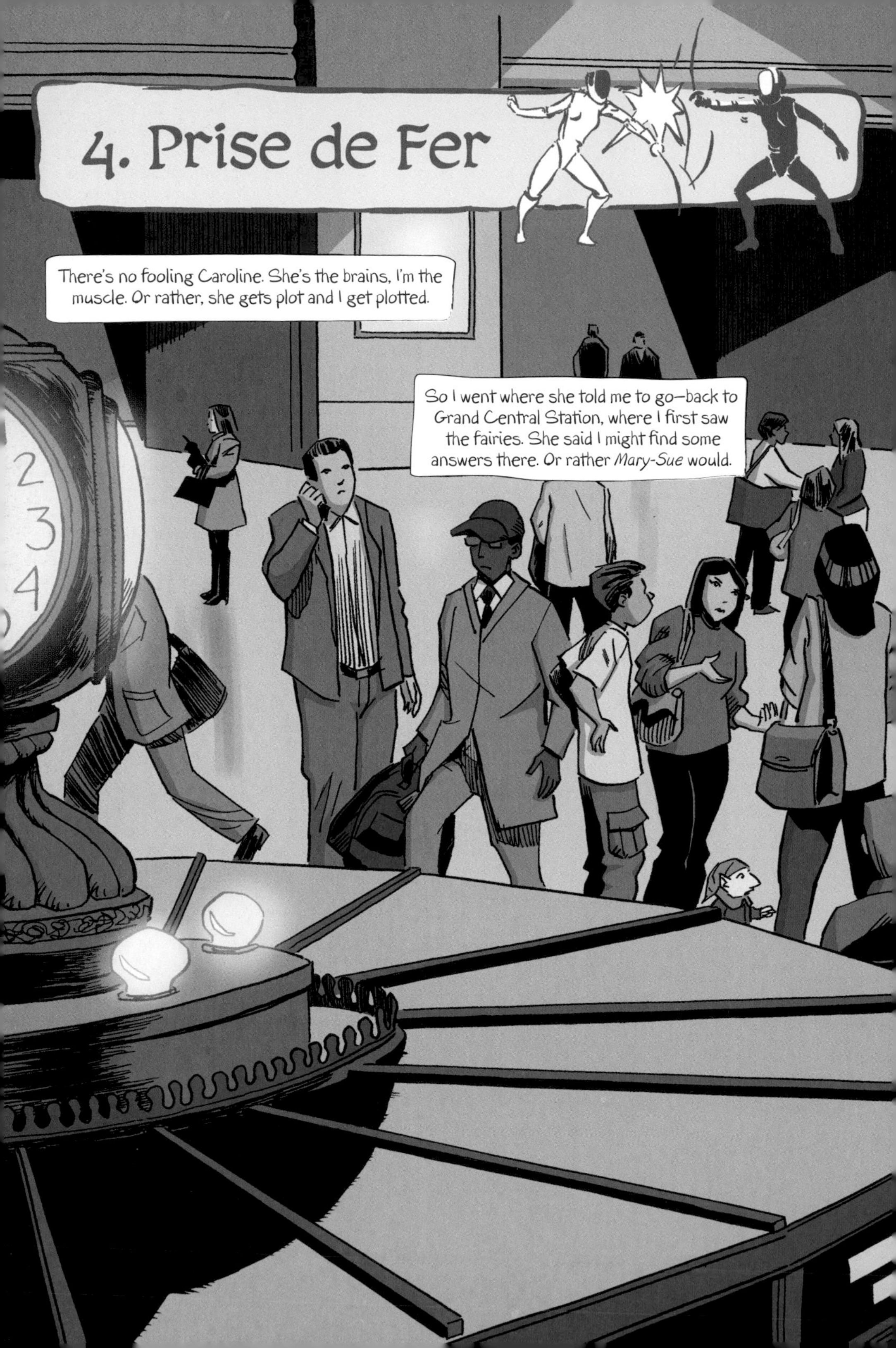

4. Prise de Fer
There's no fooling Caroline. She's the brains, I'm the muscle. Or rather, she gets plot and I get plotted.
So I went where she told me to go—back to Grand Central Station, where I first saw the fairies. She said I might find some answers there. Or rather *Mary-Sue* would.

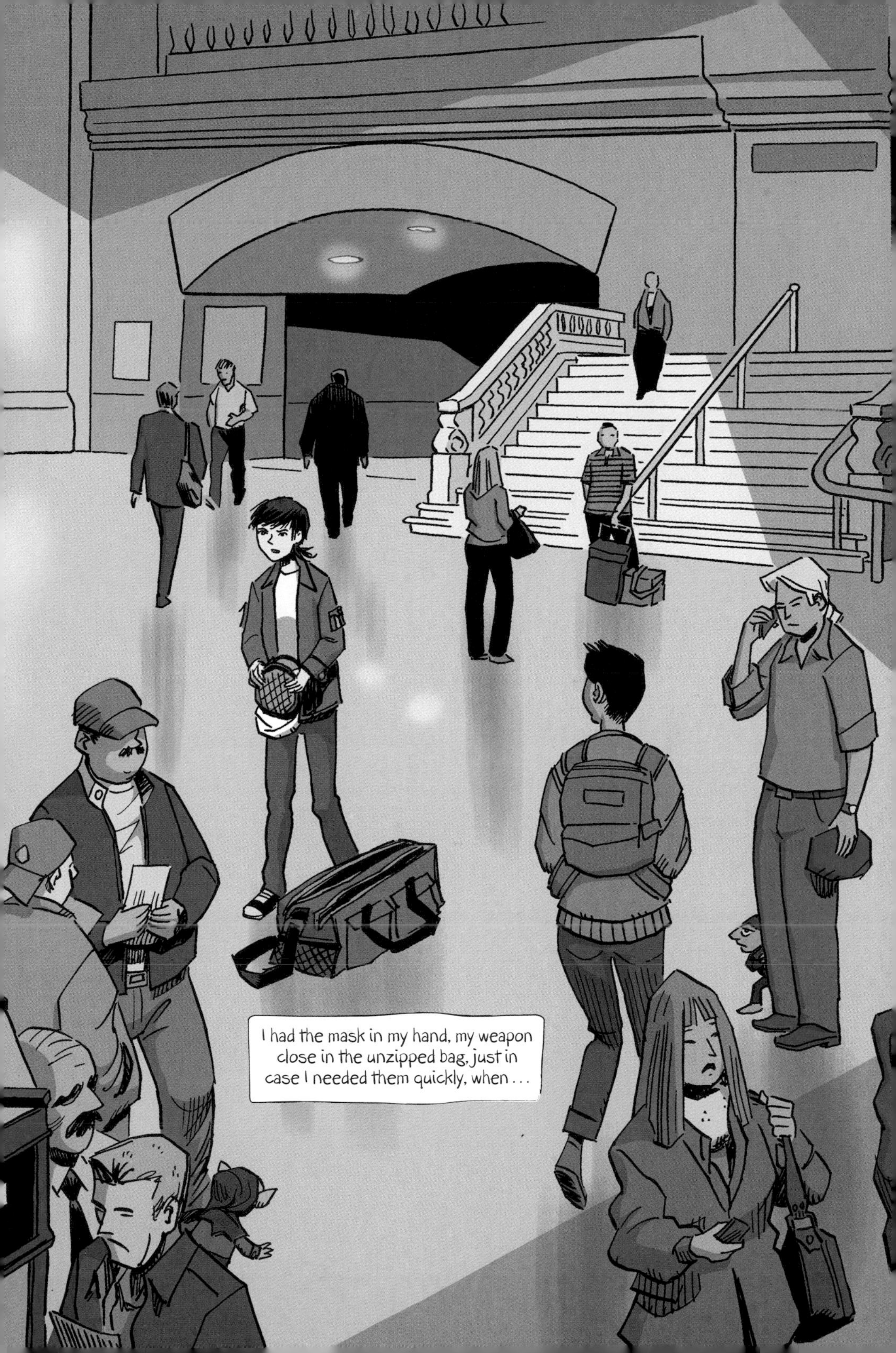
I had the mask in my hand, my weapon close in the unzipped bag, just in case I needed them quickly, when . . .

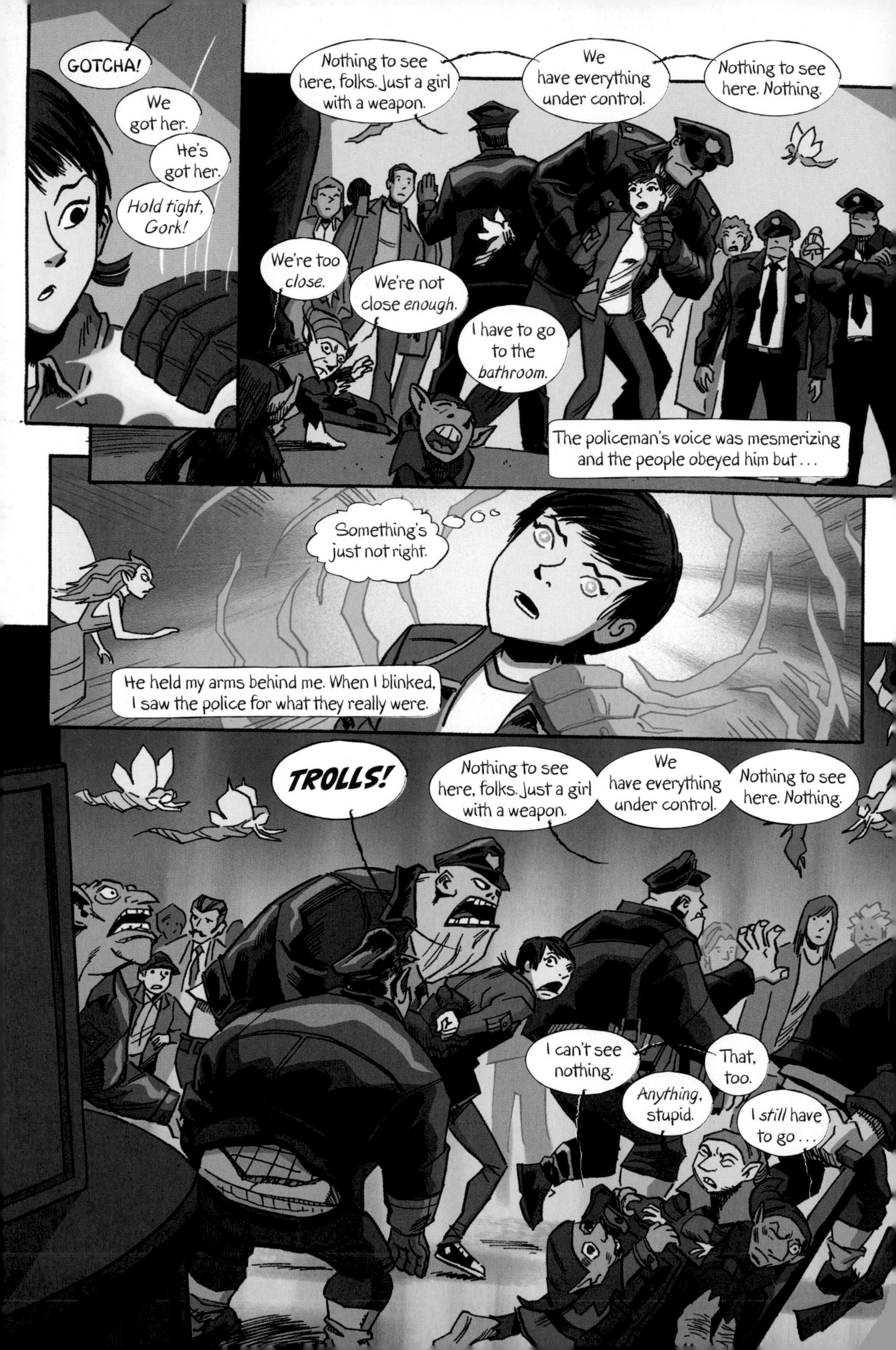
GOTCHA!
We got her.
He's got her.
Hold tight, Gork!
Nothing to see here, folks. Just a girl with a weapon.
We have everything under control.
Nothing to see here. Nothing.
We're too close.
We're not close enough.
I have to go to the bathroom.
The policeman's voice was mesmerizing and the people obeyed him but . . .
Something's just not right.
He held my arms behind me. When I blinked, I saw the police for what they really were.
TROLLS!
Nothing to see here, folks. Just a girl with a weapon.
We have everything under control.
Nothing to see here. Nothing.
I can't see nothing.
Anything, stupid.
That, too.
I still have to go . . .

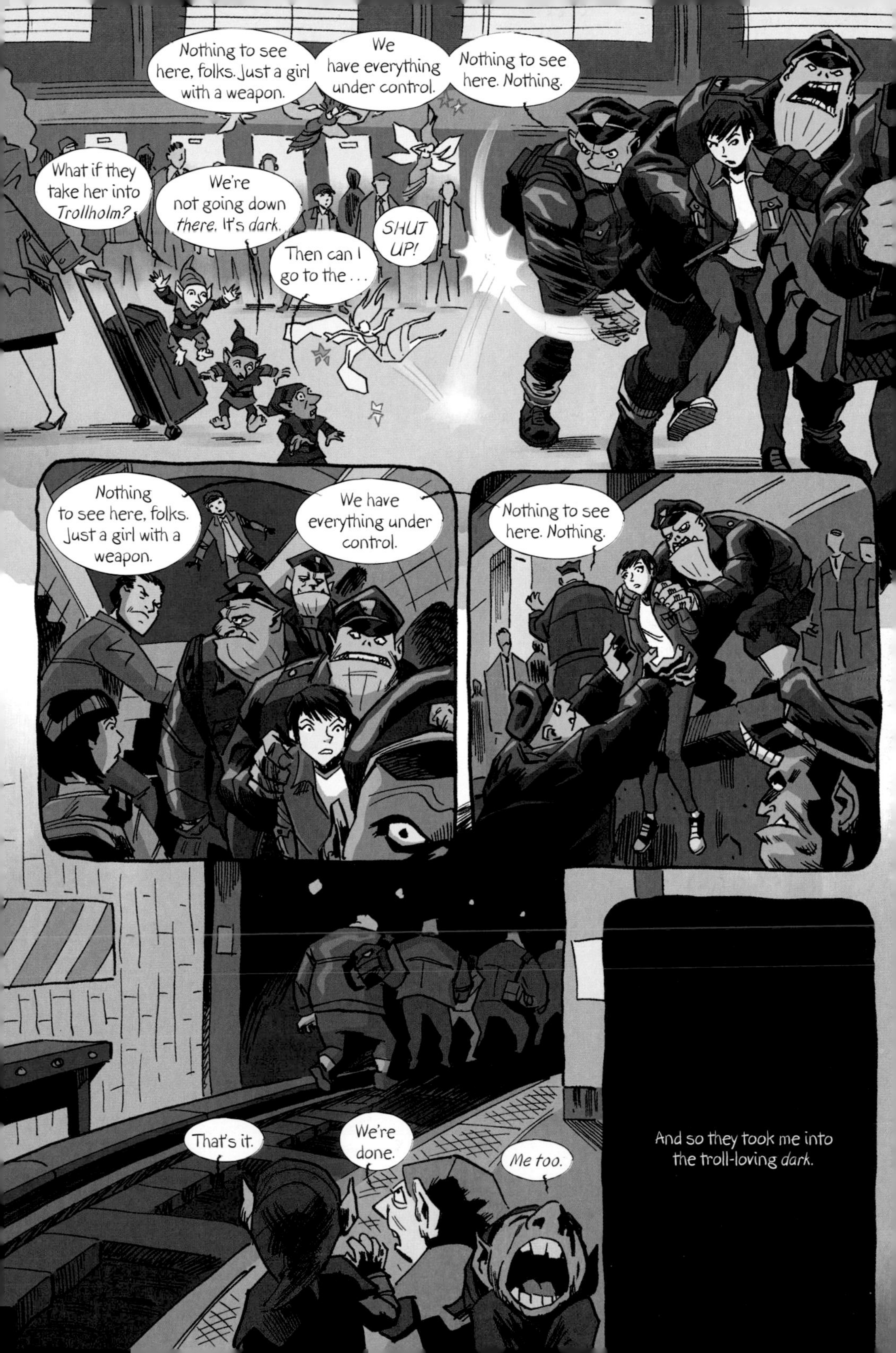
Nothing to see here, folks. Just a girl with a weapon.
We have everything under control.
Nothing to see here. Nothing.
What if they take her into *Trollholm?*
We're not going down *there*. It's *dark*.
Then can I go to the . . .
SHUT UP!
Nothing to see here, folks. Just a girl with a weapon.
We have everything under control.
Nothing to see here. Nothing.
That's it.
We're done.
Me too.
And so they took me into the troll-loving *dark*.

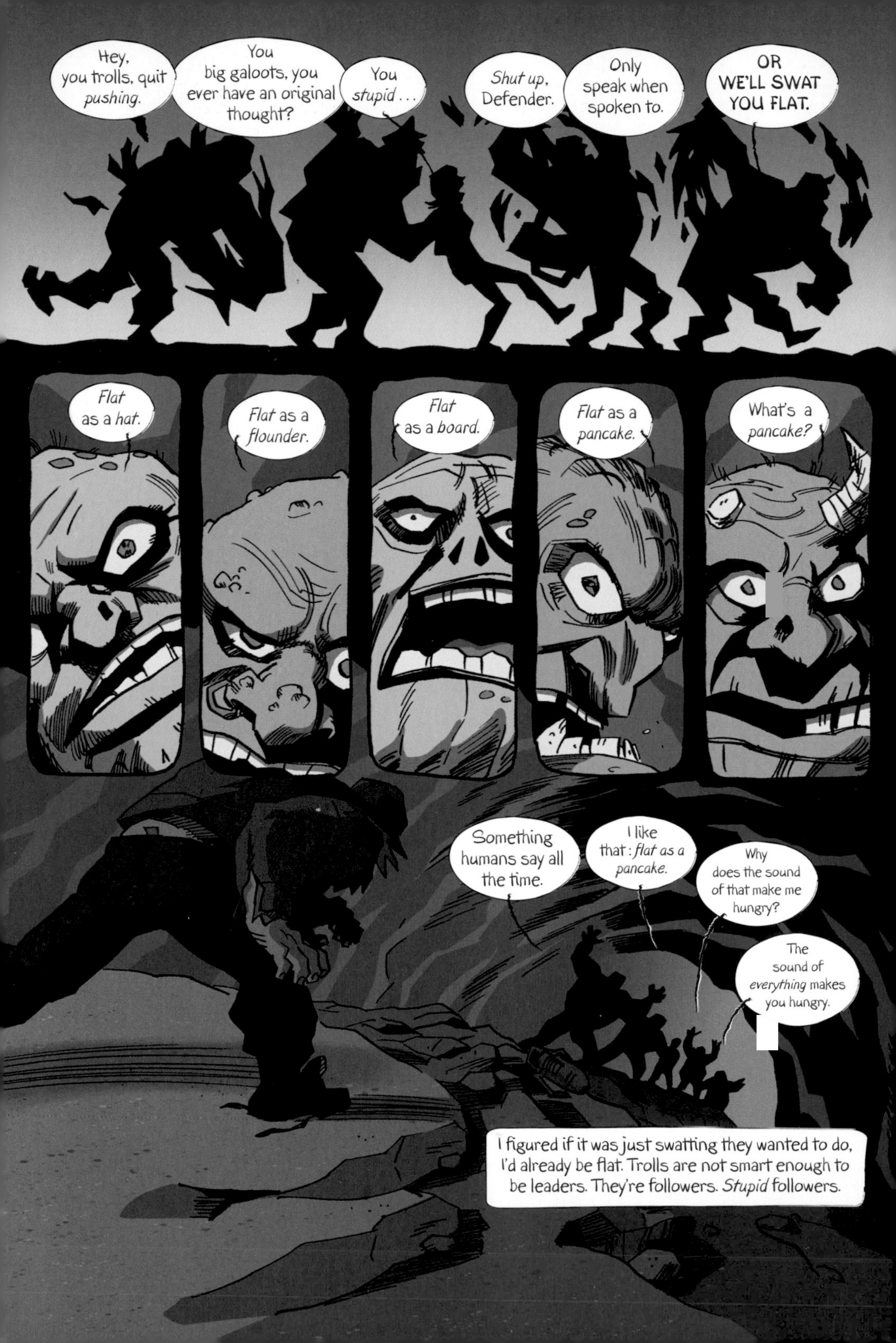
Hey, you trolls, quit pushing.
You big galoots, you ever have an original thought?
You stupid . . .
Shut up, Defender.
Only speak when spoken to.
OR WE'LL SWAT YOU FLAT.
Flat as a hat.
Flat as a flounder.
Flat as a board.
Flat as a pancake.
What's a pancake?
Something humans say all the time.
I like that: flat as a pancake.
Why does the sound of that make me hungry?
The sound of everything makes you hungry.
I figured if it was just swatting they wanted to do, I'd already be flat. Trolls are not smart enough to be leaders. They're followers. Stupid followers.

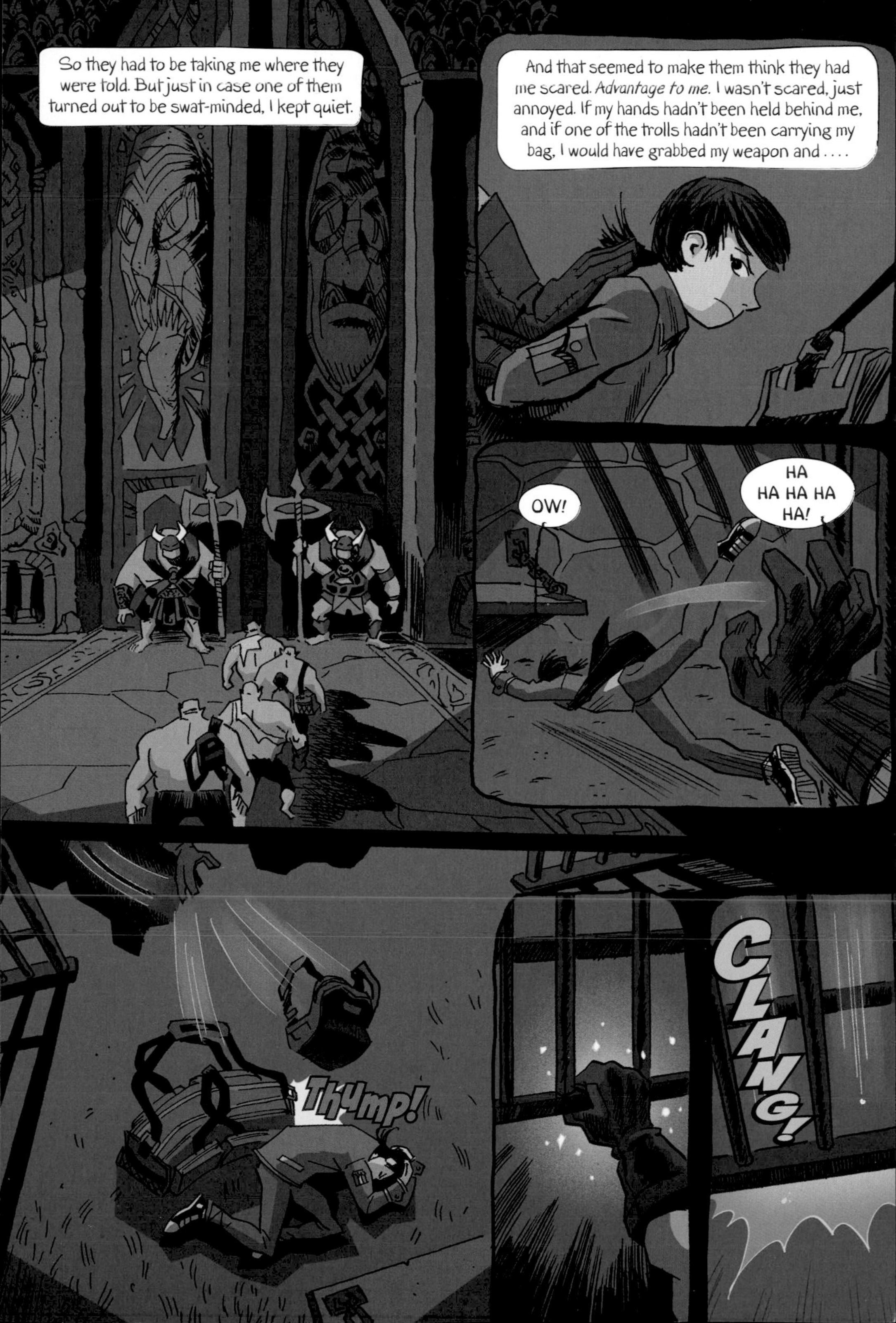
So they had to be taking me where they were told. But just in case one of them turned out to be swat-minded, I kept quiet.
And that seemed to make them think they had me scared. *Advantage to me.* I wasn't scared, just annoyed. If my hands hadn't been held behind me, and if one of the trolls hadn't been carrying my bag, I would have grabbed my weapon and . . . .
OW!
HA HA HA HA HA!
THUMP!
CLANG!

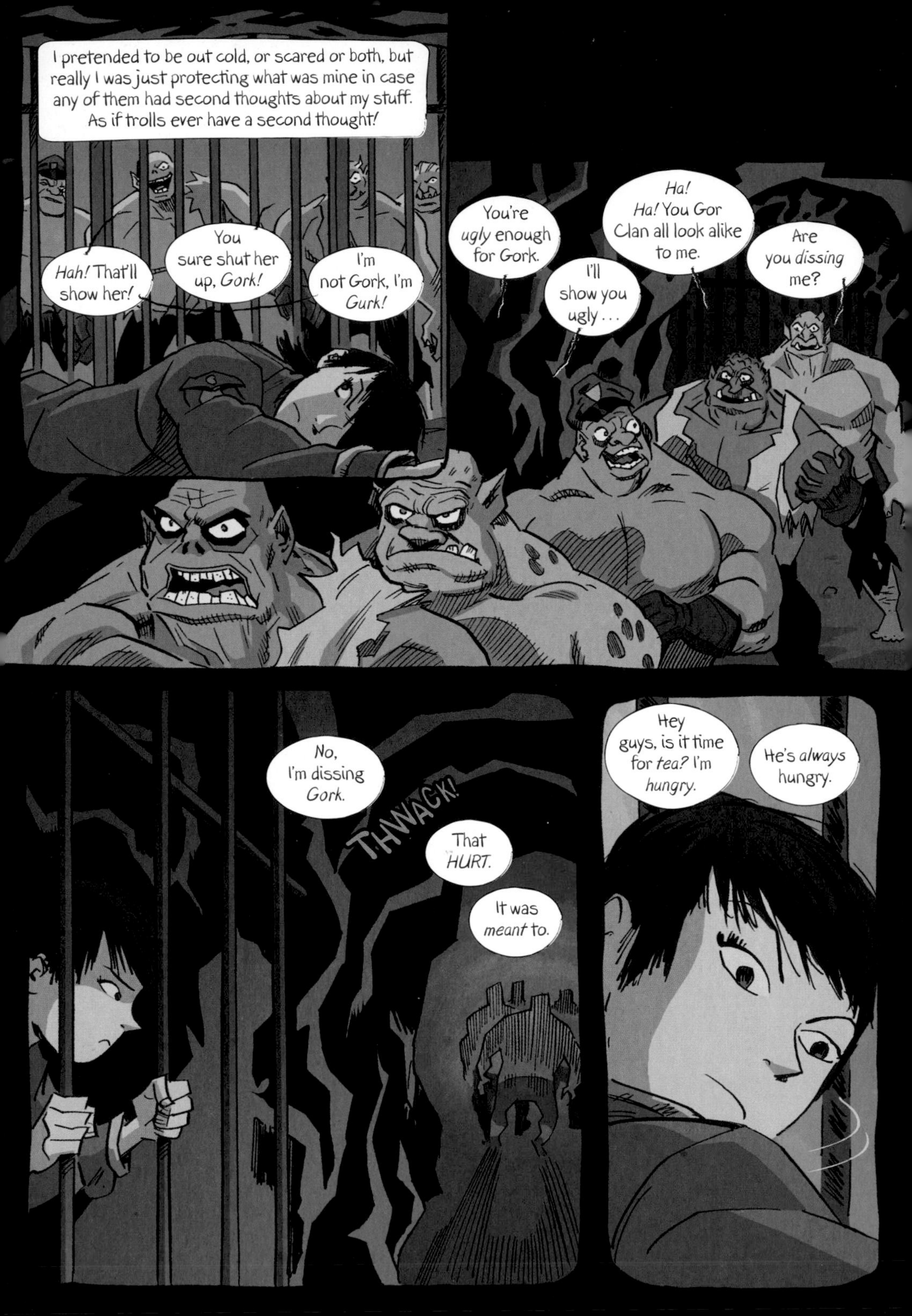

I pretended to be out cold, or scared or both, but really I was just protecting what was mine in case any of them had second thoughts about my stuff. As if trolls ever have a second thought!
Hah! That'll show her!
You sure shut her up, Gork!
I'm not Gork, I'm Gurk!
You're ugly enough for Gork.
I'll show you ugly . . .
Ha! Ha! You Gor Clan all look alike to me.
Are you dissing me?
No, I'm dissing Gork.
THWACK!
That HURT.
It was meant to.
Hey guys, is it time for tea? I'm hungry.
He's always hungry.

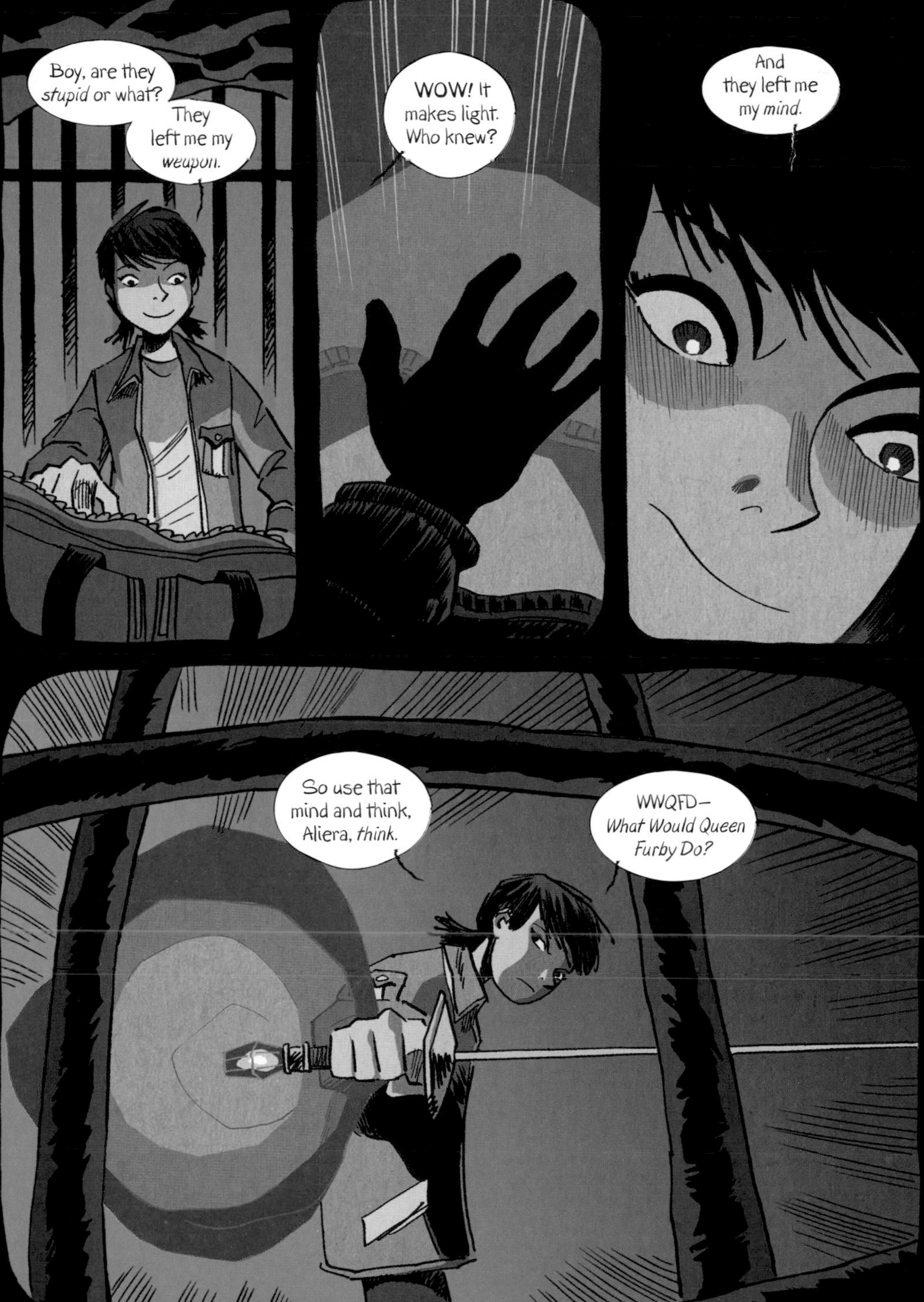
Boy, are they *stupid* or what?
They left me my *weapon*.
WOW! It makes light. Who knew?
And they left me my *mind*.
So use that mind and think, Aliera, *think*.
WWQFD—
What Would Queen Furby Do?

5. Derobement

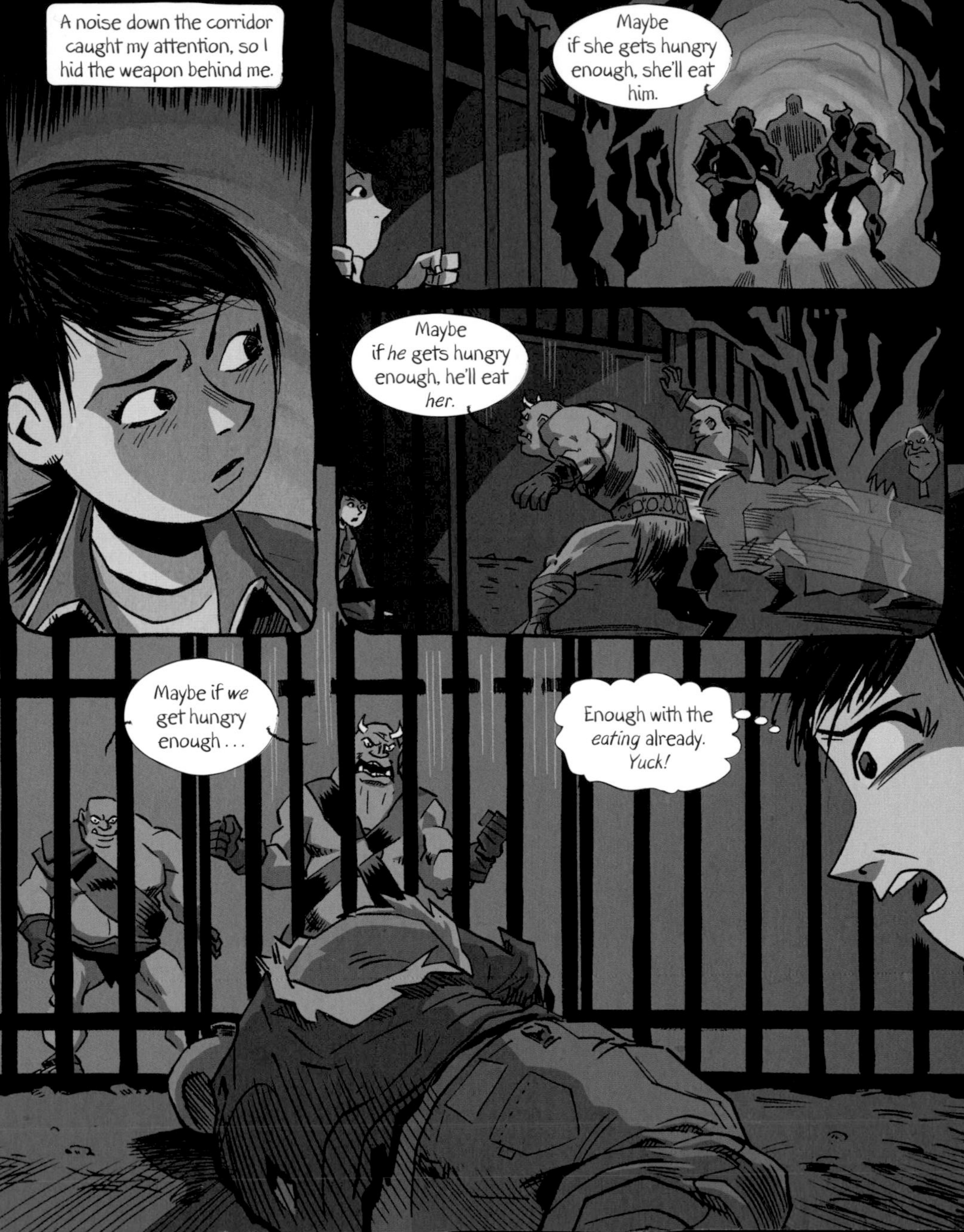
A noise down the corridor caught my attention, so I hid the weapon behind me.
Maybe if she gets hungry enough, she'll eat him.
Maybe if *he* gets hungry enough, he'll eat *her*.
Maybe if *we* get hungry enough . . .
Enough with the *eating* already. *Yuck!*

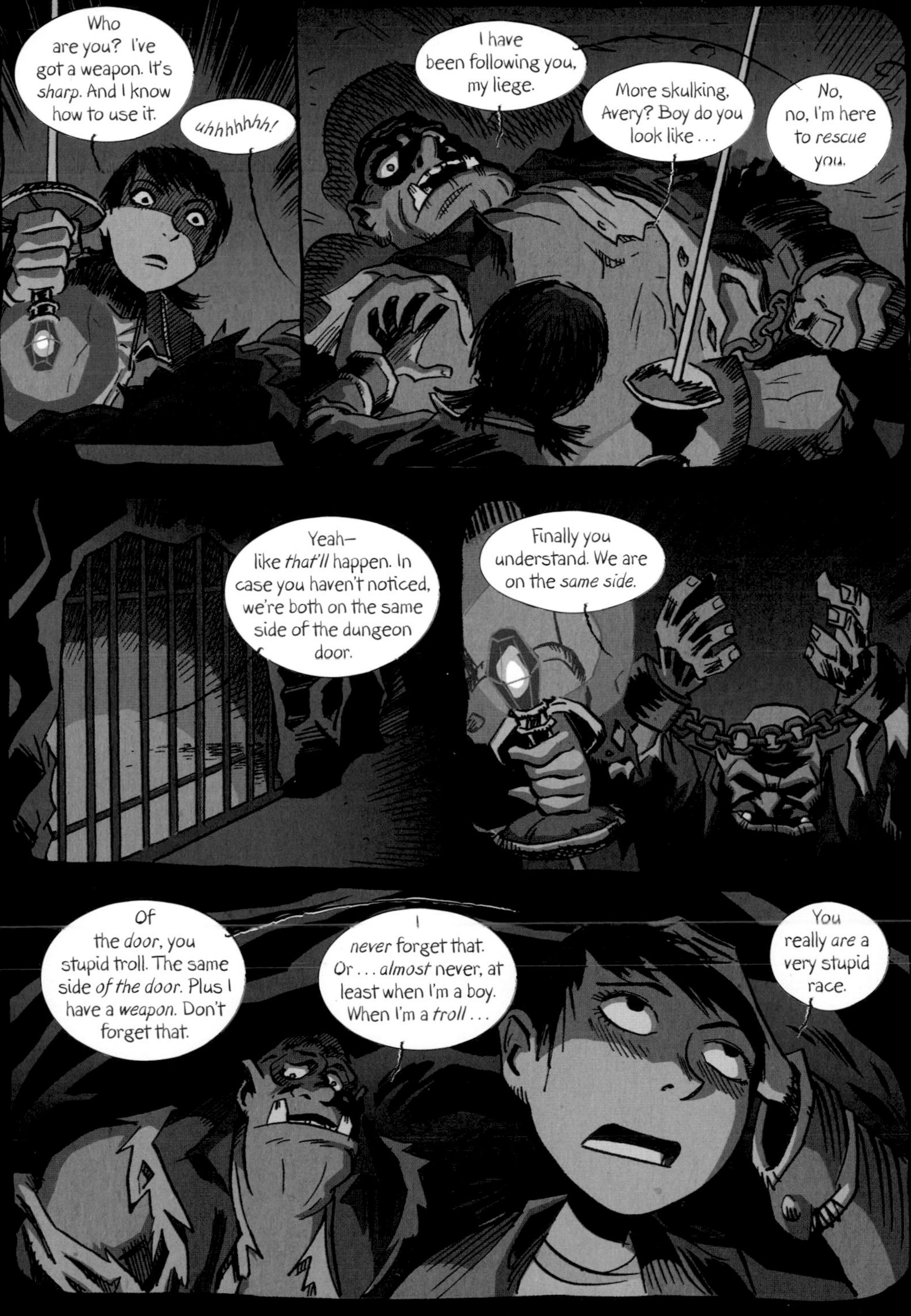
Who are you? I've got a weapon. It's *sharp*. And I know how to use it.
uhhhhhhh!
I have been following you, my liege.
More skulking, Avery? Boy do you look like . . .
No, no, I'm here to *rescue* you.
Yeah— like *that'll* happen. In case you haven't noticed, we're both on the same side of the dungeon door.
Finally you understand. We are on the *same side*.
Of the *door*, you stupid troll. The same side *of the door*. Plus I have a *weapon*. Don't forget that.
I *never* forget that. Or . . . *almost* never, at least when I'm a boy. When I'm a *troll* . . .
You really *are* a very stupid race.

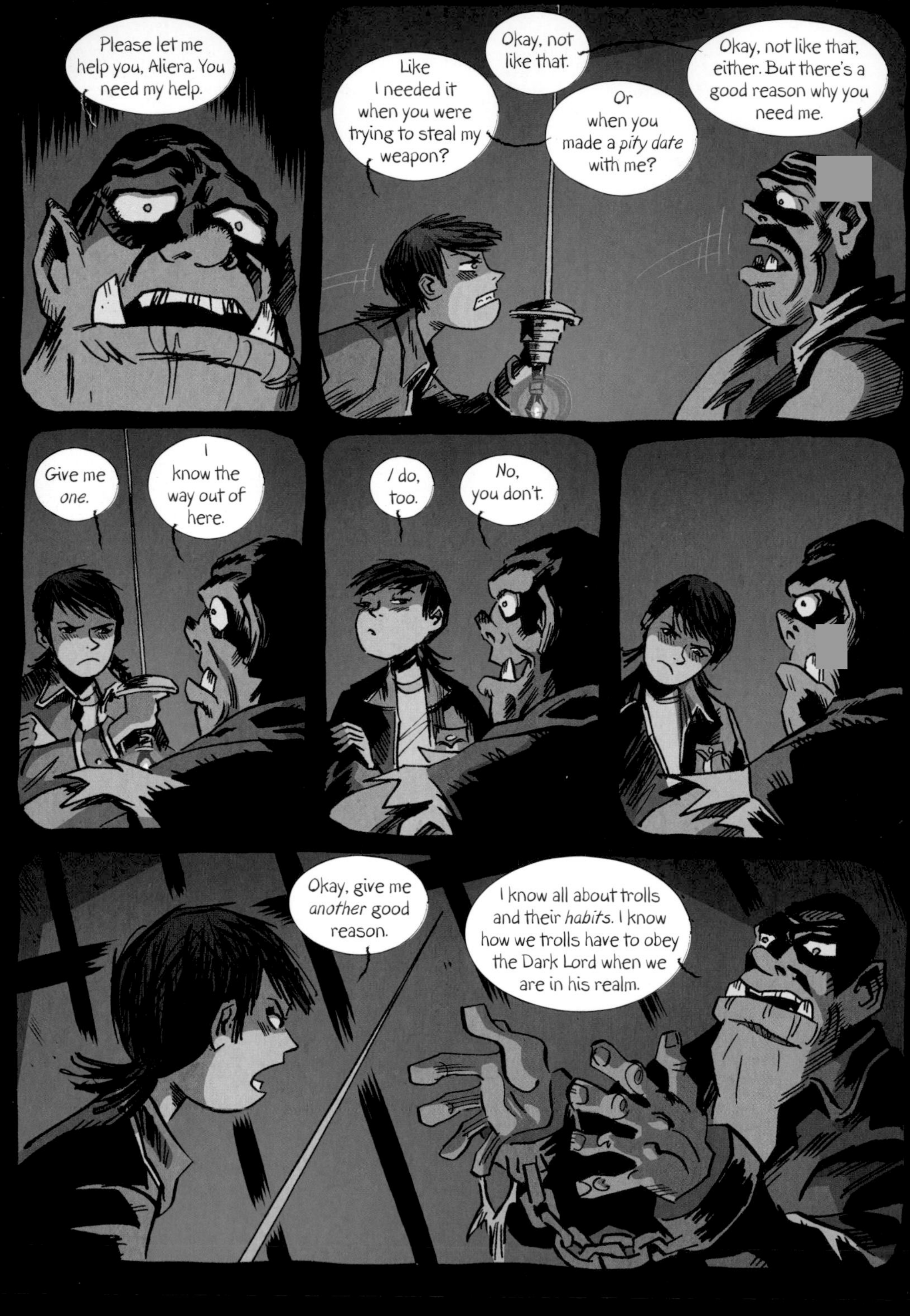
Please let me help you, Aliera. You need my help.
Like I needed it when you were trying to steal my weapon?
Okay, not like that.
Or when you made a *pity date* with me?
Okay, not like that, either. But there's a good reason why you need me.
Give me *one.*
I know the way out of here.
I do, too.
No, you don't.
Okay, give me *another* good reason.
I know all about trolls and their *habits.* I know how we trolls have to obey the Dark Lord when we are in his realm.

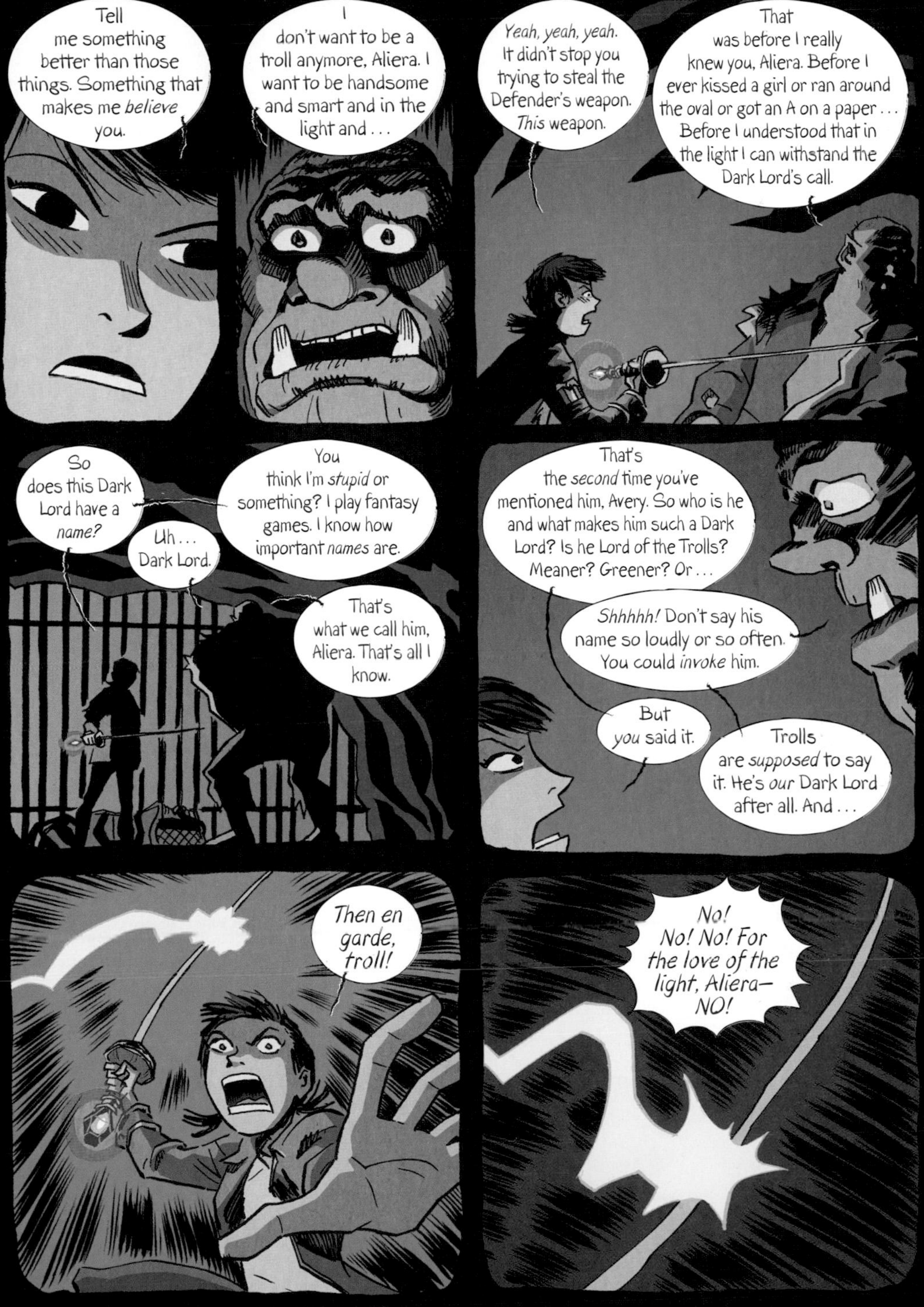
Tell me something better than those things. Something that makes me *believe* you.
I don't want to be a troll anymore, Aliera. I want to be handsome and smart and in the light and . . .
Yeah, yeah, yeah. It didn't stop you trying to steal the Defender's weapon. *This* weapon.
That was before I really knew you, Aliera. Before I ever kissed a girl or ran around the oval or got an A on a paper . . . Before I understood that in the light I can withstand the Dark Lord's call.
So does this Dark Lord have a *name?*
Uh . . . Dark Lord.
You think I'm *stupid* or something? I play fantasy games. I know how important *names* are.
That's what we call him, Aliera. That's all I know.
That's the *second* time you've mentioned him, Avery. So who is he and what makes him such a Dark Lord? Is he Lord of the Trolls? Meaner? Greener? Or . . .
Shhhhh! Don't say his name so loudly or so often. You could *invoke* him.
But *you* said it.
Trolls are *supposed* to say it. He's *our* Dark Lord after all. And . . .
Then en garde, troll!
No! No! No! For the love of the light, Aliera— NO!

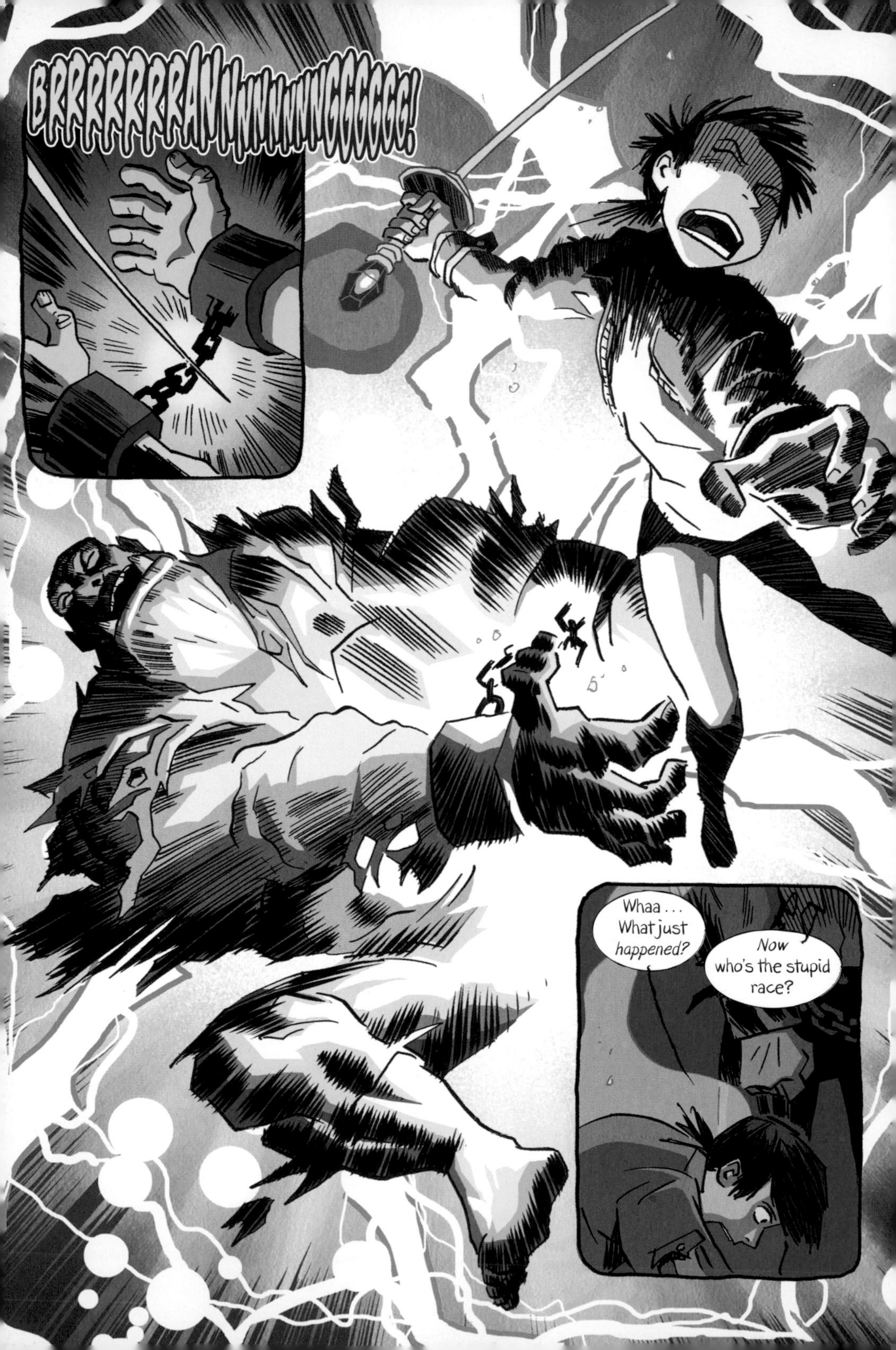
BRRRRRRRANNNNNNNGGGGGG!
Whaa . . . What just *happened?*
Now who's the stupid race?

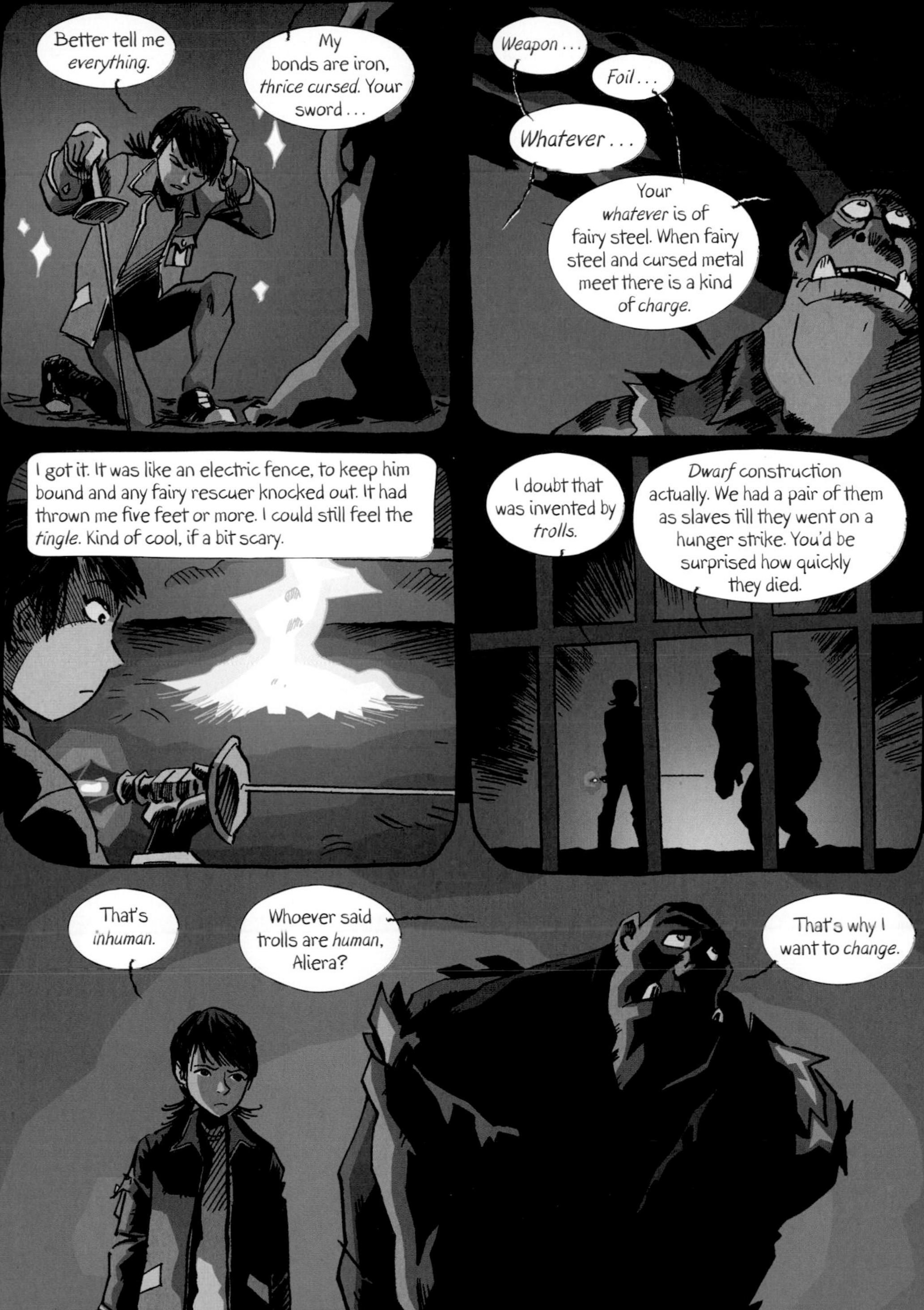
Better tell me *everything*.
My bonds are iron, *thrice cursed*. Your sword . . .
Weapon . . .
Foil . . .
Whatever . . .
Your *whatever* is of fairy steel. When fairy steel and cursed metal meet there is a kind of *charge*.
I got it. It was like an electric fence, to keep him bound and any fairy rescuer knocked out. It had thrown me five feet or more. I could still feel the *tingle*. Kind of cool, if a bit scary.
I doubt that was invented by *trolls*.
Dwarf construction actually. We had a pair of them as slaves till they went on a hunger strike. You'd be surprised how quickly they died.
That's *inhuman*.
Whoever said trolls are *human*, Aliera?
That's why I want to *change*.

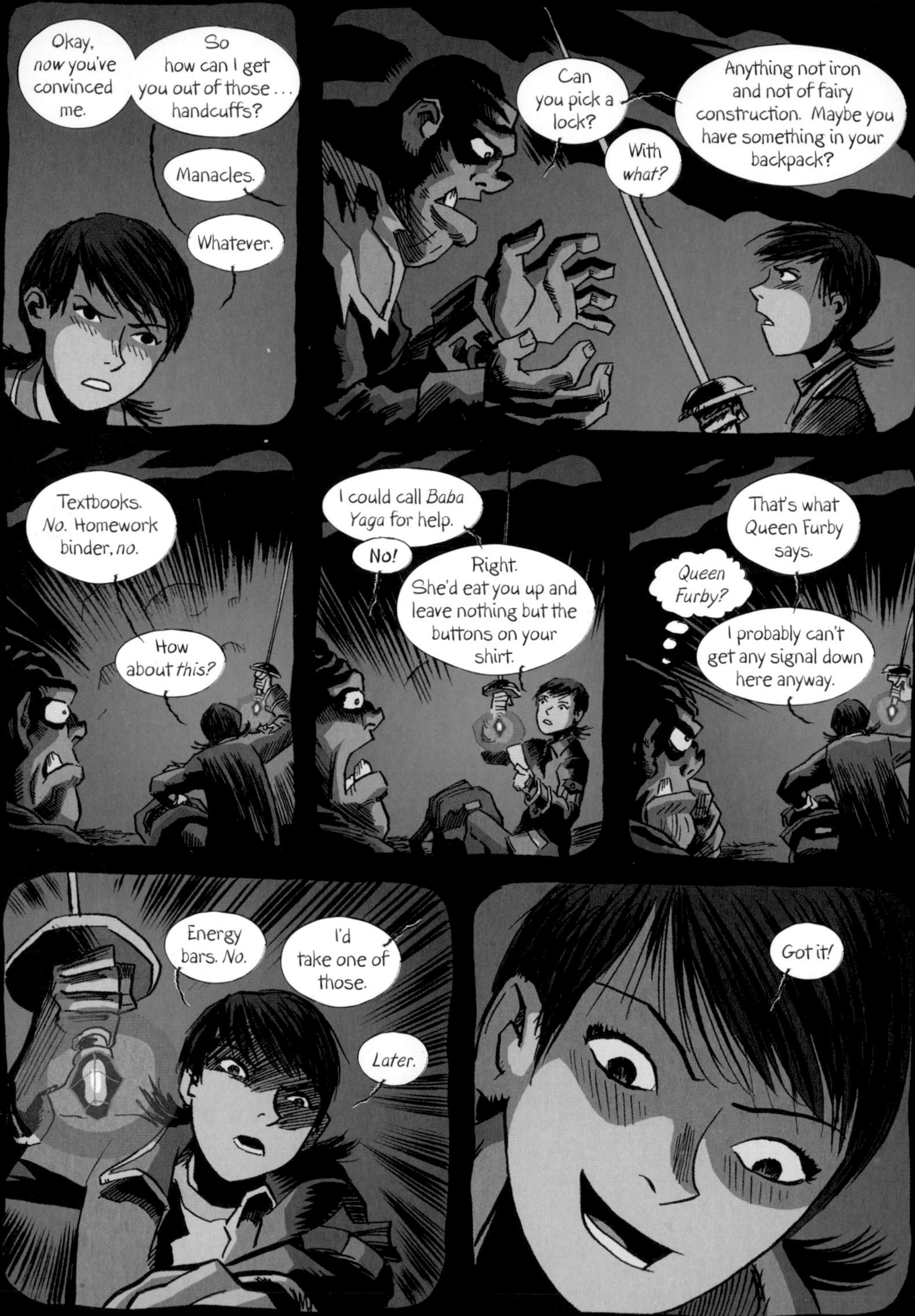
Okay, *now* you've convinced me.
So how can I get you out of those . . . handcuffs?
Manacles.
Whatever.
Can you pick a lock?
With *what?*
Anything not iron and not of fairy construction. Maybe you have something in your backpack?
Textbooks. *No.* Homework binder, *no.*
How about *this?*
I could call *Baba Yaga* for help.
No!
Right. She'd eat you up and leave nothing but the buttons on your shirt.
That's what Queen Furby says.
Queen Furby?
I probably can't get any signal down here anyway.
Energy bars. *No.*
I'd take one of those.
Later.
Got it!

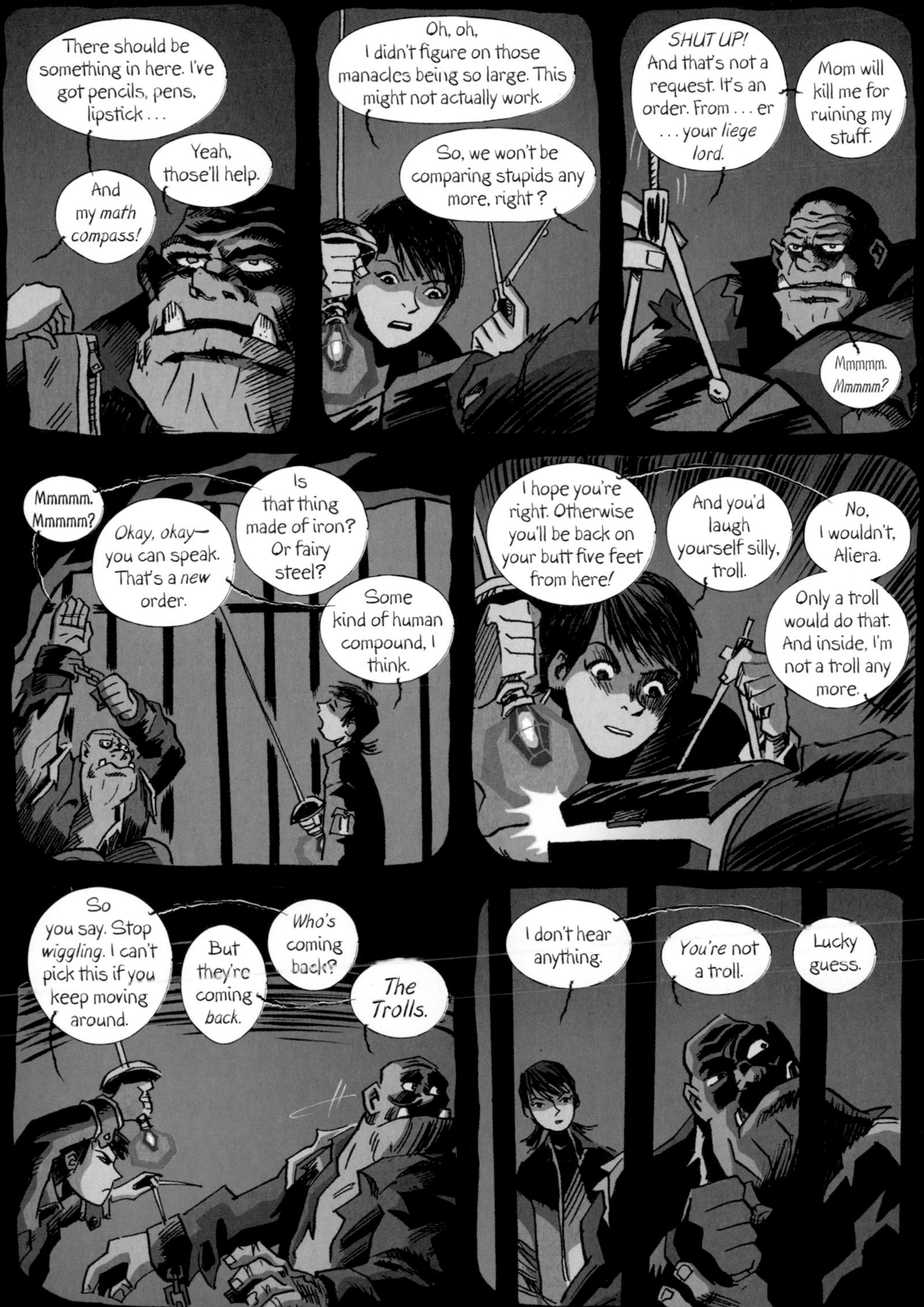
There should be something in here. I've got pencils, pens, lipstick . . .
Yeah, those'll help.
And my *math compass!*
Oh, oh, I didn't figure on those manacles being so large. This might not actually work.
So, we won't be comparing stupids any more, right ?
SHUT UP! And that's not a request. It's an order. From . . . er . . . your *liege lord.*
Mom will kill me for ruining my stuff.
Mmmmm. *Mmmmm?*
Mmmmm. Mmmmm?
Okay, okay—you can speak. That's a *new* order.
Is that thing made of iron? Or fairy steel?
Some kind of human compound, I think.
I hope you're right. Otherwise you'll be back on your butt five feet from here!
And you'd laugh yourself silly, troll.
No, I wouldn't, Aliera.
Only a troll would do that. And inside, I'm not a troll any more.
So you say. Stop *wiggling*. I can't pick this if you keep moving around.
But they're coming *back.*
Who's coming back?
The Trolls.
I don't hear anything.
You're not a troll.
Lucky guess.

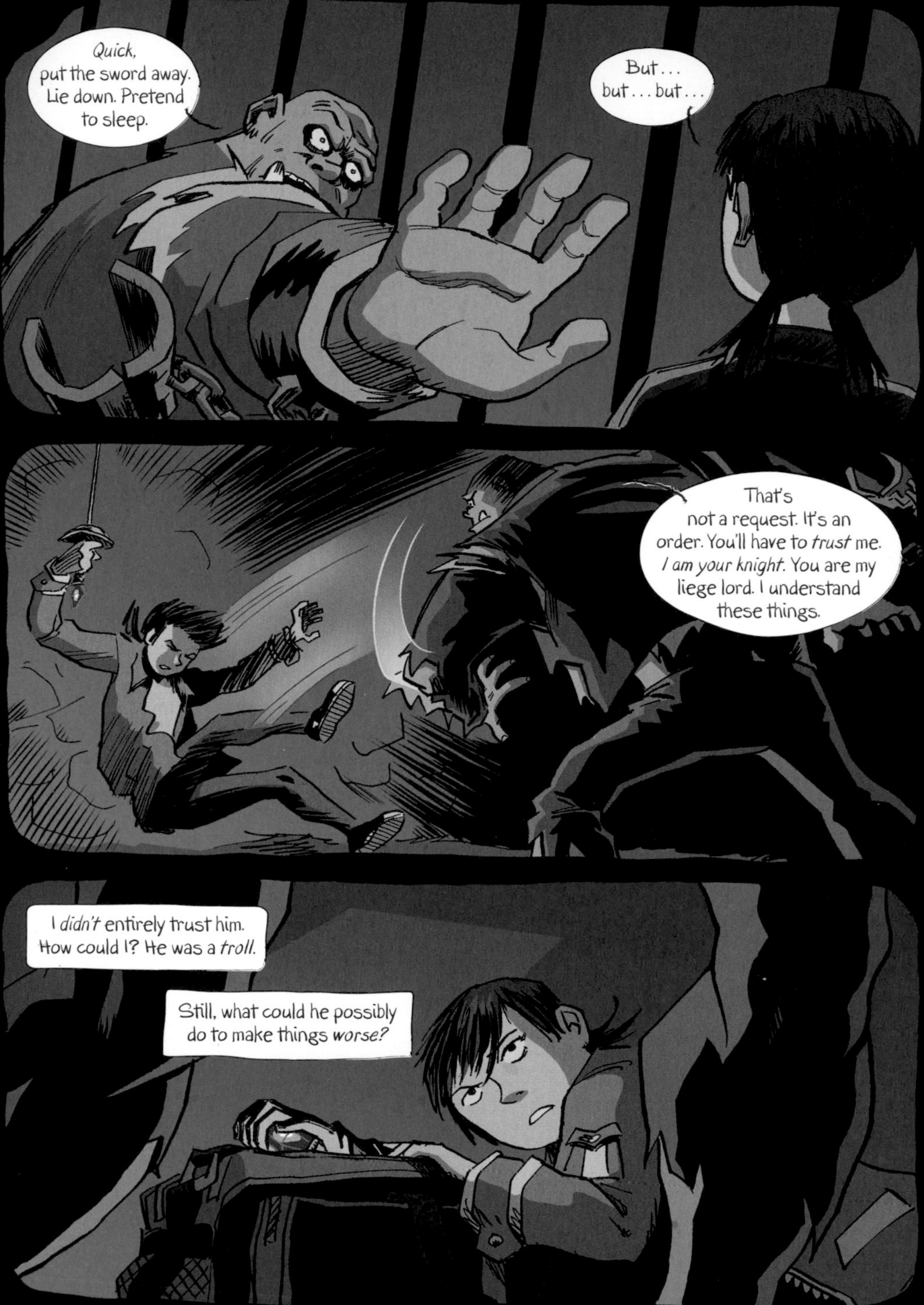
Quick, put the sword away. Lie down. Pretend to sleep.
But... but... but...
That's not a request. It's an order. You'll have to trust me. I am your knight. You are my liege lord. I understand these things.
I didn't entirely trust him. How could I? He was a troll.
Still, what could he possibly do to make things worse?

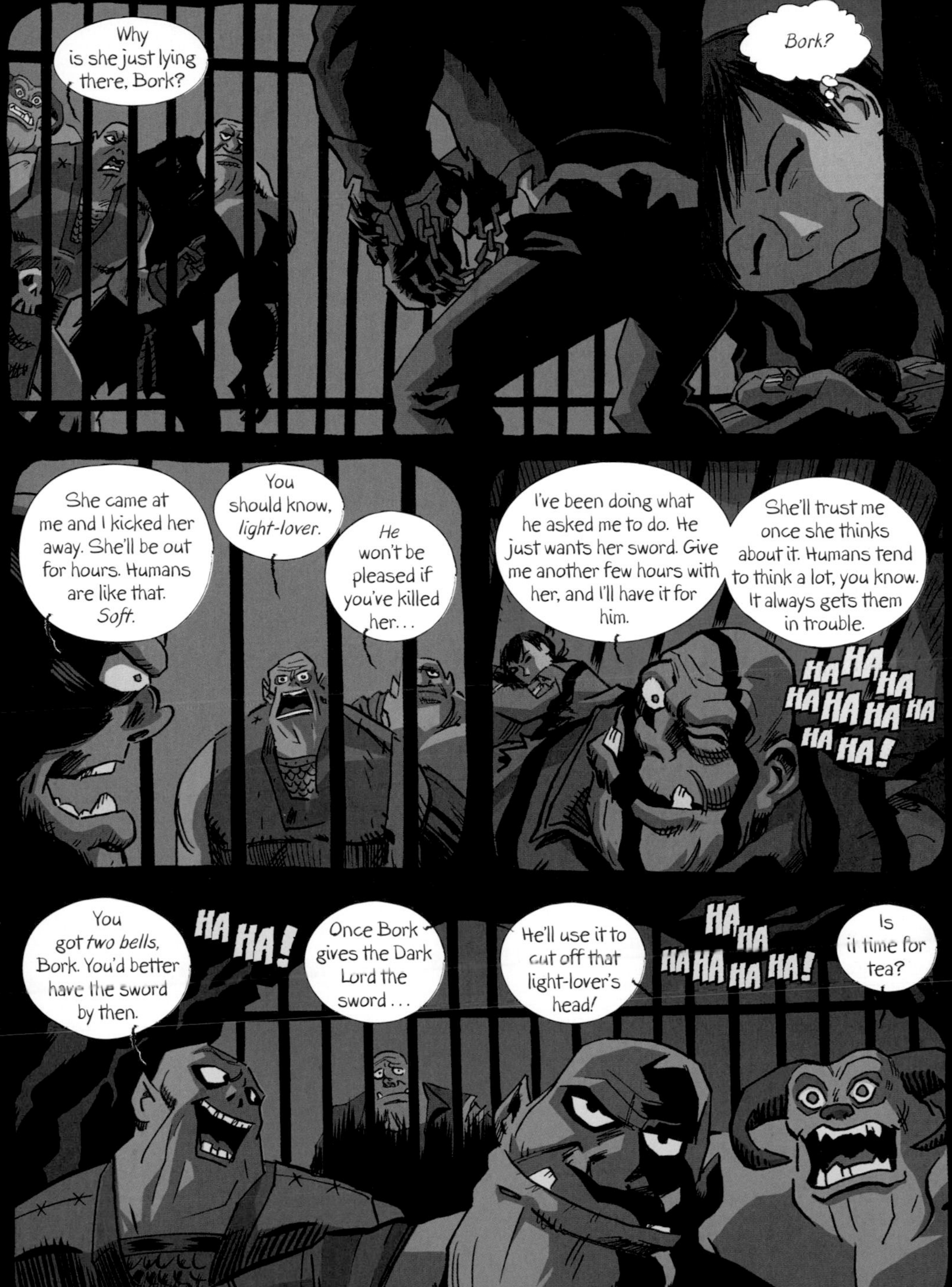
Why is she just lying there, Bork?
Bork?
She came at me and I kicked her away. She'll be out for hours. Humans are like that. *Soft*.
You should know, *light-lover*.
He won't be pleased if you've killed her...
I've been doing what he asked me to do. He just wants her sword. Give me another few hours with her, and I'll have it for him.
She'll trust me once she thinks about it. Humans tend to think a lot, you know. It always gets them in trouble.
HA HA HA HA HA HA HA HA HA HA!
You got *two bells*, Bork. You'd better have the sword by then.
HA HA!
Once Bork gives the Dark Lord the sword...
He'll use it to cut off that light-lover's head!
HA HA HA HA HA HA!
Is it time for tea?

6. Lunge

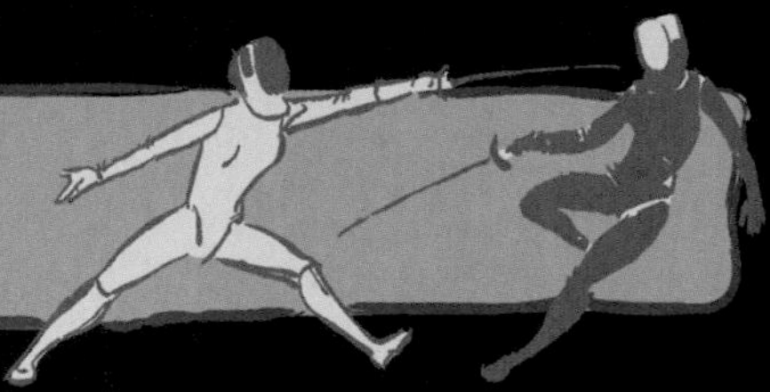

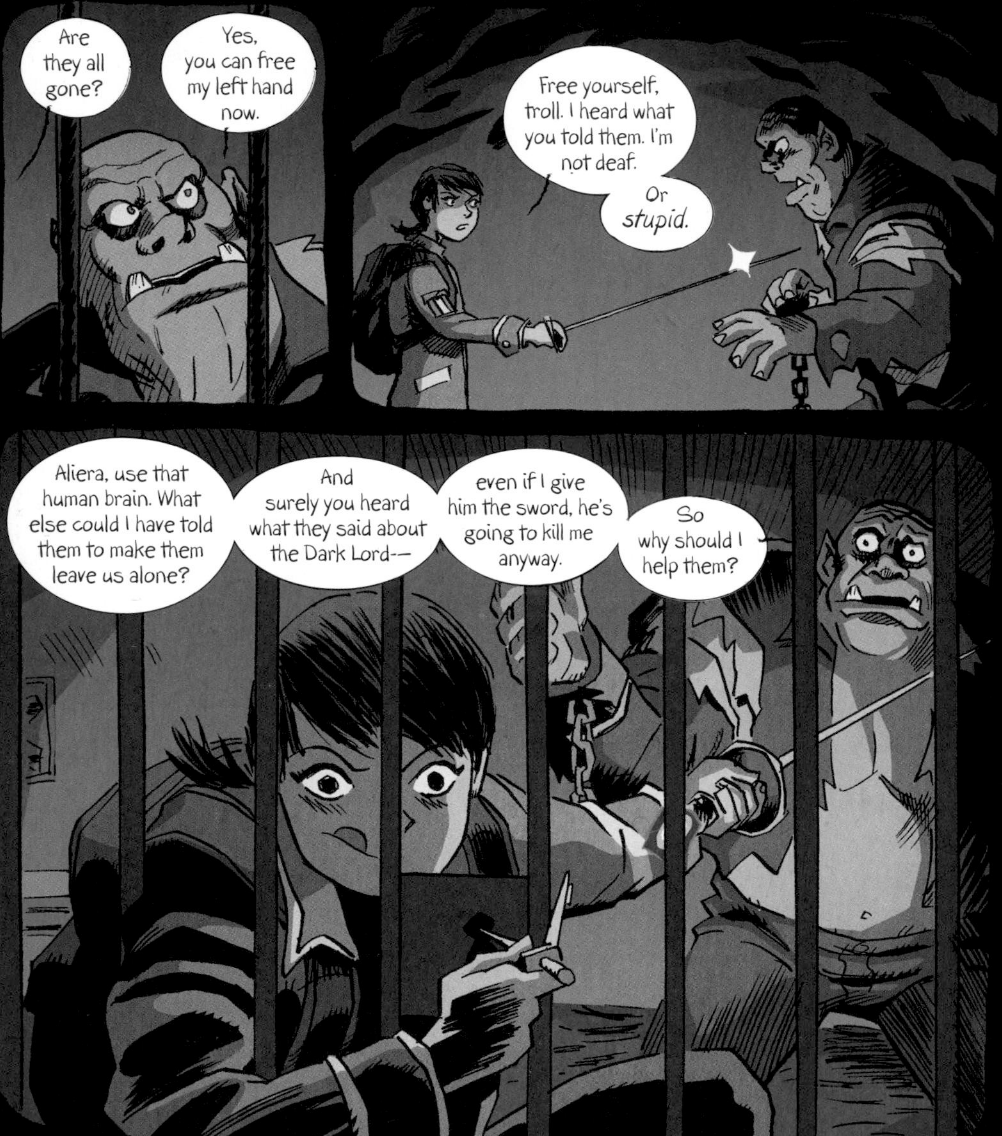

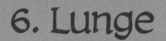

Are they all gone?
Yes, you can free my left hand now.
Free yourself, troll. I heard what you told them. I'm not deaf.
Or *stupid.*
Aliera, use that human brain. What else could I have told them to make them leave us alone?
And surely you heard what they said about the Dark Lord--
even if I give him the sword, he's going to kill me anyway.
So why should I help them?

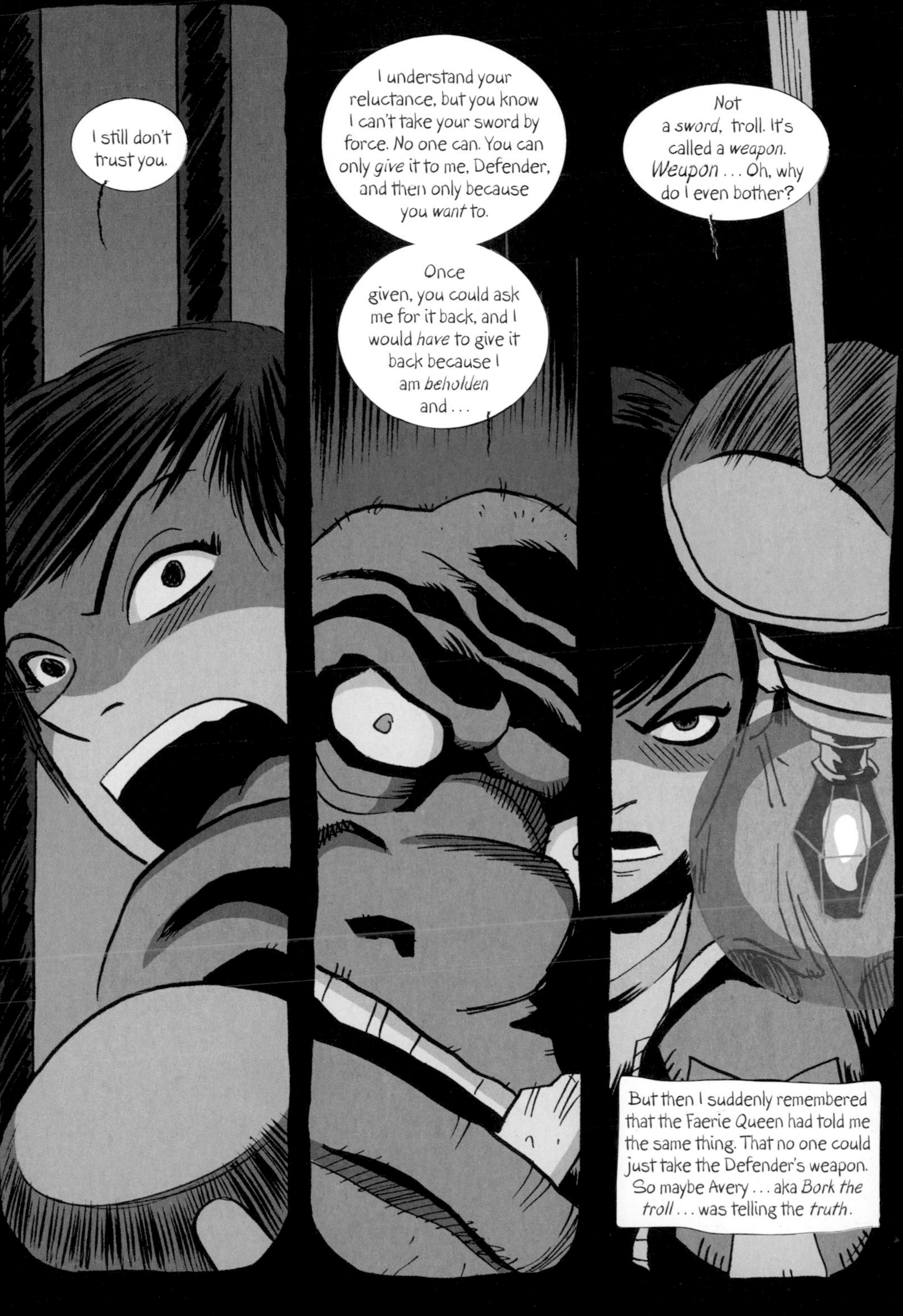
I still don't trust you.
I understand your reluctance, but you know I can't take your sword by force. No one can. You can only *give* it to me, Defender, and then only because you *want* to.
Once given, you could ask me for it back, and I would *have* to give it back because I am *beholden* and . . .
Not a *sword*, troll. It's called a *weapon*. *Weapon* . . . Oh, why do I even bother?
But then I suddenly remembered that the Faerie Queen had told me the same thing. That no one could just take the Defender's weapon. So maybe Avery . . . aka *Bork the troll* . . . was telling the *truth*.

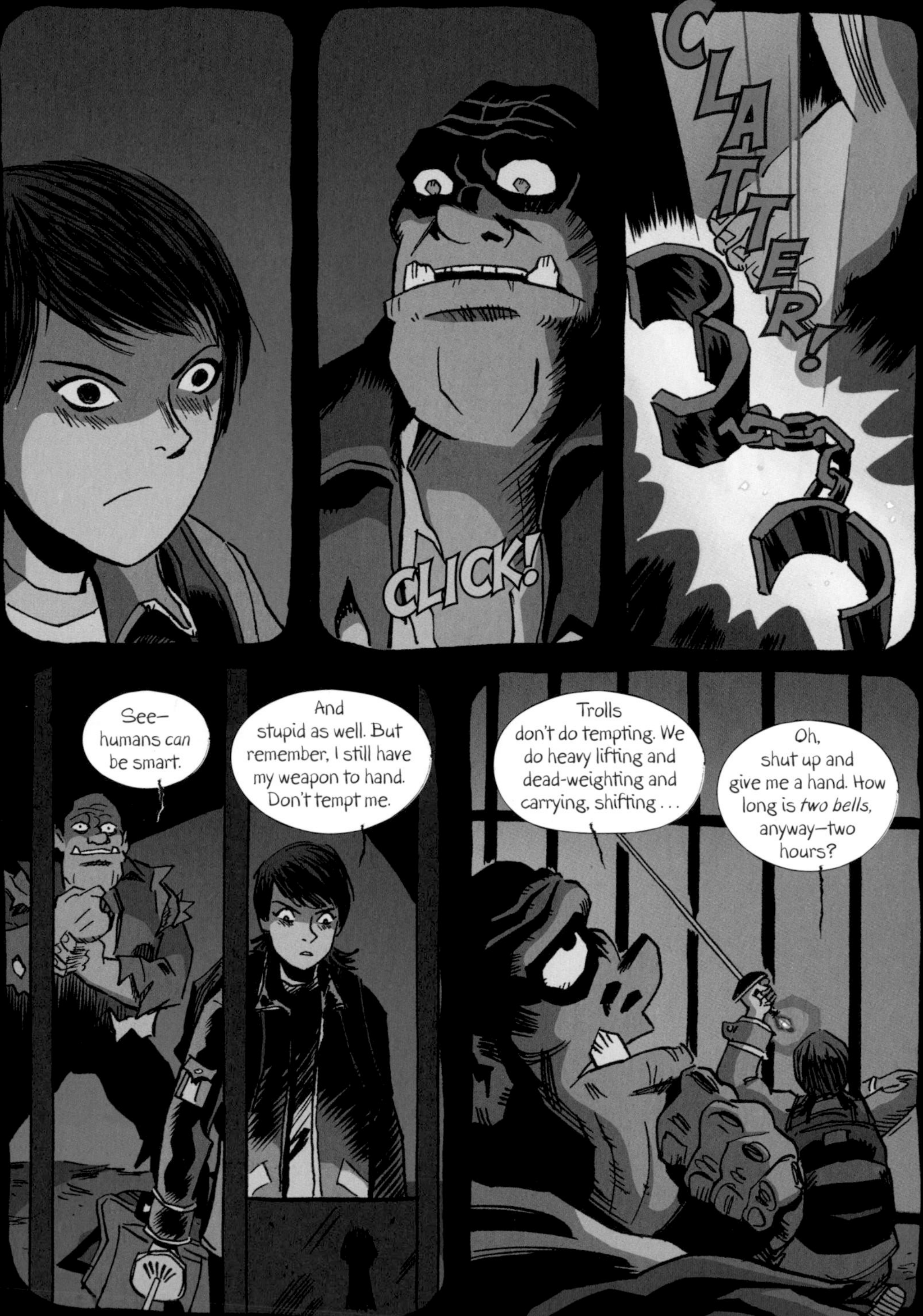
CLICK!
CLATTER!
See— humans *can* be smart.
And stupid as well. But remember, I still have my weapon to hand. Don't tempt me.
Trolls don't do tempting. We do heavy lifting and dead-weighting and carrying, shifting . . .
Oh, shut up and give me a hand. How long is *two bells,* anyway—two hours?

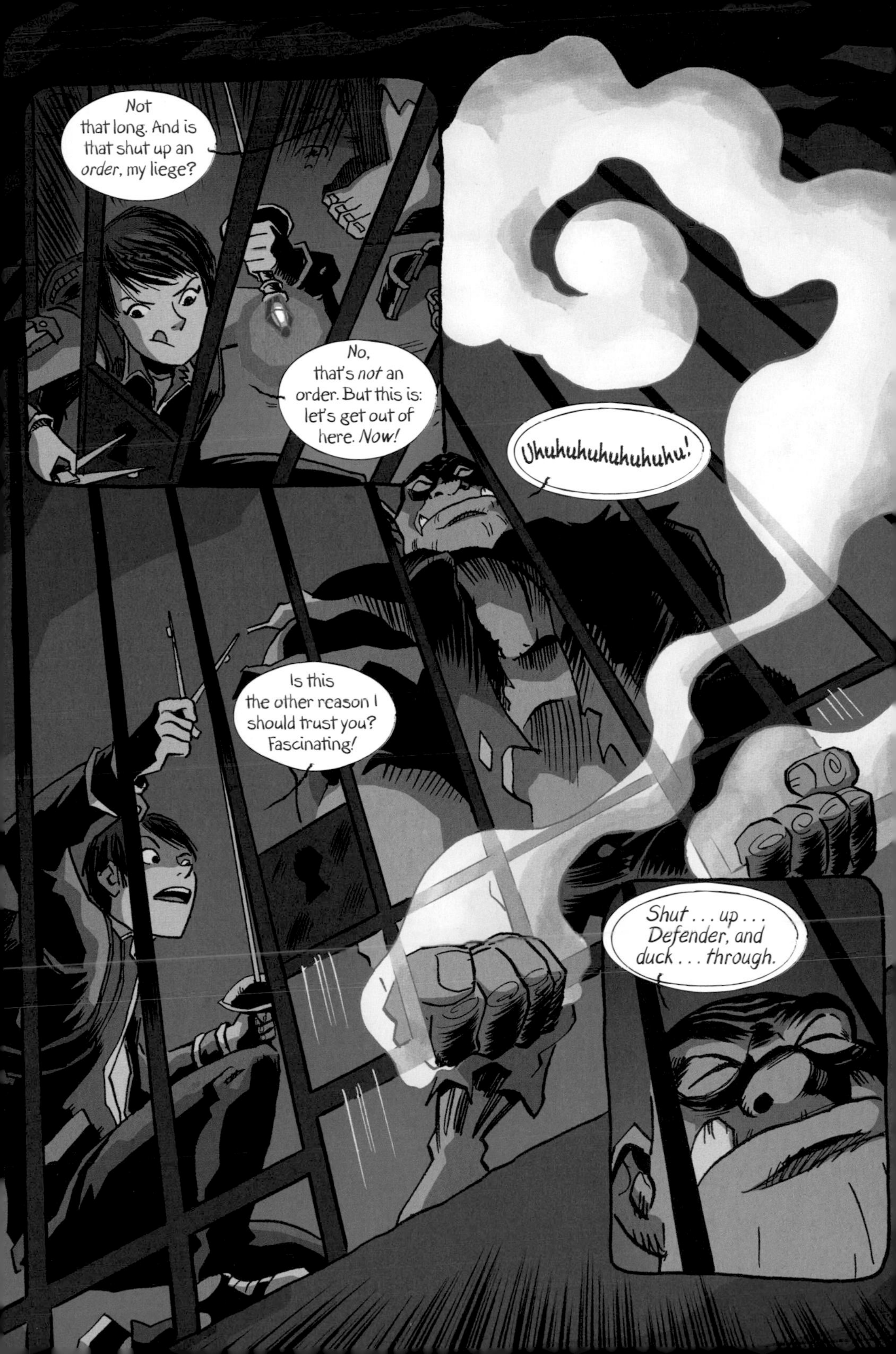

Not that long. And is that shut up an *order*, my liege?
No, that's *not* an order. But this is: let's get out of here. *Now!*
Uhuhuhuhuhuhuhu!
Is this the other reason I should trust you? Fascinating!
Shut . . . up . . . Defender, and duck . . . through.

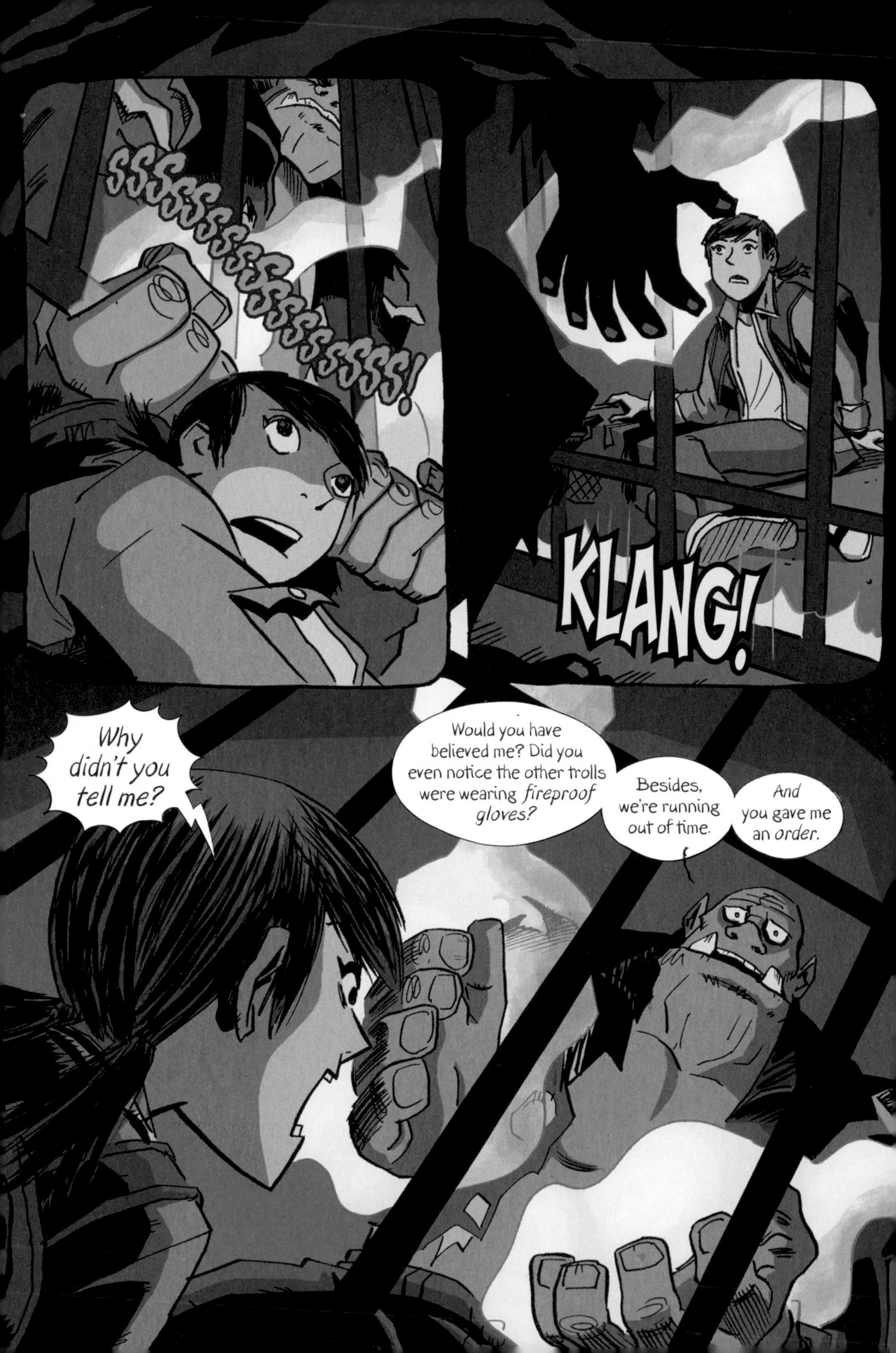
SSSSSSSSSSSSSSSSSSSSSSS!
KLANG!
Why didn't you tell me?
Would you have believed me? Did you even notice the other trolls were wearing *fireproof gloves?*
Besides, we're running out of time.
And you gave me an *order*.

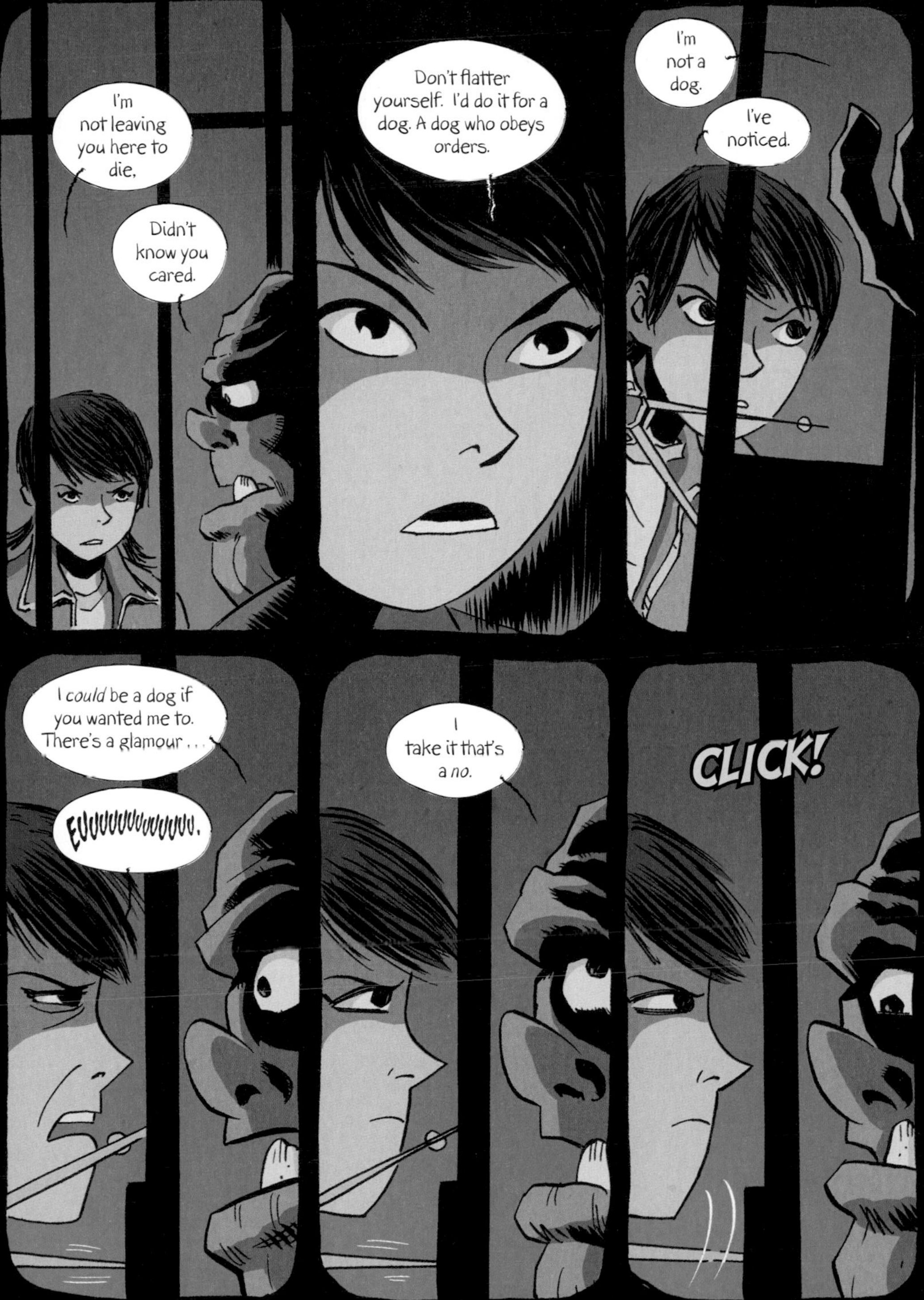
I'm not leaving you here to die,
Didn't know you cared.
Don't flatter yourself. I'd do it for a dog. A dog who obeys orders.
I'm not a dog.
I've noticed.
I *could* be a dog if you wanted me to. There's a glamour . . .
EUUUUUUUUUUUUU.
I take it that's a *no.*
CLICK!

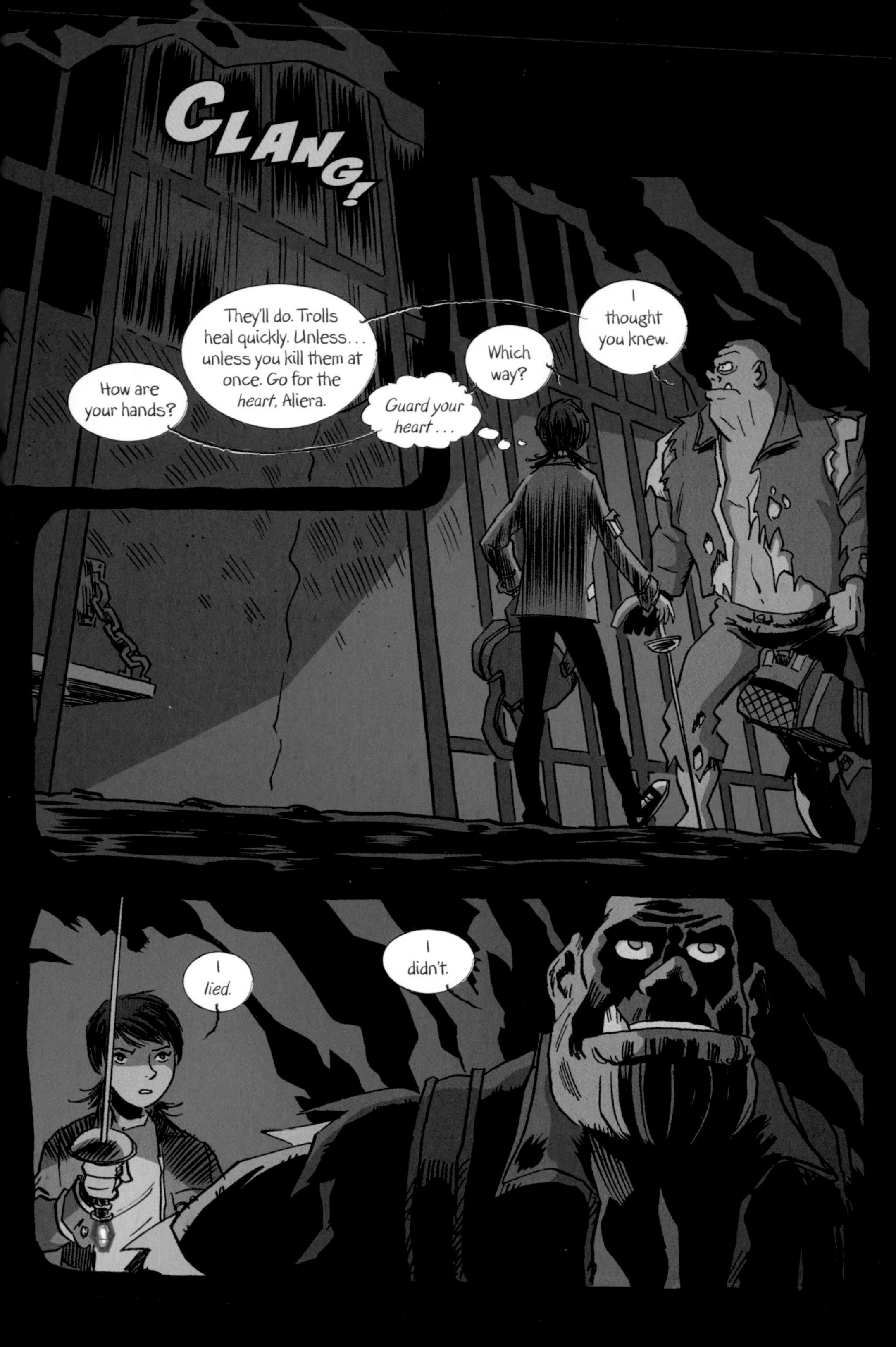
CLANG!
How are your hands?
They'll do. Trolls heal quickly. Unless... unless you kill them at once. Go for the heart, Aliera.
Guard your heart...
Which way?
I thought you knew.
I lied.
I didn't.

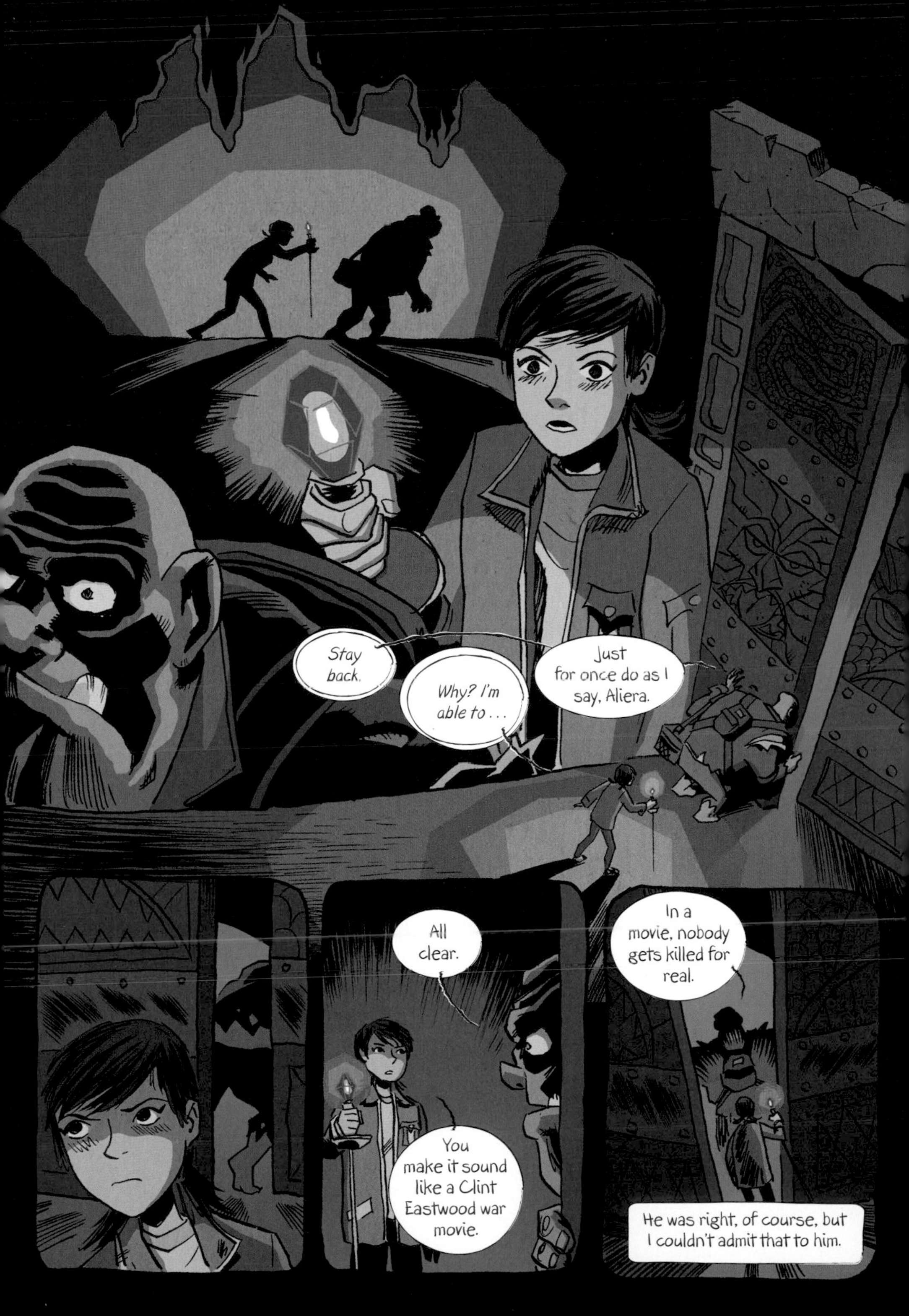
Stay back.
Why? I'm able to . . .
Just for once do as I say, Aliera.
All clear.
You make it sound like a Clint Eastwood war movie.
In a movie, nobody gets killed for real.
He was right, of course, but I couldn't admit that to him.

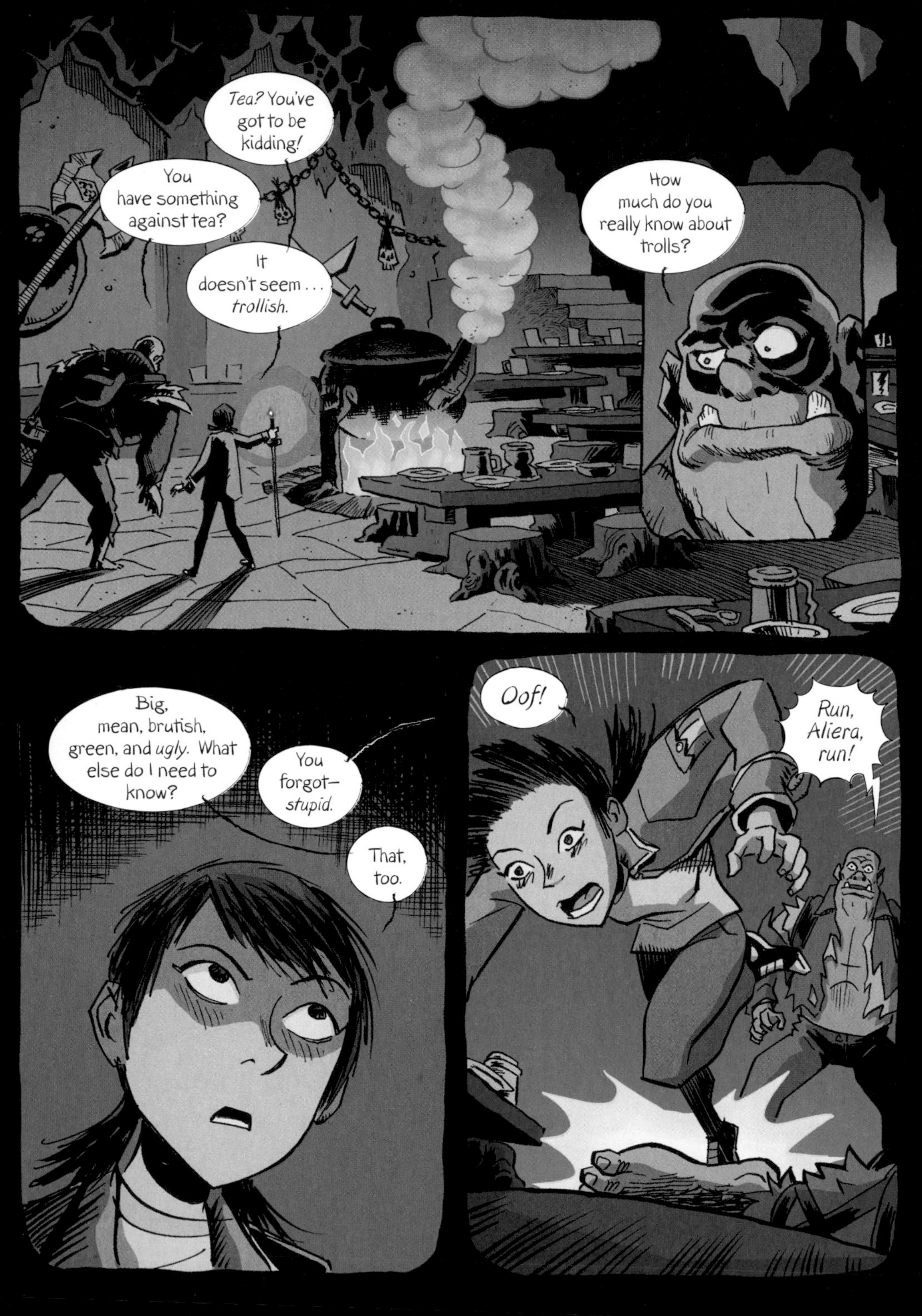
You have something against tea?
Tea? You've got to be kidding!
It doesn't seem . . . *trollish.*
How much do you really know about trolls?
Big, mean, brutish, green, and *ugly.* What else do I need to know?
You forgot—*stupid.*
That, too.
Oof!
Run, Aliera, run!

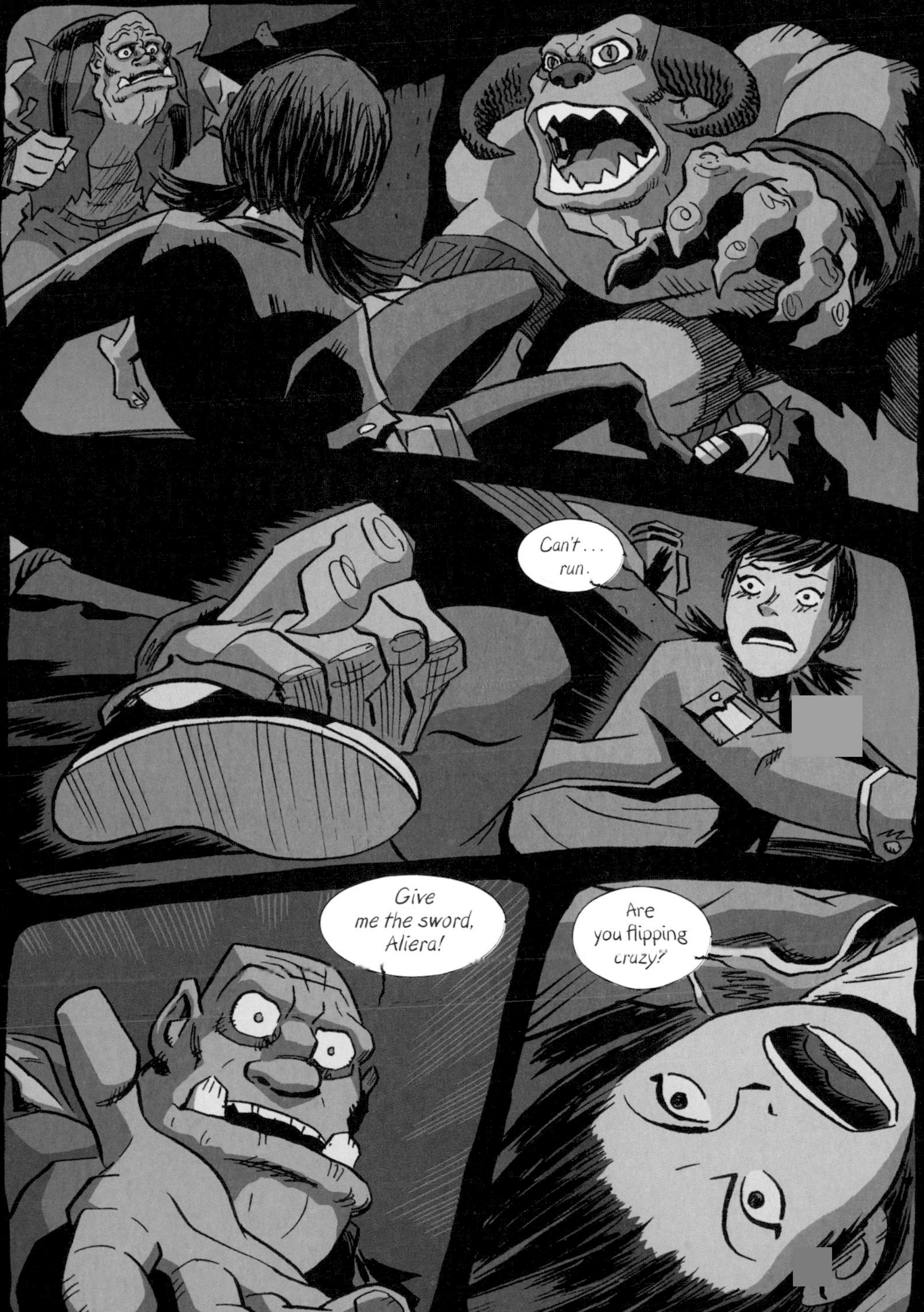
Can't . . . run.
Give me the sword, Aliera!
Are you flipping crazy?

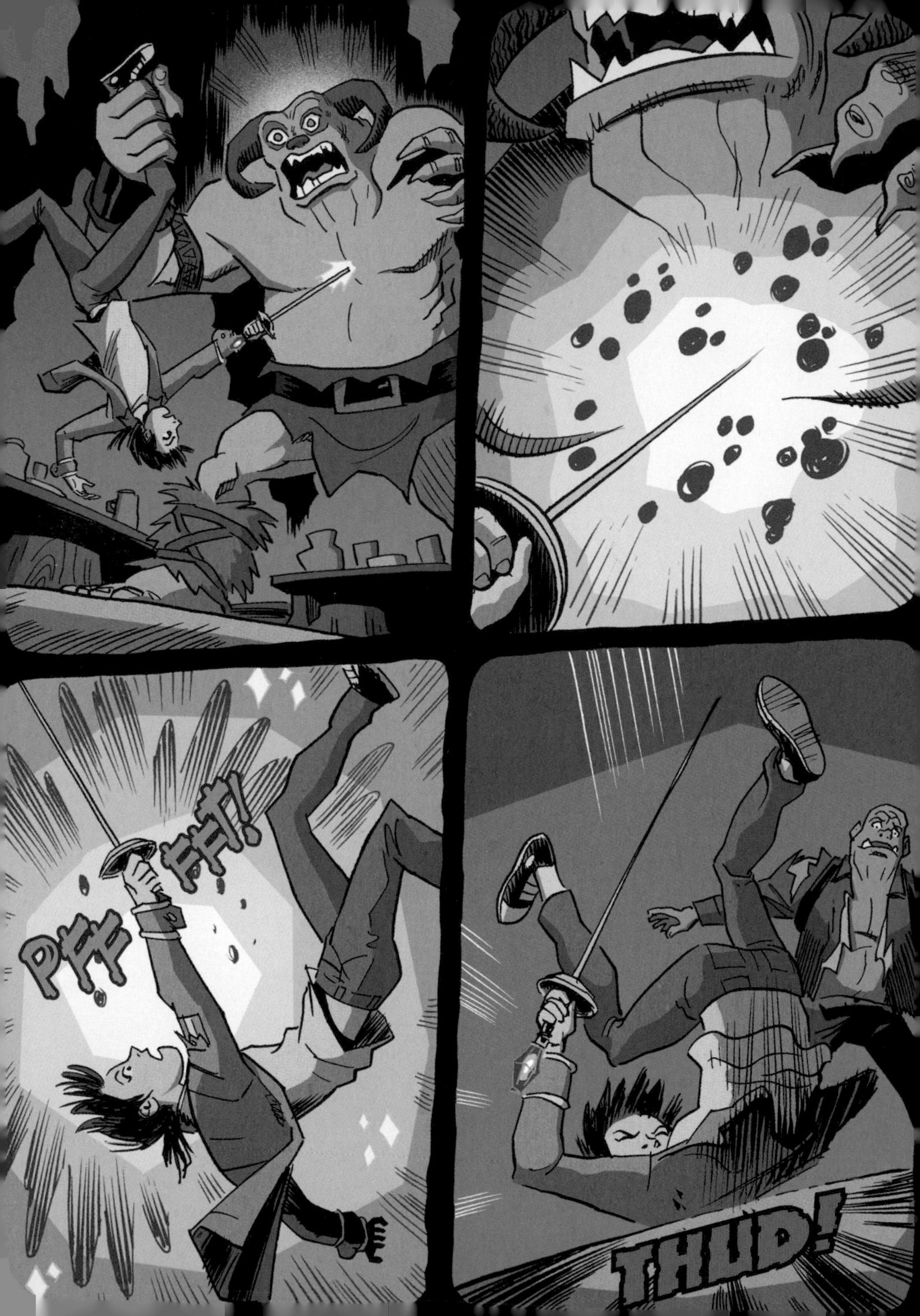
PFFFFT!
THUD!

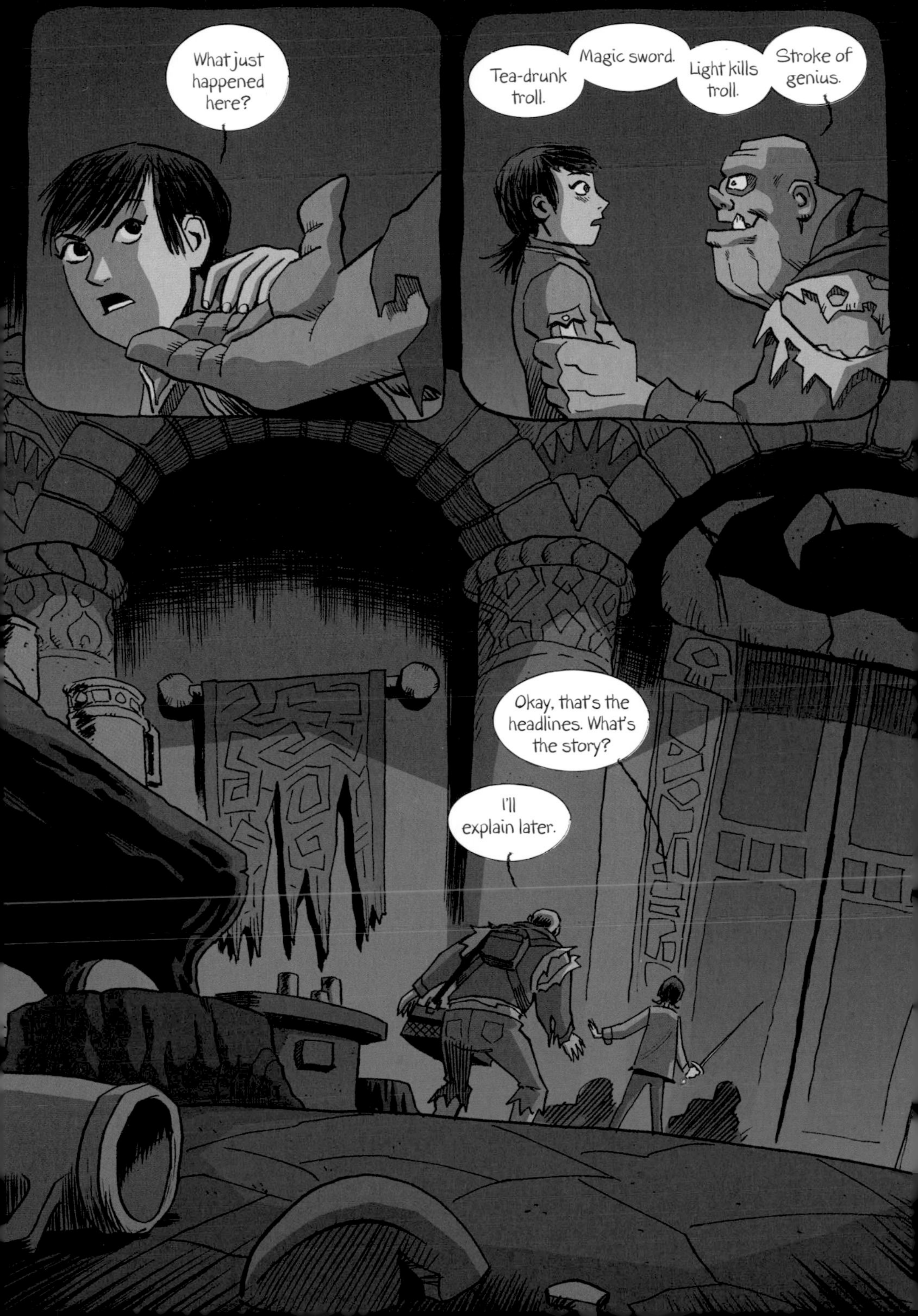
What just happened here?
Tea-drunk troll.
Magic sword.
Light kills troll.
Stroke of genius.
Okay, that's the headlines. What's the story?
I'll explain later.

7. Parry-riposte

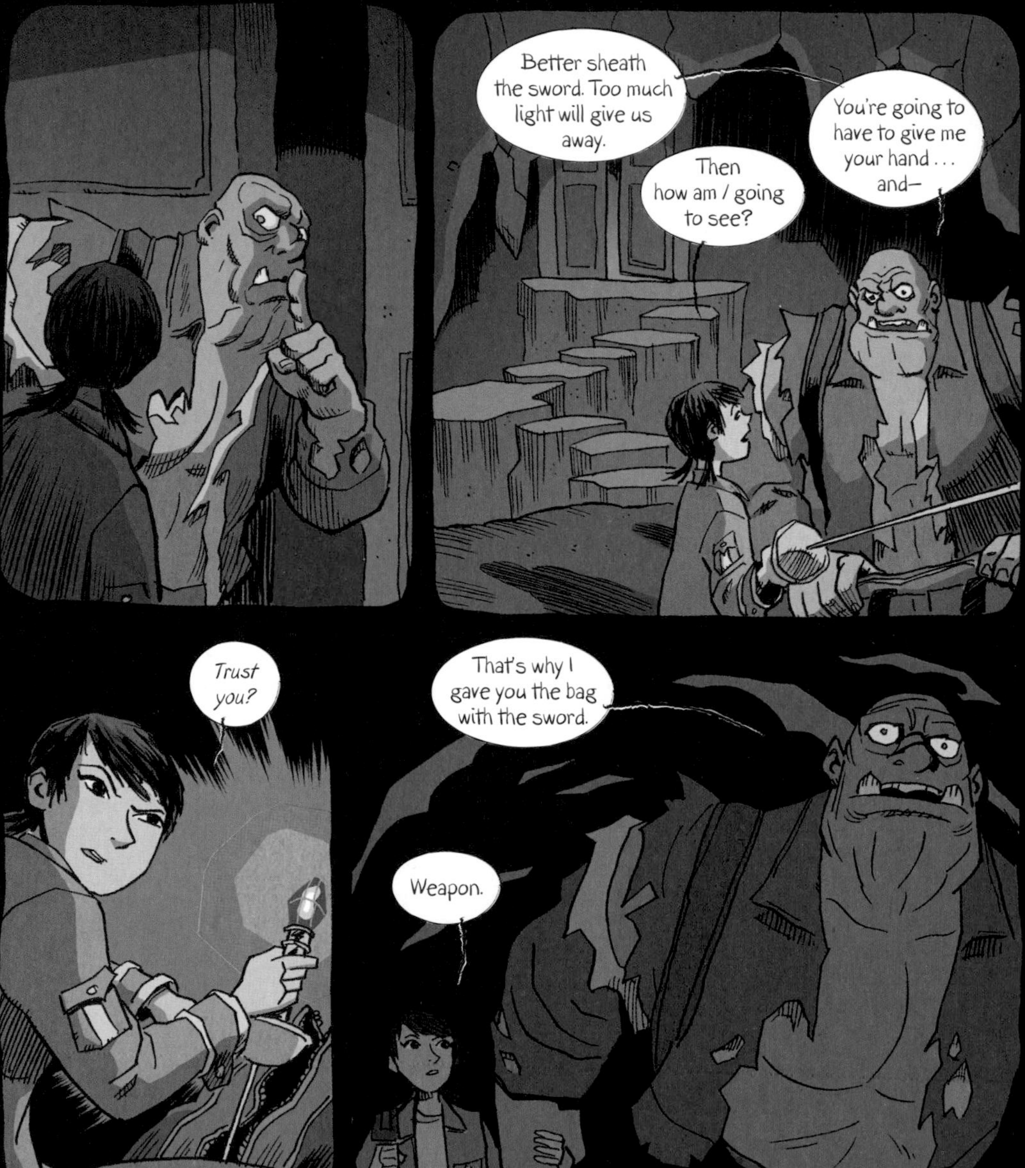
Better sheath the sword. Too much light will give us away.
Then how am I going to see?
You're going to have to give me your hand . . . and–
Trust you?
That's why I gave you the bag with the sword.
Weapon.

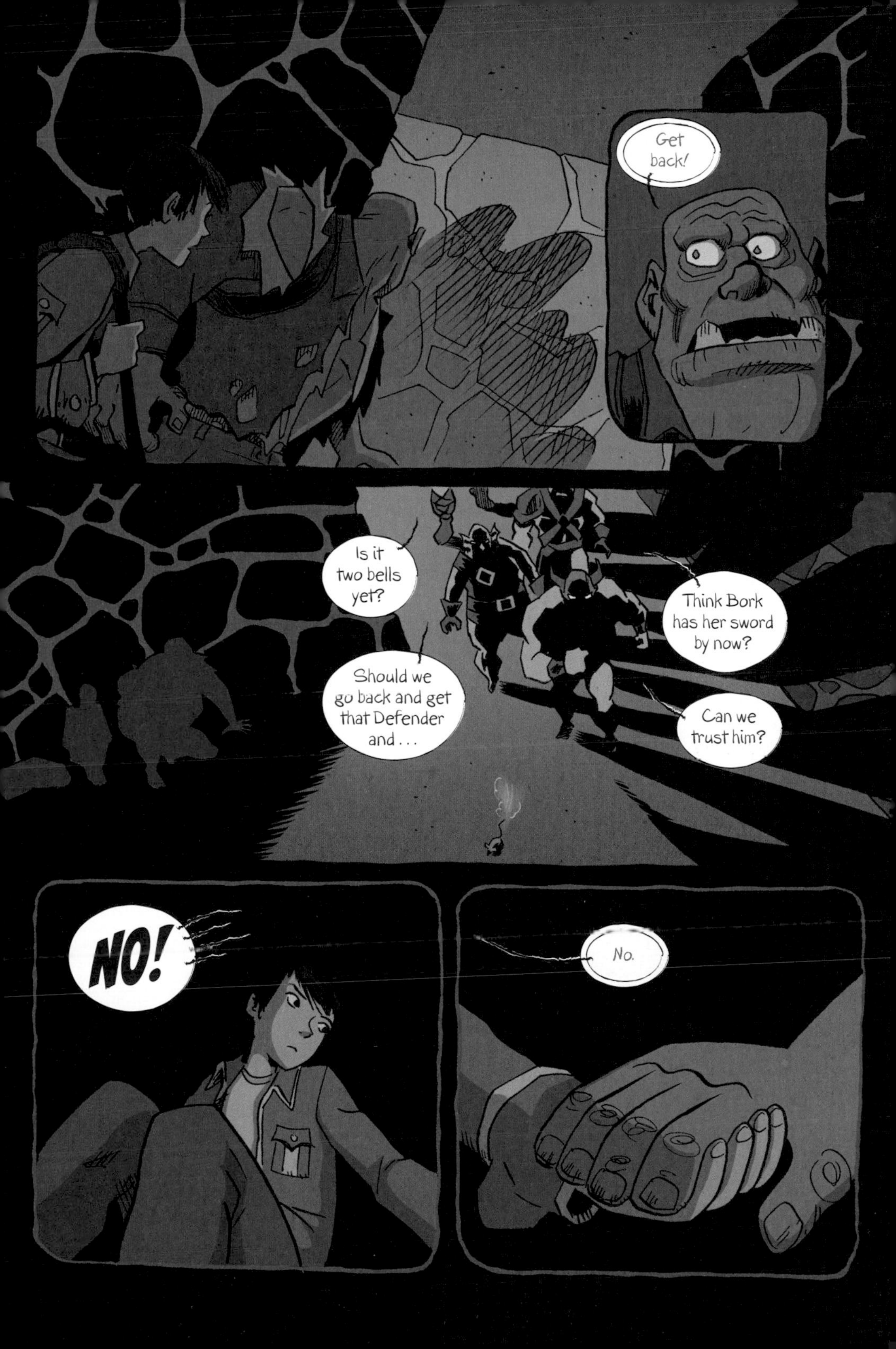
Get back!
Is it two bells yet?
Think Bork has her sword by now?
Should we go back and get that Defender and . . .
Can we trust him?
NO!
No.

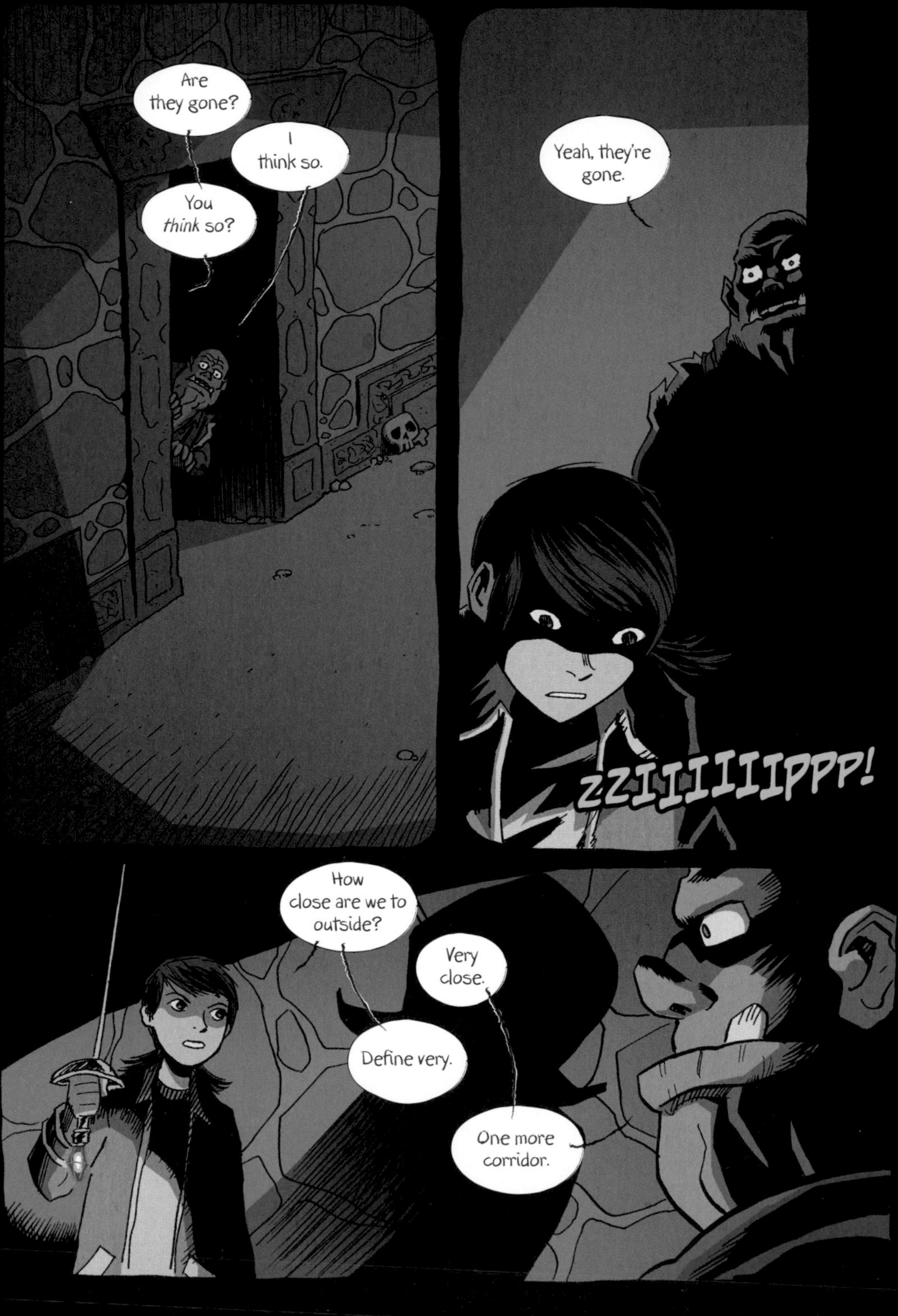
Are they gone?
I think so.
You *think* so?
Yeah, they're gone.
ZZIIIIIIPPP!
How close are we to outside?
Very close.
Define very.
One more corridor.

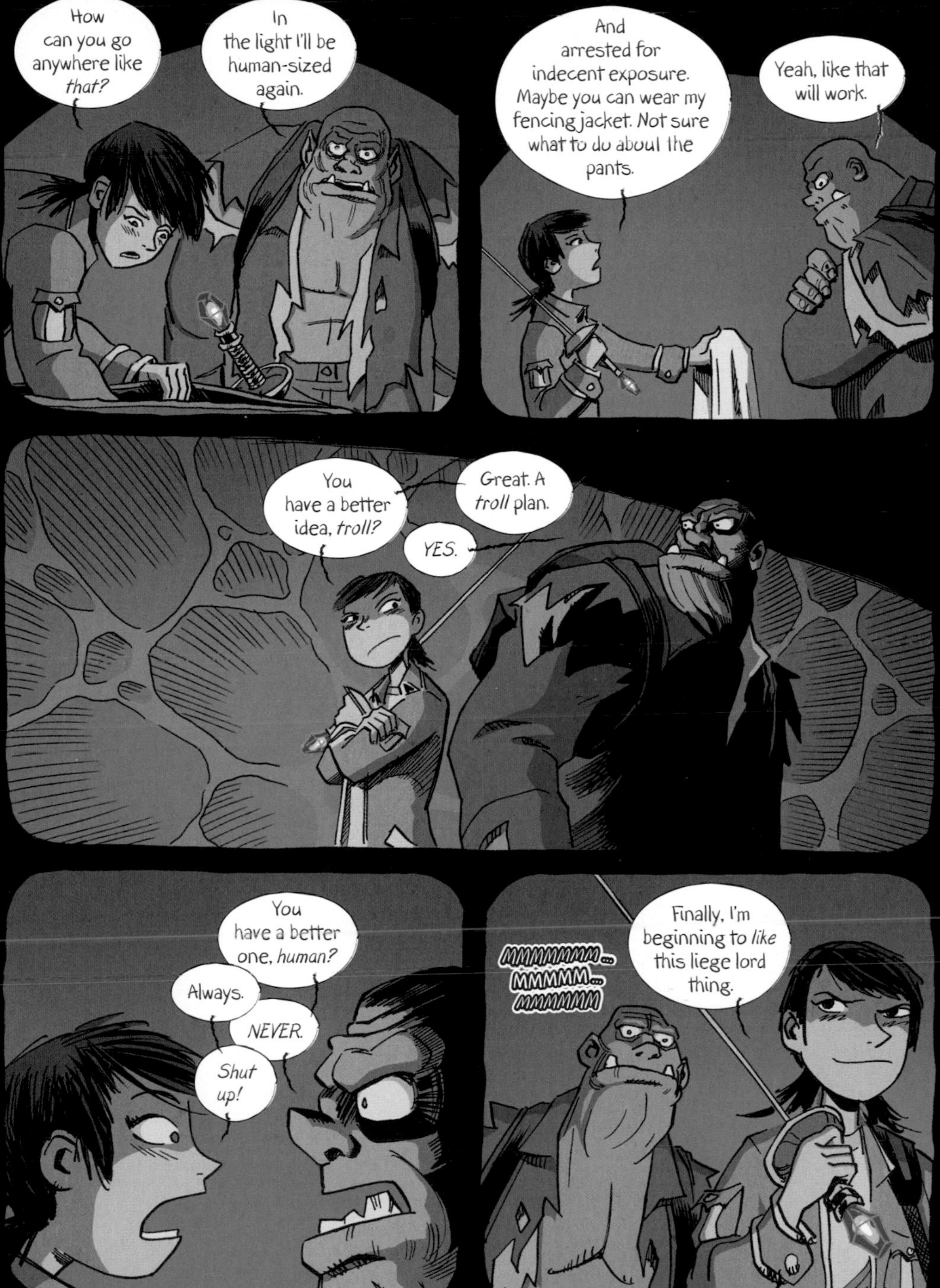
How can you go anywhere like *that?*
In the light I'll be human-sized again.
And arrested for indecent exposure. Maybe you can wear my fencing jacket. Not sure what to do about the pants.
Yeah, like that will work.
You have a better idea, *troll?*
Great. A *troll* plan.
YES.
You have a better one, *human?*
Always.
NEVER.
Shut up!
MMMMMMM... MMMMM... MMMMMM
Finally, I'm beginning to *like* this liege lord thing.

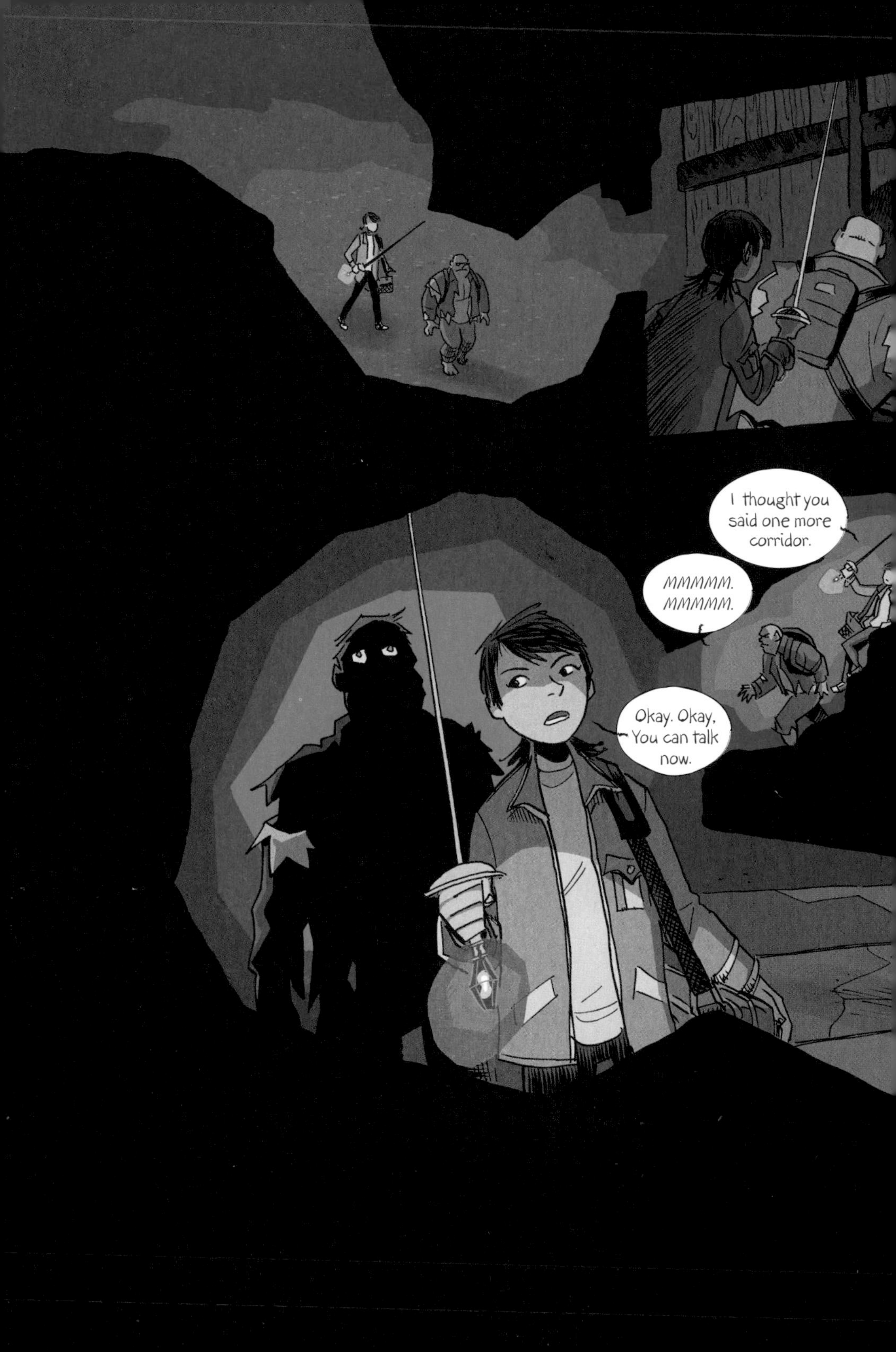
I thought you said one more corridor.
MMMMM. MMMMM.
Okay. Okay, You can talk now.

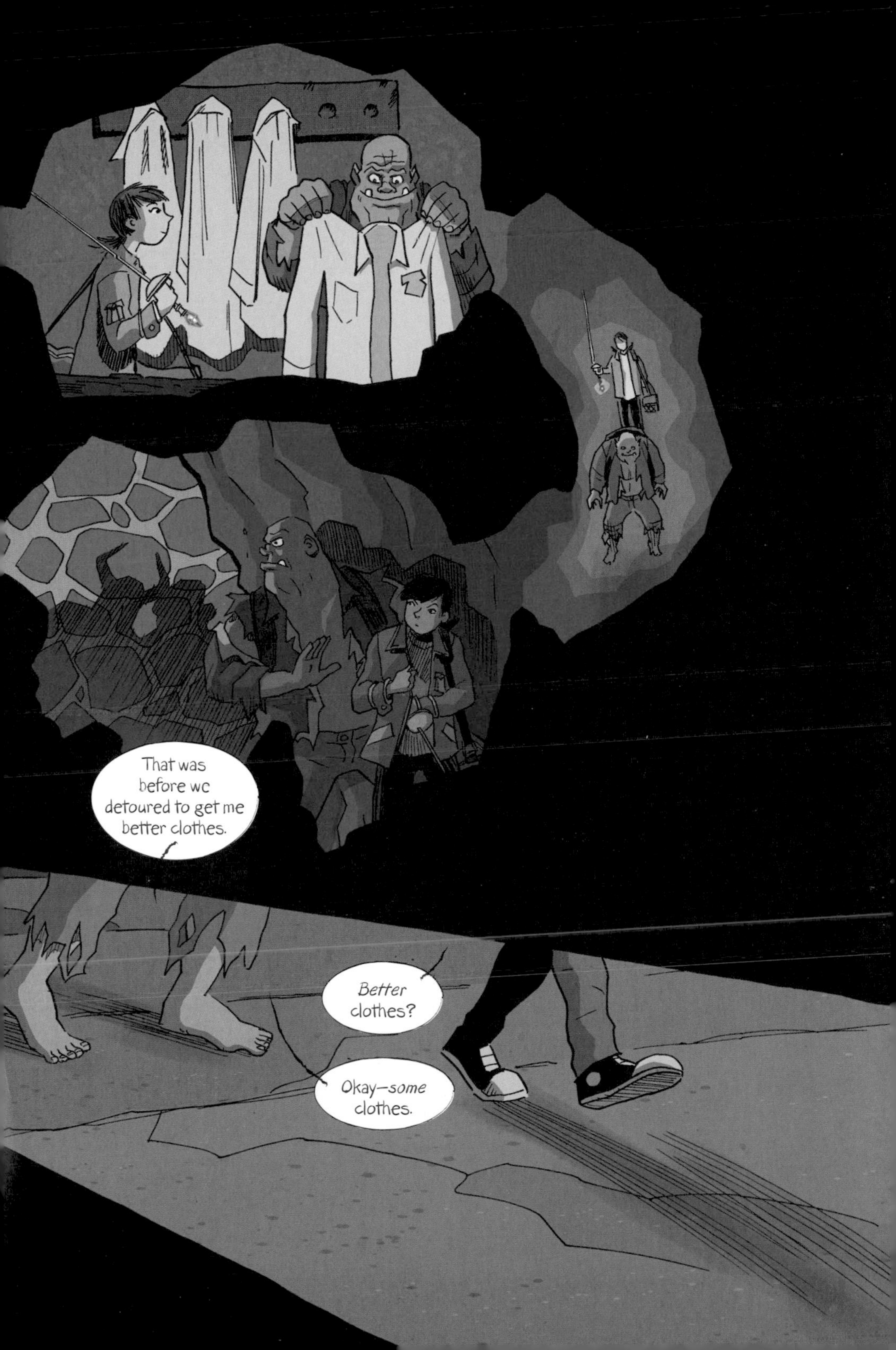
That was before wc detoured to get me better clothes.
Better clothes?
Okay—*some* clothes.

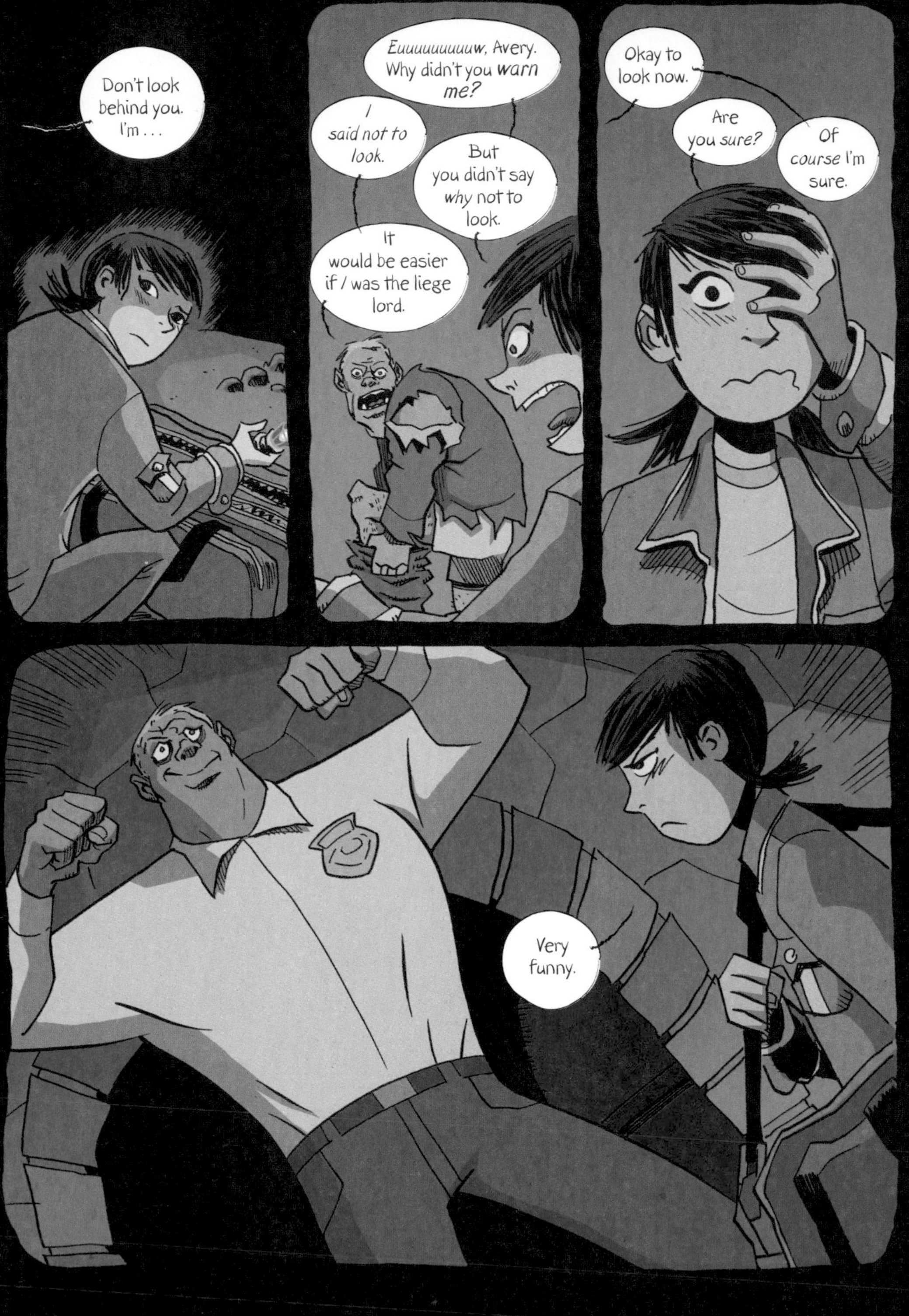
Don't look behind you. I'm . . .
Euuuuuuuuuw, Avery. Why didn't you warn me?
I said not to look.
But you didn't say why not to look.
It would be easier if I was the liege lord.
Okay to look now.
Are you sure?
Of course I'm sure.
Very funny.

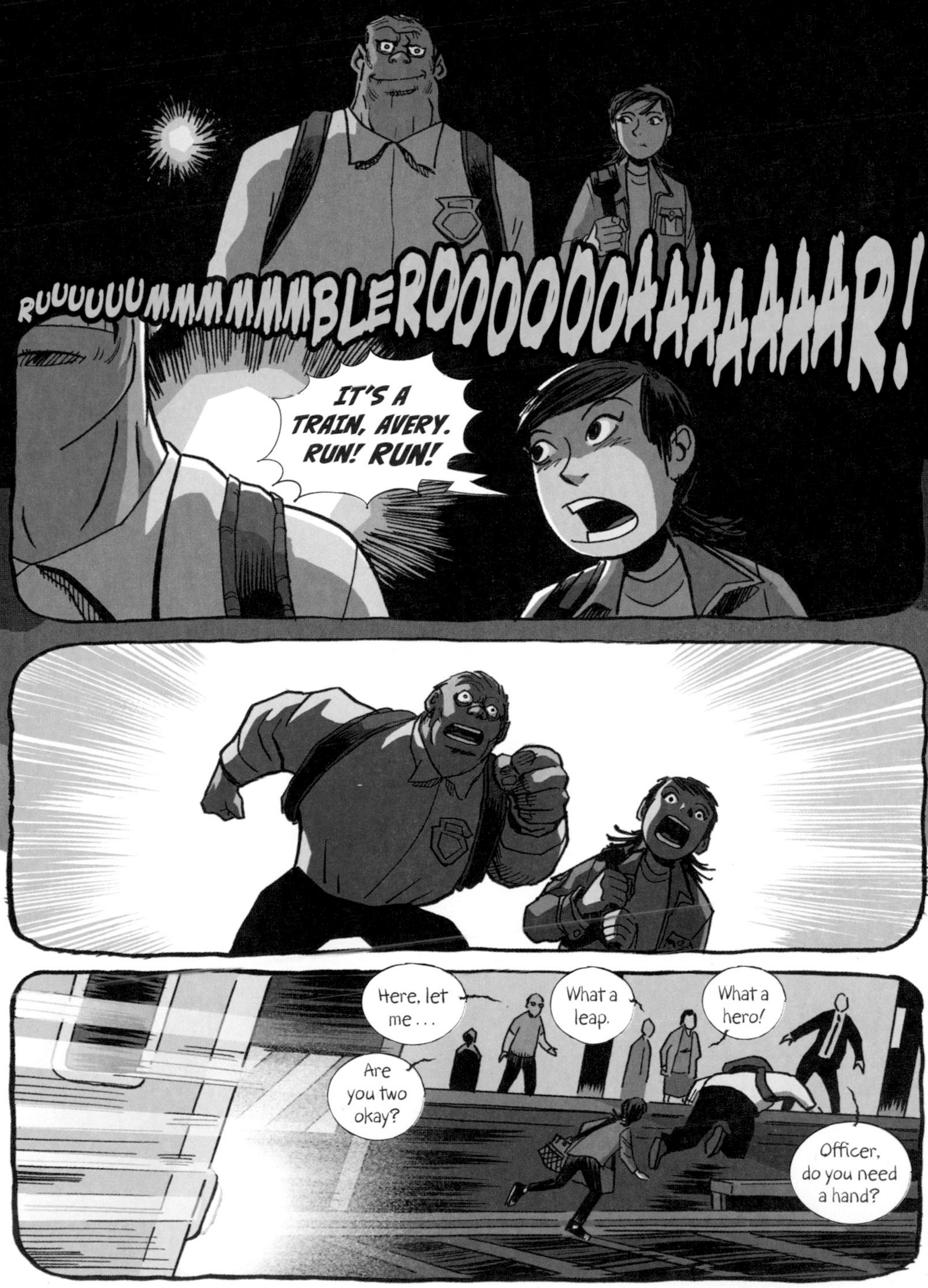
RUUUUUUMMMMMMBLEROOOOOOAAAAAAR!
IT'S A TRAIN, AVERY. RUN! RUN!
Here, let me . . .
What a leap.
What a hero!
Are you two okay?
Officer, do you need a hand?

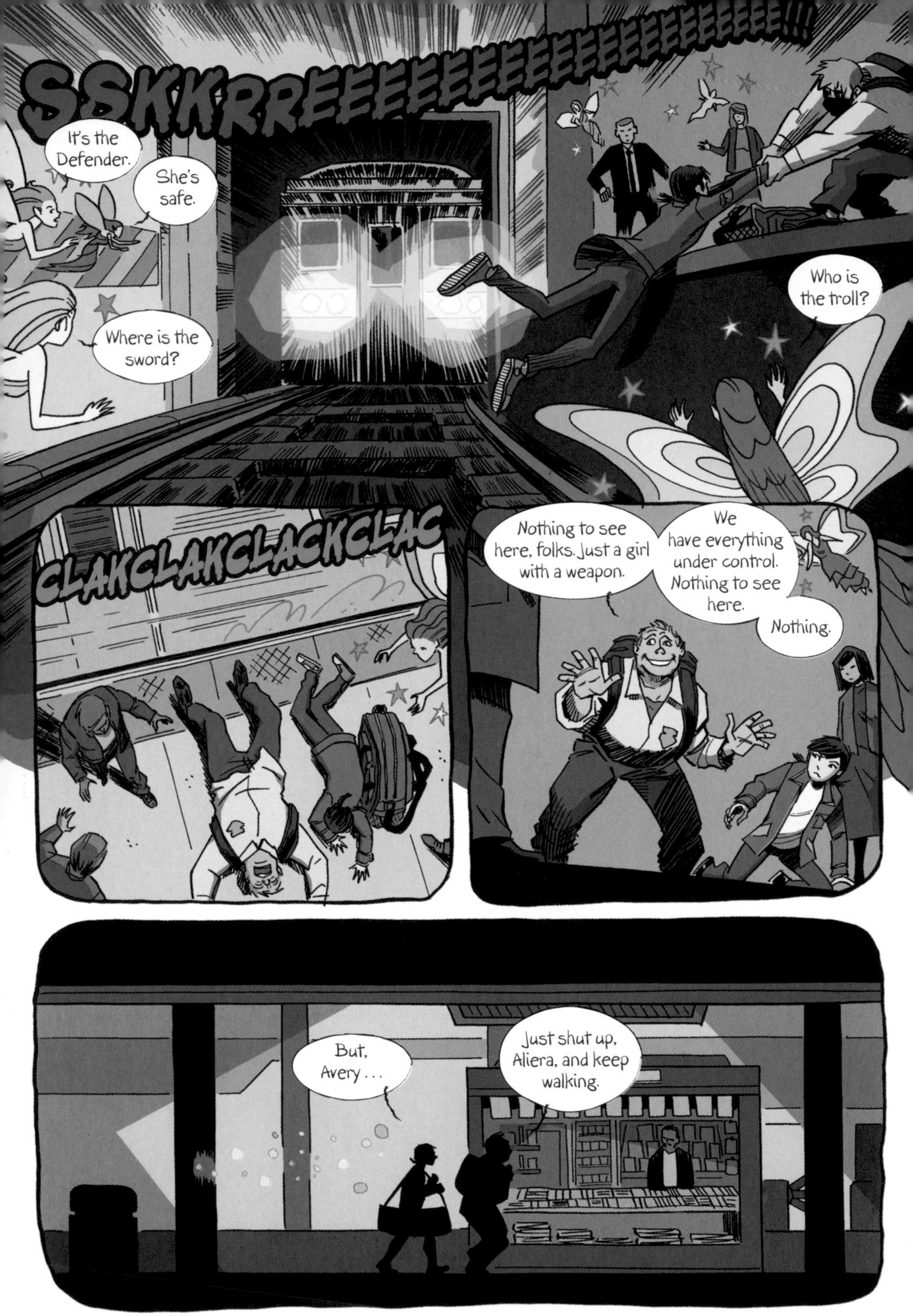
SSKKRREEEEEEEEEEEEEEEEEEEEEEEEEE!!!
It's the Defender.
She's safe.
Where is the sword?
Who is the troll?
CLAKCLAKCLACKCLAC
Nothing to see here, folks. Just a girl with a weapon.
We have everything under control. Nothing to see here.
Nothing.
But, Avery . . .
Just shut up, Aliera, and keep walking.

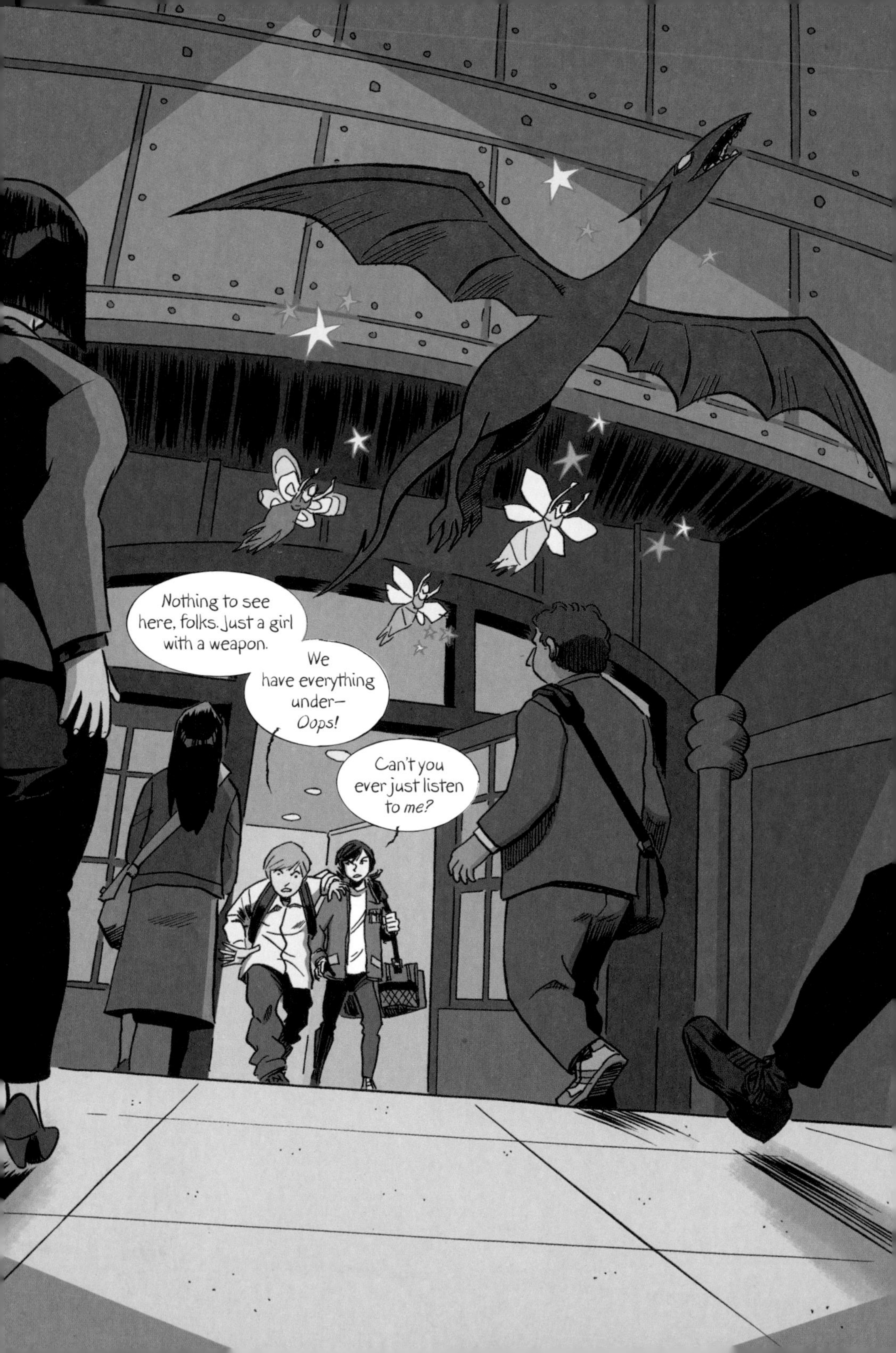
Nothing to see here, folks. Just a girl with a weapon.
We have everything under— Oops!
Can't you ever just listen to *me?*

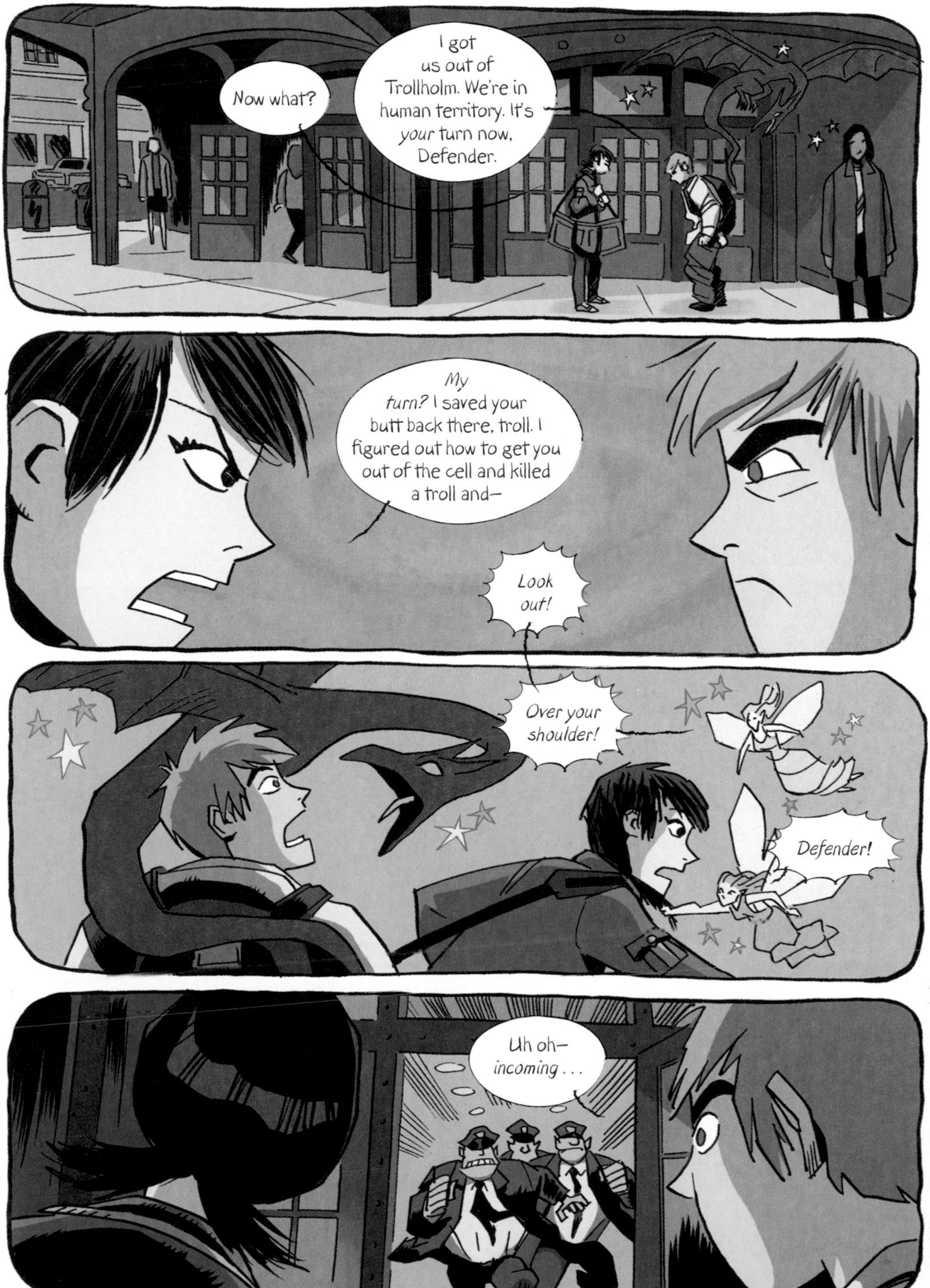
Now what?
I got us out of Trollholm. We're in human territory. It's *your* turn now, Defender.
My turn? I saved your butt back there, troll. I figured out how to get you out of the cell and killed a troll and—
Look out!
Over your shoulder!
Defender!
Uh oh— *incoming . . .*

8. Counter-riposte

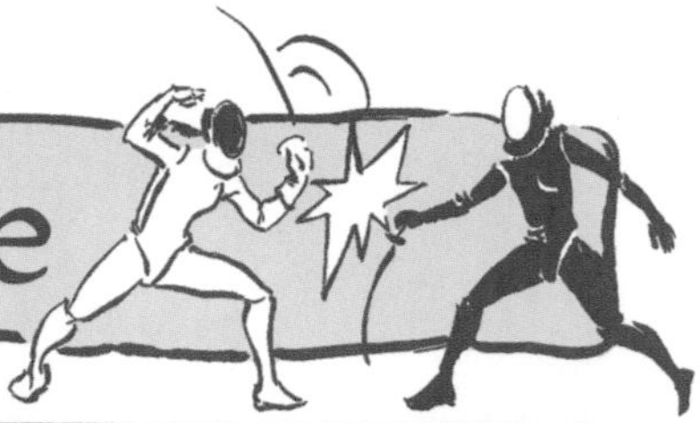

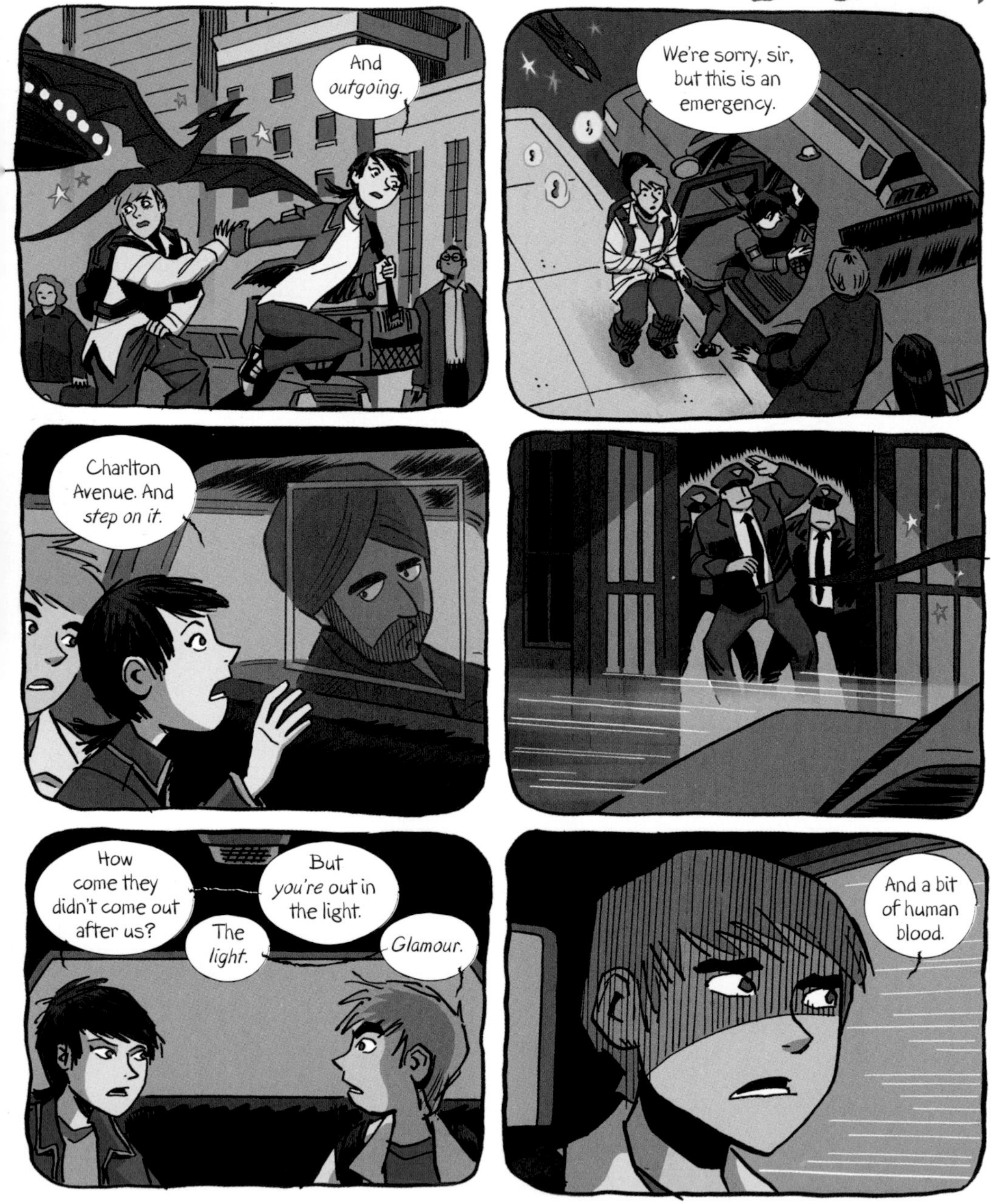
And *outgoing.*
We're sorry, sir, but this is an emergency.
Charlton Avenue. And *step on it.*
How come they didn't come out after us?
The *light.*
But *you're* out in the light.
Glamour.
And a bit of human blood.

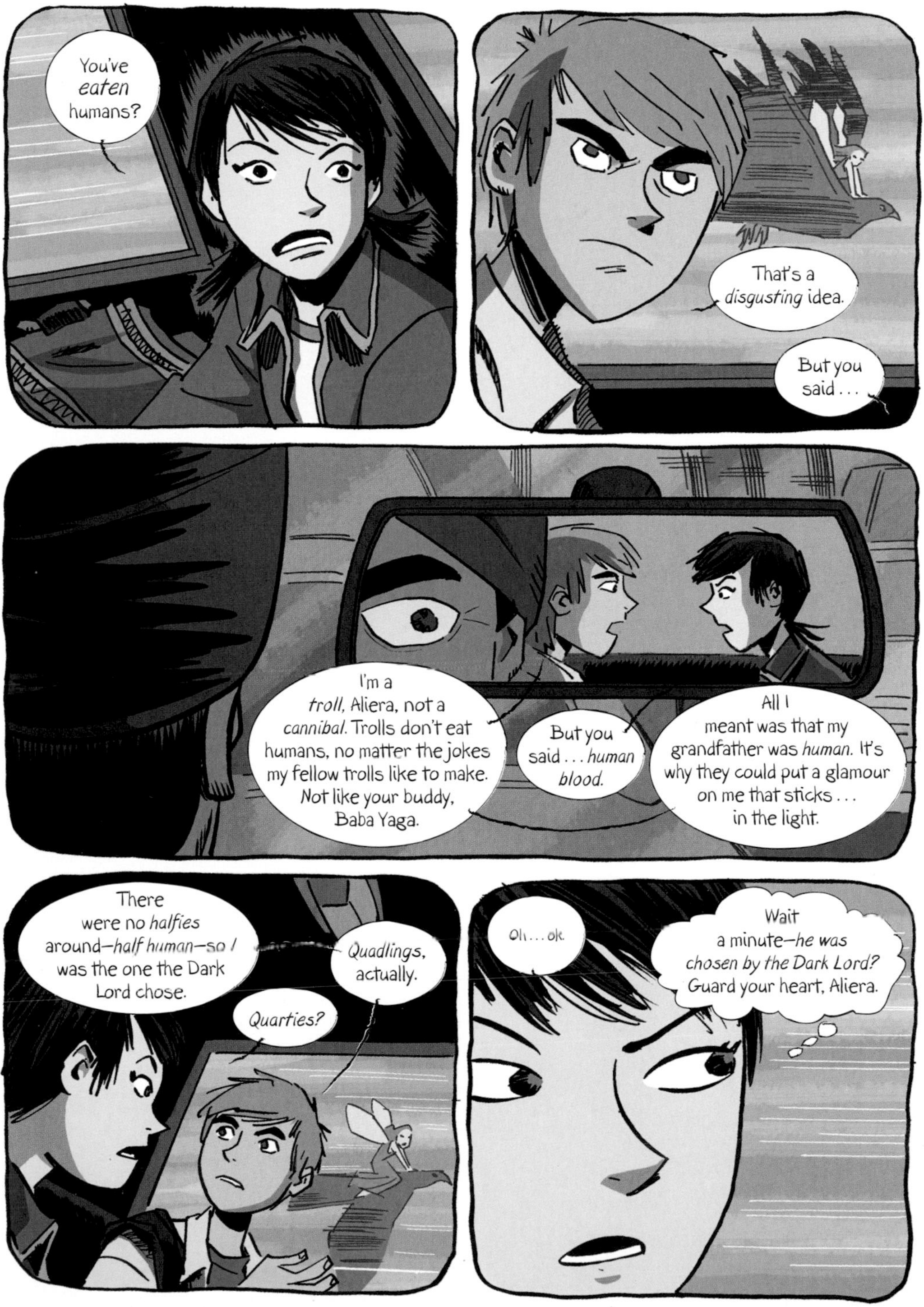
You've *eaten* humans?
That's a *disgusting* idea.
But you said . . .
I'm a *troll,* Aliera, not a *cannibal.* Trolls don't eat humans, no matter the jokes my fellow trolls like to make. Not like your buddy, Baba Yaga.
But you said . . . *human blood.*
All I meant was that my grandfather was *human.* It's why they could put a glamour on me that sticks . . . in the light.
There were no *halfies* around—*half human*—so *I* was the one the Dark Lord chose.
Quadlings, actually.
Quarties?
Oh . . . ok.
Wait a minute—*he was chosen by the Dark Lord?* Guard your heart, Aliera.

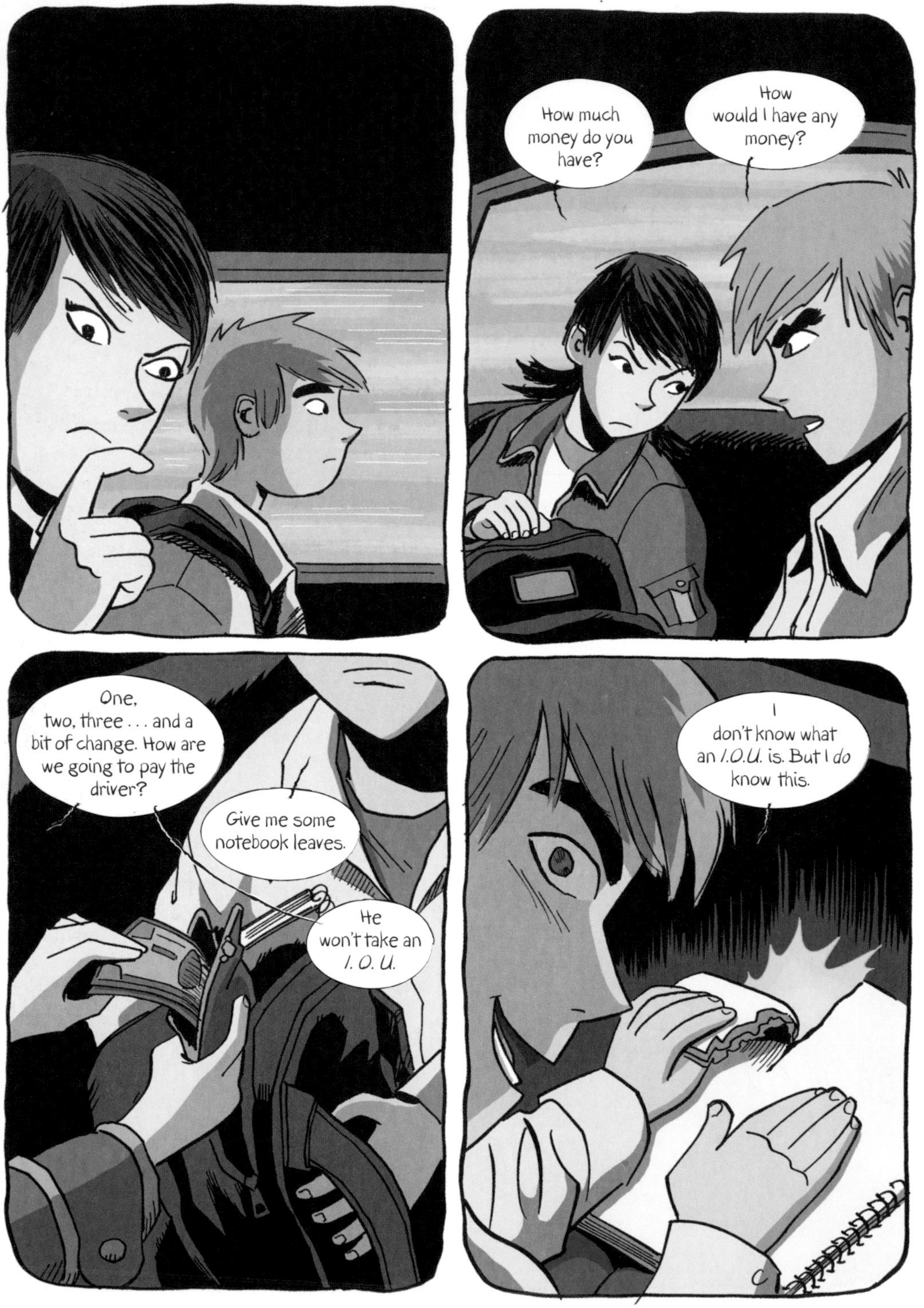
How much money do you have?
How would I have any money?
One, two, three . . . and a bit of change. How are we going to pay the driver?
Give me some notebook leaves.
He won't take an *I. O. U.*
I don't know what an *I.O.U.* is. But I *do* know this.

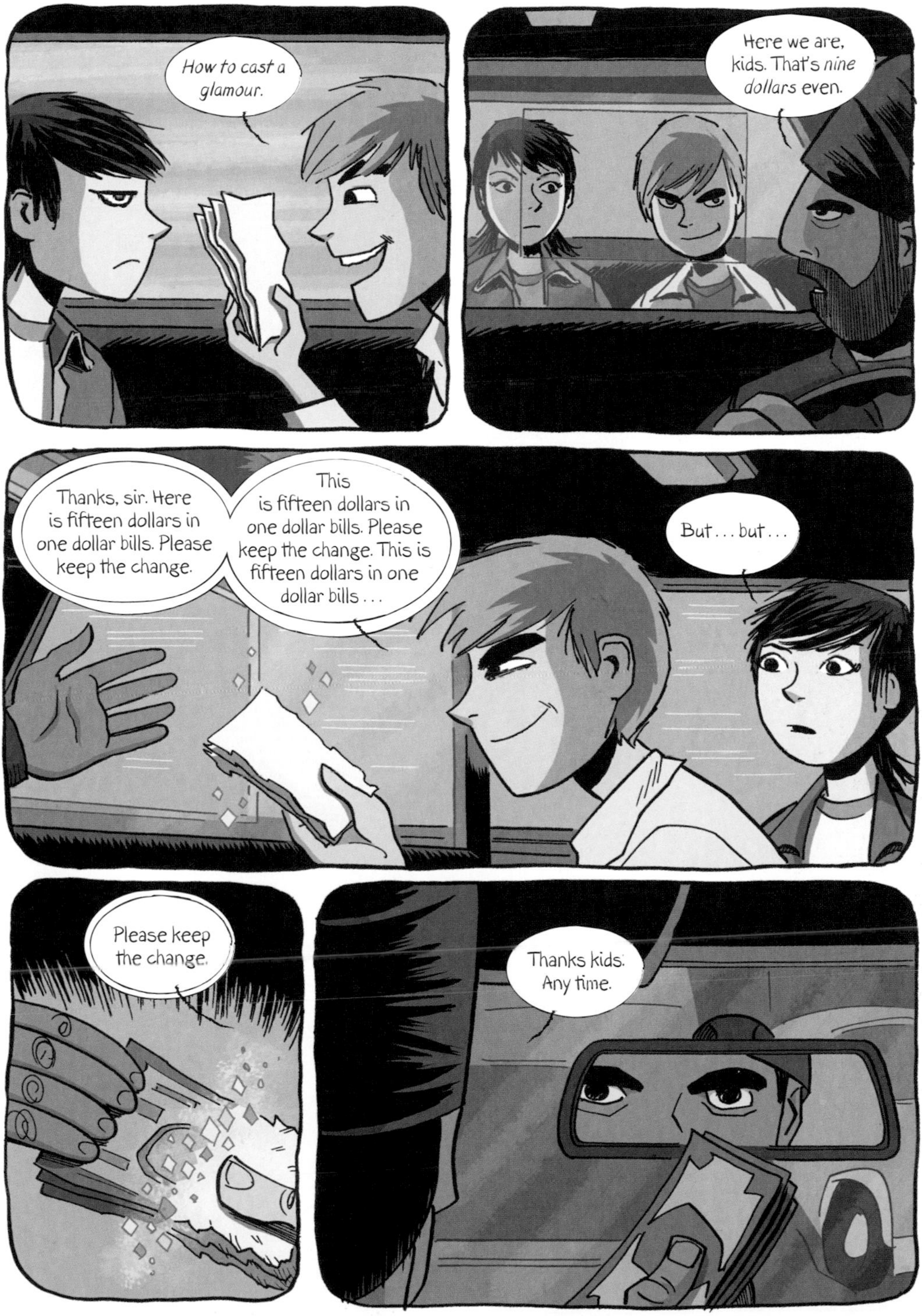
How to cast a *glamour.*
Here we are, kids. That's *nine dollars* even.
Thanks, sir. Here is fifteen dollars in one dollar bills. Please keep the change.
This is fifteen dollars in one dollar bills. Please keep the change. This is fifteen dollars in one dollar bills . . .
But . . . but . . .
Please keep the change.
Thanks kids. Any time.

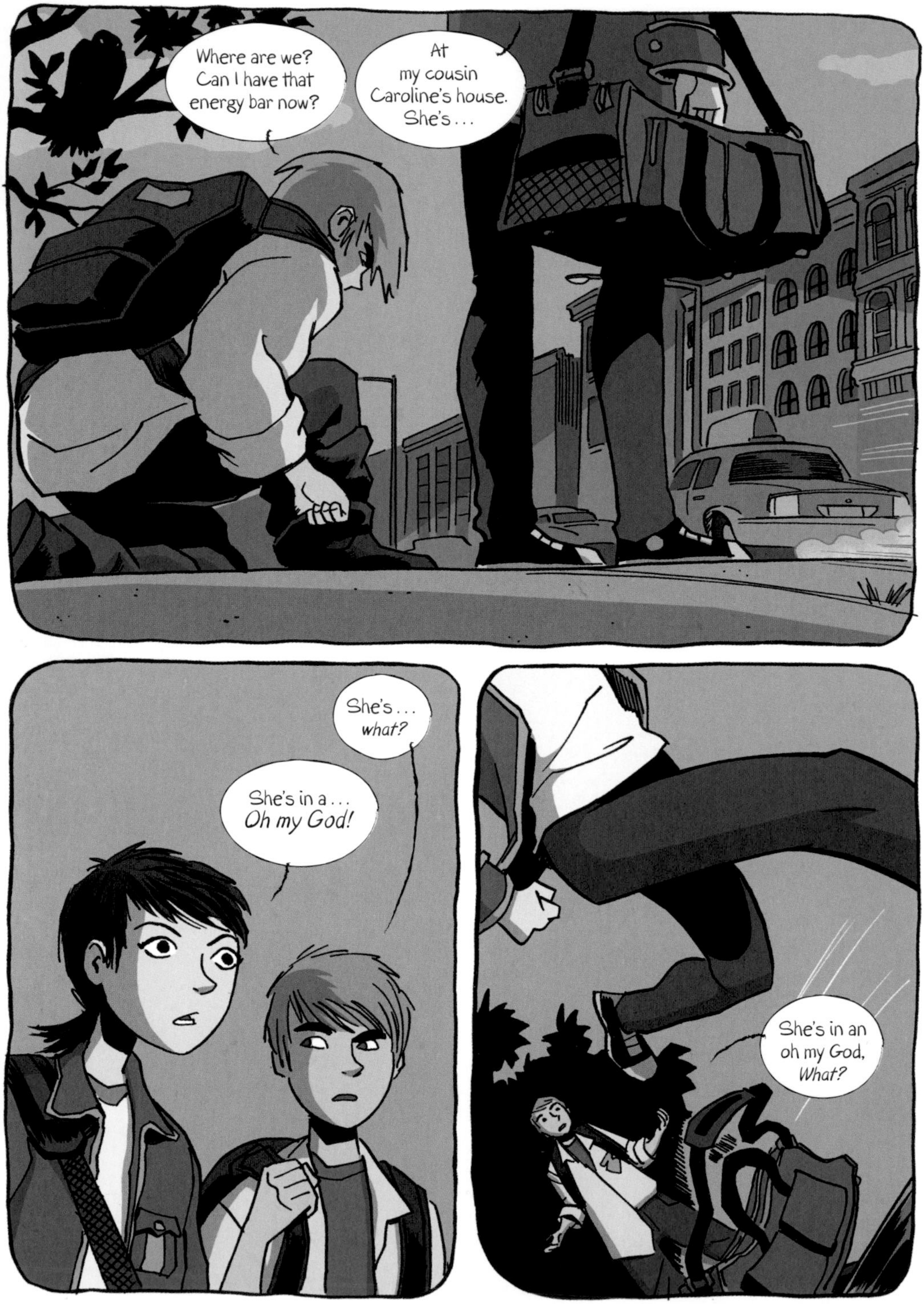
Where are we? Can I have that energy bar now?
At my cousin Caroline's house. She's . . .
She's . . . *what?*
She's in a . . . *Oh my God!*
She's in an oh my God, *What?*

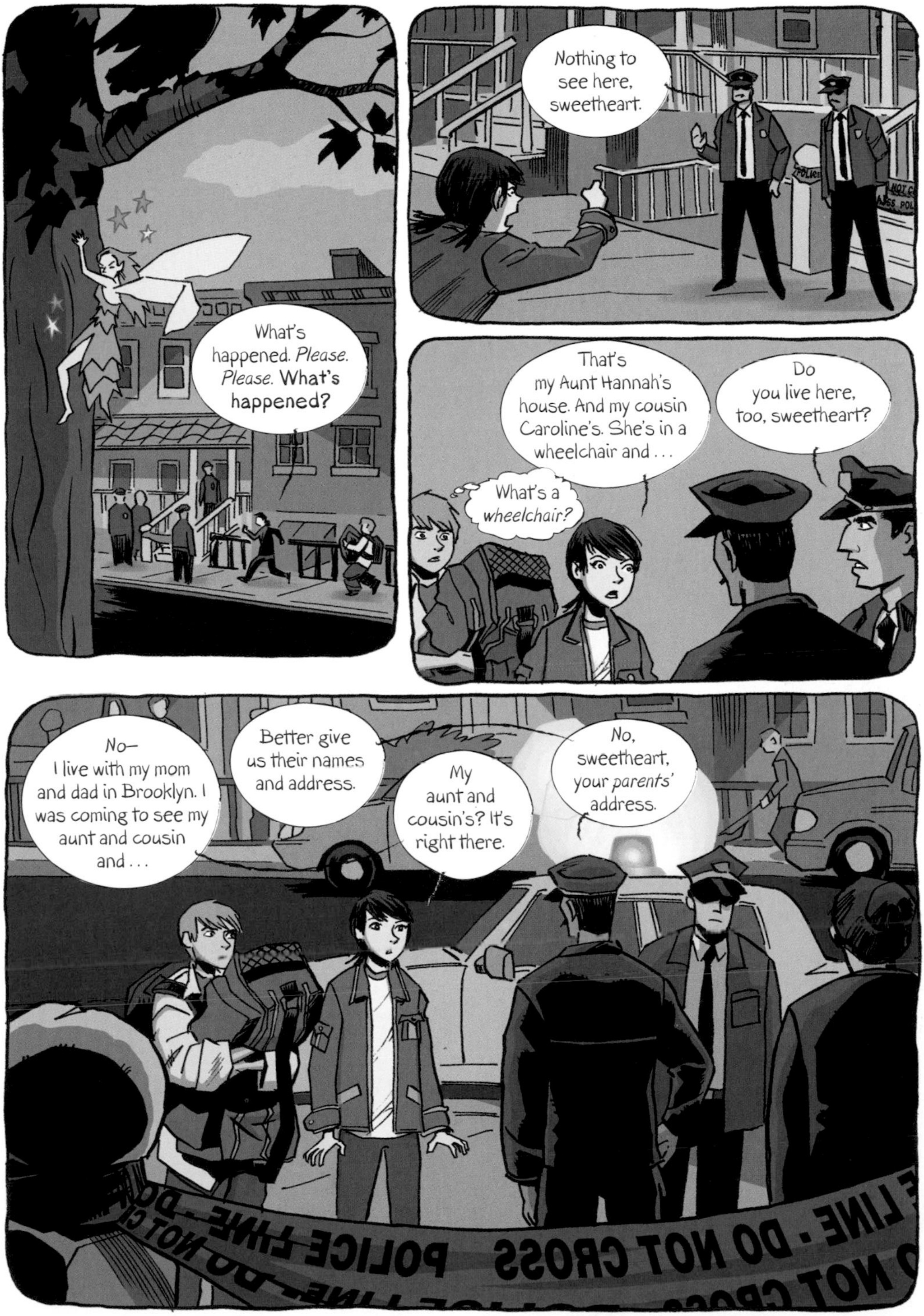
What's happened. *Please. Please.* **What's happened?**
Nothing to see here, sweetheart.
That's my Aunt Hannah's house. And my cousin Caroline's. She's in a wheelchair and . . .
Do you live here, too, sweetheart?
What's a *wheelchair?*
No—
I live with my mom and dad in Brooklyn. I was coming to see my aunt and cousin and . . .
Better give us their names and address.
My aunt and cousin's? It's right there.
No, sweetheart, your *parents'* address.

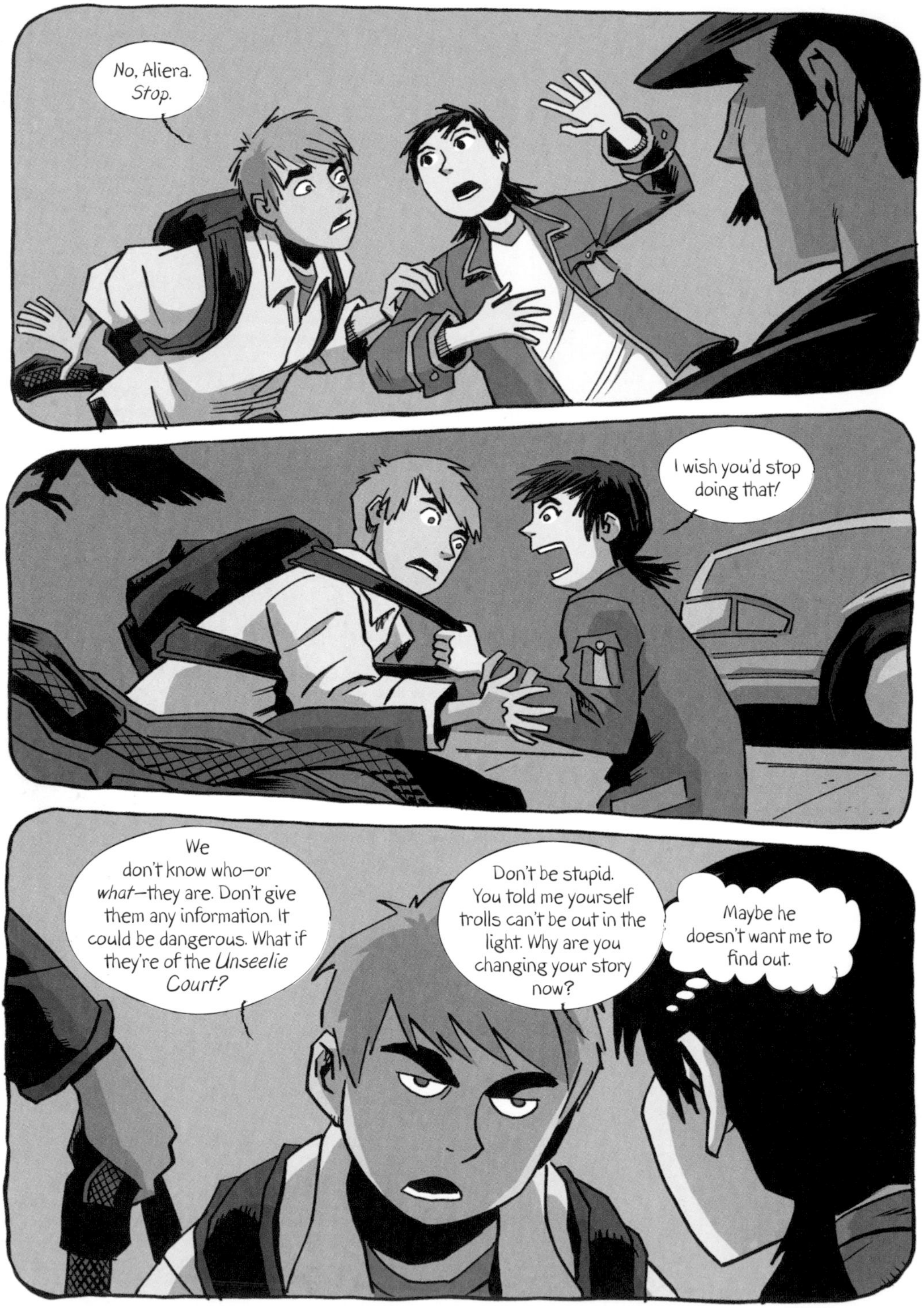
No, Aliera. *Stop.*
I wish you'd stop doing that!
We don't know who—or *what*—they are. Don't give them any information. It could be dangerous. What if they're of the *Unseelie Court?*
Don't be stupid. You told me yourself trolls can't be out in the light. Why are you changing your story now?
Maybe he doesn't want me to find out.

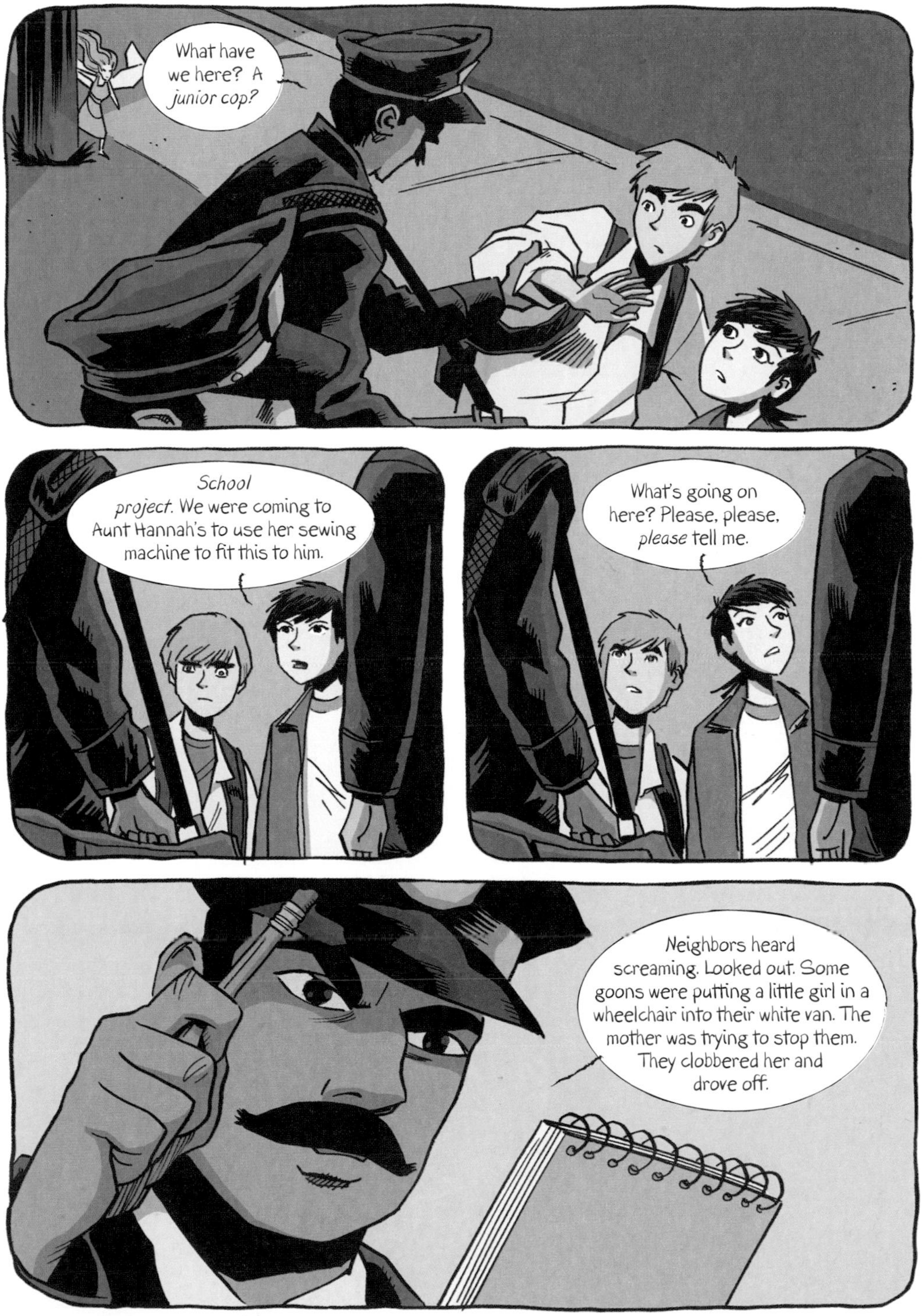
What have we here? A *junior cop?*
School project. We were coming to Aunt Hannah's to use her sewing machine to fit this to him.
What's going on here? Please, please, *please* tell me.
Neighbors heard screaming. Looked out. Some goons were putting a little girl in a wheelchair into their white van. The mother was trying to stop them. They clobbered her and drove off.

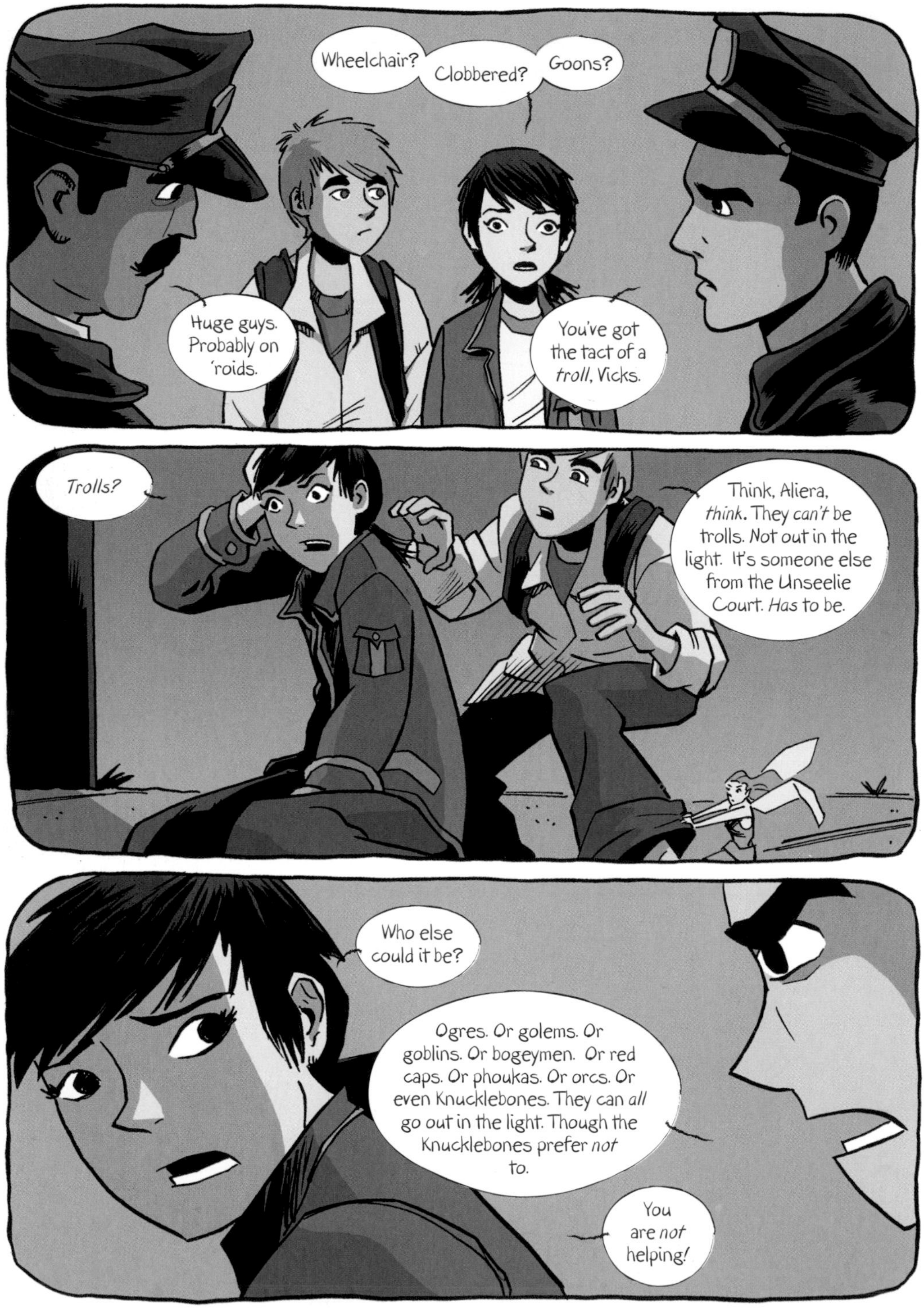
Wheelchair?
Clobbered?
Goons?
Huge guys. Probably on 'roids.
You've got the tact of a *troll*, Vicks.
Trolls?
Think, Aliera, *think*. They *can't* be trolls. Not out in the light. It's someone else from the Unseelie Court. *Has* to be.
Who else could it be?
Ogres. Or golems. Or goblins. Or bogeymen. Or red caps. Or phoukas. Or orcs. Or even Knucklebones. They can *all* go out in the light. Though the Knucklebones prefer *not* to.
You are *not* helping!

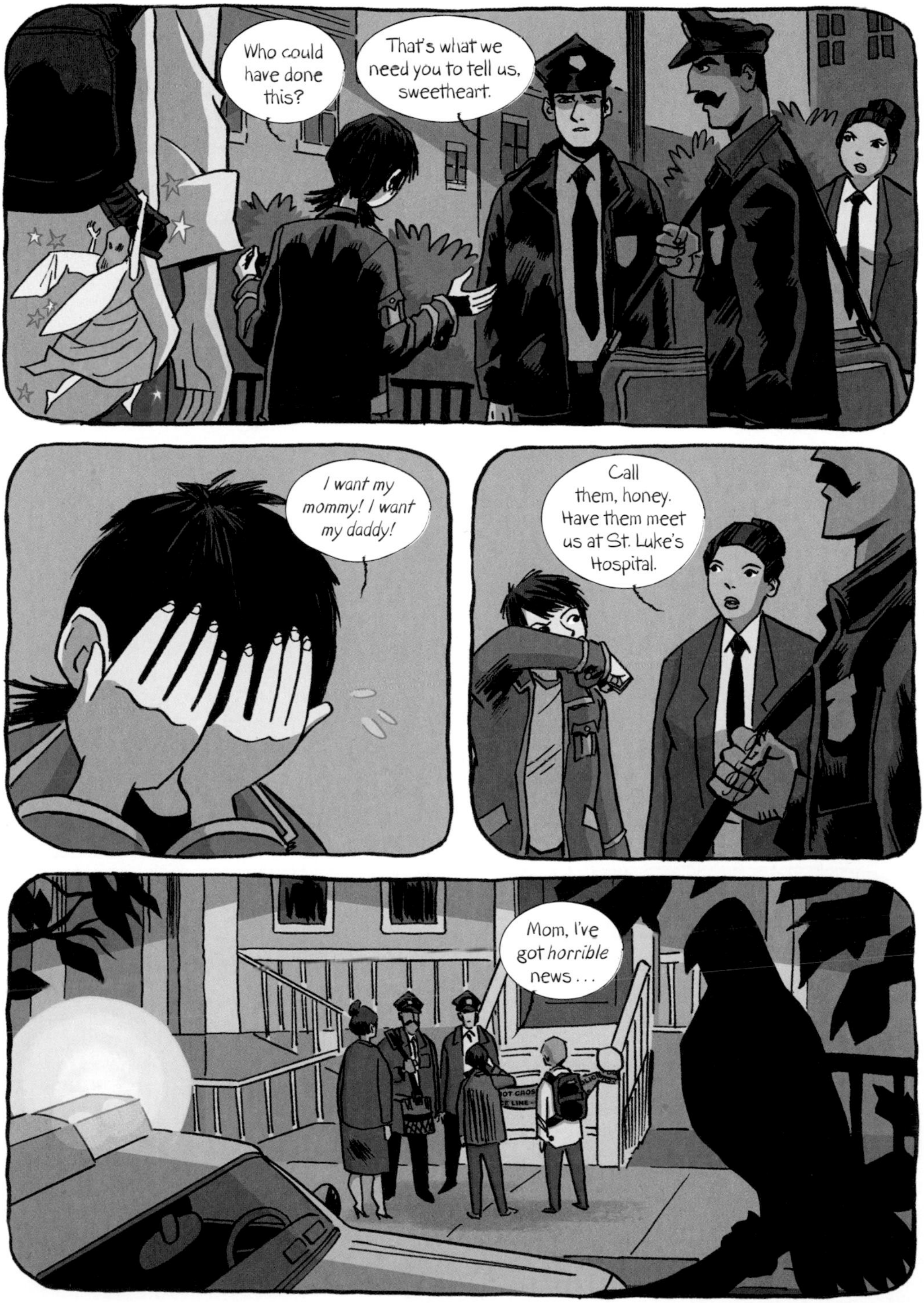
Who could have done this?
That's what we need you to tell us, sweetheart.
I want my mommy! I want my daddy!
Call them, honey. Have them meet us at St. Luke's Hospital.
Mom, I've got *horrible* news . . .

9. Coup de Temps

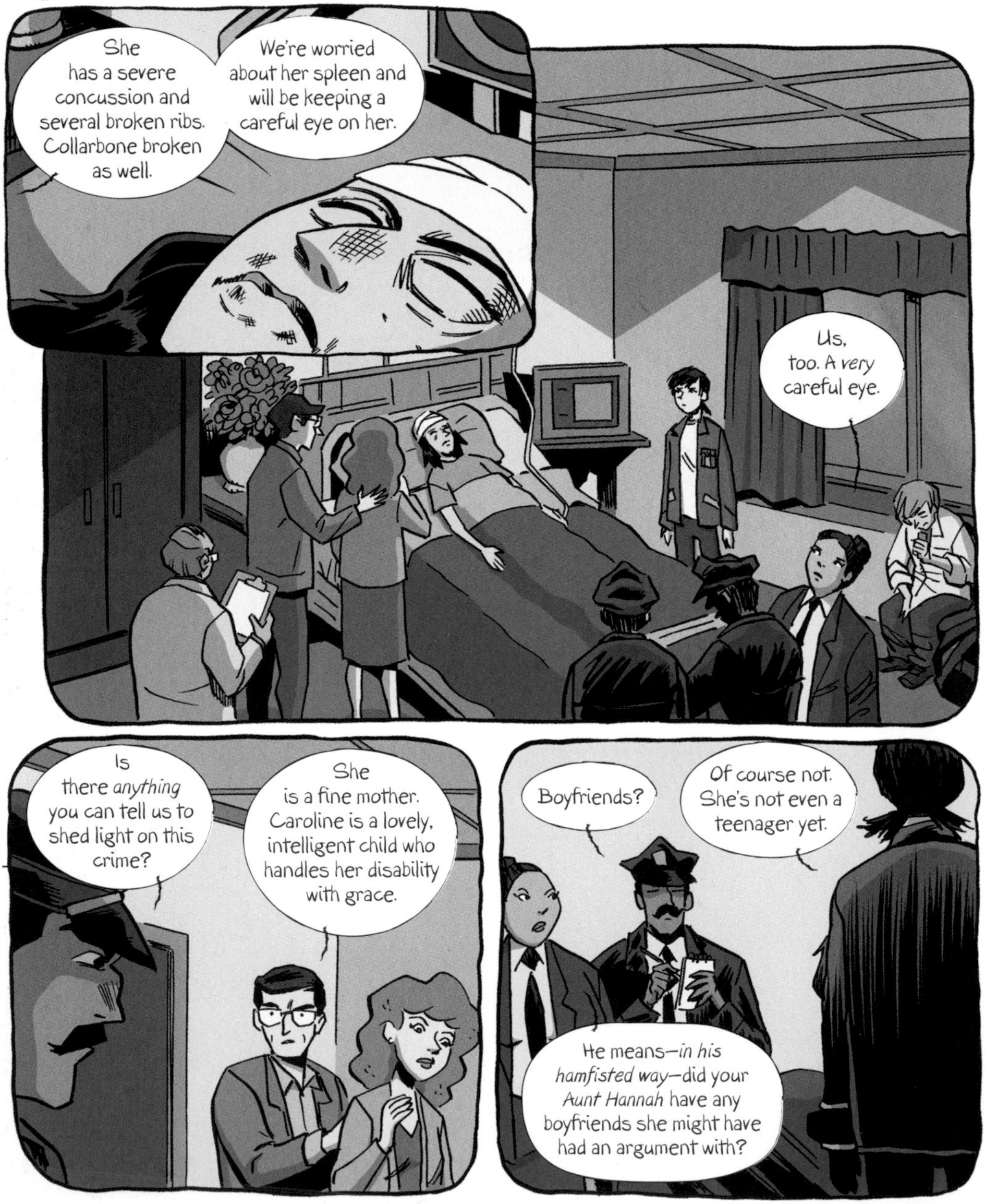
She has a severe concussion and several broken ribs. Collarbone broken as well.
We're worried about her spleen and will be keeping a careful eye on her.
Us, too. A *very* careful eye.
Is there *anything* you can tell us to shed light on this crime?
She is a fine mother. Caroline is a lovely, intelligent child who handles her disability with grace.
Boyfriends?
Of course not. She's not even a teenager yet.
He means—*in his hamfisted way*—did your *Aunt Hannah* have any boyfriends she might have had an argument with?

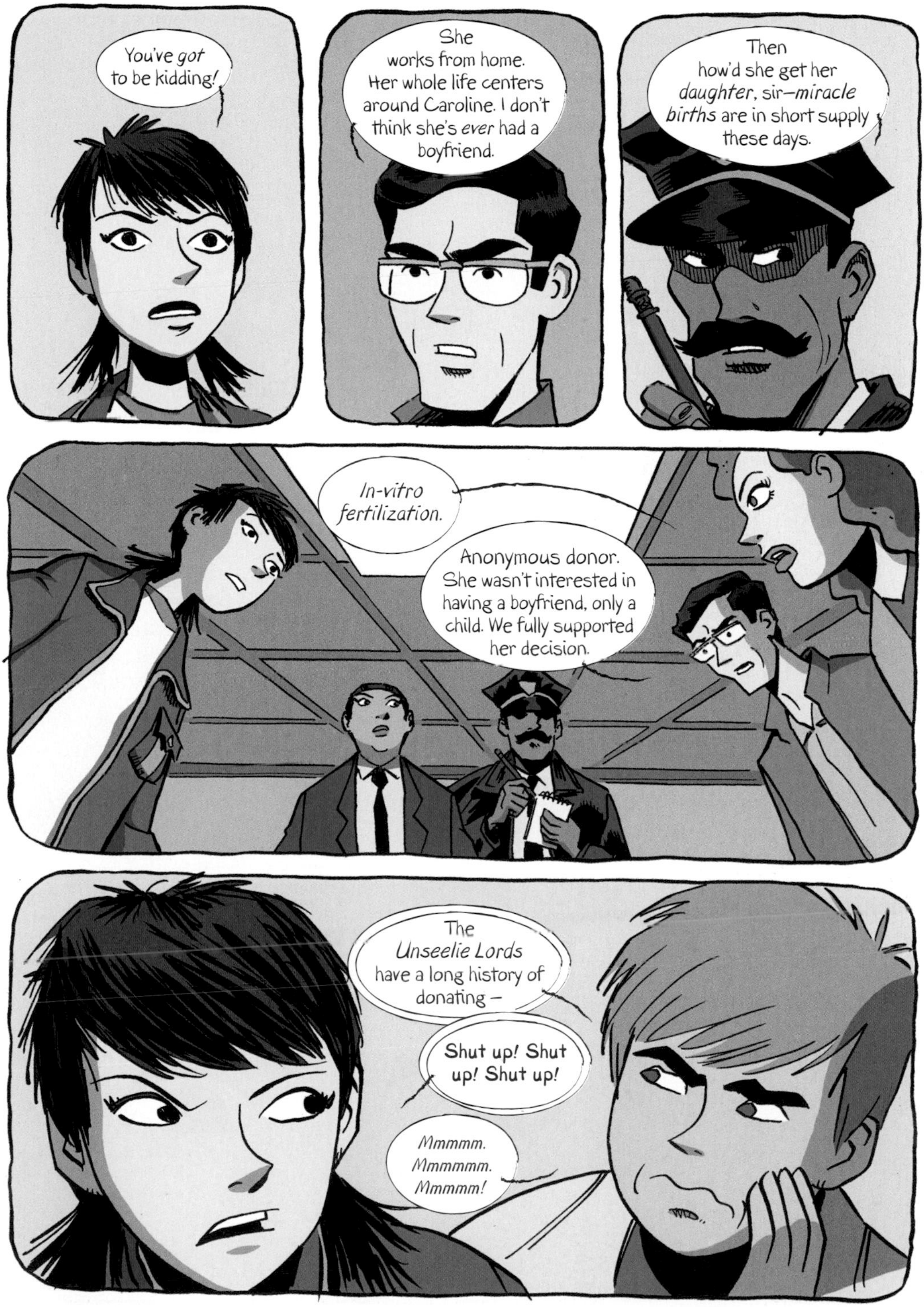

You've *got* to be kidding!
She works from home. Her whole life centers around Caroline. I don't think she's *ever* had a boyfriend.
Then how'd she get her *daughter*, sir—*miracle births* are in short supply these days.
In-vitro fertilization.
Anonymous donor. She wasn't interested in having a boyfriend, only a child. We fully supported her decision.
The *Unseelie Lords* have a long history of donating –
Shut up! Shut up! Shut up!
Mmmmm. Mmmmmm. Mmmmm!

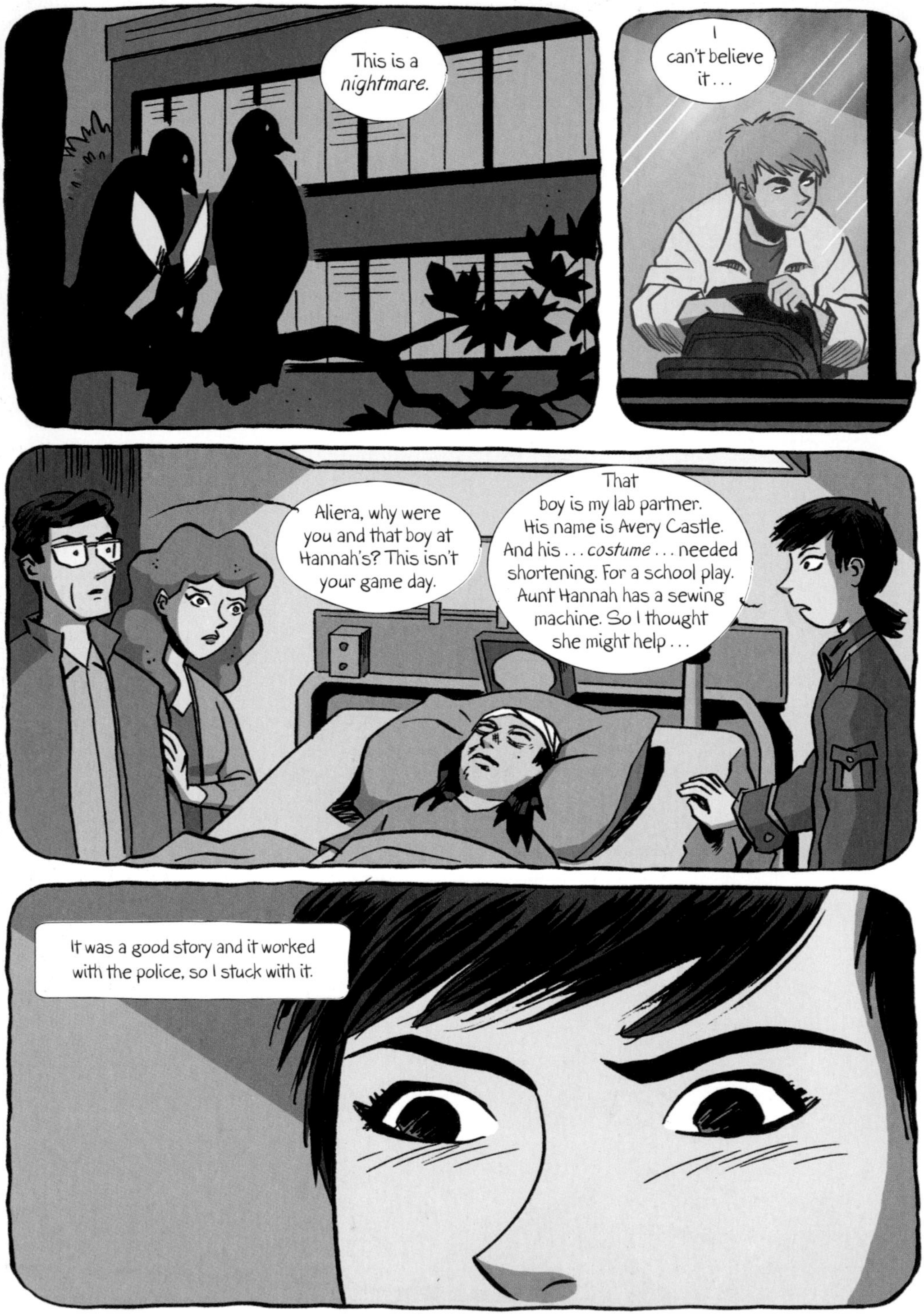
This is a *nightmare.*
I can't believe it . . .
Aliera, why were you and that boy at Hannah's? This isn't your game day.
That boy is my lab partner. His name is Avery Castle. And his . . . *costume* . . . needed shortening. For a school play. Aunt Hannah has a sewing machine. So I thought she might help . . .
It was a good story and it worked with the police, so I stuck with it.

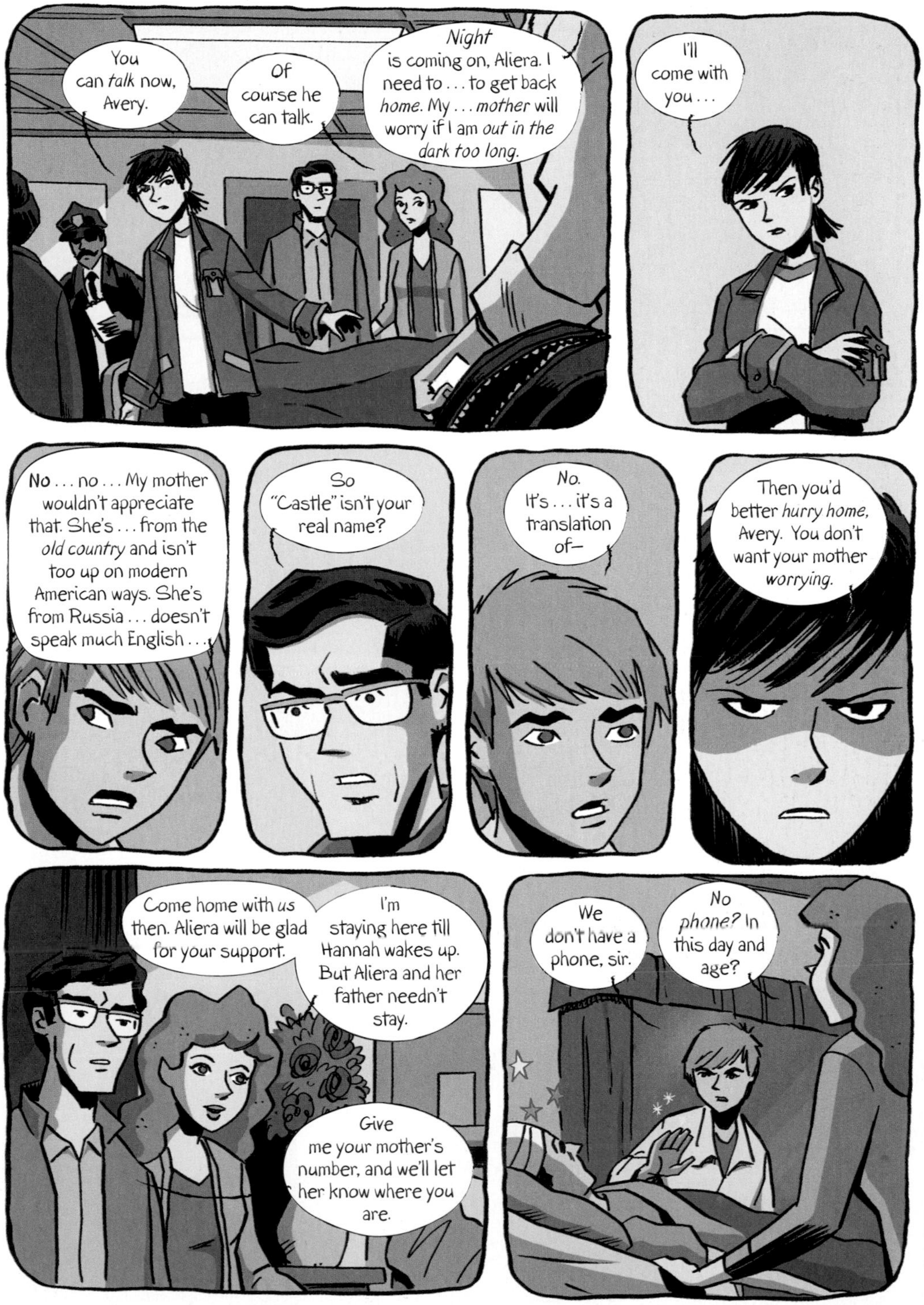
You can *talk* now, Avery.
Of course he can talk.
Night is coming on, Aliera. I need to . . . to get back *home.* My . . . *mother* will worry if I am *out in the dark too long.*
I'll come with you . . .
No . . . no . . . My mother wouldn't appreciate that. She's . . . from the *old country* and isn't too up on modern American ways. She's from Russia . . . doesn't speak much English . . .
So "Castle" isn't your real name?
No. It's . . . it's a translation of—
Then you'd better *hurry home,* Avery. You don't want your mother *worrying.*
Come home with *us* then. Aliera will be glad for your support.
I'm staying here till Hannah wakes up. But Aliera and her father needn't stay.
Give me your mother's number, and we'll let her know where you are.
We don't have a phone, sir.
No *phone?* In this day and age?

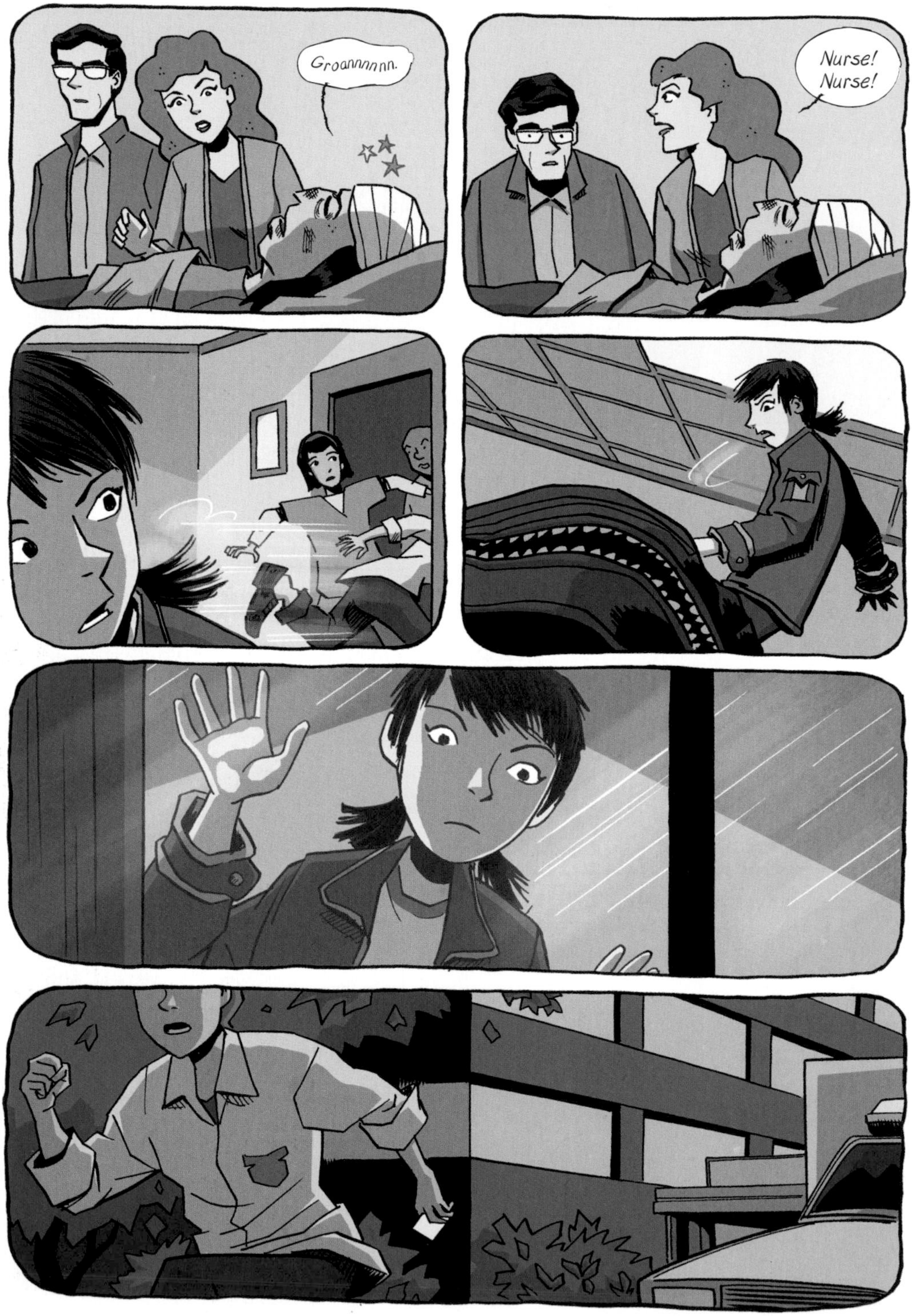
Groannnnnn.
Nurse! Nurse!

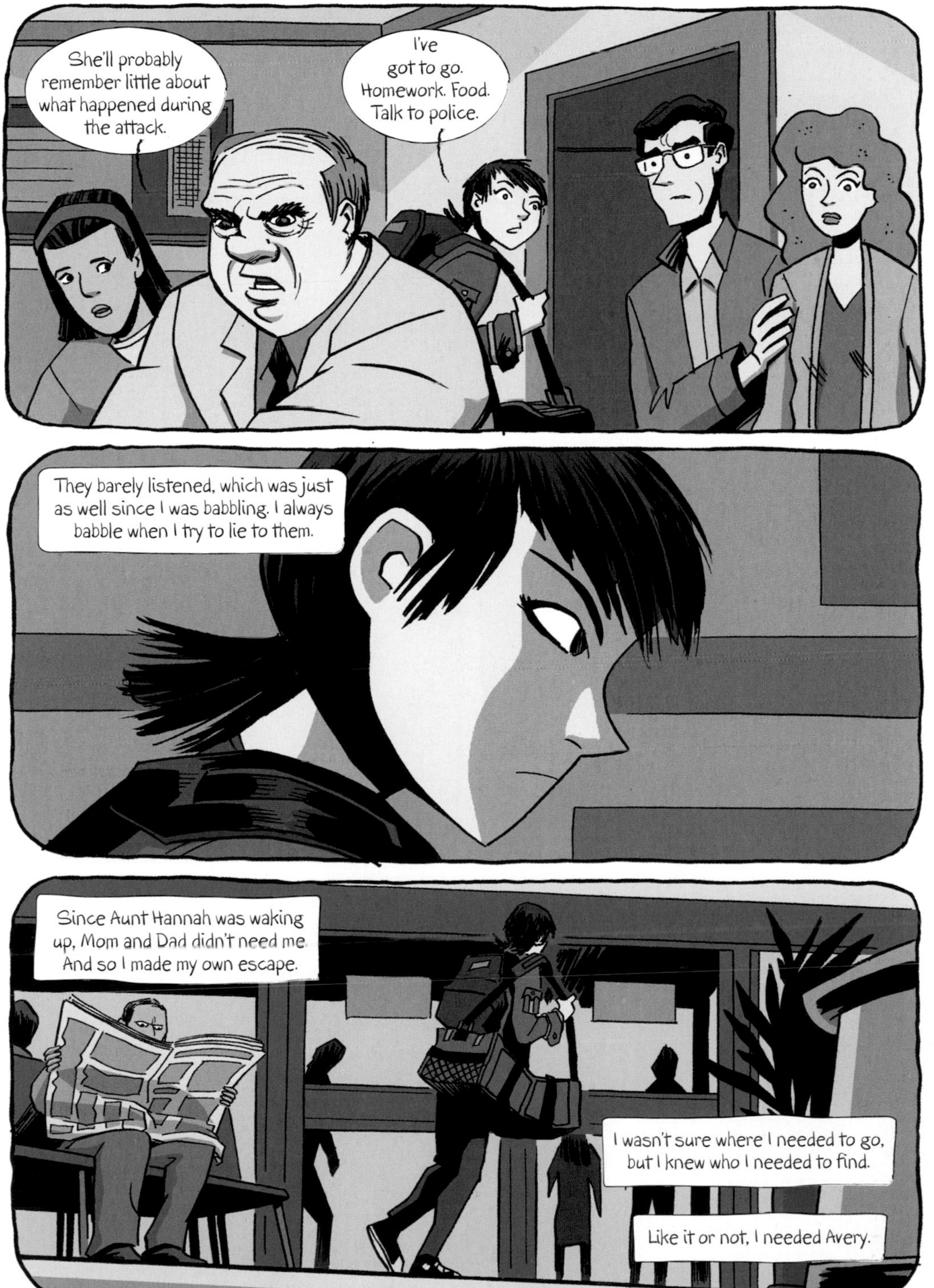
She'll probably remember little about what happened during the attack.
I've got to go. Homework. Food. Talk to police.
They barely listened, which was just as well since I was babbling. I always babble when I try to lie to them.
Since Aunt Hannah was waking up, Mom and Dad didn't need me. And so I made my own escape.
I wasn't sure where I needed to go, but I knew who I needed to find.
Like it or not, I needed Avery.

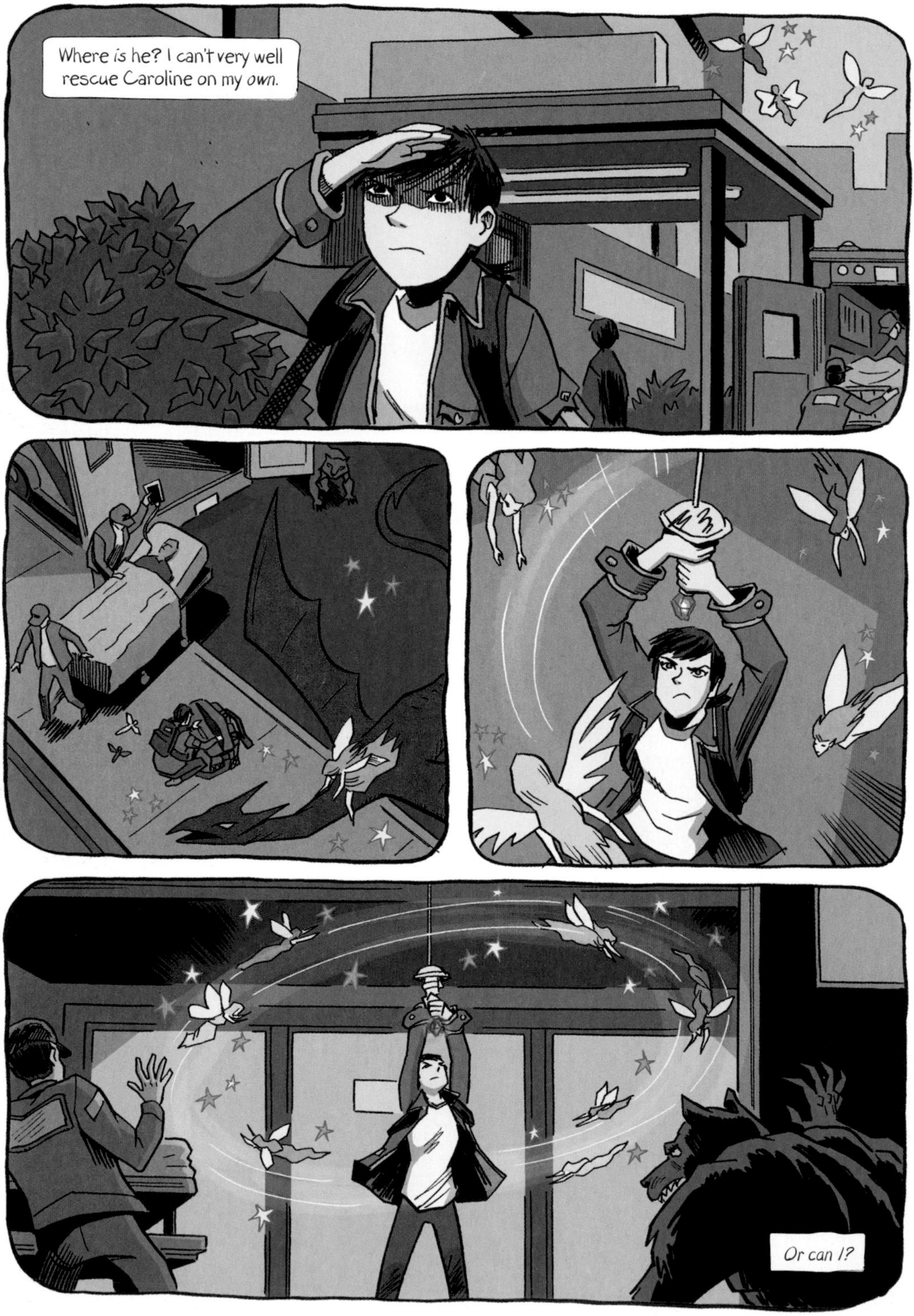
Where *is* he? I can't very well rescue Caroline on my *own*.
Or can I?

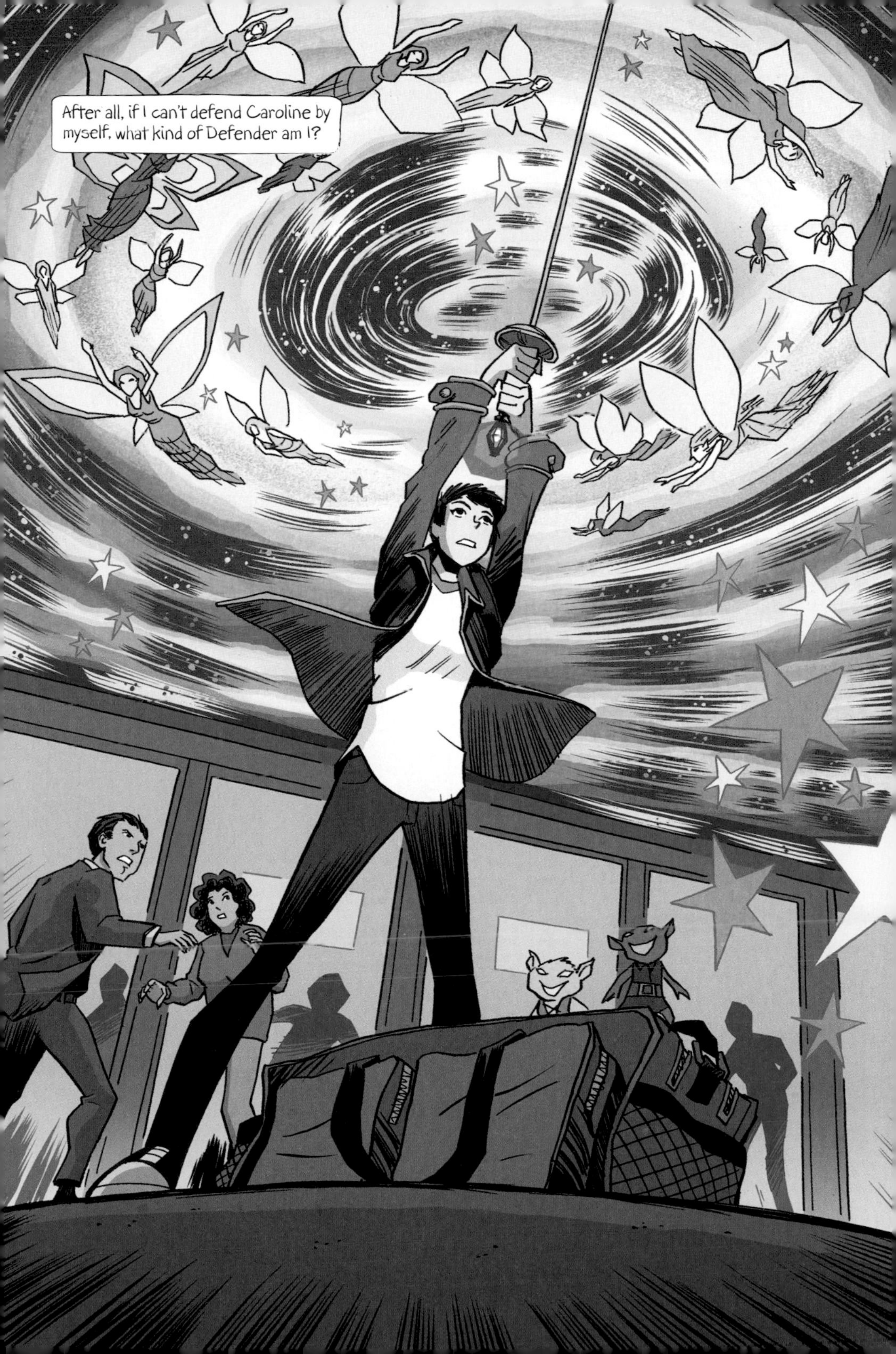
After all, if I can't defend Caroline by myself, what kind of Defender am I?

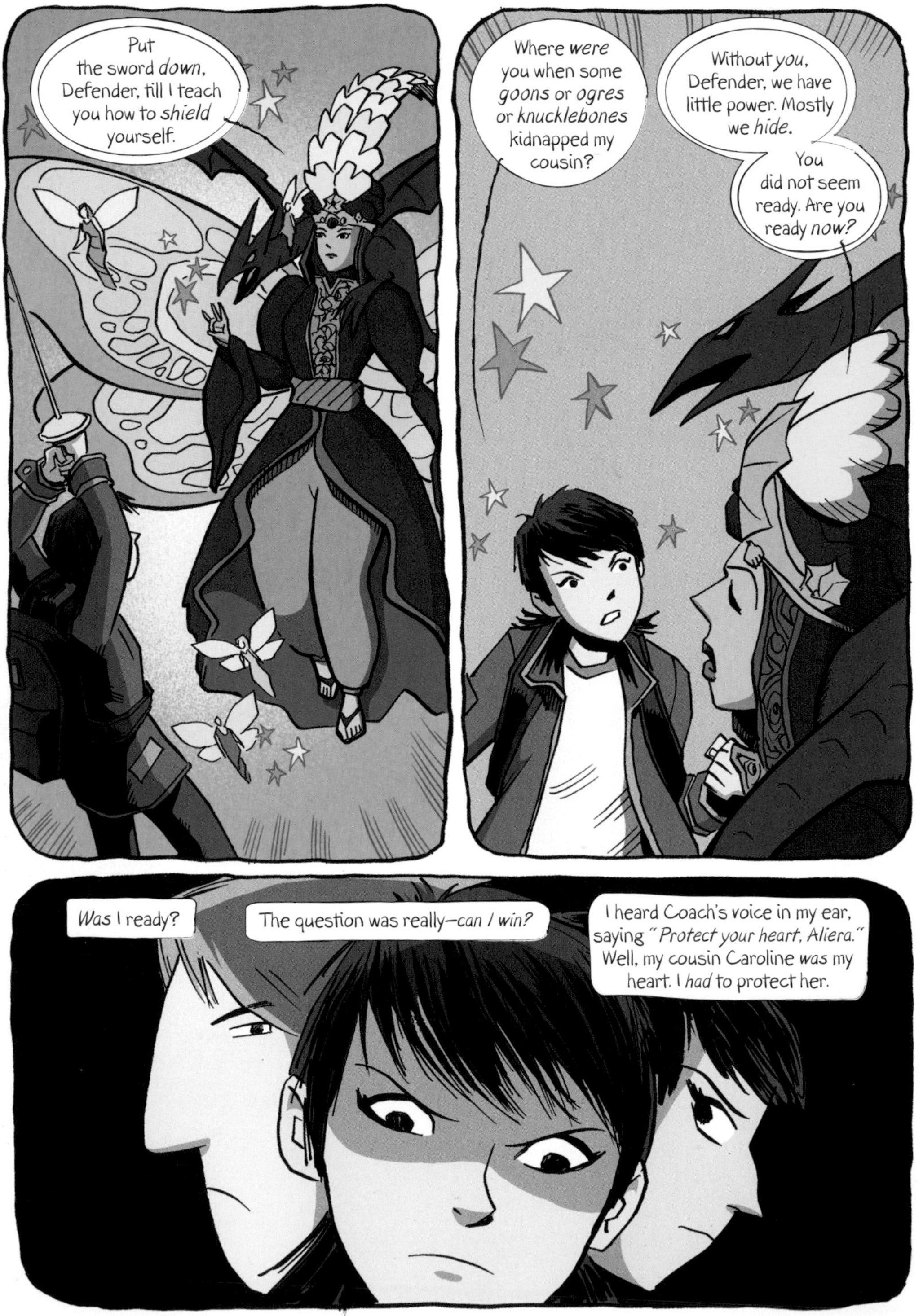
Put the sword *down*, Defender, till I teach you how to *shield* yourself.
Where *were* you when some *goons* or *ogres* or *knucklebones* kidnapped my cousin?
Without *you*, Defender, we have little power. Mostly we *hide*.
You did not seem ready. Are you ready *now?*
Was I ready?
The question was really—*can I win?*
I heard Coach's voice in my ear, saying *"Protect your heart, Aliera."* Well, my cousin Caroline *was* my heart. I *had* to protect her.

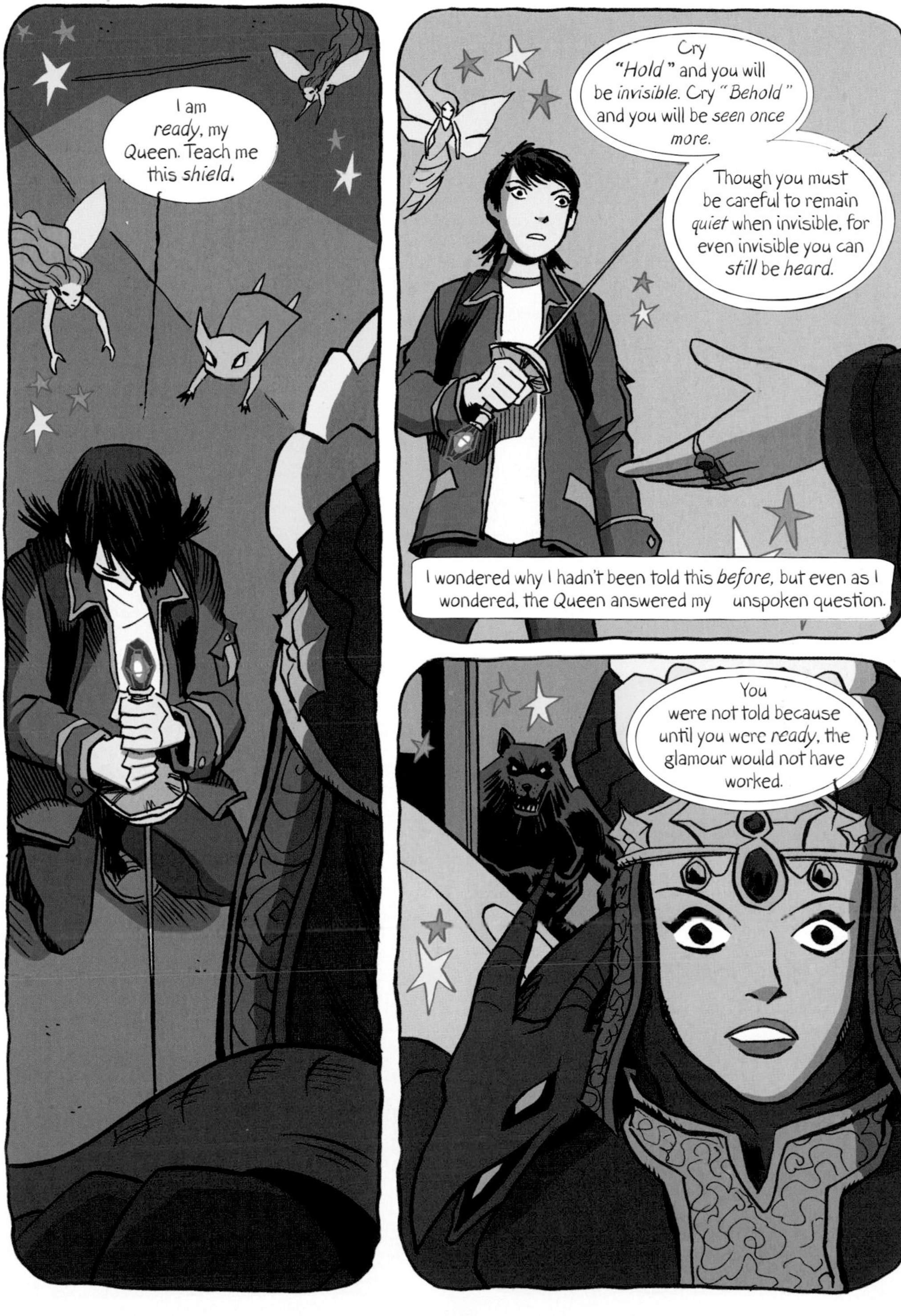
I am *ready*, my Queen. Teach me this *shield.*
Cry "*Hold*" and you will be *invisible.* Cry "*Behold*" and you will be *seen once more.*
Though you must be careful to remain *quiet* when invisible, for even invisible you can *still* be *heard.*
I wondered why I hadn't been told this *before,* but even as I wondered, the Queen answered my unspoken question.
You were not told because until you were *ready*, the glamour would not have worked.

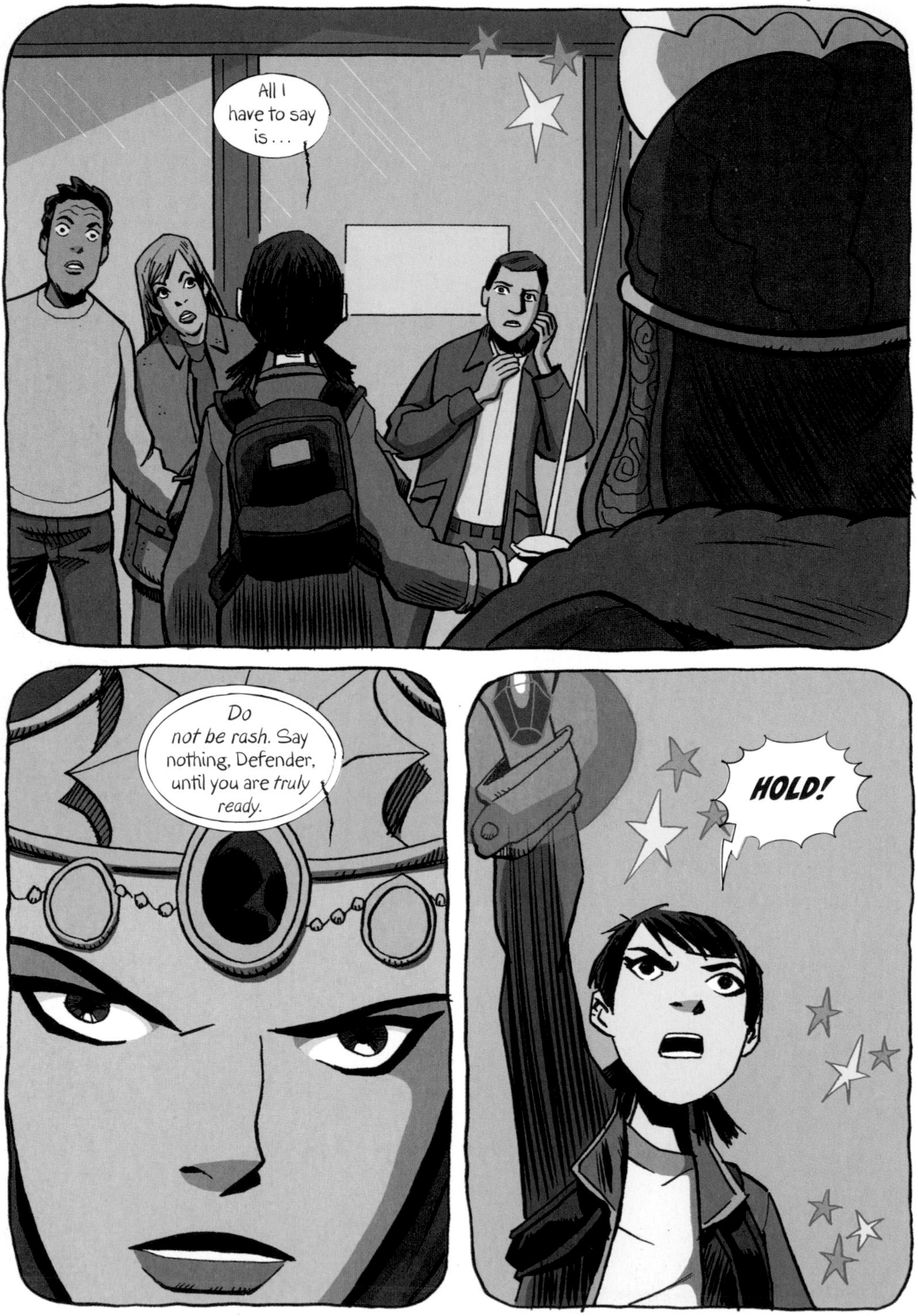
All I have to say is . . .
Do not be rash. Say nothing, Defender, until you are truly ready.
HOLD!

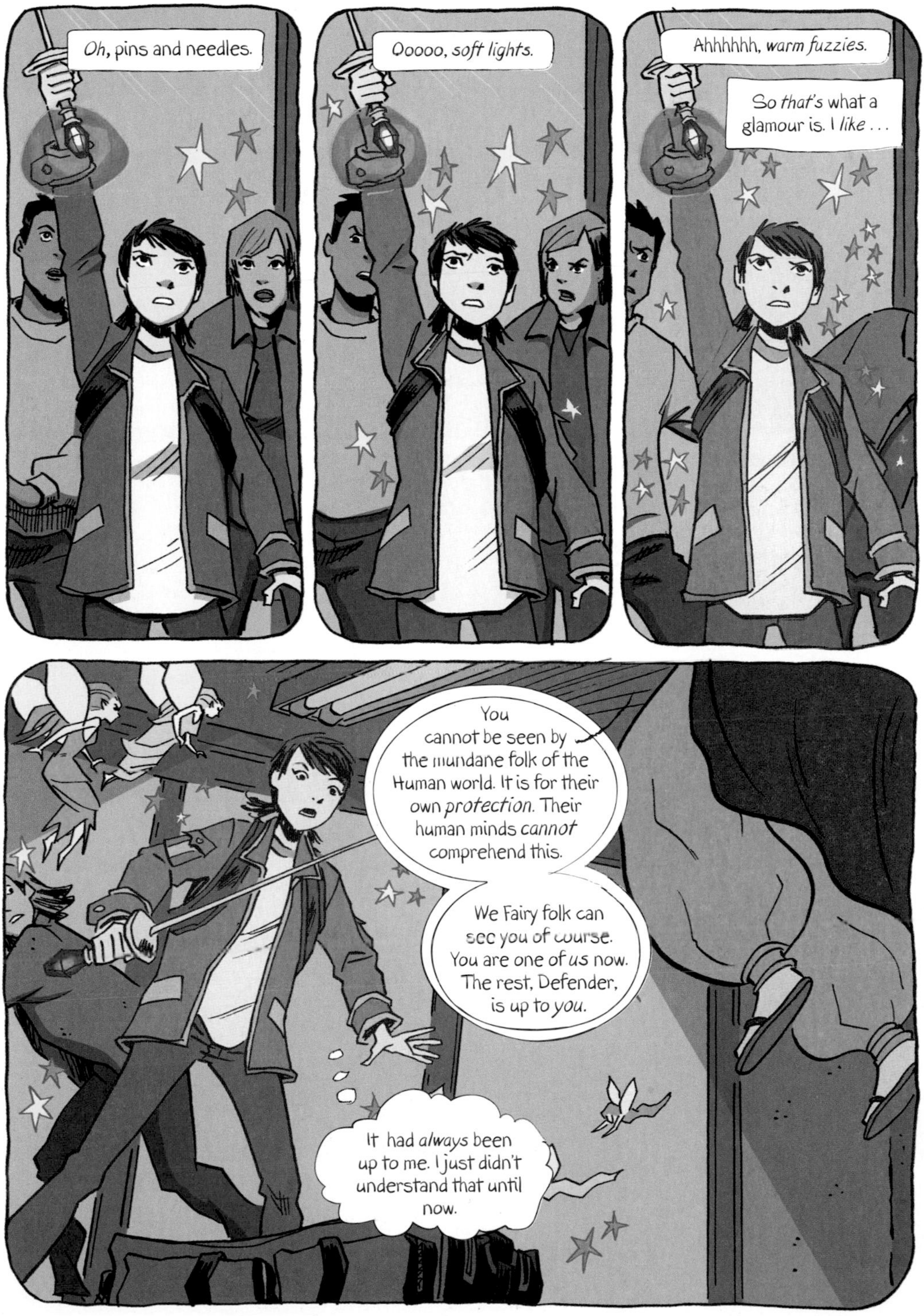
Oh, pins and needles.
Ooooo, soft lights.
Ahhhhhh, warm fuzzies.
So that's what a glamour is. I like . . .
You cannot be seen by the mundane folk of the Human world. It is for their own protection. Their human minds cannot comprehend this.
We Fairy folk can see you of course. You are one of us now. The rest, Defender, is up to you.
It had always been up to me. I just didn't understand that until now.

10. Esquive

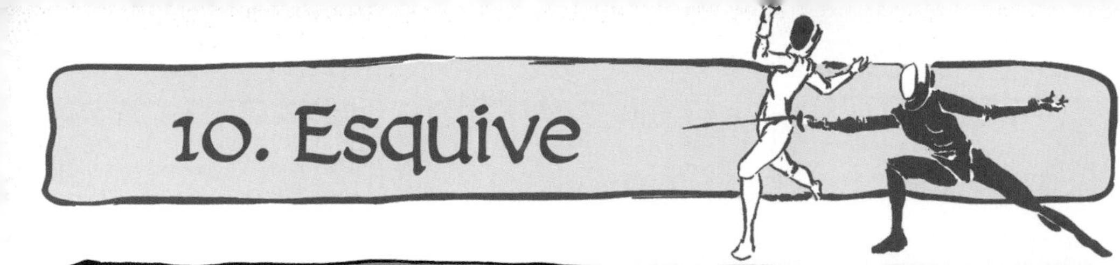

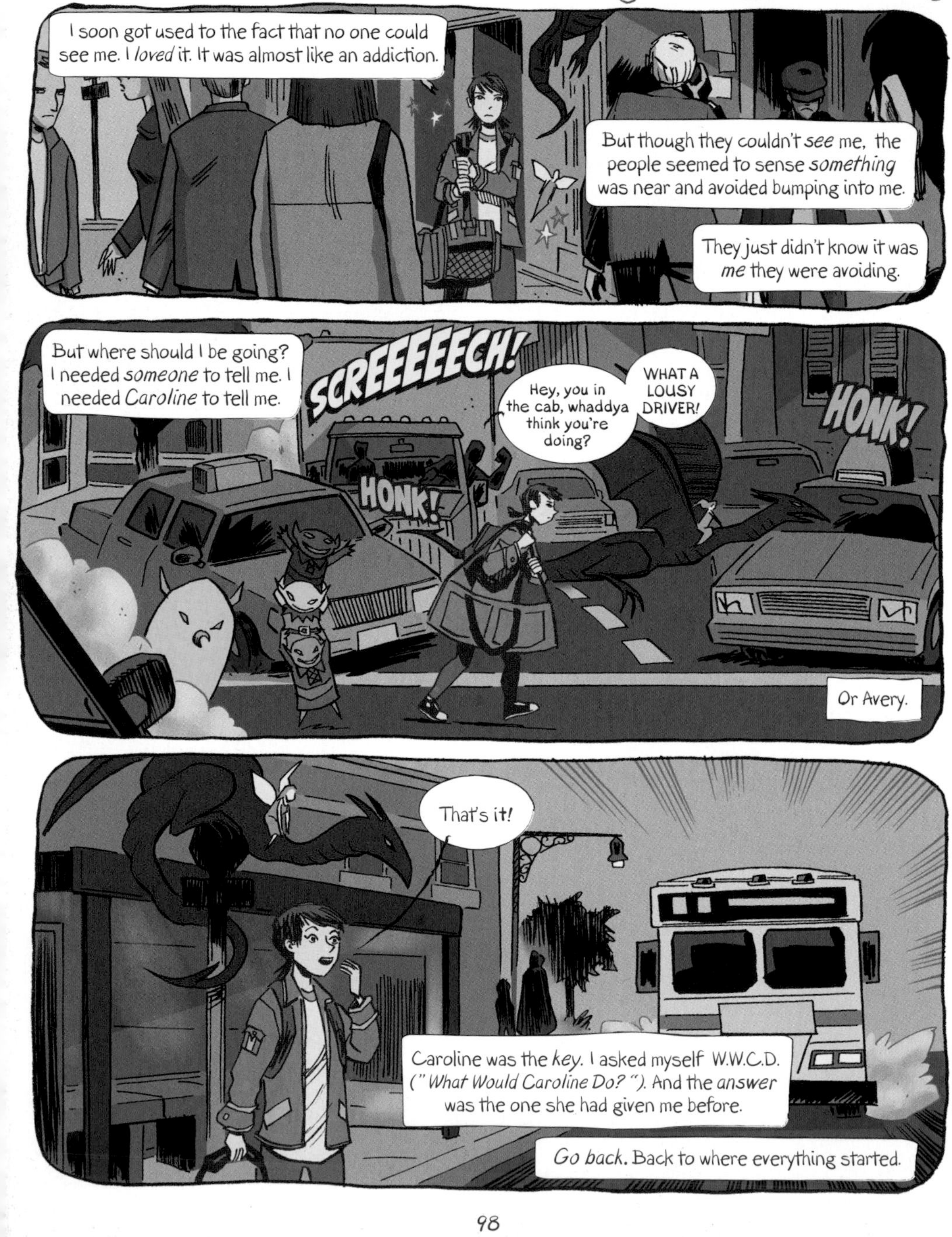
I soon got used to the fact that no one could see me. I *loved* it. It was almost like an addiction.
But though they couldn't *see* me, the people seemed to sense *something* was near and avoided bumping into me.
They just didn't know it was *me* they were avoiding.
But where should I be going? I needed *someone* to tell me. I needed *Caroline* to tell me.
SCREEEEEECH!
Hey, you in the cab, whaddya think you're doing?
WHAT A LOUSY DRIVER!
HONK!
HONK!
Or Avery.
That's it!
Caroline was the *key*. I asked myself W.W.C.D. ("*What Would Caroline Do?*"). And the *answer* was the one she had given me before.
Go back. Back to where everything started.

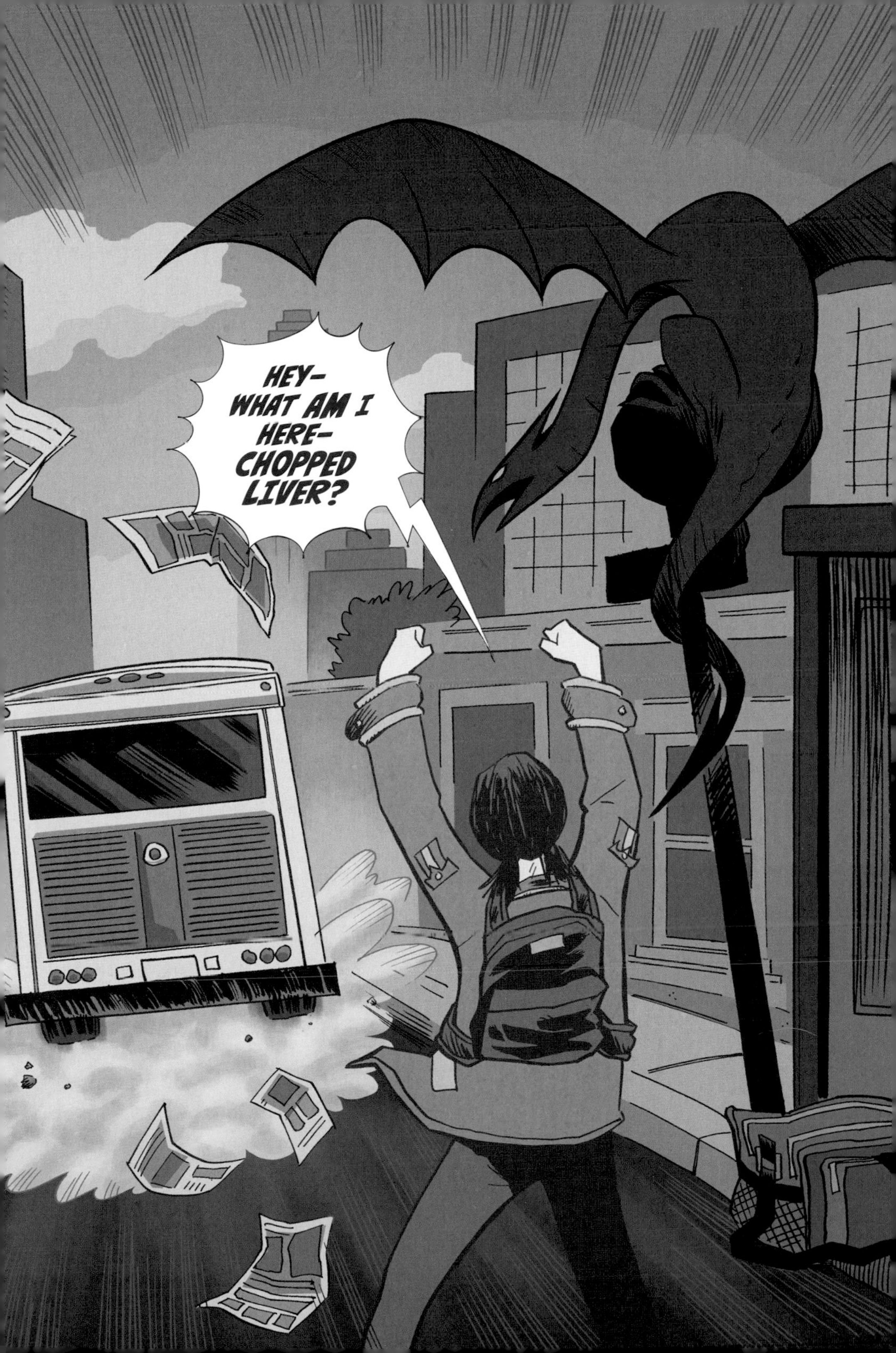
HEY- WHAT AM I HERE- CHOPPED LIVER?

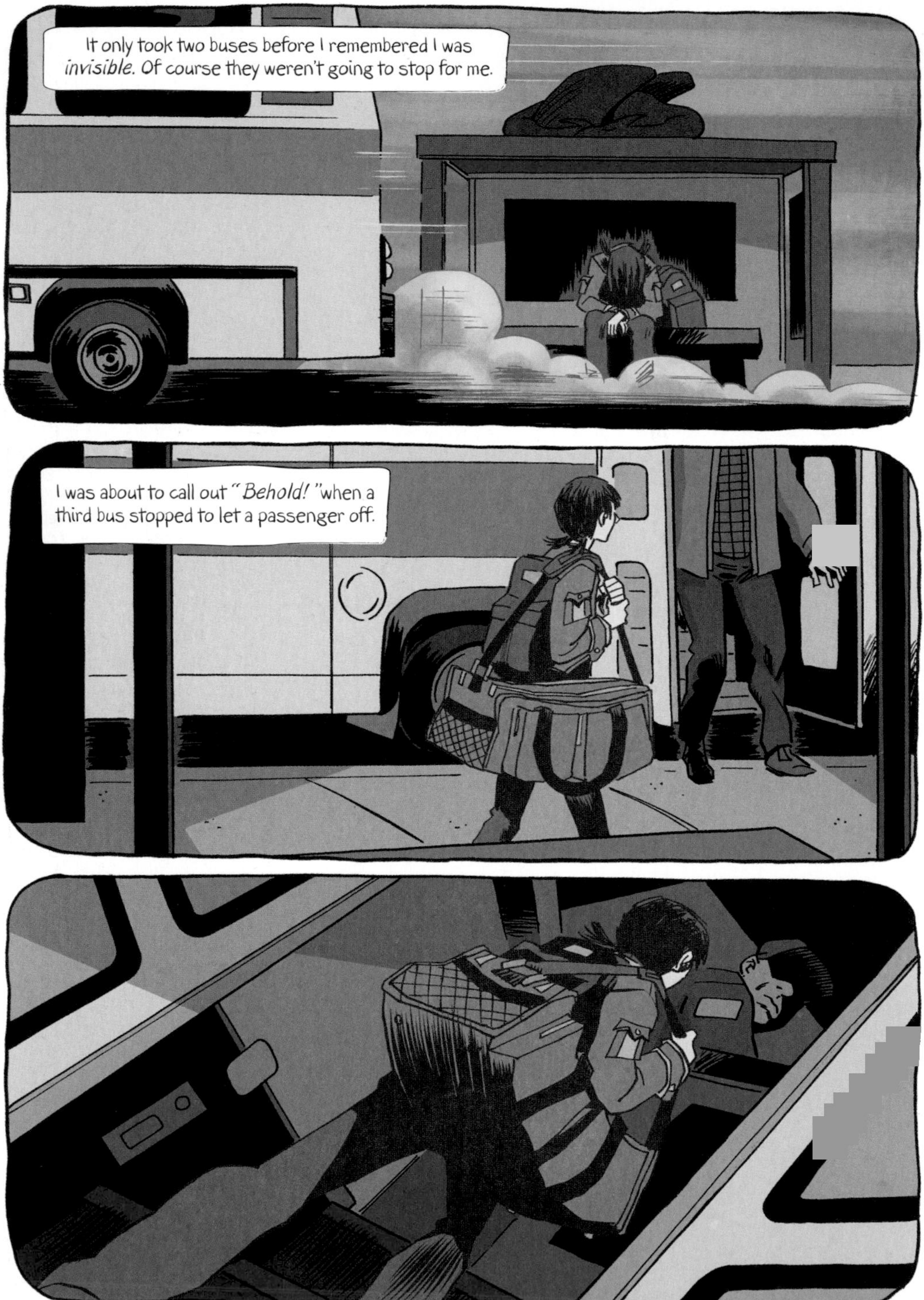
It only took two buses before I remembered I was *invisible.* Of course they weren't going to stop for me.
I was about to call out "*Behold!*" when a third bus stopped to let a passenger off.

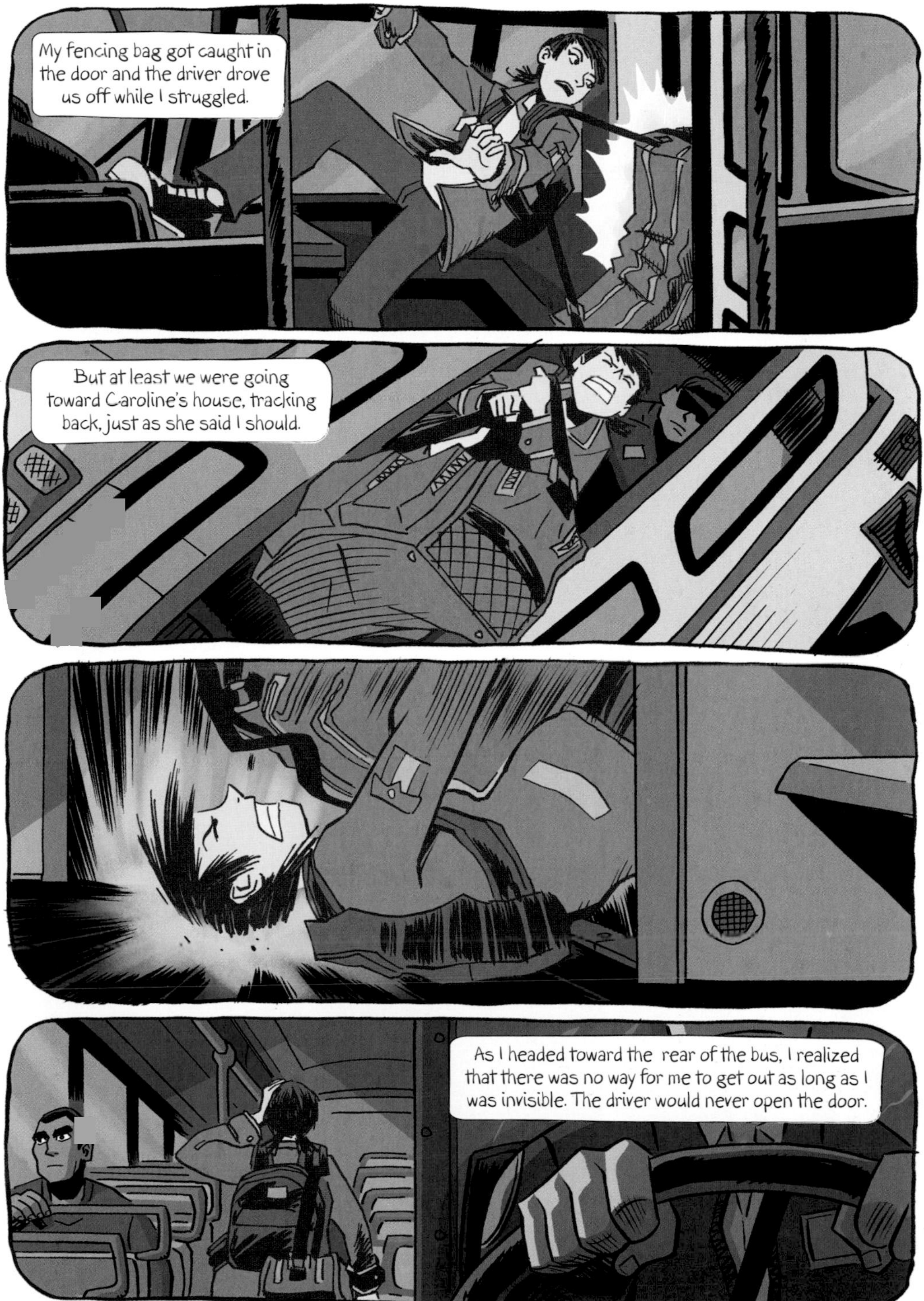
My fencing bag got caught in the door and the driver drove us off while I struggled.
But at least we were going toward Caroline's house, tracking back, just as she said I should.
As I headed toward the rear of the bus, I realized that there was no way for me to get out as long as I was invisible. The driver would never open the door.

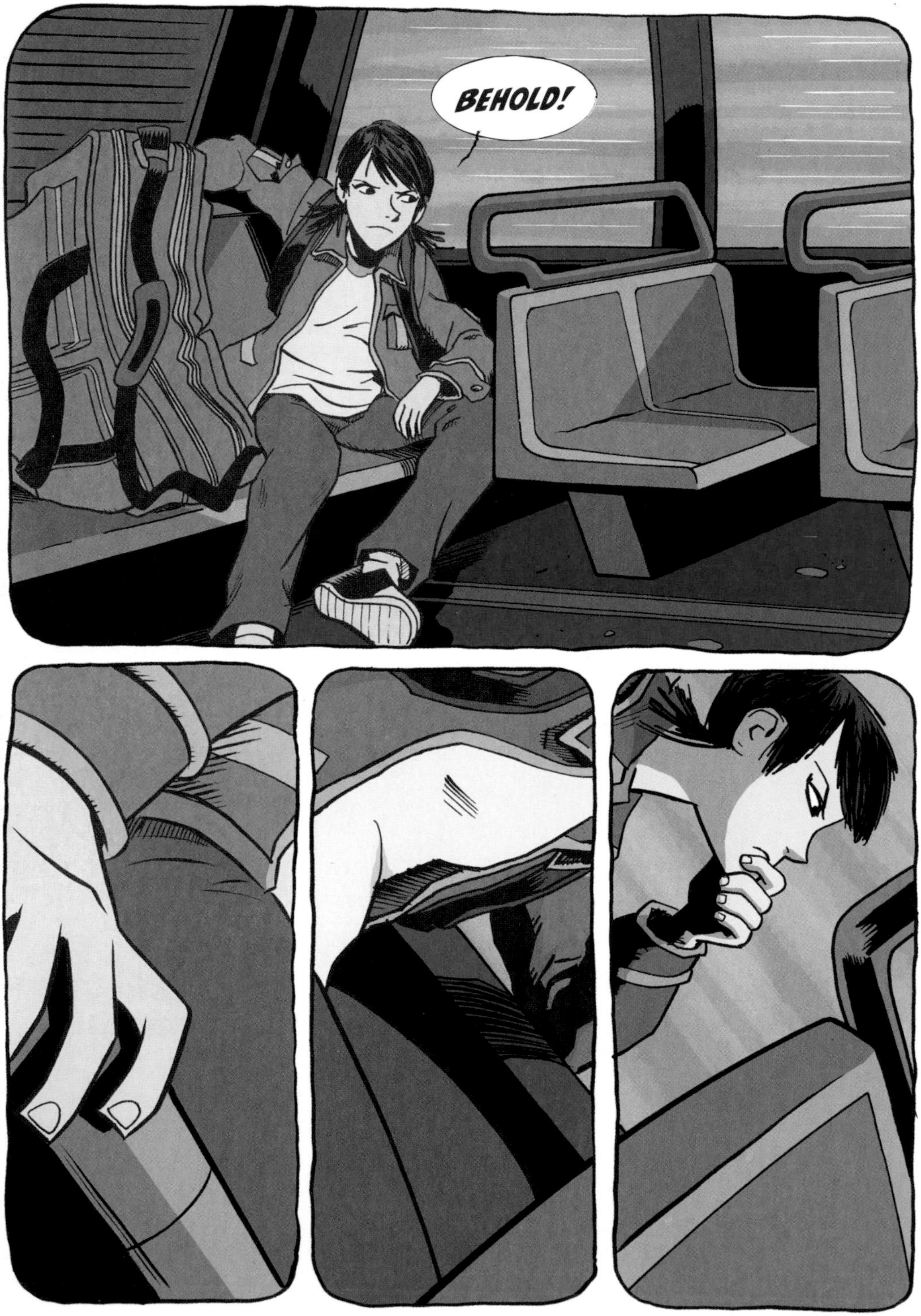
BEHOLD!

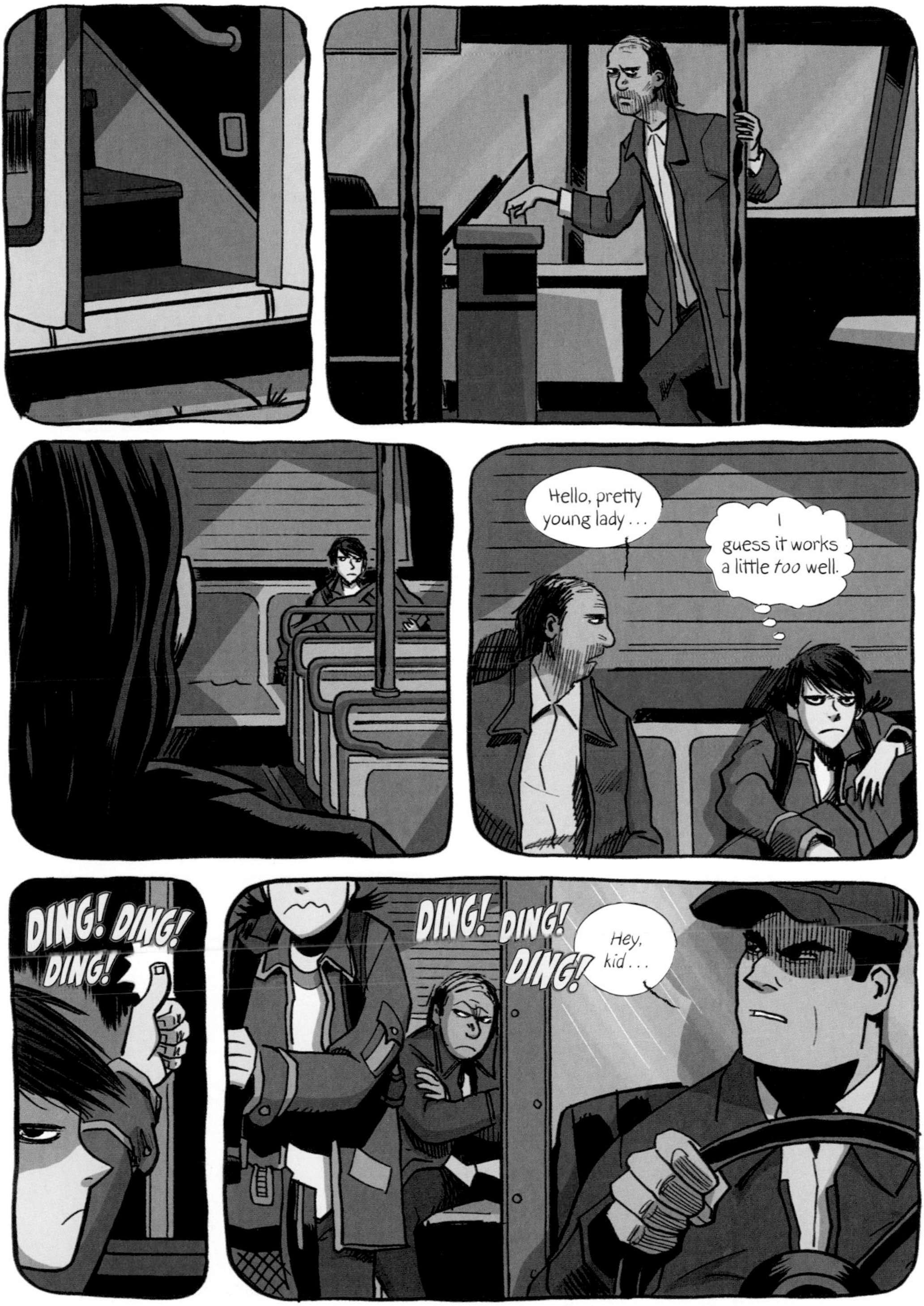
Hello, pretty young lady . . .
I guess it works a little *too* well.
DING! DING! DING!
DING! DING! DING!
Hey, kid . . .

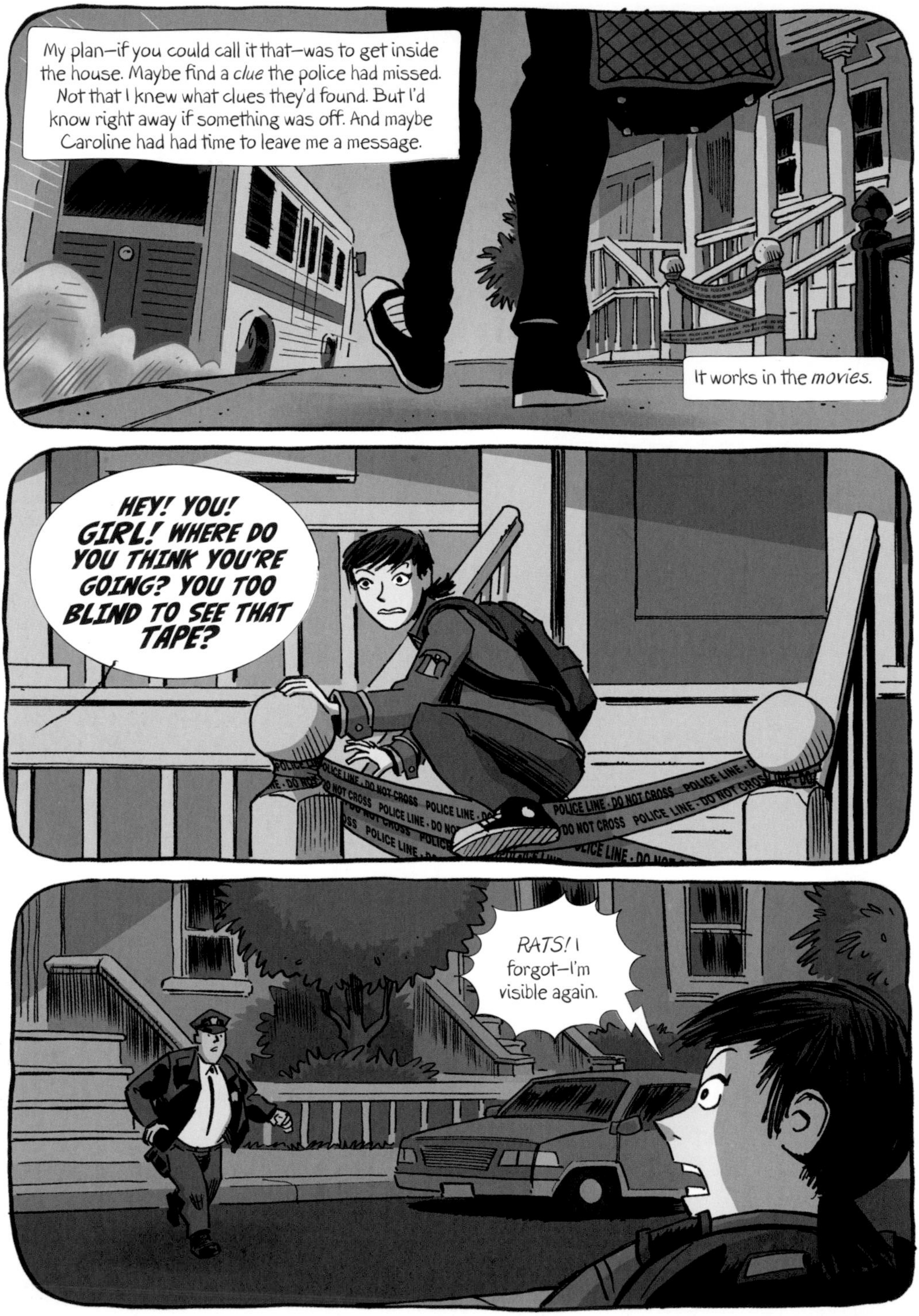
My plan—if you could call it that—was to get inside the house. Maybe find a *clue* the police had missed. Not that I knew what clues they'd found. But I'd know right away if something was off. And maybe Caroline had had time to leave me a message.
It works in the *movies*.
HEY! YOU! GIRL! WHERE DO YOU THINK YOU'RE GOING? YOU TOO BLIND TO SEE THAT TAPE?
POLICE LINE - DO NOT CROSS
RATS! I forgot—I'm visible again.

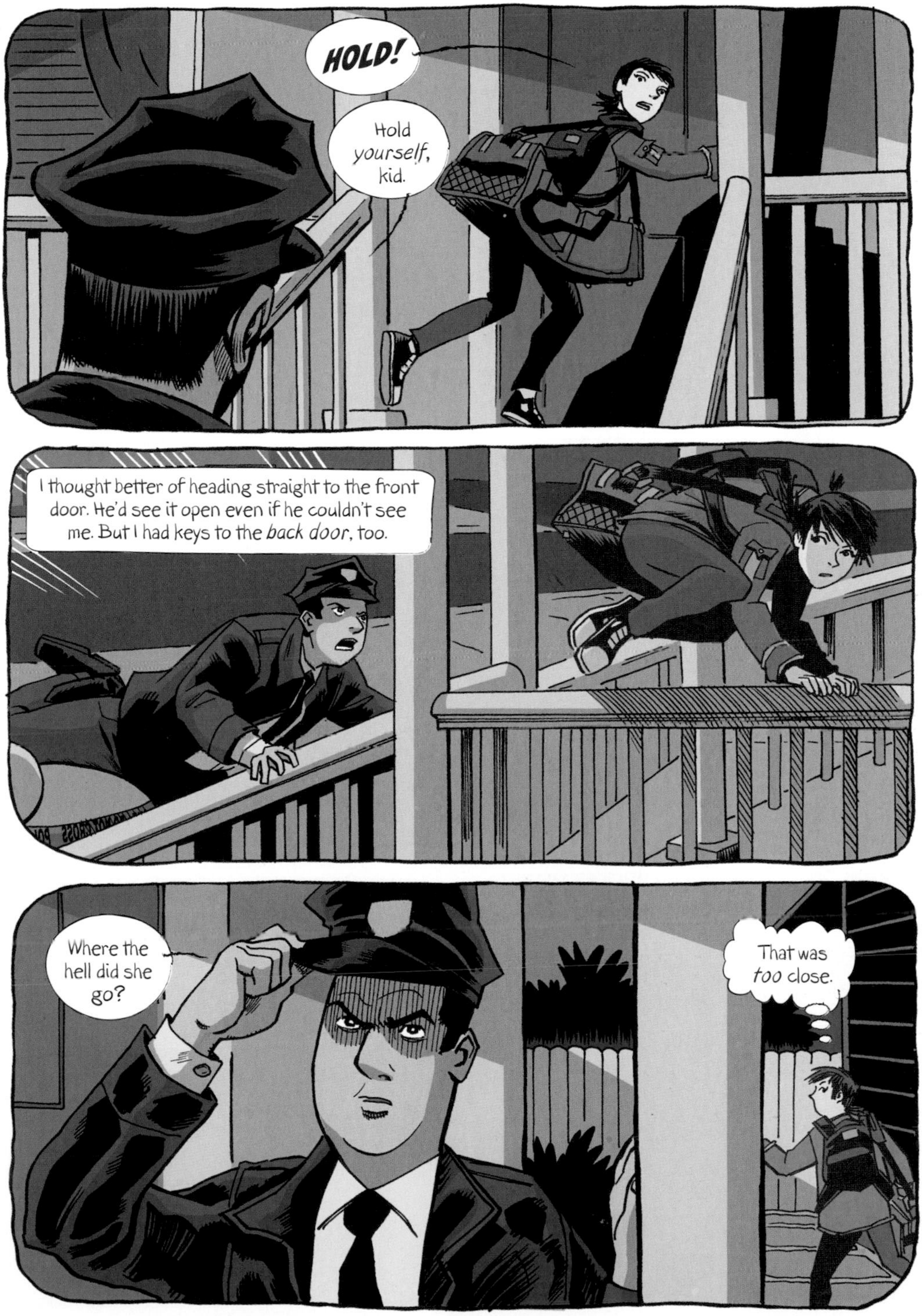
HOLD!
Hold *yourself*, kid.
I thought better of heading straight to the front door. He'd see it open even if he couldn't see me. But I had keys to the *back door*, too.
Where the hell did she go?
That was *too* close.

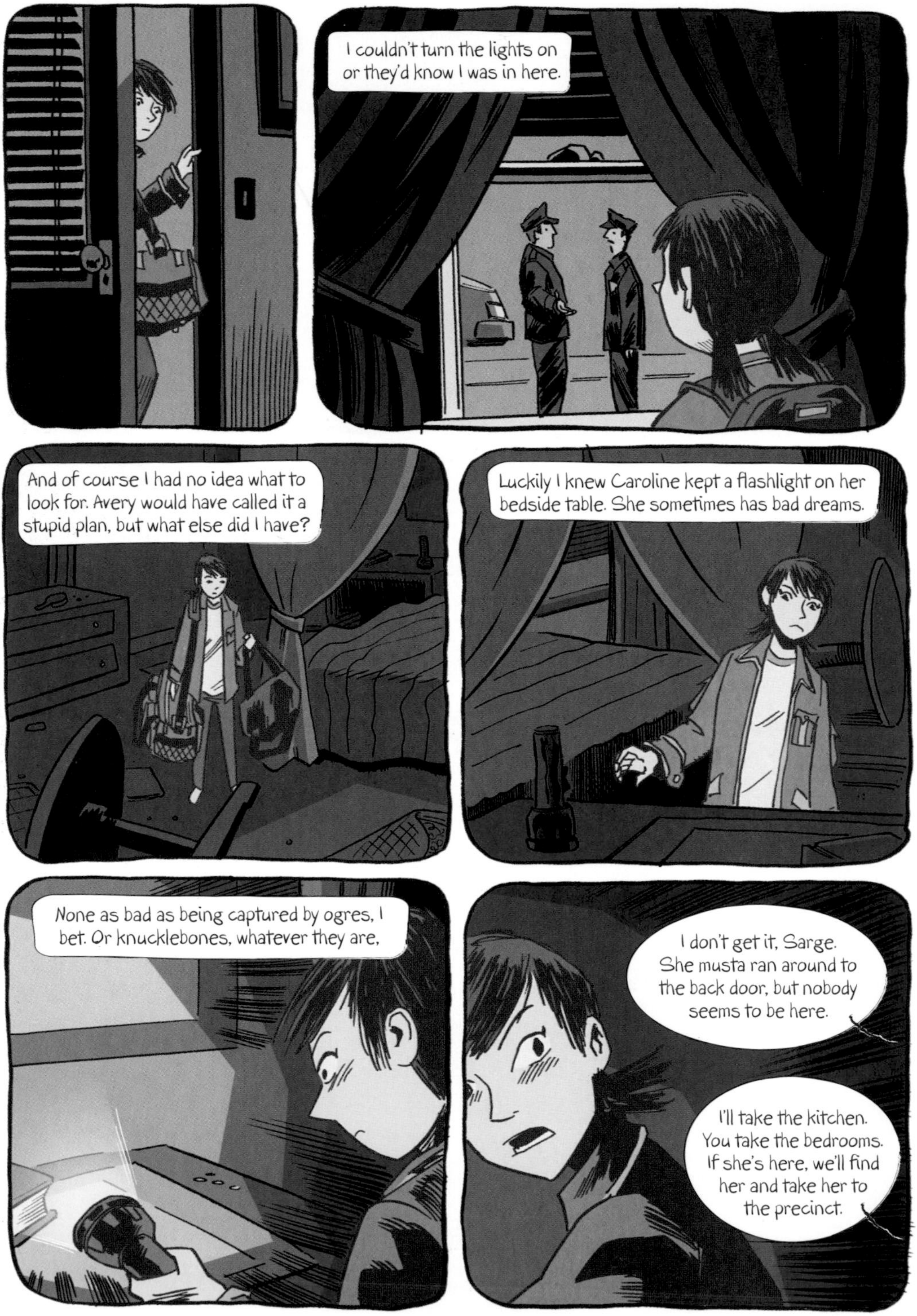
I couldn't turn the lights on or they'd know I was in here.
And of course I had no idea what to look for. Avery would have called it a stupid plan, but what else did I have?
Luckily I knew Caroline kept a flashlight on her bedside table. She sometimes has bad dreams.
None as bad as being captured by ogres, I bet. Or knucklebones, whatever they are.
I don't get it, Sarge. She musta ran around to the back door, but nobody seems to be here.
I'll take the kitchen. You take the bedrooms. If she's here, we'll find her and take her to the precinct.

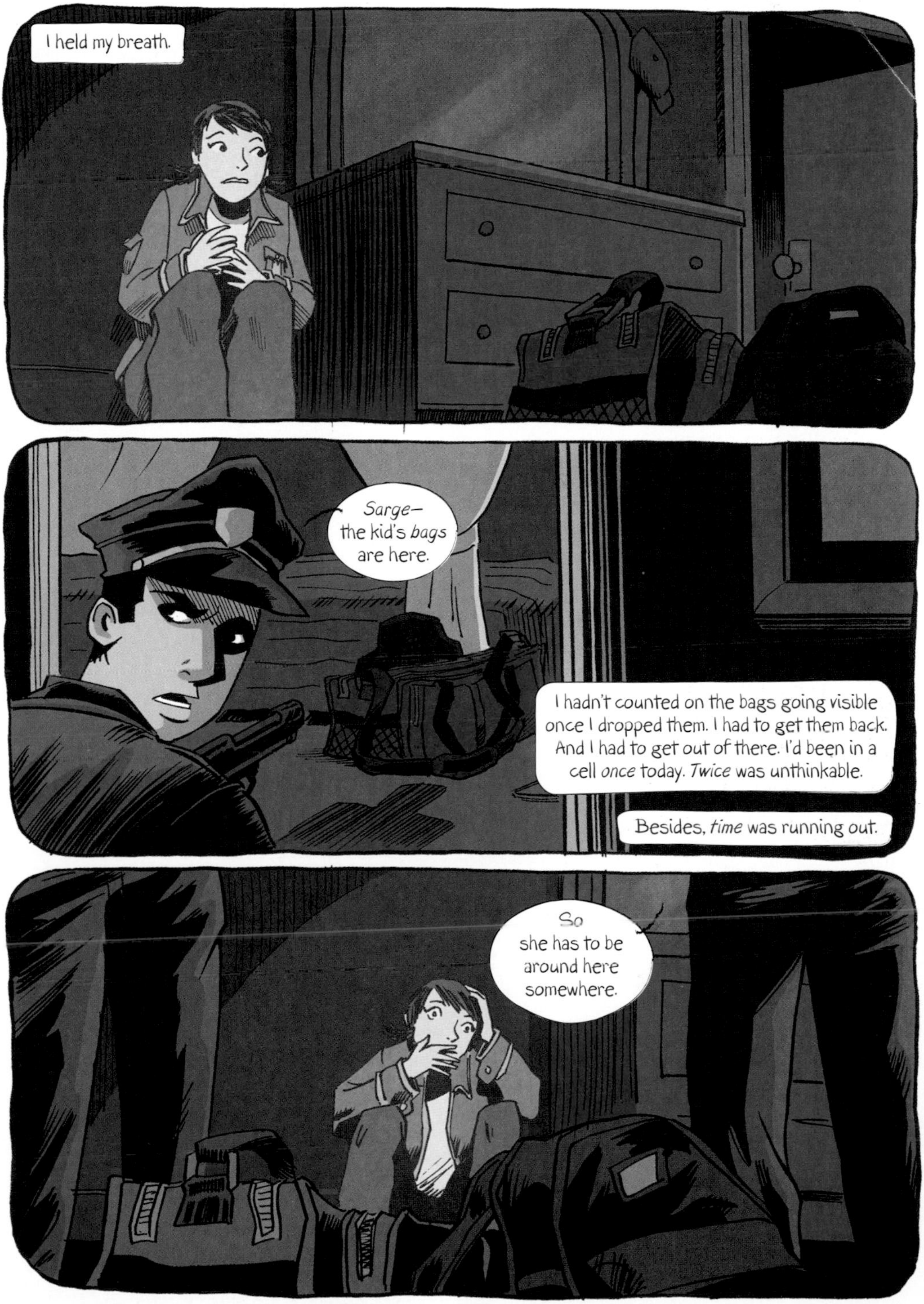
I held my breath.
Sarge— the kid's *bags* are here.
I hadn't counted on the bags going visible once I dropped them. I had to get them back. And I had to get out of there. I'd been in a cell *once* today. *Twice* was unthinkable.
Besides, *time* was running out.
So she has to be around here somewhere.

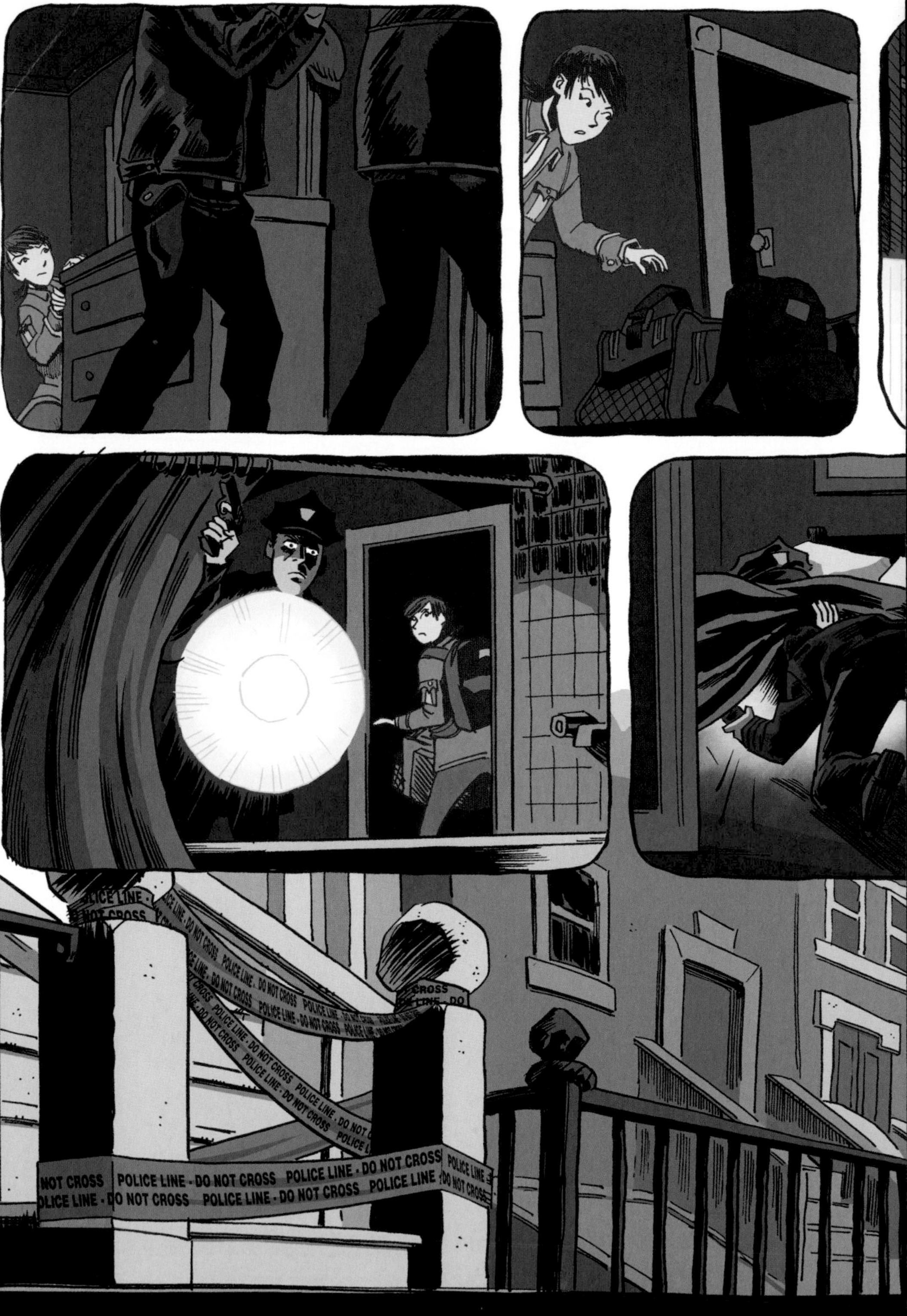
NOT CROSS POLICE LINE - DO NOT CROSS POLICE LINE - DO NOT CROSS
OLICE LINE - DO NOT CROSS POLICE LINE - DO NOT CROSS POLICE LINE
POLICE LINE
DO NOT CROSS
POLICE LINE - DO NOT CROSS

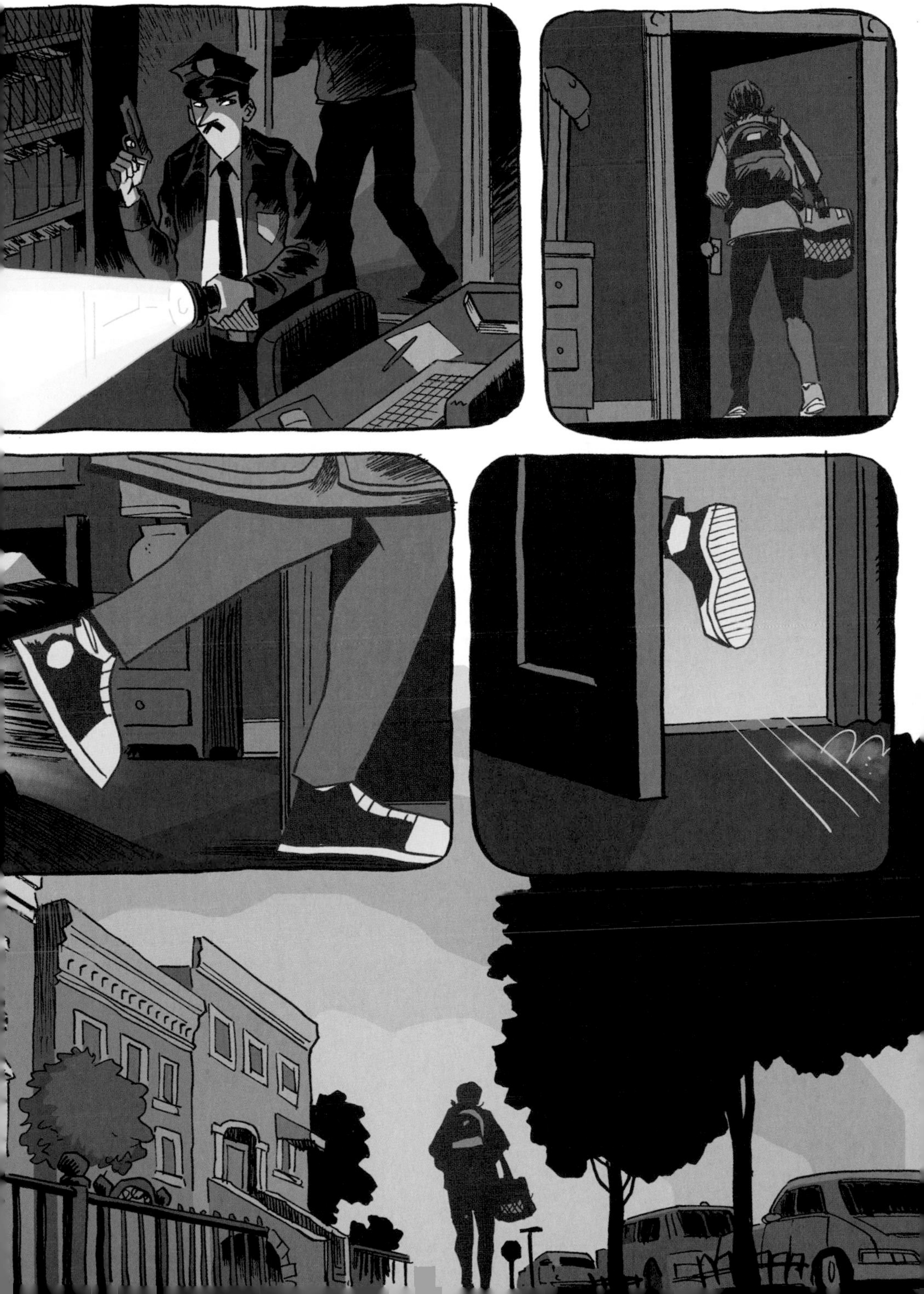

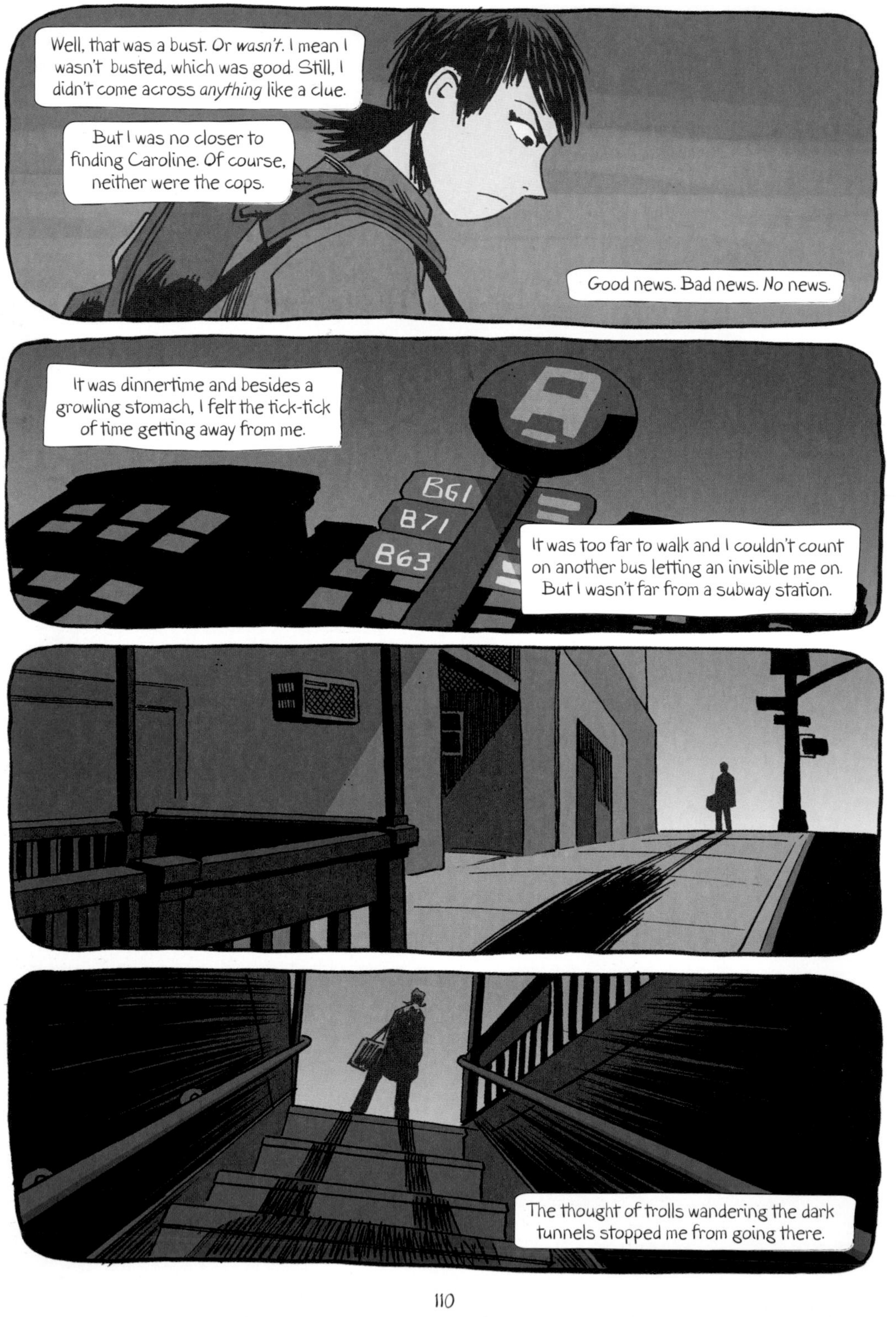
Well, that was a bust. Or *wasn't*. I mean I wasn't busted, which was good. Still, I didn't come across *anything* like a clue.
But I was no closer to finding Caroline. Of course, neither were the cops.
Good news. Bad news. No news.
It was dinnertime and besides a growling stomach, I felt the tick-tick of time getting away from me.
B61
B71
B63
It was too far to walk and I couldn't count on another bus letting an invisible me on. But I wasn't far from a subway station.
The thought of trolls wandering the dark tunnels stopped me from going there.

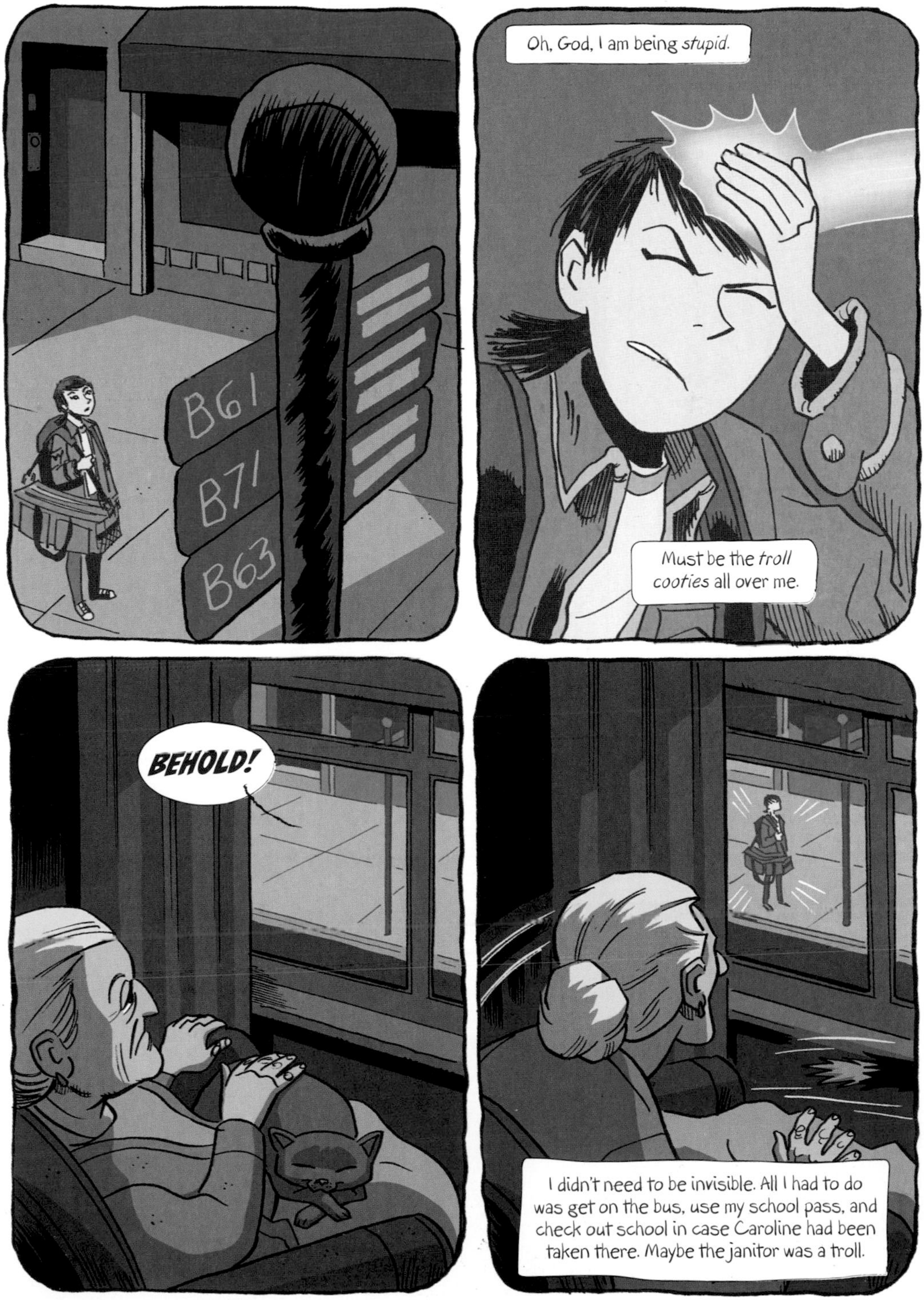
B61
B71
B63
Oh, God, I am being *stupid*.
Must be the *troll cooties* all over me.
BEHOLD!
I didn't need to be invisible. All I had to do was get on the bus, use my school pass, and check out school in case Caroline had been taken there. Maybe the janitor was a troll.

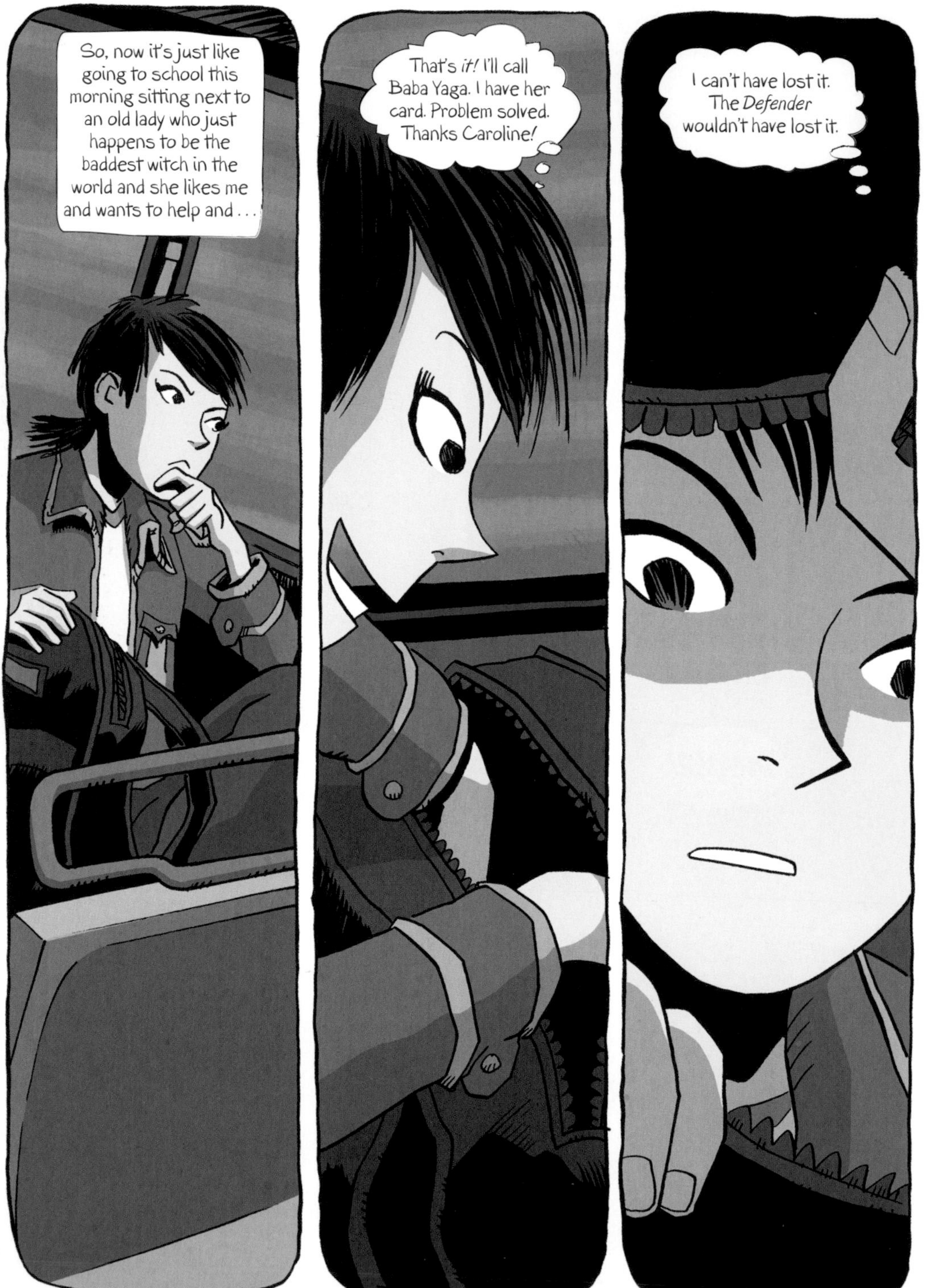
So, now it's just like going to school this morning sitting next to an old lady who just happens to be the baddest witch in the world and she likes me and wants to help and . . .
That's *it!* I'll call Baba Yaga. I have her card. Problem solved. Thanks Caroline!
I can't have lost it. The *Defender* wouldn't have lost it.

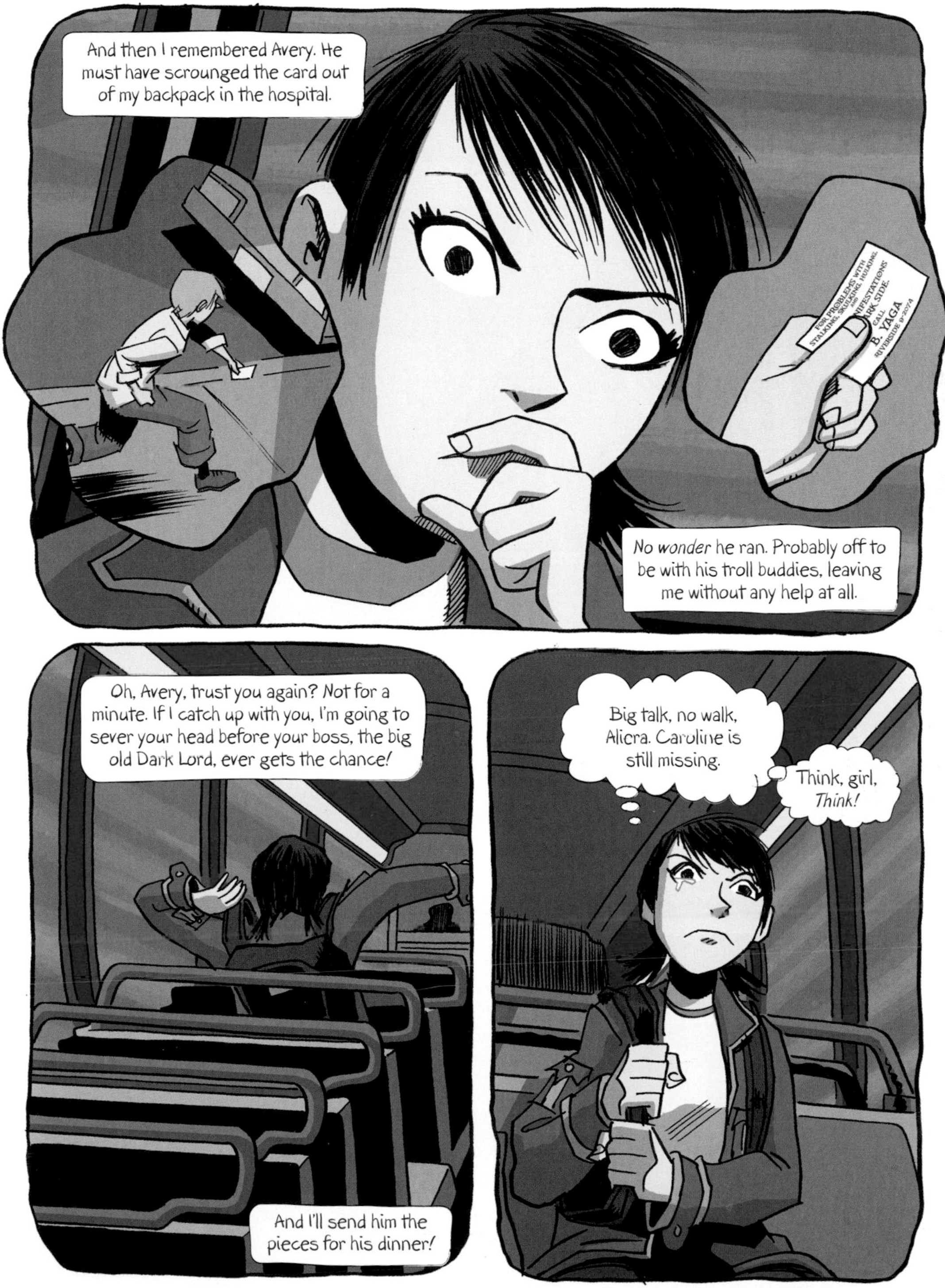
And then I remembered Avery. He must have scrounged the card out of my backpack in the hospital.
FOR PROBLEMS WITH
STALKING, SKULKING, HULKING
CALL
B. YAGA
RIVERSIDE 9-2074
No *wonder* he ran. Probably off to be with his troll buddies, leaving me without any help at all.
Oh, Avery, trust you again? Not for a minute. If I catch up with you, I'm going to sever your head before your boss, the big old Dark Lord, ever gets the chance!
And I'll send him the pieces for his dinner!
Big talk, no walk, Alicra. Caroline is still missing.
Think, girl, *Think!*

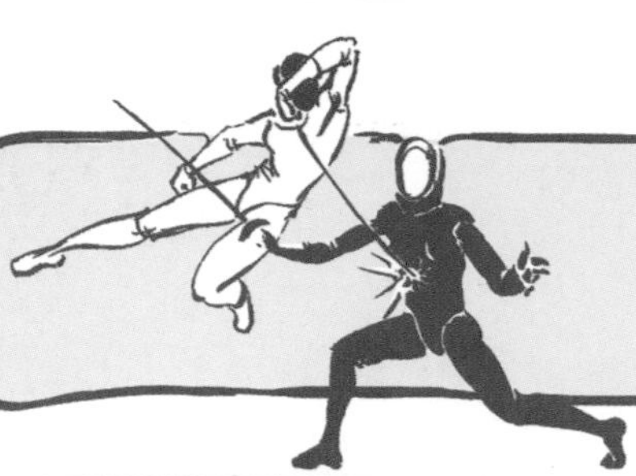

11. Remise

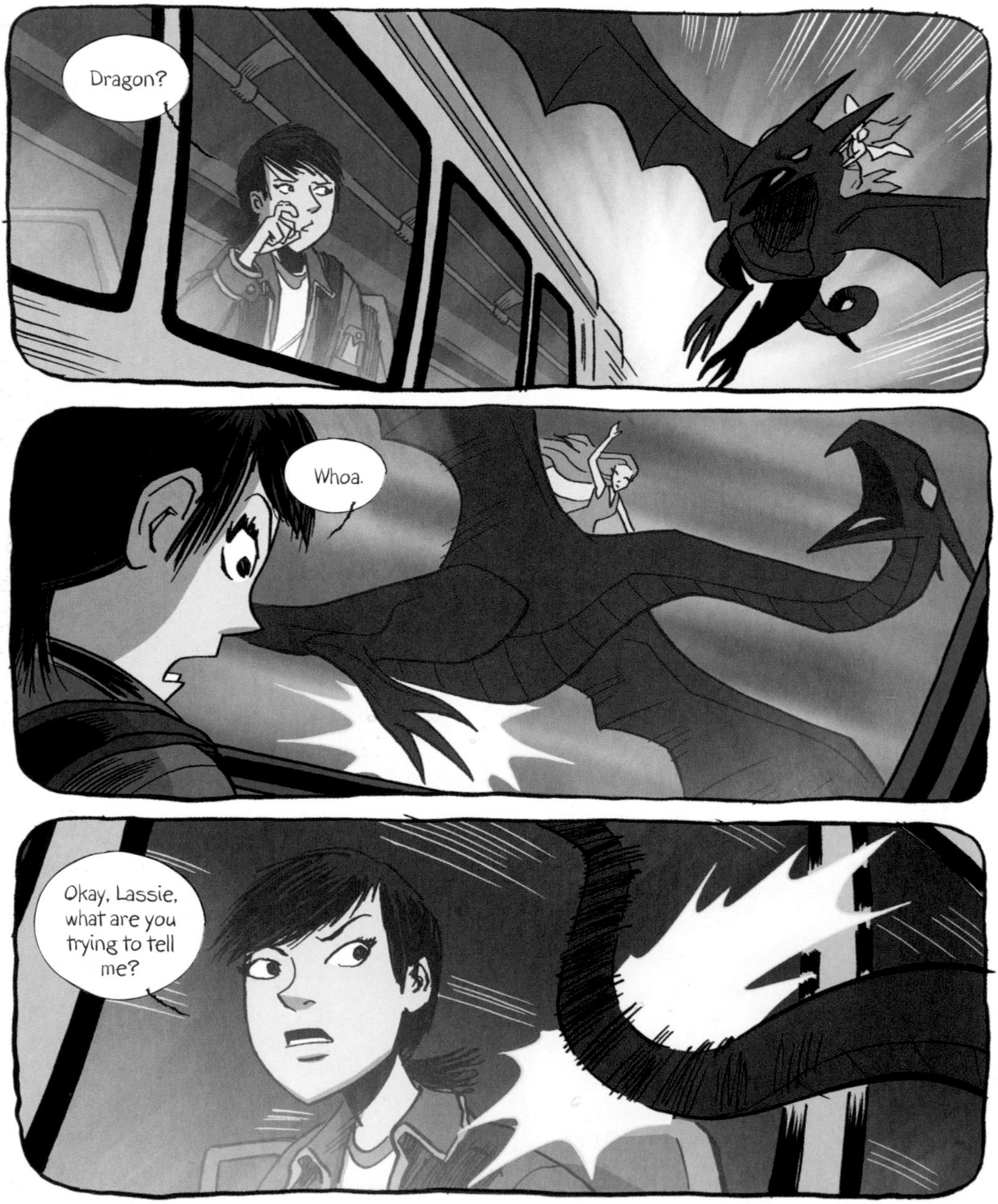
Dragon?
Whoa.
Okay, Lassie, what are you trying to tell me?

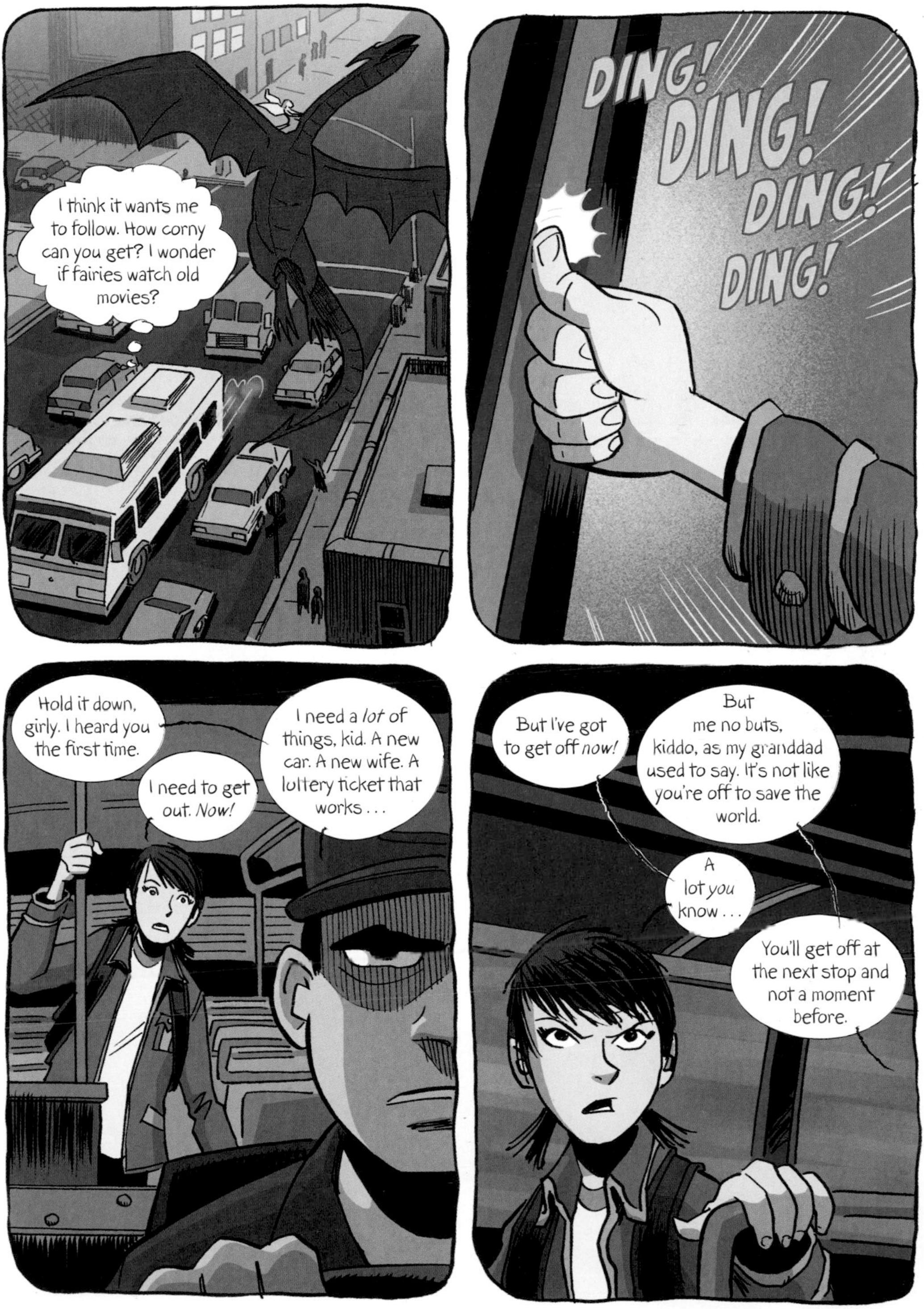
I think it wants me to follow. How corny can you get? I wonder if fairies watch old movies?
DING! DING! DING! DING!
Hold it down, girly. I heard you the first time.
I need to get out. *Now!*
I need a *lot* of things, kid. A new car. A new wife. A lottery ticket that works . . .
But I've got to get off *now!*
But me no buts, kiddo, as my granddad used to say. It's not like you're off to save the world.
A lot *you* know . . .
You'll get off at the next stop and not a moment before.

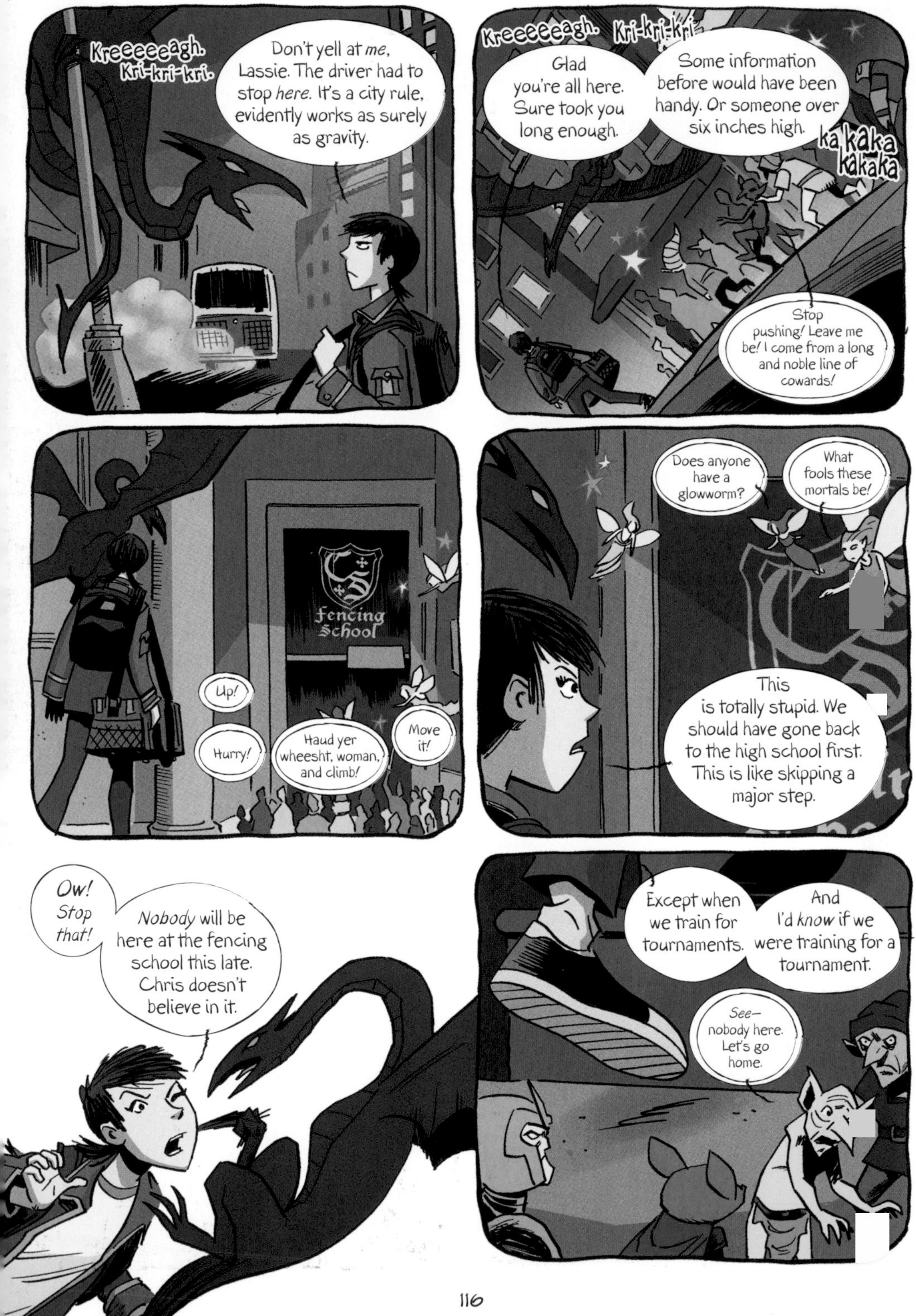

Kreeeeeagh.
Kri-kri-kri.
Don't yell at *me*, Lassie. The driver had to stop *here*. It's a city rule, evidently works as surely as gravity.
Kreeeeeagh.
Kri-kri-kri
Glad you're all here. Sure took you long enough.
Some information before would have been handy. Or someone over six inches high.
ka kaka kakaka
Stop pushing! Leave me be! I come from a long and noble line of cowards!
Fencing School
Up!
Hurry!
Haud yer wheesht, woman, and climb!
Move it!
Does anyone have a glowworm?
What fools these mortals be!
This is totally stupid. We should have gone back to the high school first. This is like skipping a major step.
Ow! Stop that!
Nobody will be here at the fencing school this late. Chris doesn't believe in it.
Except when we train for tournaments.
And I'd *know* if we were training for a tournament.
See— nobody here. Let's go home.

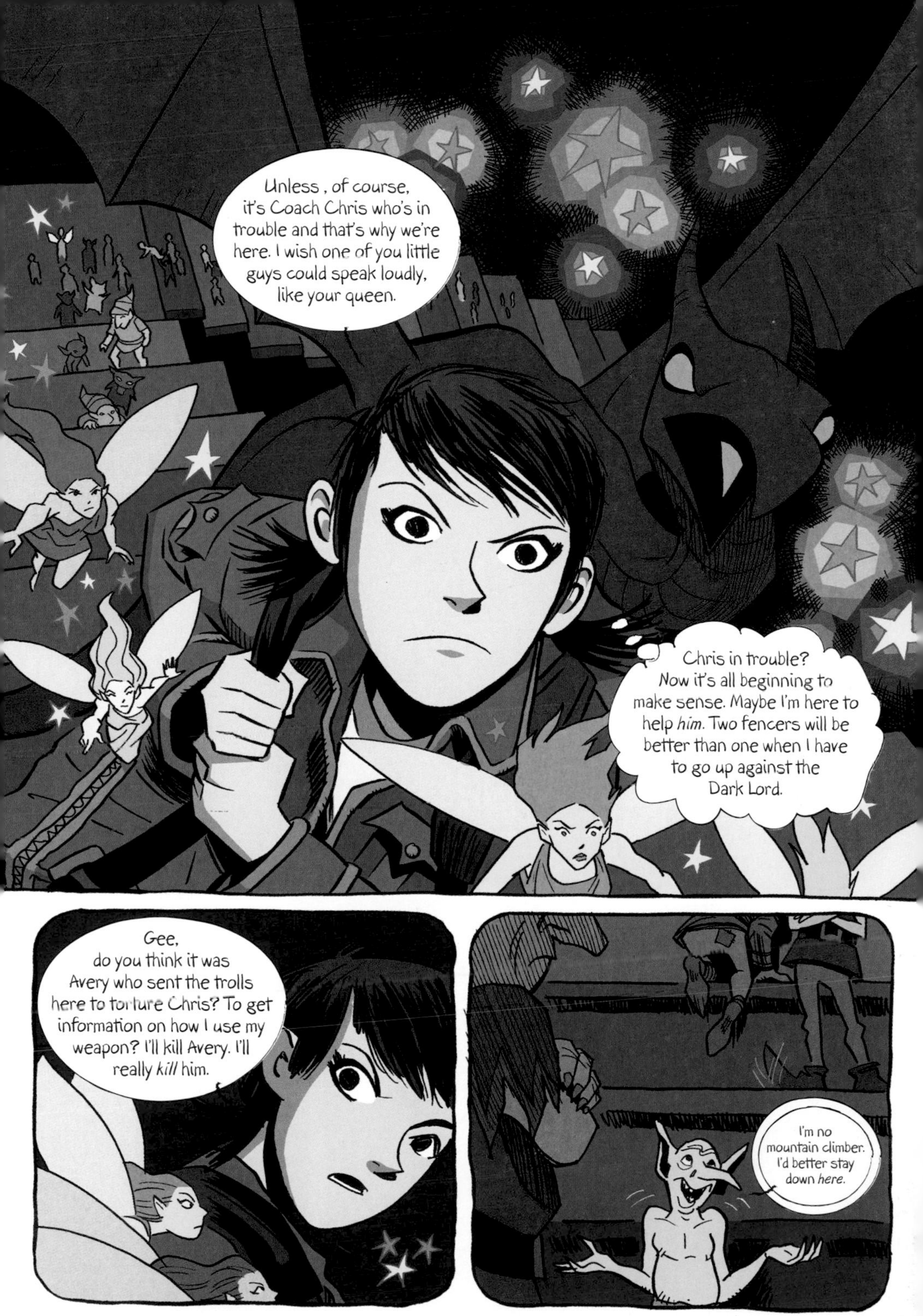
Unless , of course, it's Coach Chris who's in trouble and that's why we're here. I wish one of you little guys could speak loudly, like your queen.
Chris in trouble? Now it's all beginning to make sense. Maybe I'm here to help *him*. Two fencers will be better than one when I have to go up against the Dark Lord.
Gee, do you think it was Avery who sent the trolls here to torture Chris? To get information on how I use my weapon? I'll kill Avery. I'll really *kill* him.
I'm no mountain climber. I'd better stay down *here*.

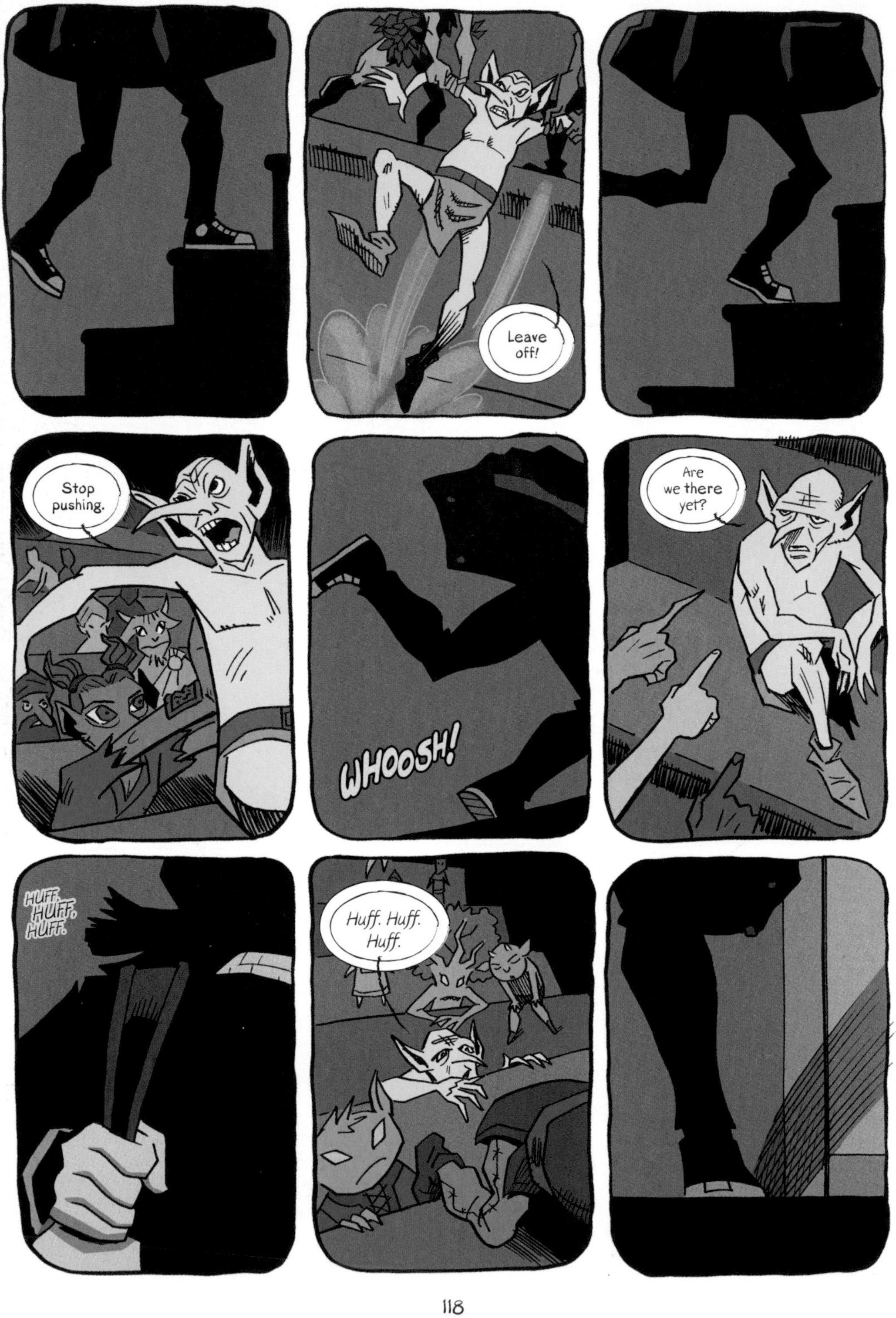
Leave off!
Stop pushing.
WHOOSH!
Are we there yet?
HUFF. HUFF. HUFF.
Huff. Huff. Huff.

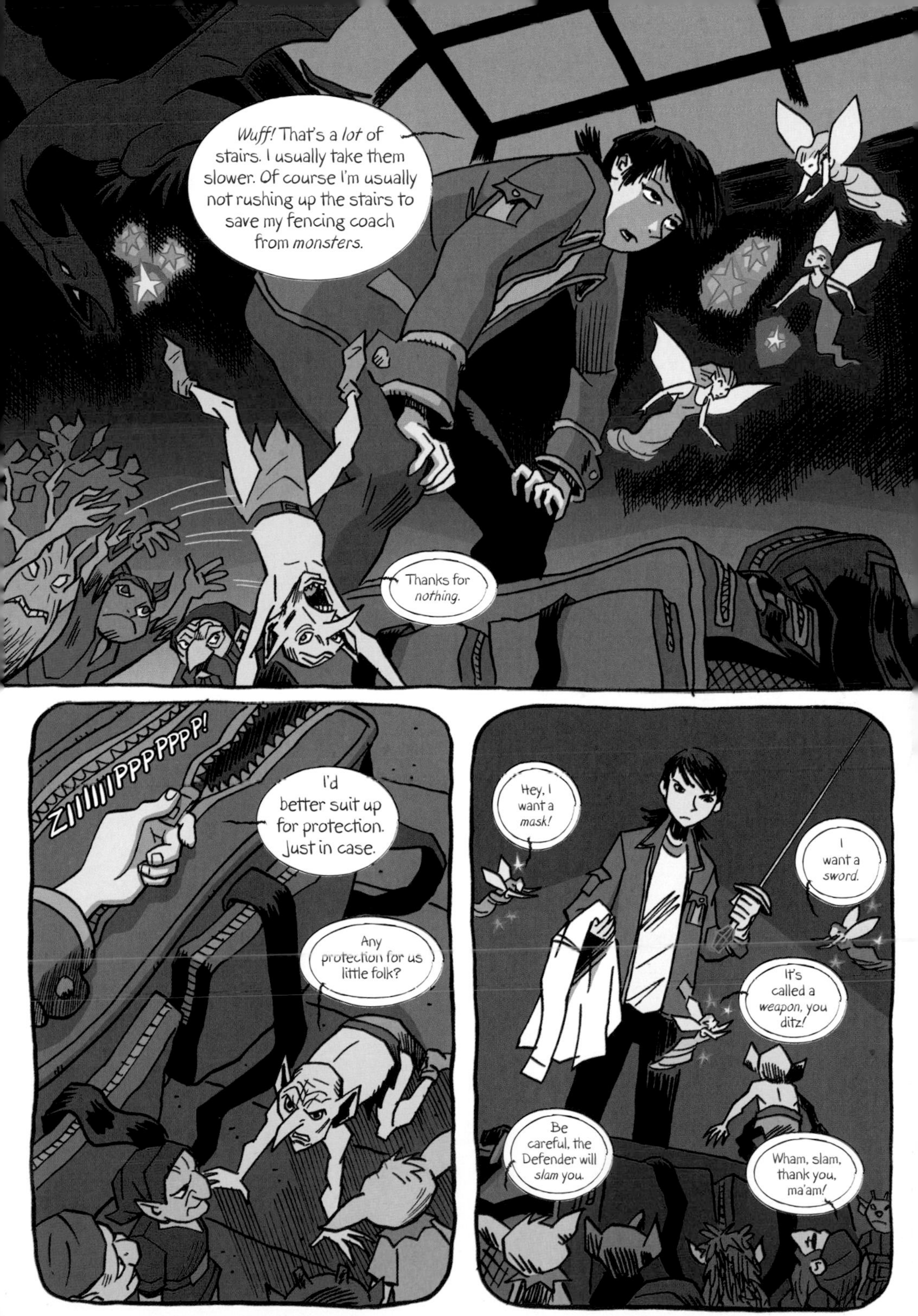

Wuff! That's a lot of stairs. I usually take them slower. Of course I'm usually not rushing up the stairs to save my fencing coach from monsters.
Thanks for nothing.
ZIIIIIIPPPPPPP!
I'd better suit up for protection. Just in case.
Any protection for us little folk?
Hey, I want a mask!
I want a sword.
It's called a weapon, you ditz!
Be careful, the Defender will slam you.
Wham, slam, thank you, ma'am!

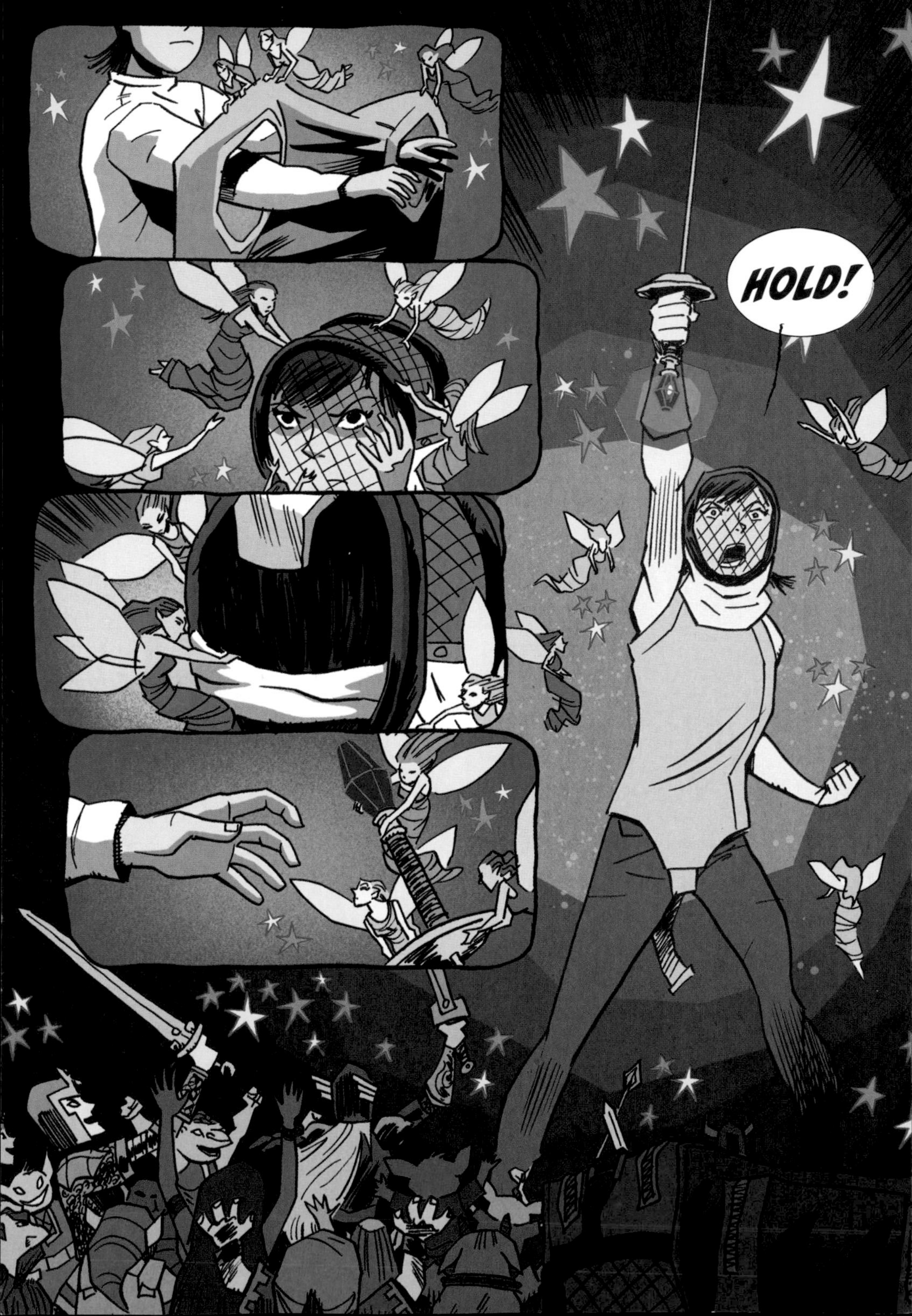
HOLD!

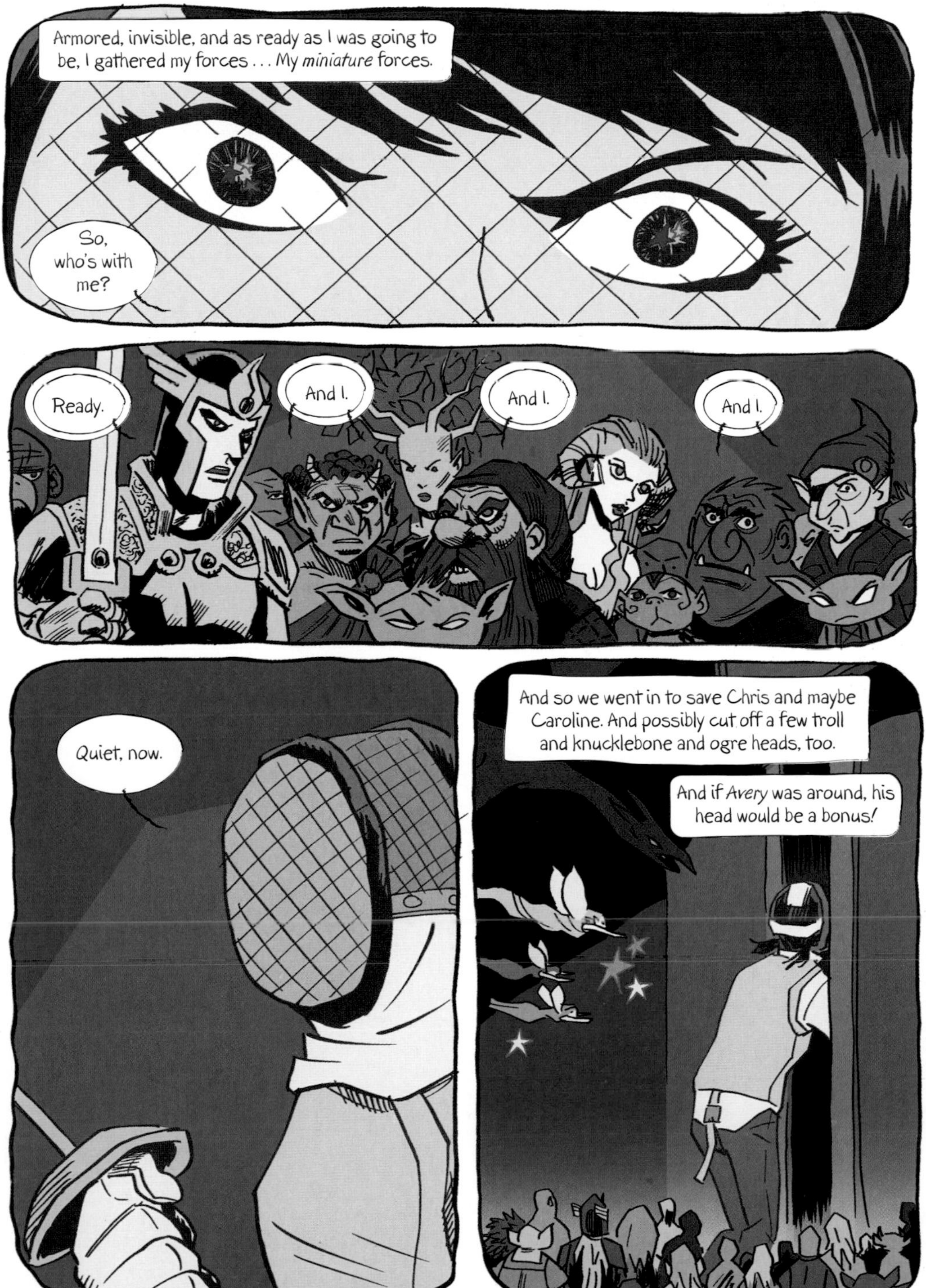
Armored, invisible, and as ready as I was going to be, I gathered my forces . . . My *miniature* forces.
So, who's with me?
Ready.
And I.
And I.
And I.
Quiet, now.
And so we went in to save Chris and maybe Caroline. And possibly cut off a few troll and knucklebone and ogre heads, too.
And if *Avery* was around, his head would be a bonus!

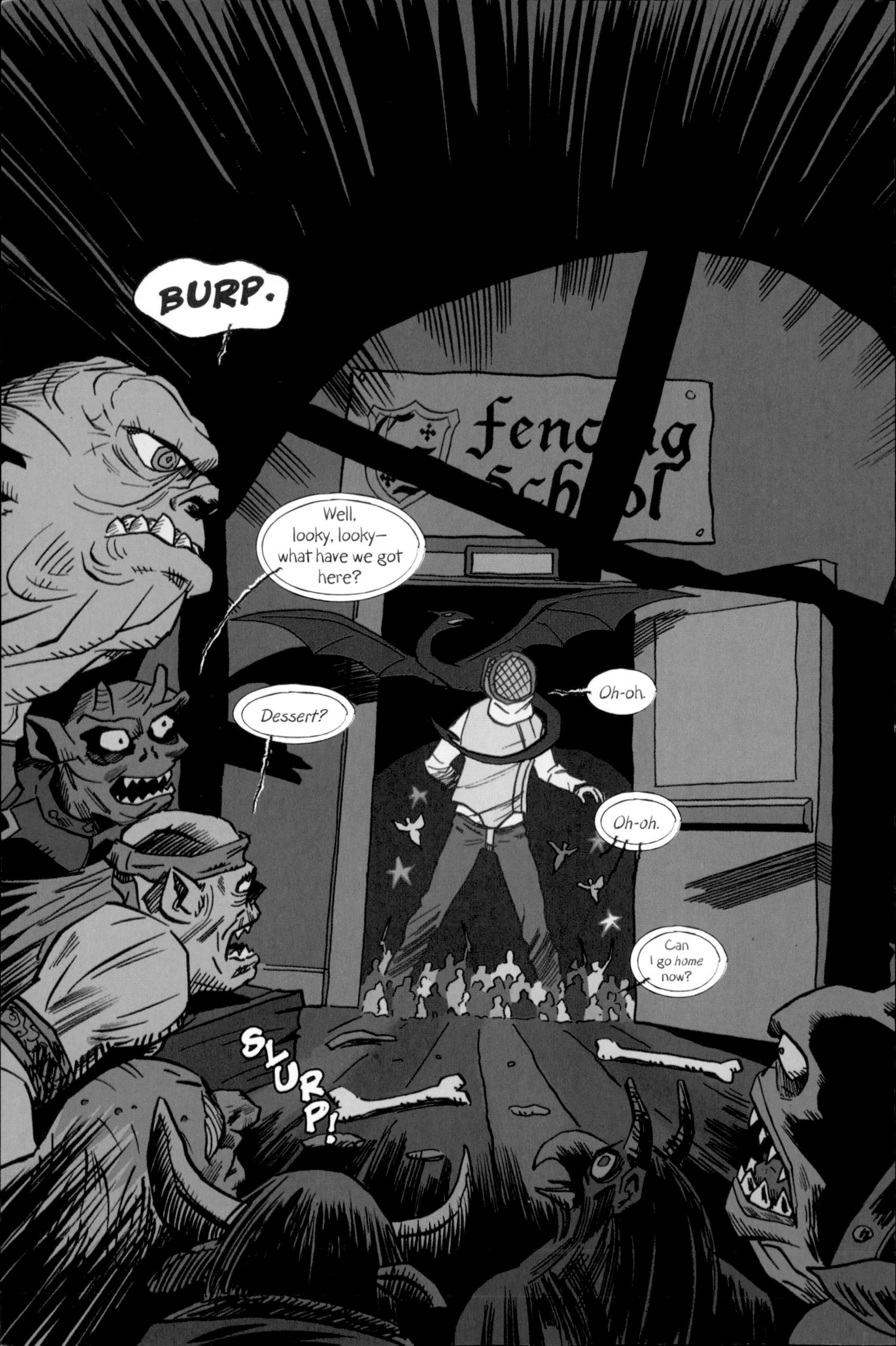
BURP.
Well, looky, looky— what have we got here?
Fencing School
Dessert?
Oh-oh.
Oh-oh.
Can I go *home* now?
SLURP!

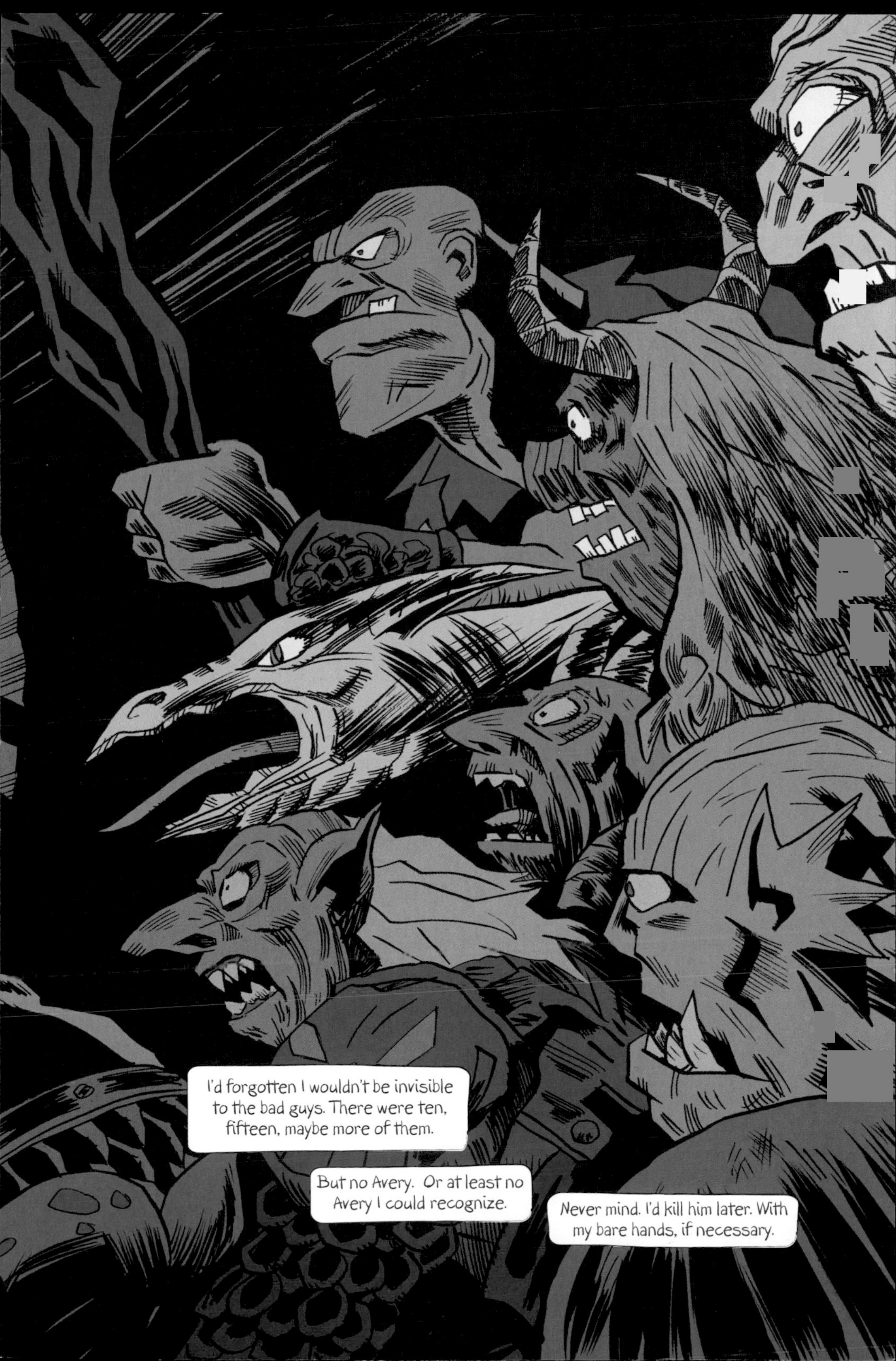
I'd forgotten I wouldn't be invisible to the bad guys. There were ten, fifteen, maybe more of them.
But no Avery. Or at least no Avery I could recognize.
Never mind. I'd kill him later. With my bare hands, if necessary.

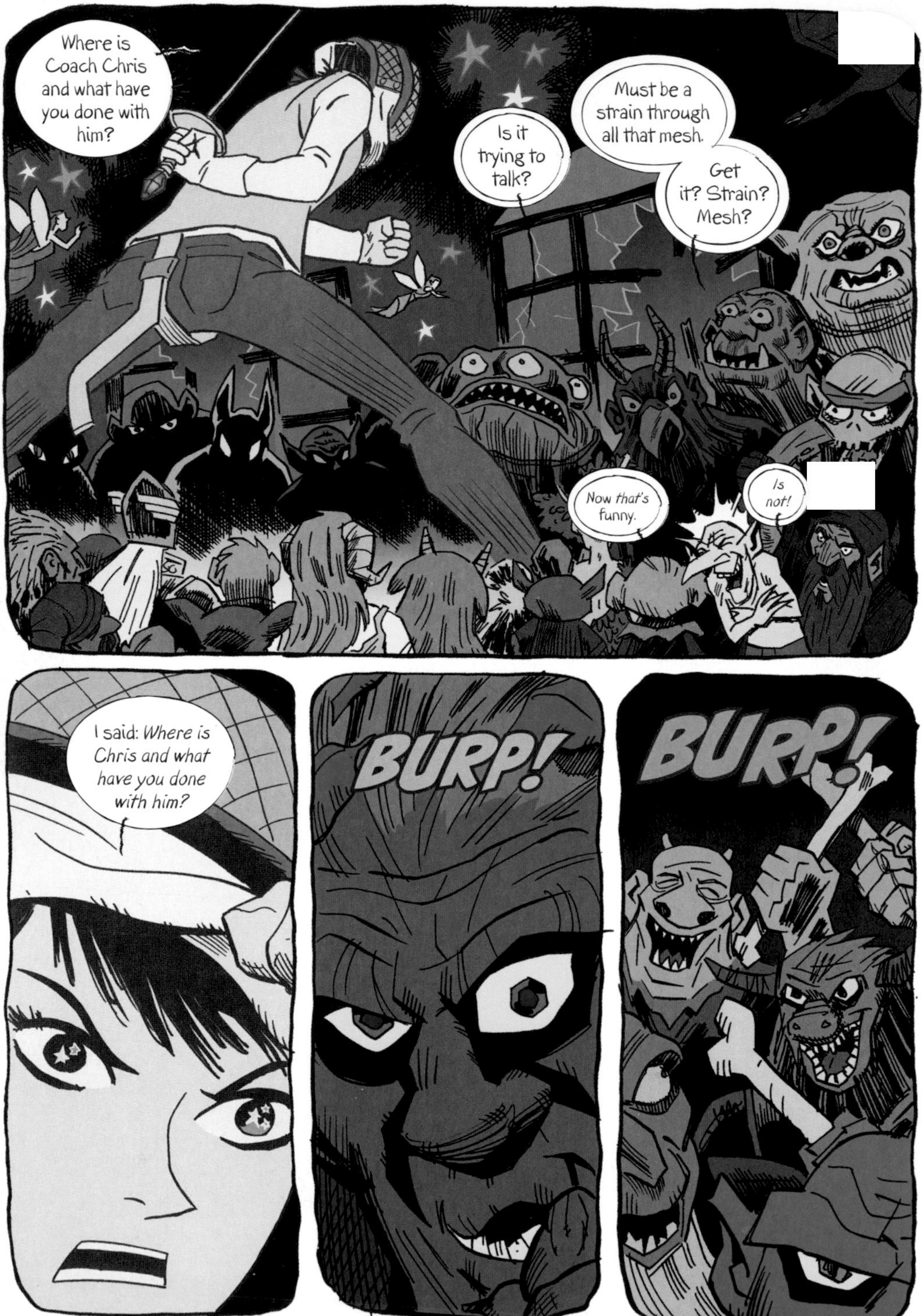
Where is Coach Chris and what have you done with him?
Is it trying to talk?
Must be a strain through all that mesh.
Get it? Strain? Mesh?
Now *that's* funny.
Is not!
I said: *Where is Chris and what have you done with him?*
BURP!
BURP!

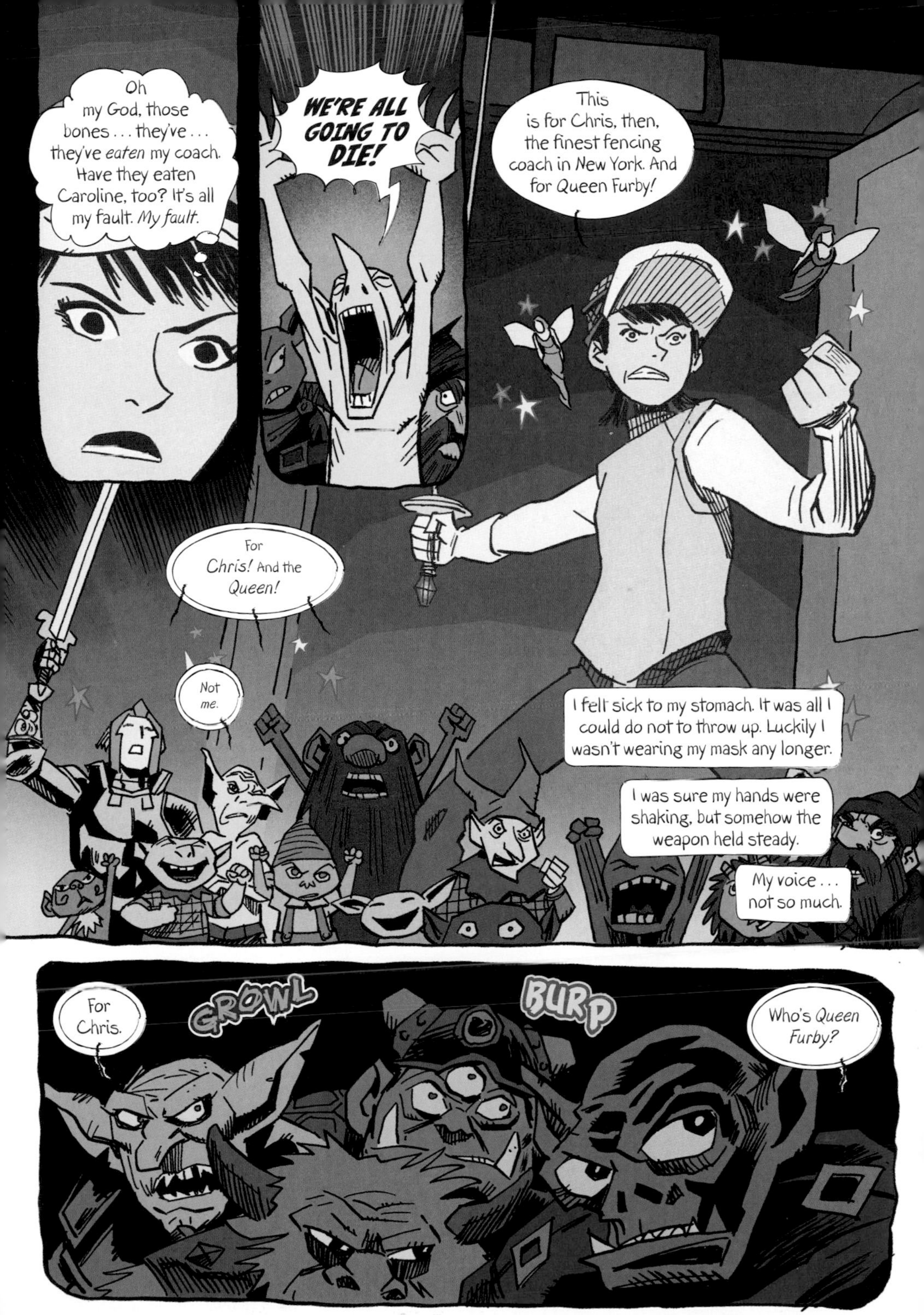
Oh my God, those bones . . . they've . . . they've *eaten* my coach. Have they eaten Caroline, too? It's all my fault. *My fault.*
WE'RE ALL GOING TO DIE!
This is for Chris, then, the finest fencing coach in New York. And for Queen Furby!
For *Chris!* And the *Queen!*
Not *me.*
I felt sick to my stomach. It was all I could do not to throw up. Luckily I wasn't wearing my mask any longer.
I was sure my hands were shaking, but somehow the weapon held steady.
My voice . . . not so much.
For Chris.
GROWL
BURP
Who's *Queen Furby?*

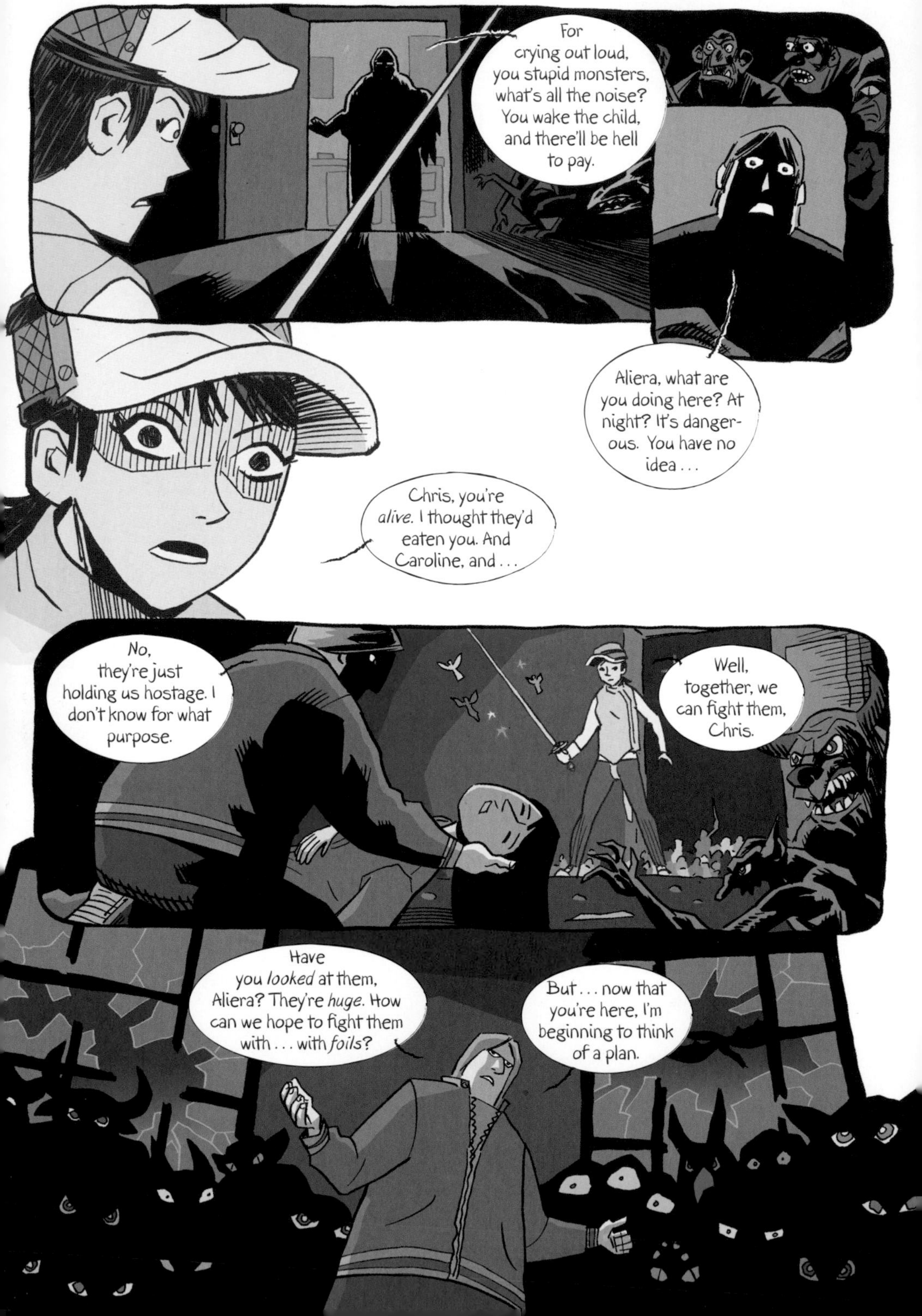

For crying out loud, you stupid monsters, what's all the noise? You wake the child, and there'll be hell to pay.
Aliera, what are you doing here? At night? It's danger-ous. You have no idea . . .
Chris, you're *alive*. I thought they'd eaten you. And Caroline, and . . .
No, they're just holding us hostage. I don't know for what purpose.
Well, together, we can fight them, Chris.
Have you *looked* at them, Aliera? They're *huge*. How can we hope to fight them with . . . with *foils*?
But . . . now that you're here, I'm beginning to think of a plan.

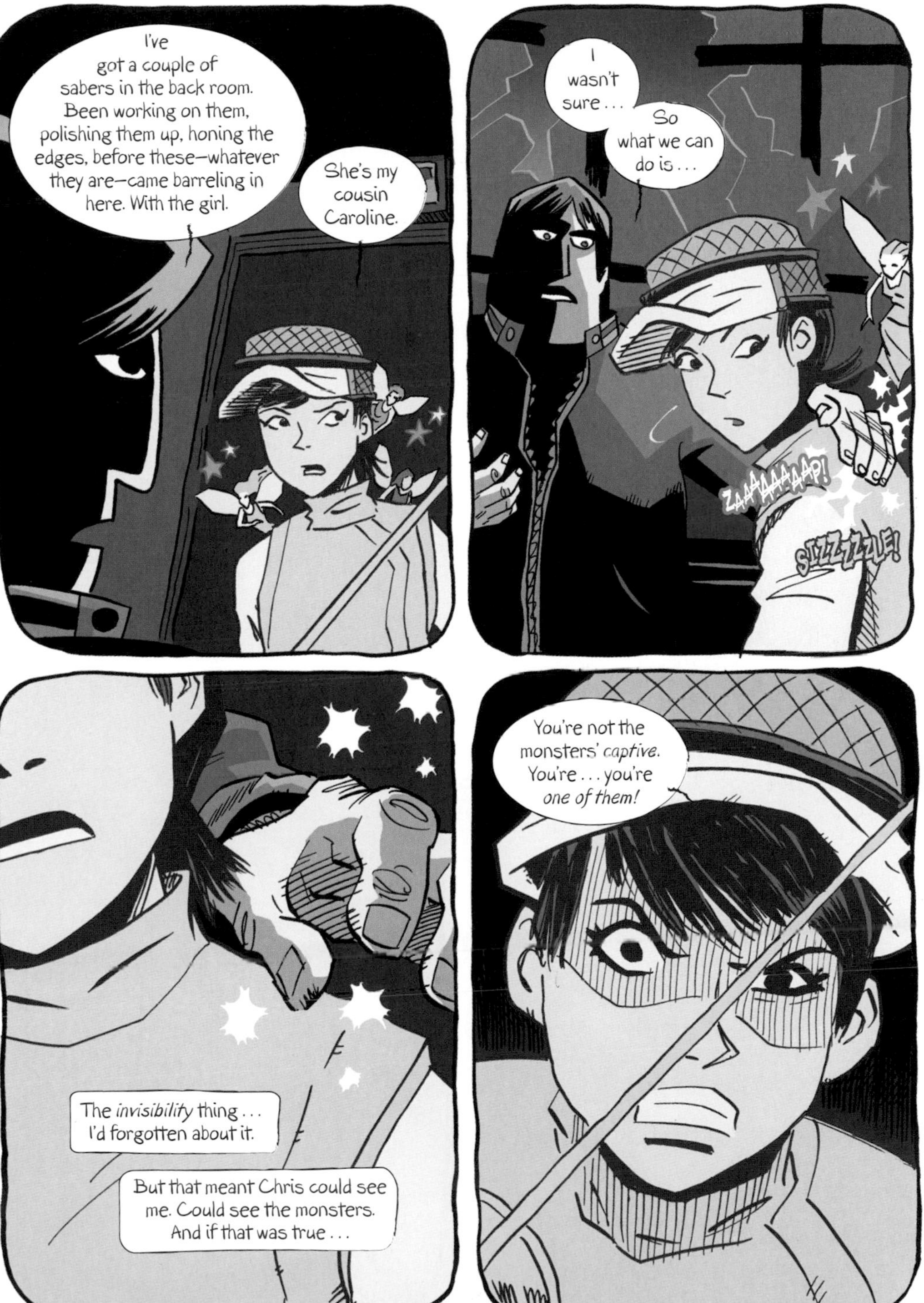
I've got a couple of sabers in the back room. Been working on them, polishing them up, honing the edges, before these—whatever they are—came barreling in here. With the girl.
She's my cousin Caroline.
I wasn't sure . . .
So what we can do is . . .
ZAAAAAAAAP!
SIZZZZZLE!
The *invisibility* thing . . . I'd forgotten about it.
But that meant Chris could see me. Could see the monsters. And if that was true . . .
You're not the monsters' *captive*. You're . . . you're *one of them!*

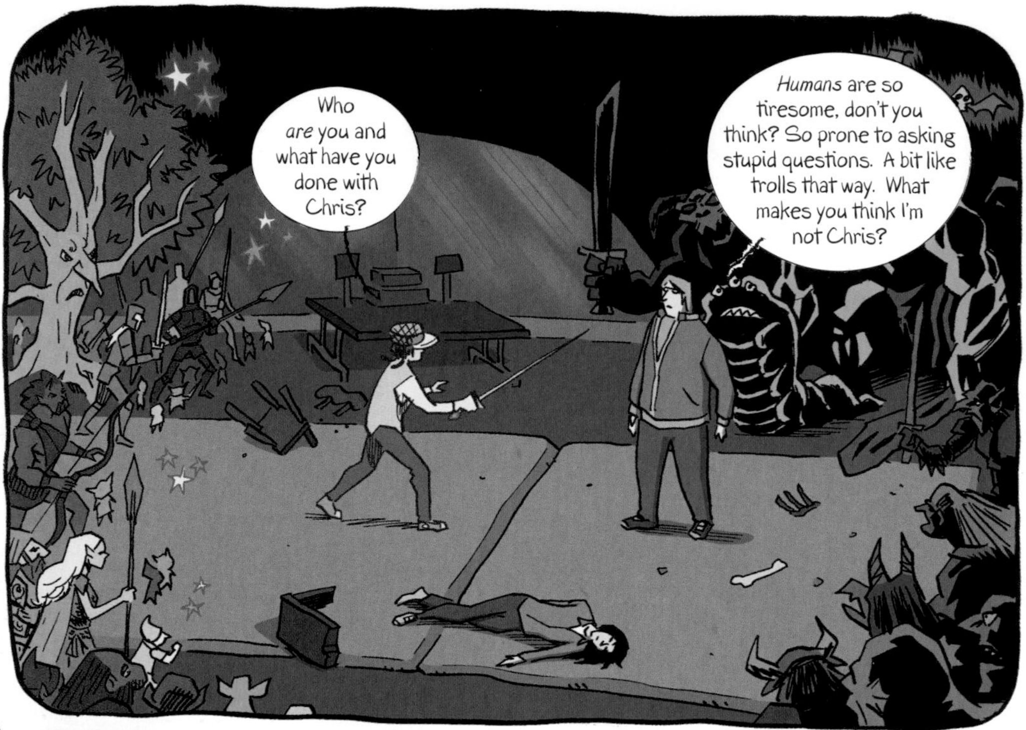
Who *are* you and what have you done with Chris?
Humans are so tiresome, don't you think? So prone to asking stupid questions. A bit like trolls that way. What makes you think I'm not Chris?

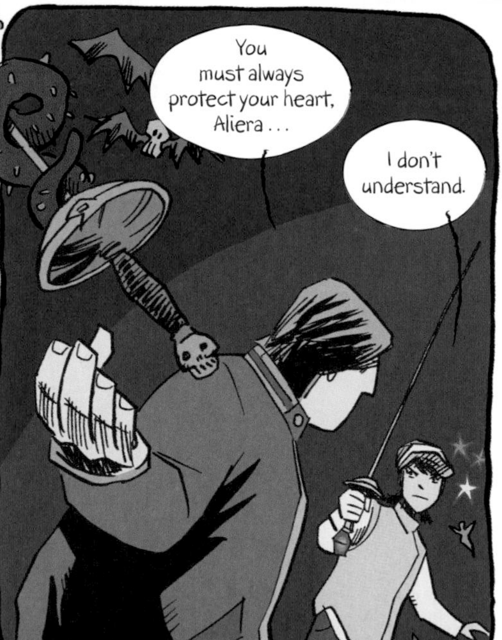
You must always protect your heart, Aliera . . .
I don't understand.

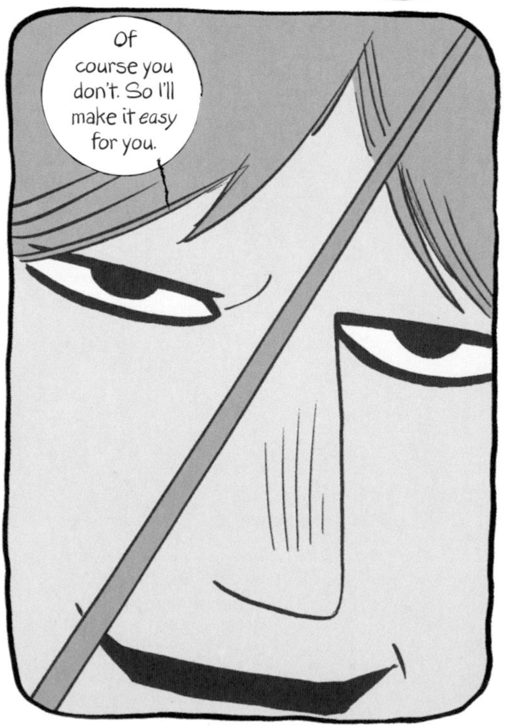
Of course you don't. So I'll make it *easy* for you.

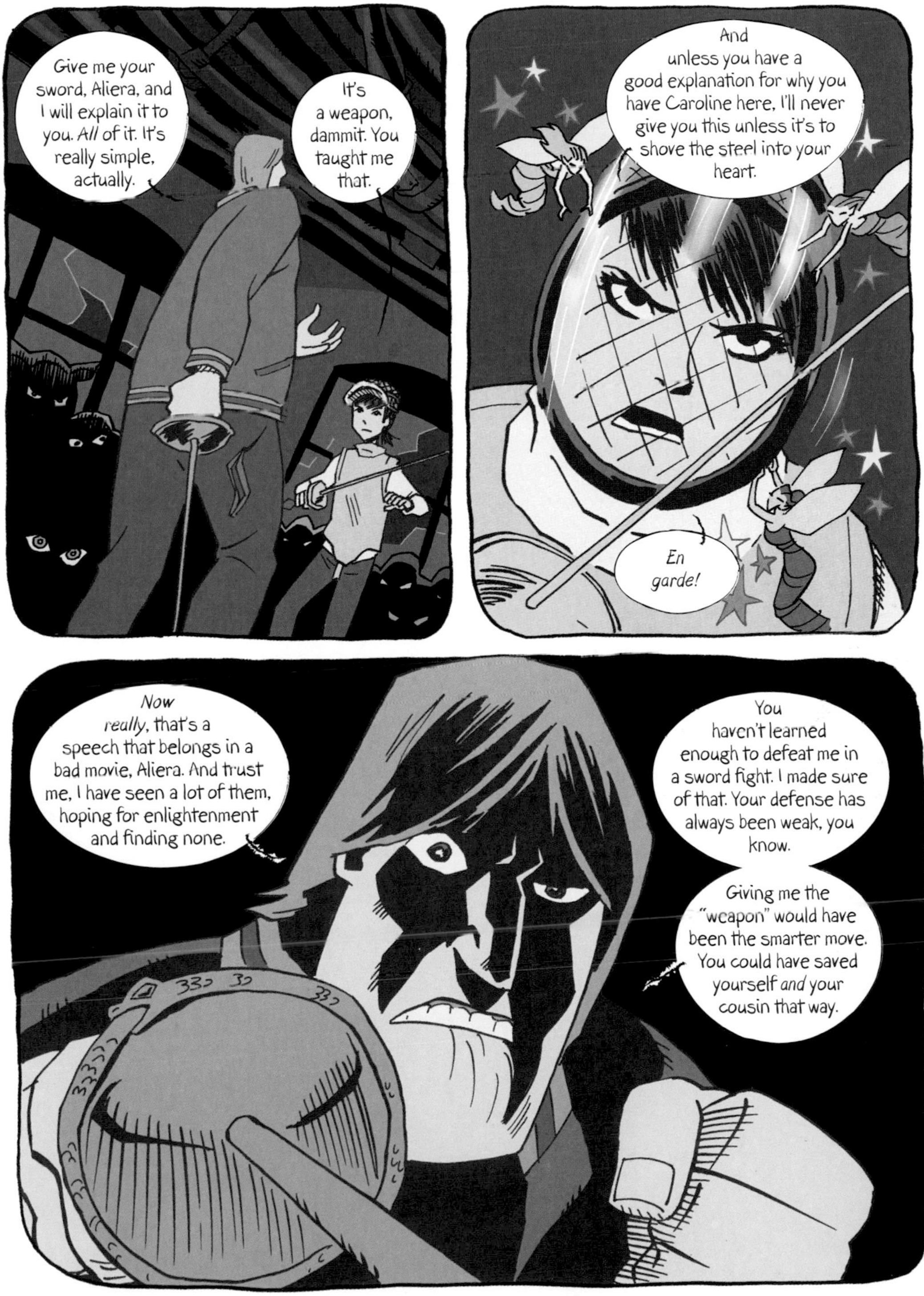
Give me your sword, Aliera, and I will explain it to you. *All* of it. It's really simple, actually.
It's a weapon, dammit. You taught me that.
And unless you have a good explanation for why you have Caroline here, I'll never give you this unless it's to shove the steel into your heart.
En garde!
Now *really*, that's a speech that belongs in a bad movie, Aliera. And trust me, I have seen a lot of them, hoping for enlightenment and finding none.
You haven't learned enough to defeat me in a sword fight. I made sure of that. Your defense has always been weak, you know.
Giving me the "weapon" would have been the smarter move. You could have saved yourself *and* your cousin that way.

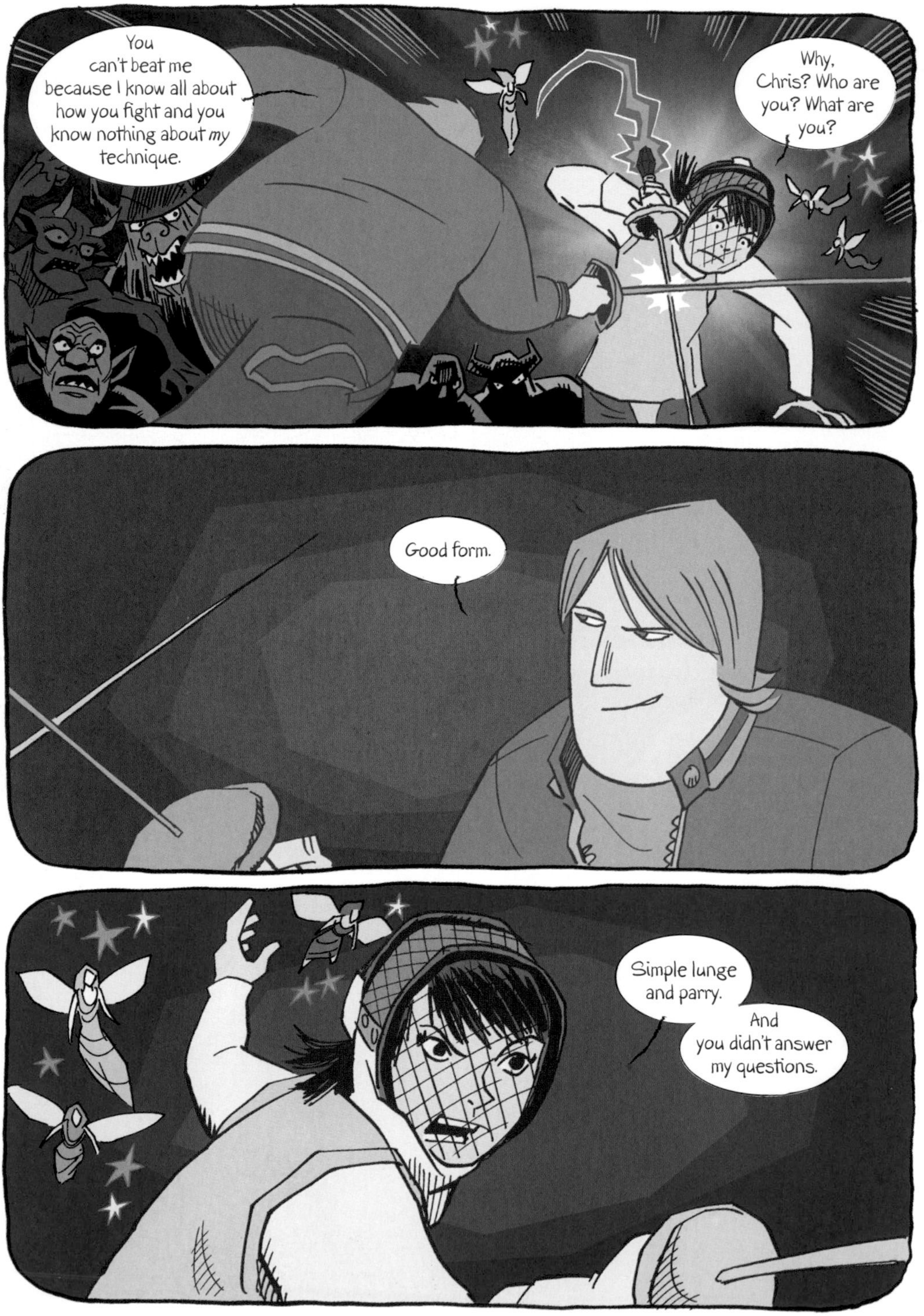
You can't beat me because I know all about how you fight and you know nothing about *my* technique.
Why, Chris? Who are you? What are you?
Good form.
Simple lunge and parry.
And you didn't answer my questions.

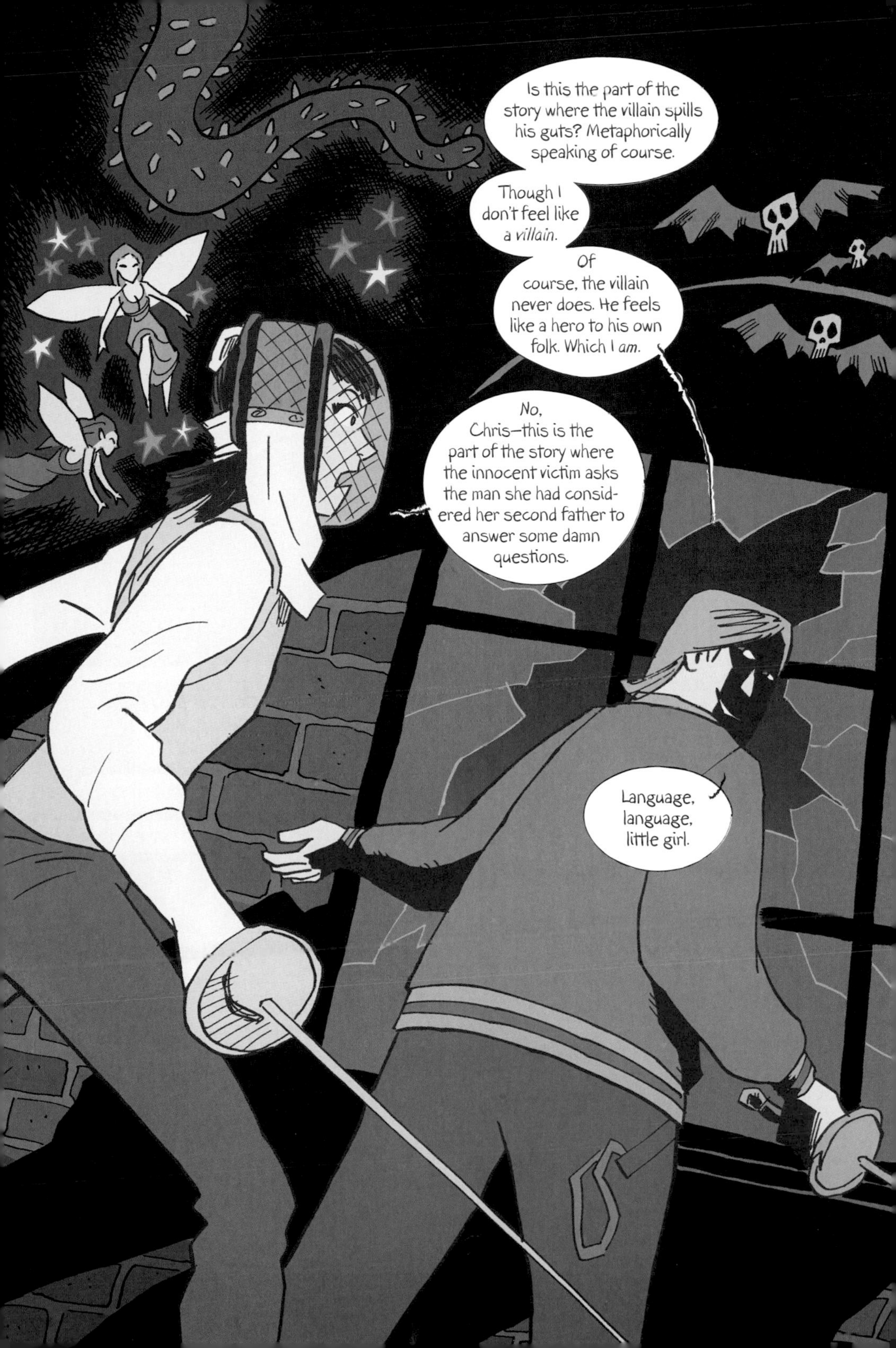
Is this the part of the story where the villain spills his guts? Metaphorically speaking of course.
Though I don't feel like a *villain*.
Of course, the villain never does. He feels like a hero to his own folk. Which I *am*.
No, Chris—this is the part of the story where the innocent victim asks the man she had considered her second father to answer some damn questions.
Language, language, little girl.

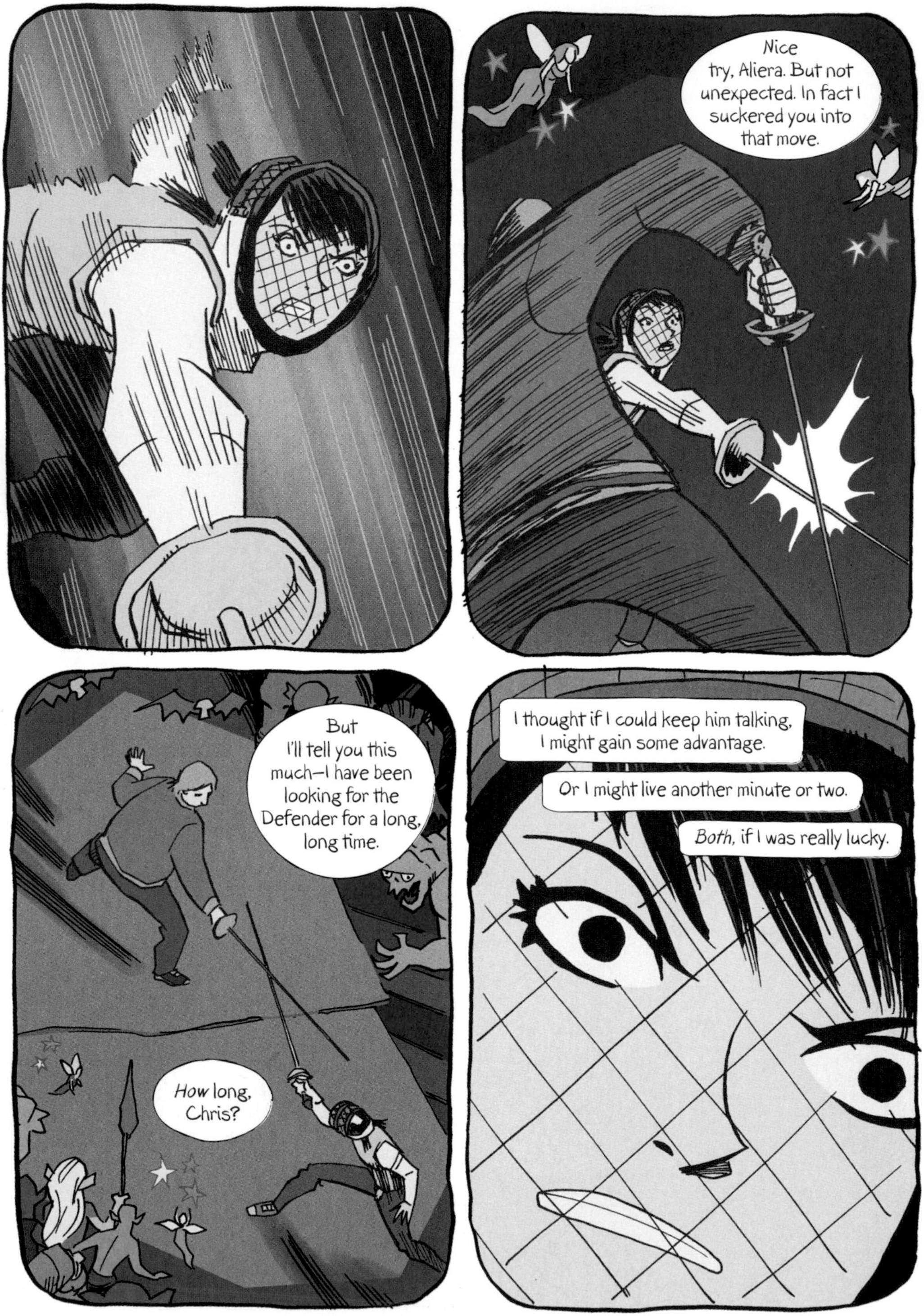
Nice try, Aliera. But not unexpected. In fact I suckered you into that move.
But I'll tell you this much—I have been looking for the Defender for a long, long time.
How long, Chris?
I thought if I could keep him talking, I might gain some advantage.
Or I might live another minute or two.
Both, if I was really lucky.

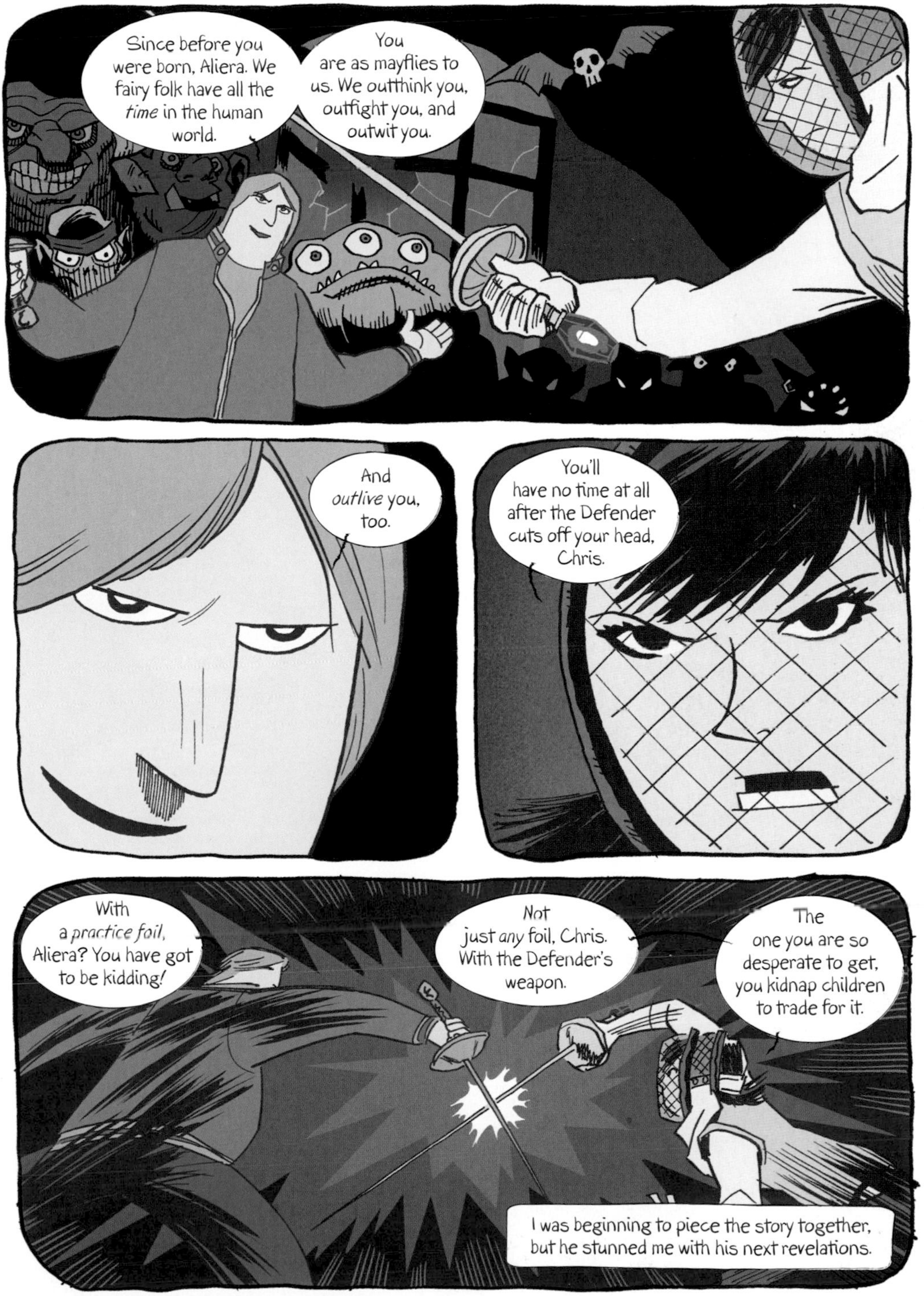
Since before you were born, Aliera. We fairy folk have all the *time* in the human world.
You are as mayflies to us. We outthink you, outfight you, and outwit you.
And *outlive* you, too.
You'll have no time at all after the Defender cuts off your head, Chris.
With a *practice foil*, Aliera? You have got to be kidding!
Not just *any* foil, Chris. With the Defender's weapon.
The one you are so desperate to get, you kidnap children to trade for it.
I was beginning to piece the story together, but he stunned me with his next revelations.

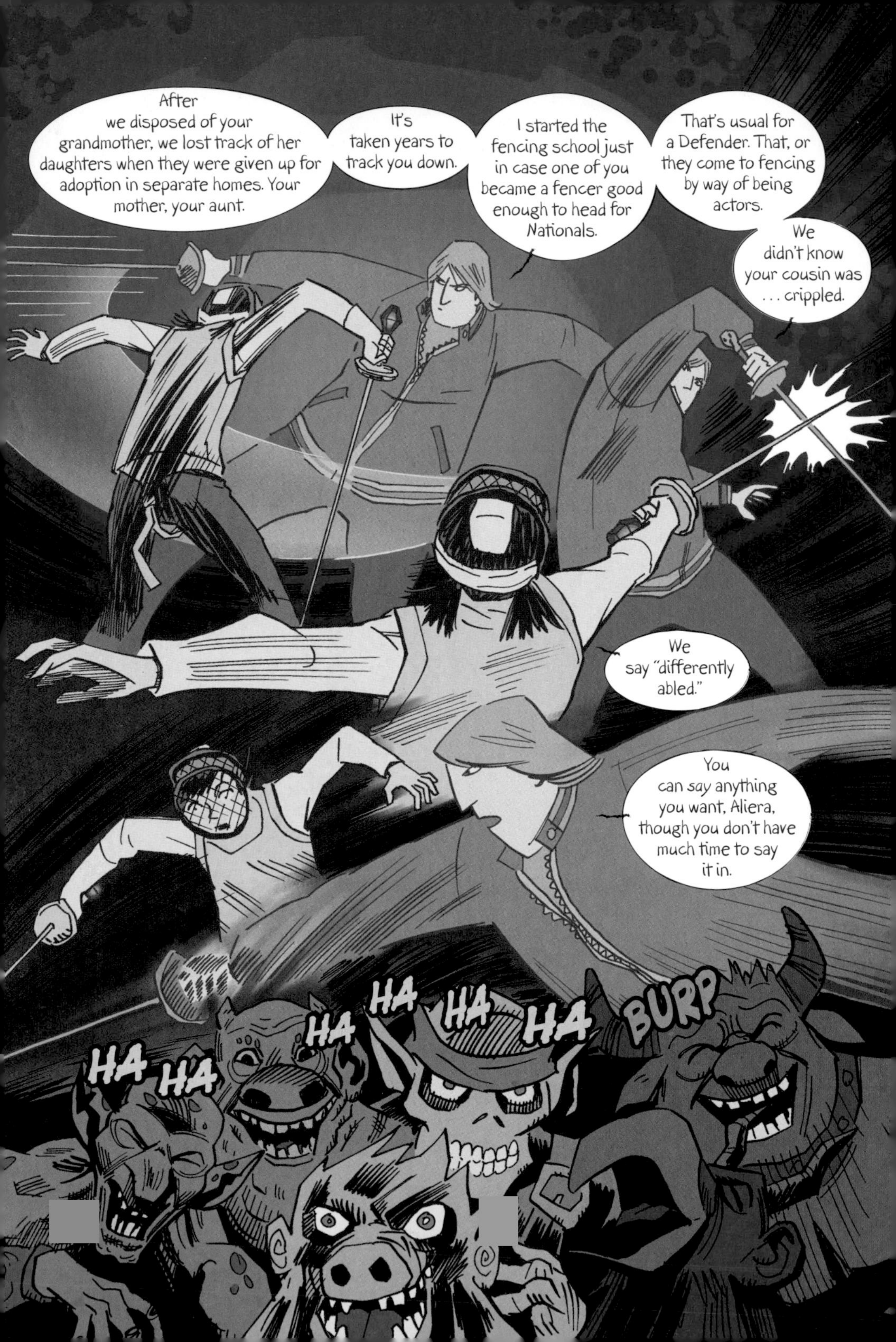
After we disposed of your grandmother, we lost track of her daughters when they were given up for adoption in separate homes. Your mother, your aunt.
It's taken years to track you down.
I started the fencing school just in case one of you became a fencer good enough to head for Nationals.
That's usual for a Defender. That, or they come to fencing by way of being actors.
We didn't know your cousin was . . . crippled.
We say "differently abled."
You can *say* anything you want, Aliera, though you don't have much time to say it in.
HA
HA
HA
HA
HA
HA
BURP

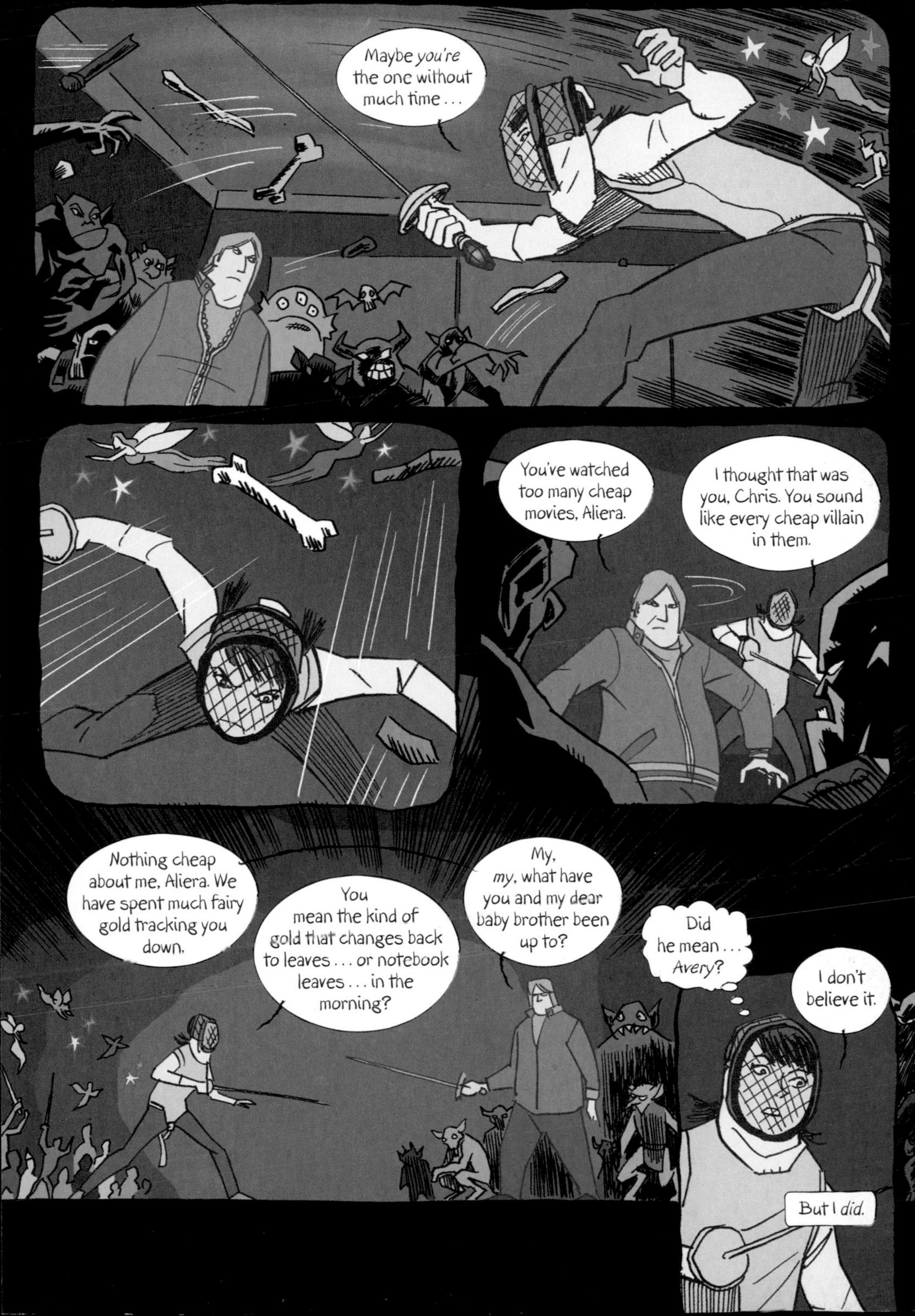
Maybe *you're* the one without much time . . .
You've watched too many cheap movies, Aliera.
I thought that was you, Chris. You sound like every cheap villain in them.
Nothing cheap about me, Aliera. We have spent much fairy gold tracking you down.
You mean the kind of gold that changes back to leaves . . . or notebook leaves . . . in the morning?
My, *my*, what have you and my dear baby brother been up to?
Did he mean . . . *Avery*?
I don't believe it.
But I *did*.

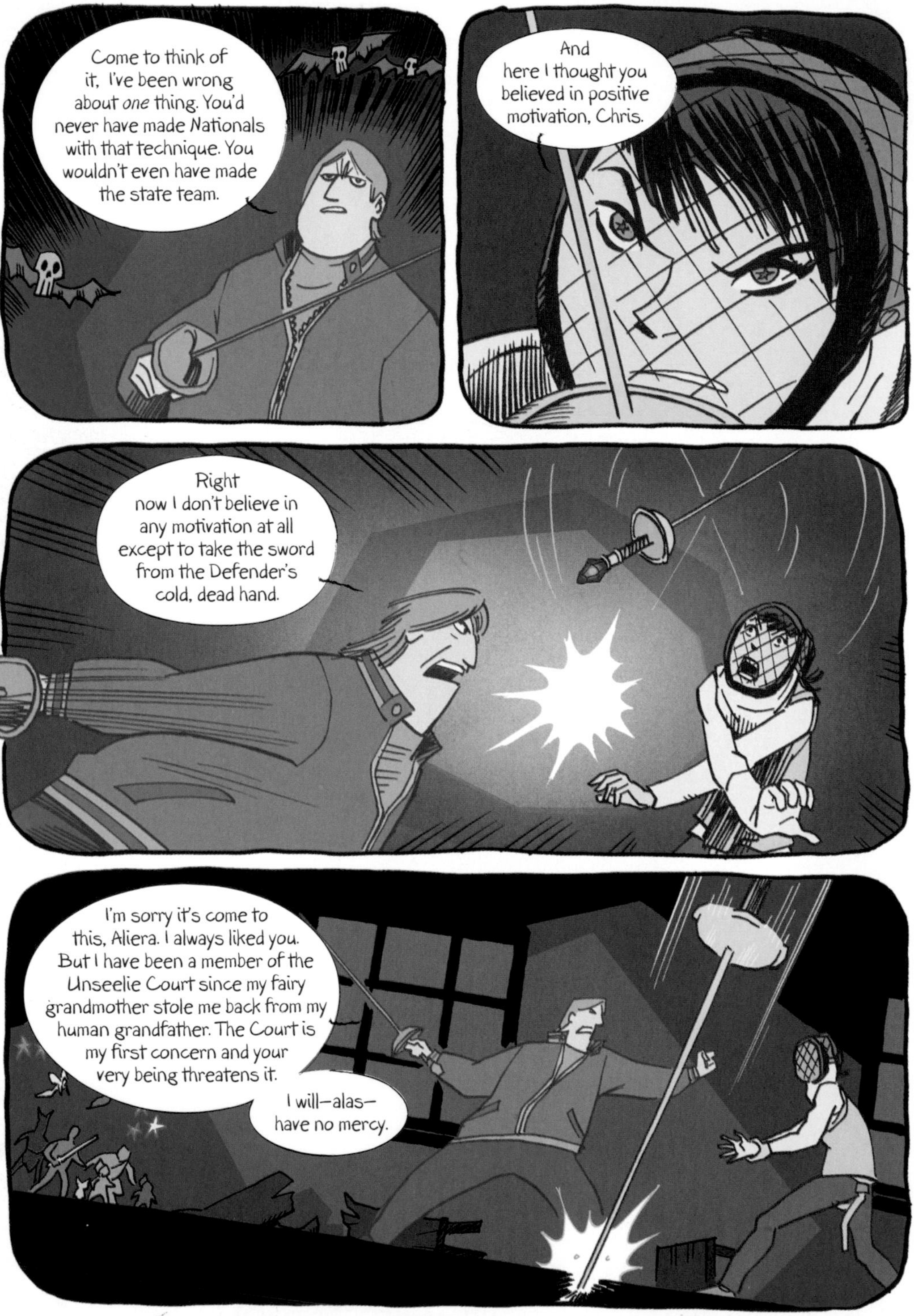
Come to think of it, I've been wrong about *one* thing. You'd never have made Nationals with that technique. You wouldn't even have made the state team.
And here I thought you believed in positive motivation, Chris.
Right now I don't believe in any motivation at all except to take the sword from the Defender's cold, dead hand.
I'm sorry it's come to this, Aliera. I always liked you. But I have been a member of the Unseelie Court since my fairy grandmother stole me back from my human grandfather. The Court is my first concern and your very being threatens it.
I will—alas—have no mercy.

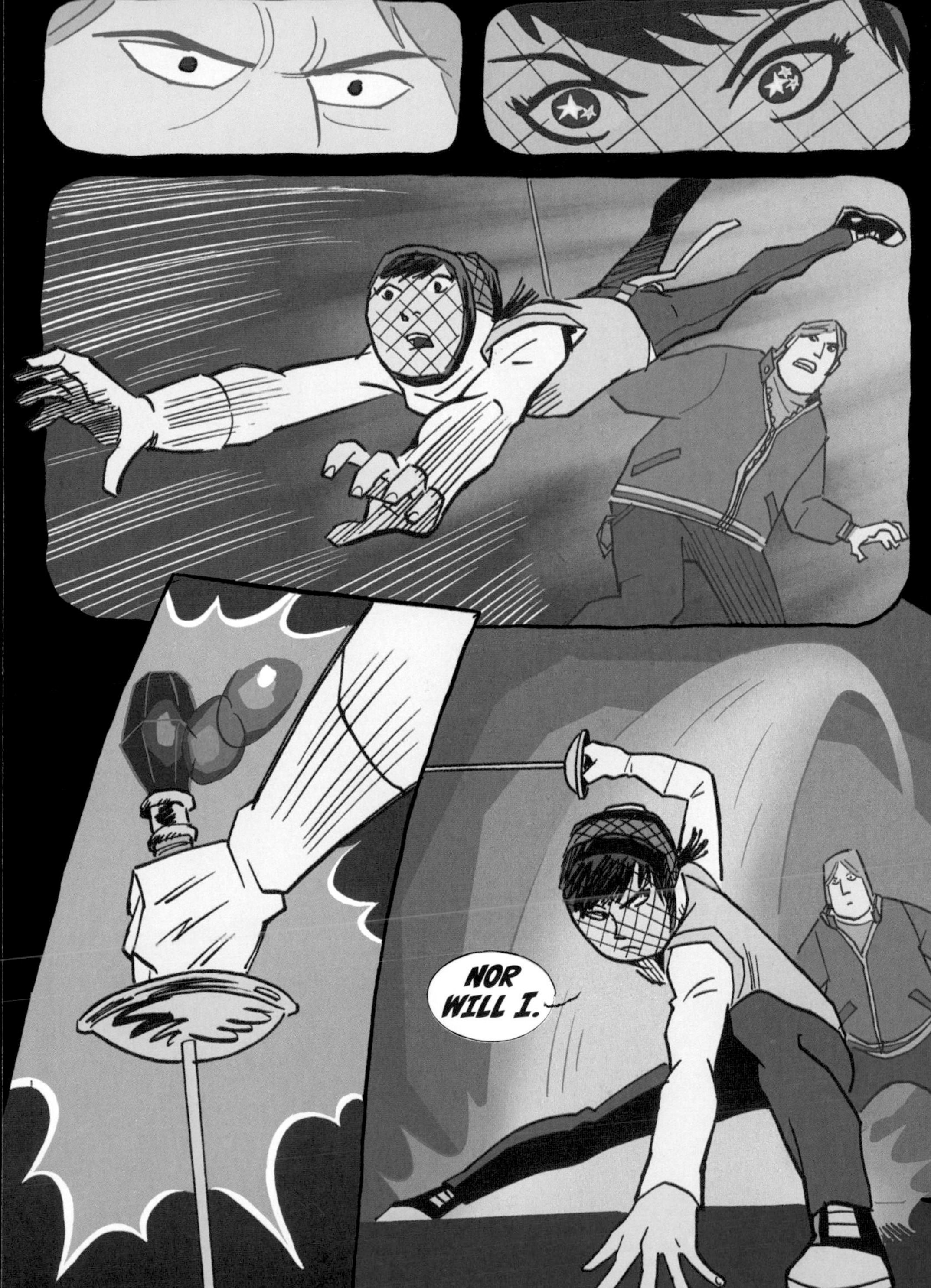
NOR WILL I.

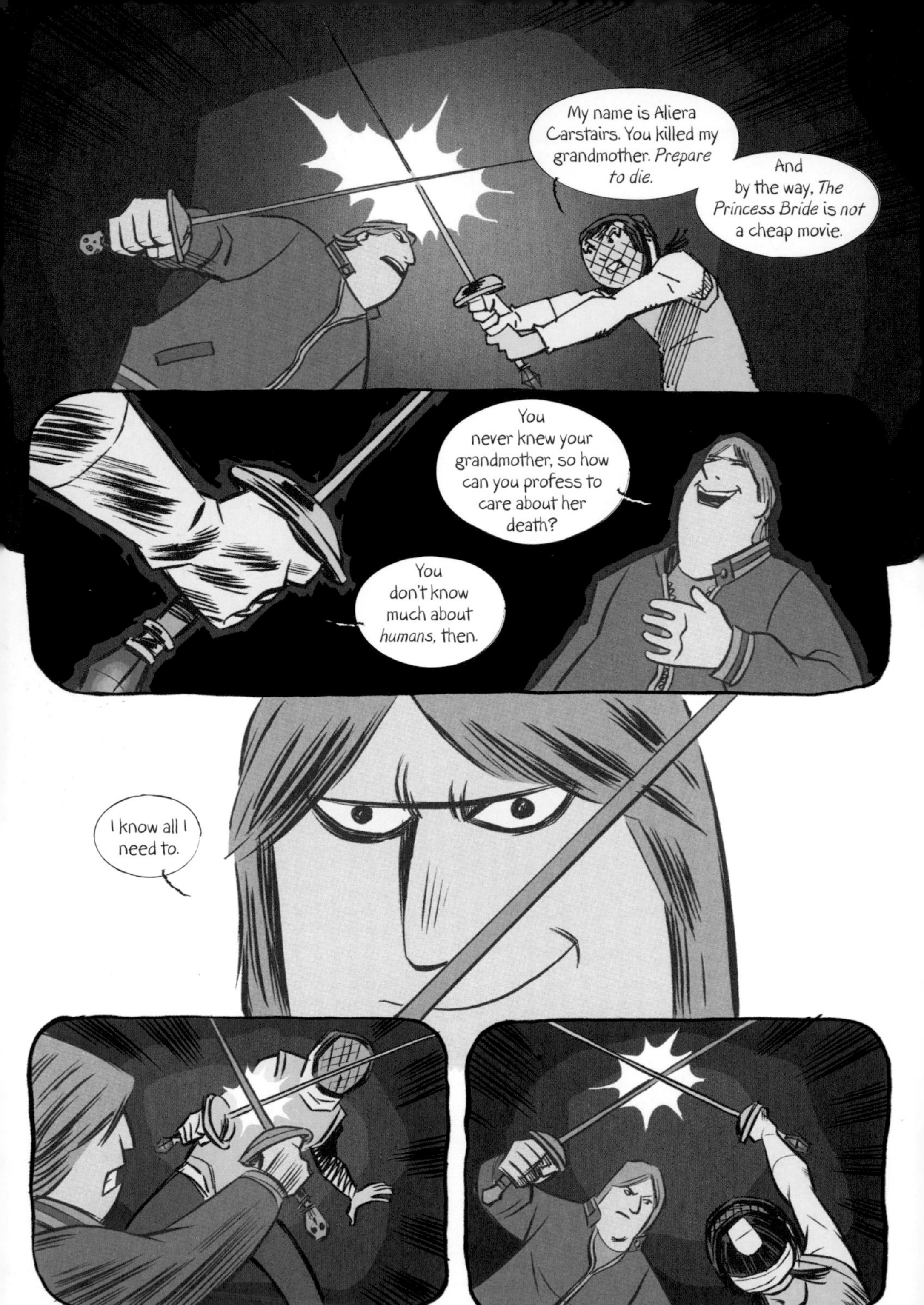
My name is Aliera Carstairs. You killed my grandmother. *Prepare to die.*
And by the way, *The Princess Bride* is not a cheap movie.
You never knew your grandmother, so how can you profess to care about her death?
You don't know much about *humans,* then.
I know all I need to.

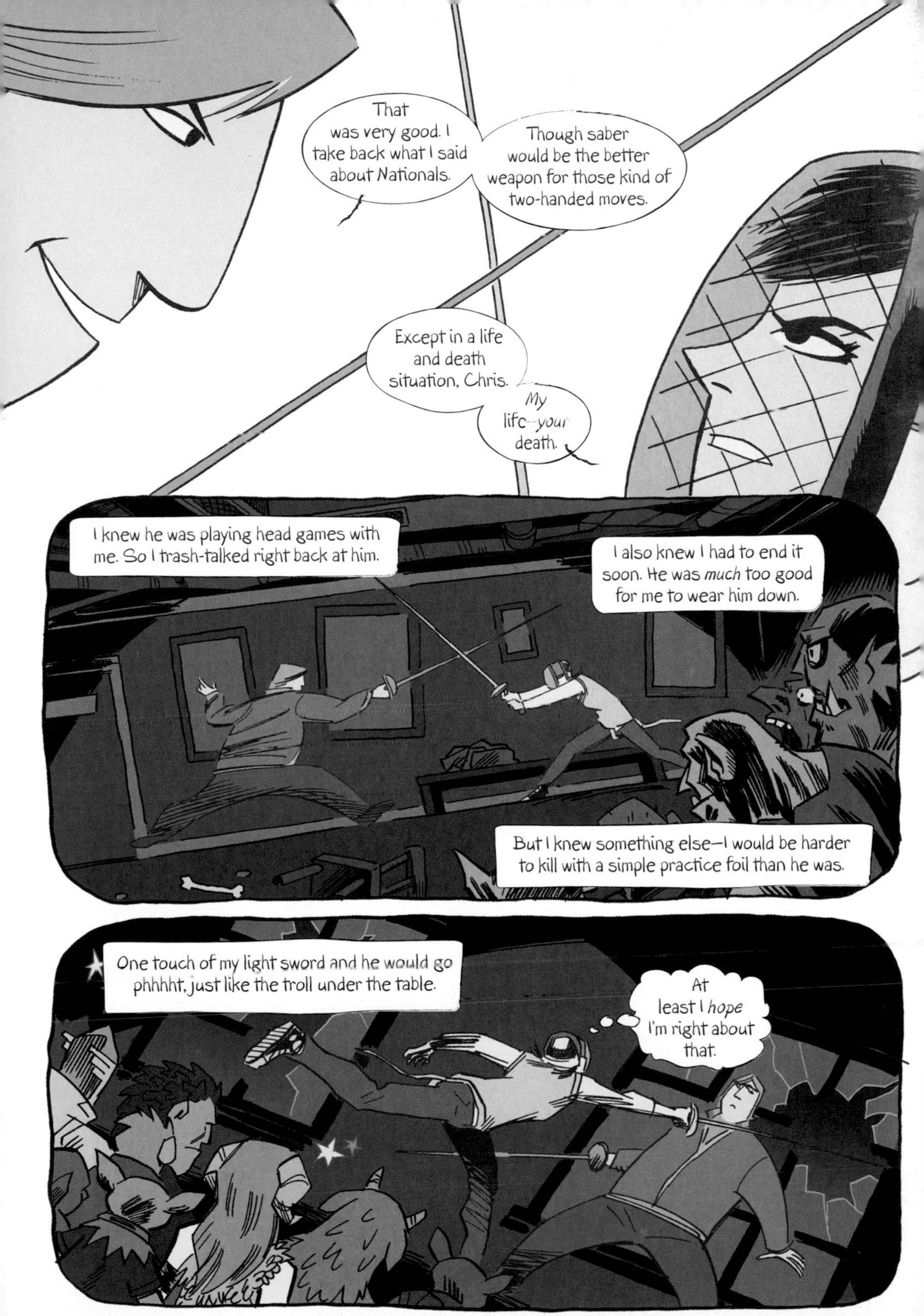
That was very good. I take back what I said about Nationals.
Though saber would be the better weapon for those kind of two-handed moves.
Except in a life and death situation, Chris.
My life—your death.
I knew he was playing head games with me. So I trash-talked right back at him.
I also knew I had to end it soon. He was *much* too good for me to wear him down.
But I knew something else—I would be harder to kill with a simple practice foil than he was.
One touch of my light sword and he would go phhhht, just like the troll under the table.
At least I *hope* I'm right about that.

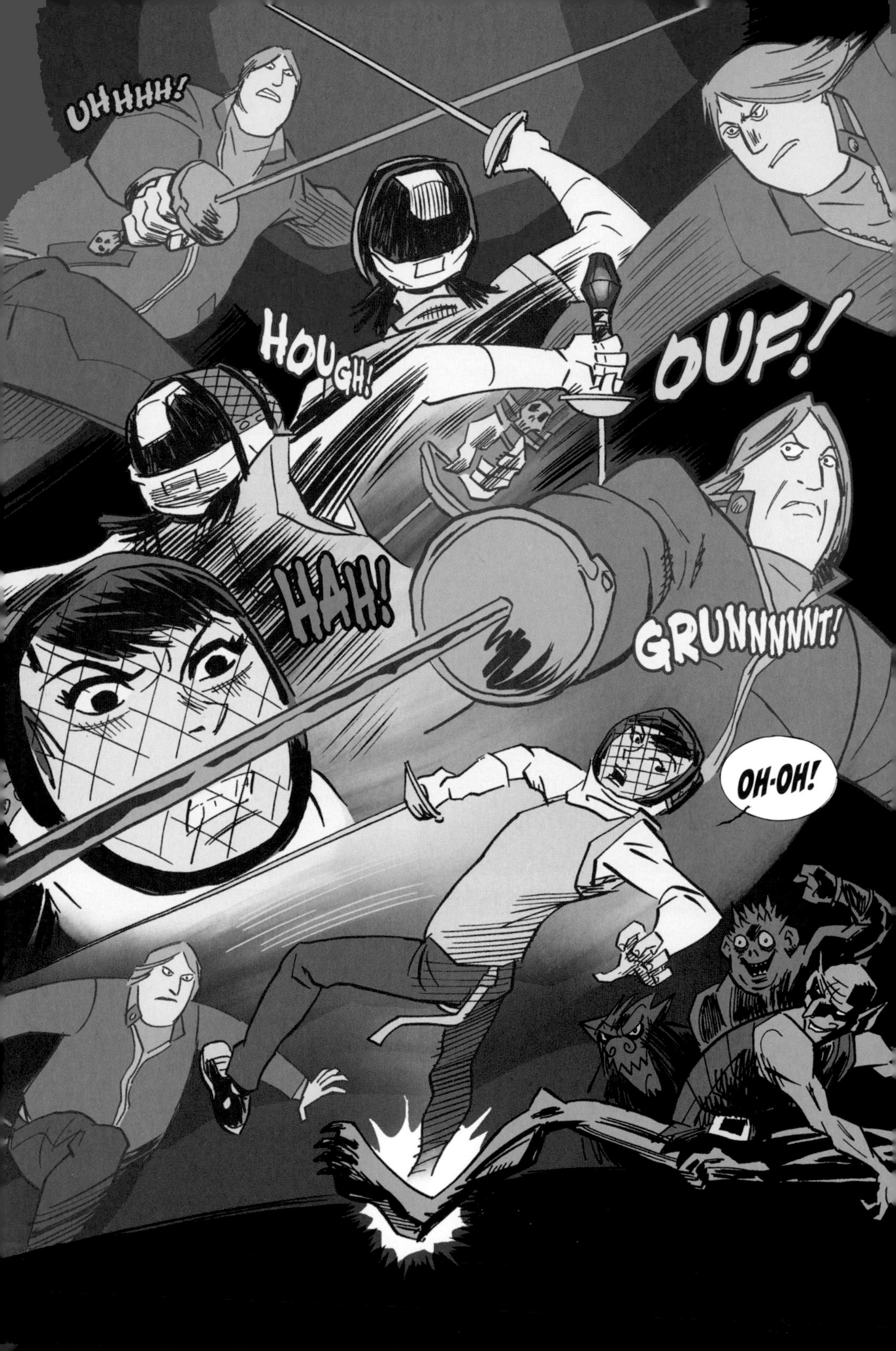
UHHHH!
HOUGH!
OUF!
HAH!
GRUNNNNNT!
OH-OH!

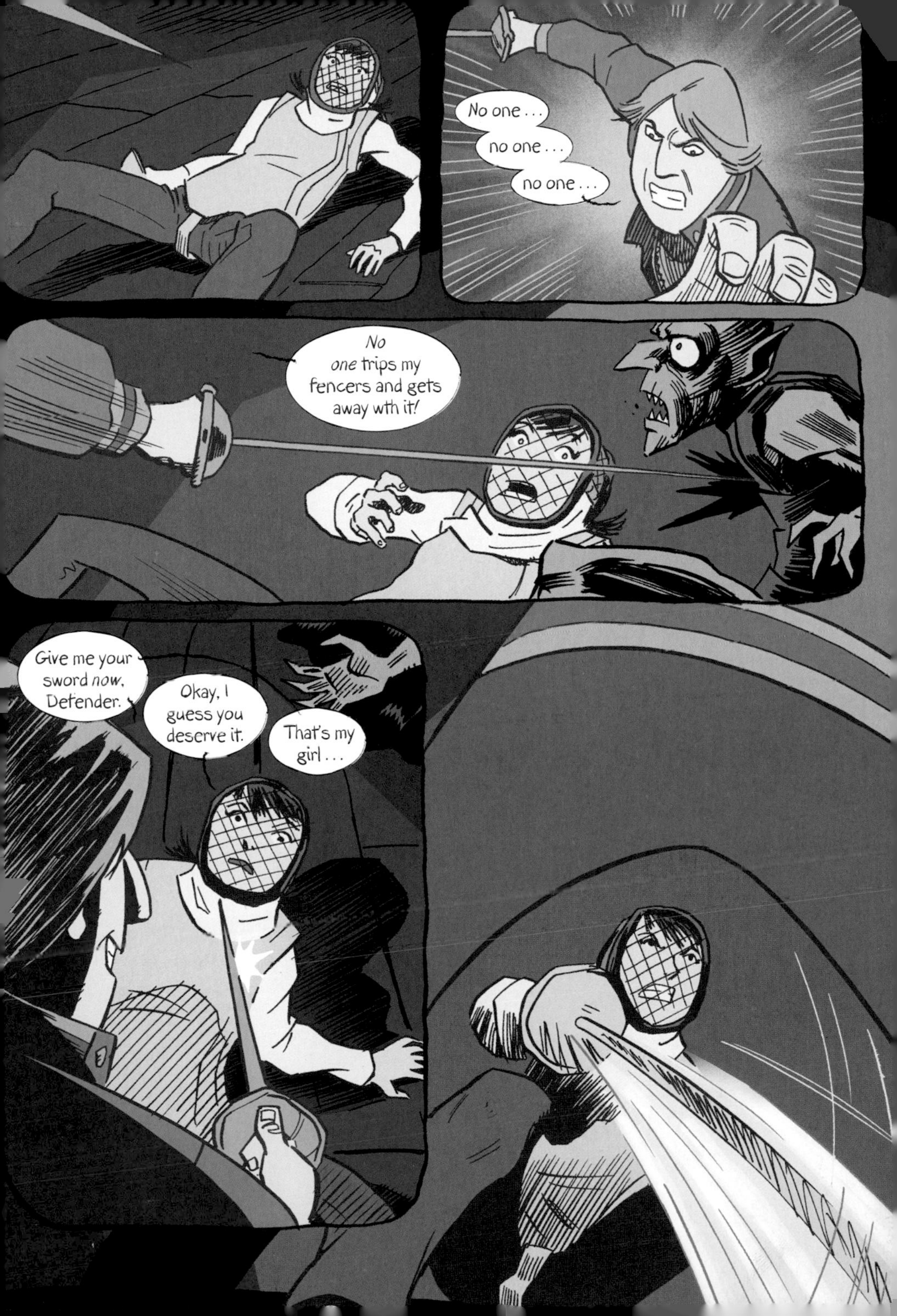
No one . . .
no one . . .
no one . . .
No one trips my fencers and gets away wth it!
Give me your sword *now*, Defender.
Okay, I guess you deserve it.
That's my girl . . .

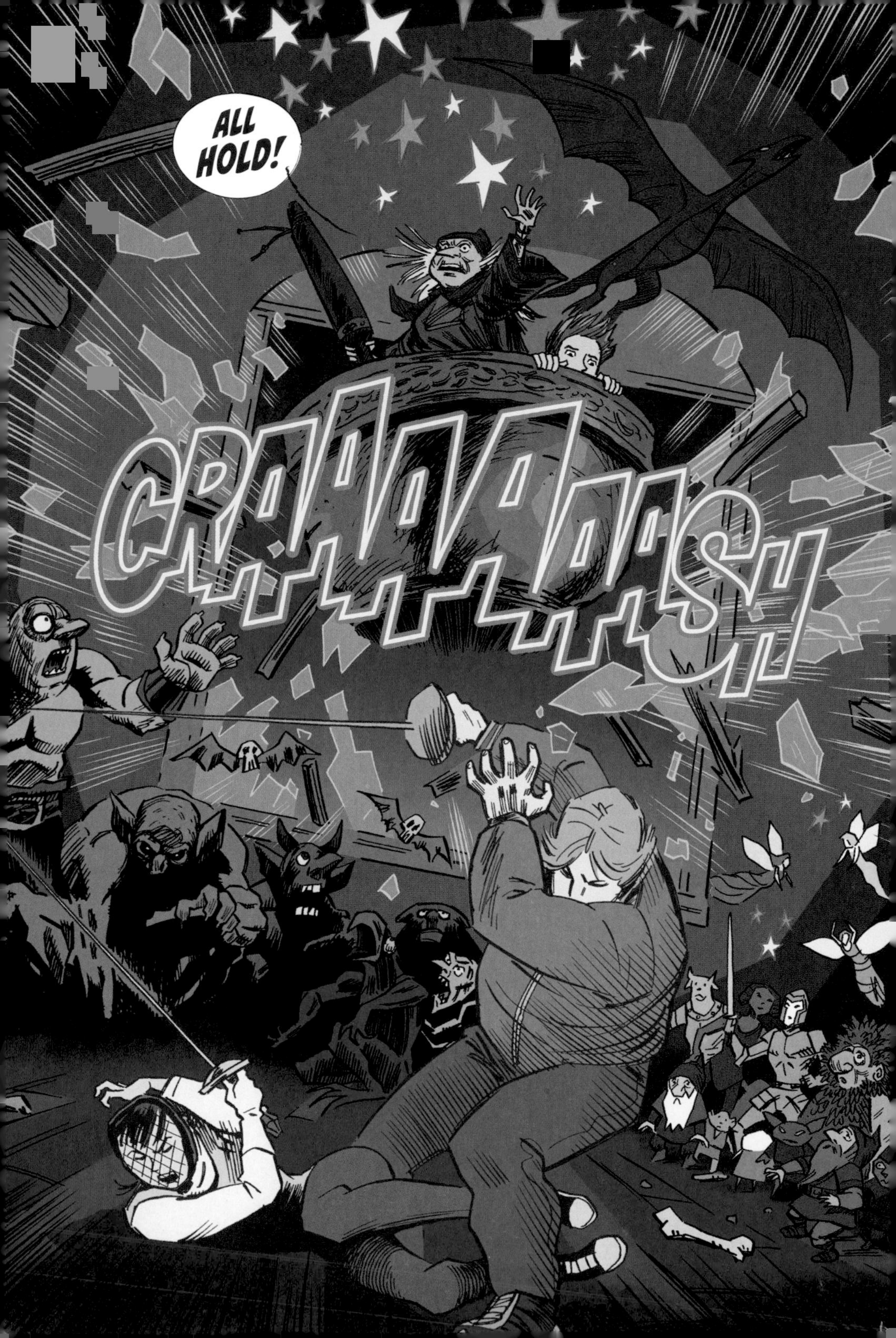
ALL HOLD!
CRAAAAASH

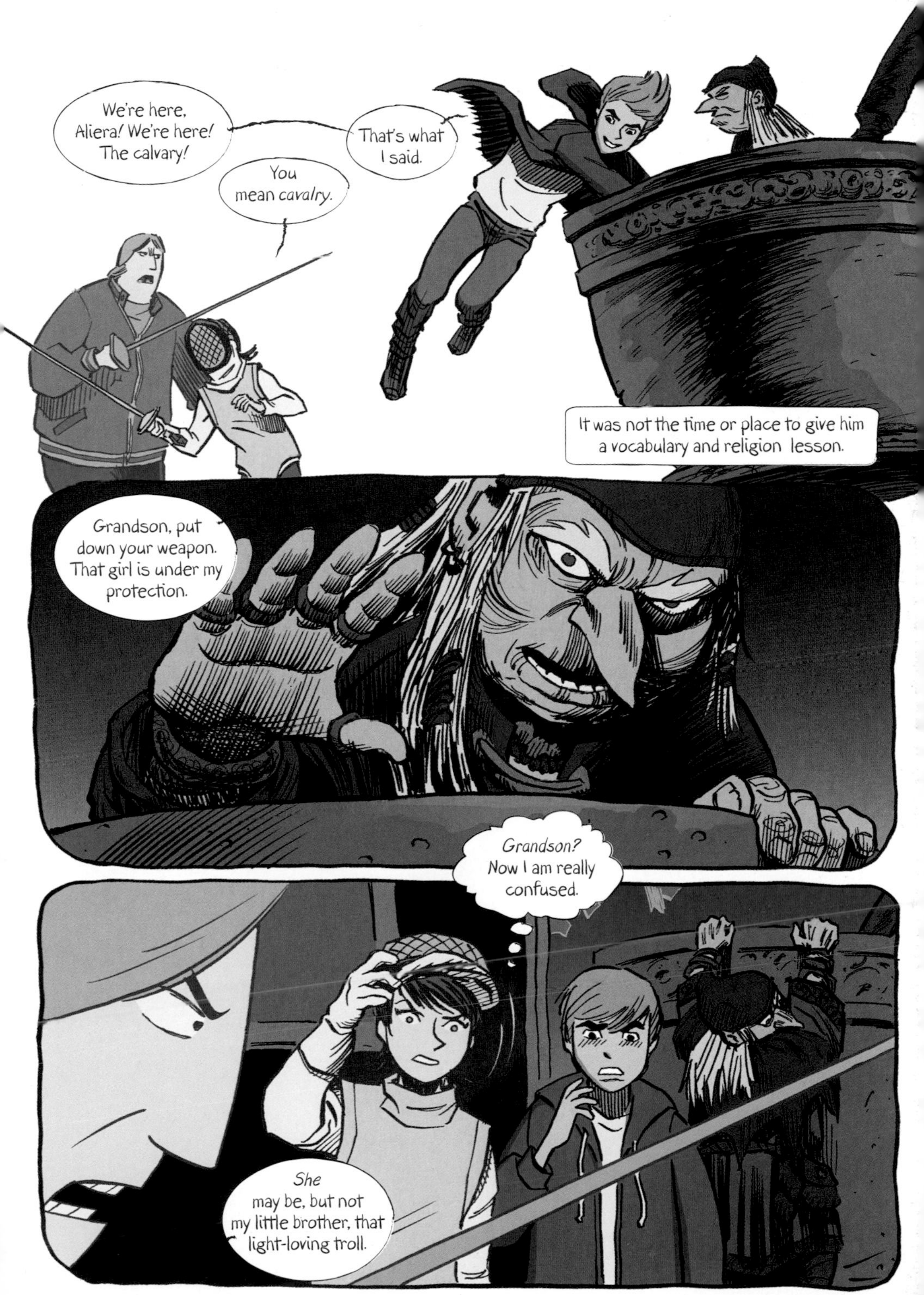
We're here, Aliera! We're here! The calvary!
That's what I said.
You mean cavalry.
It was not the time or place to give him a vocabulary and religion lesson.
Grandson, put down your weapon. That girl is under my protection.
Grandson? Now I am really confused.
She may be, but not my little brother, that light-loving troll.

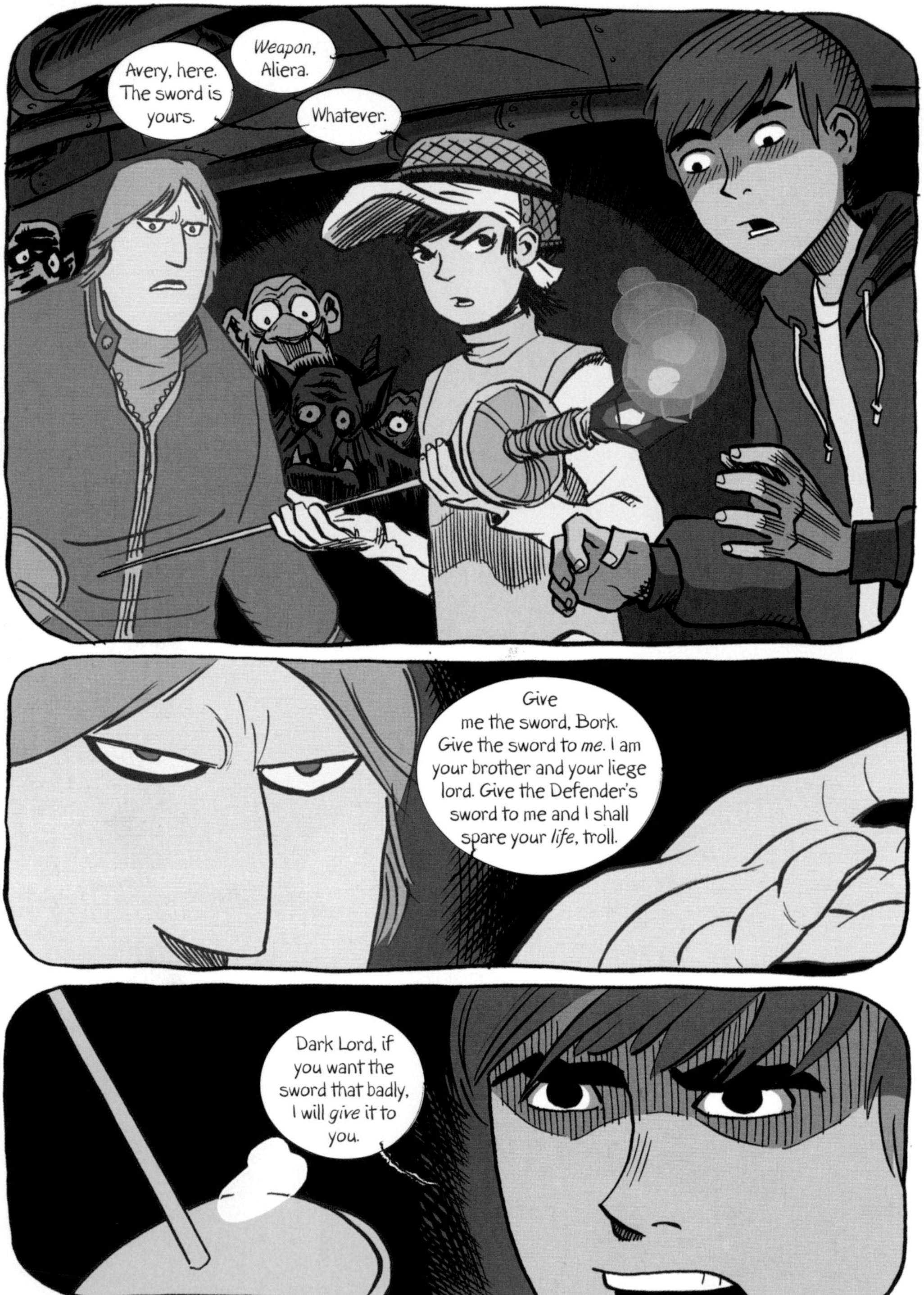

Avery, here. The sword is yours.
Weapon, Aliera.
Whatever.
Give me the sword, Bork. Give the sword to *me*. I am your brother and your liege lord. Give the Defender's sword to me and I shall spare your *life*, troll.
Dark Lord, if you want the sword that badly, I will *give* it to you.

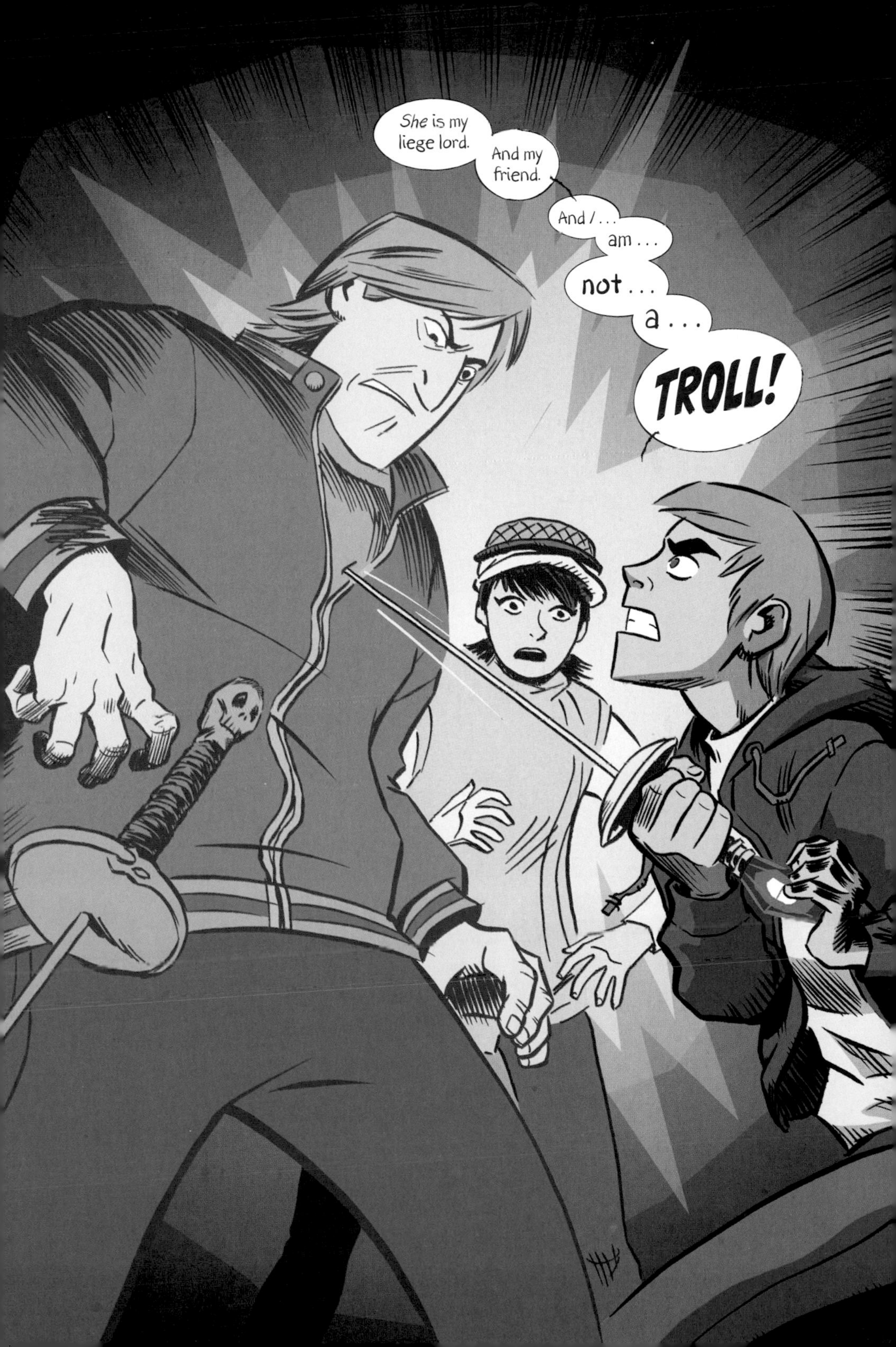
She is my liege lord.
And my friend.
And I . . .
am . . .
not . . .
a . . .
TROLL!

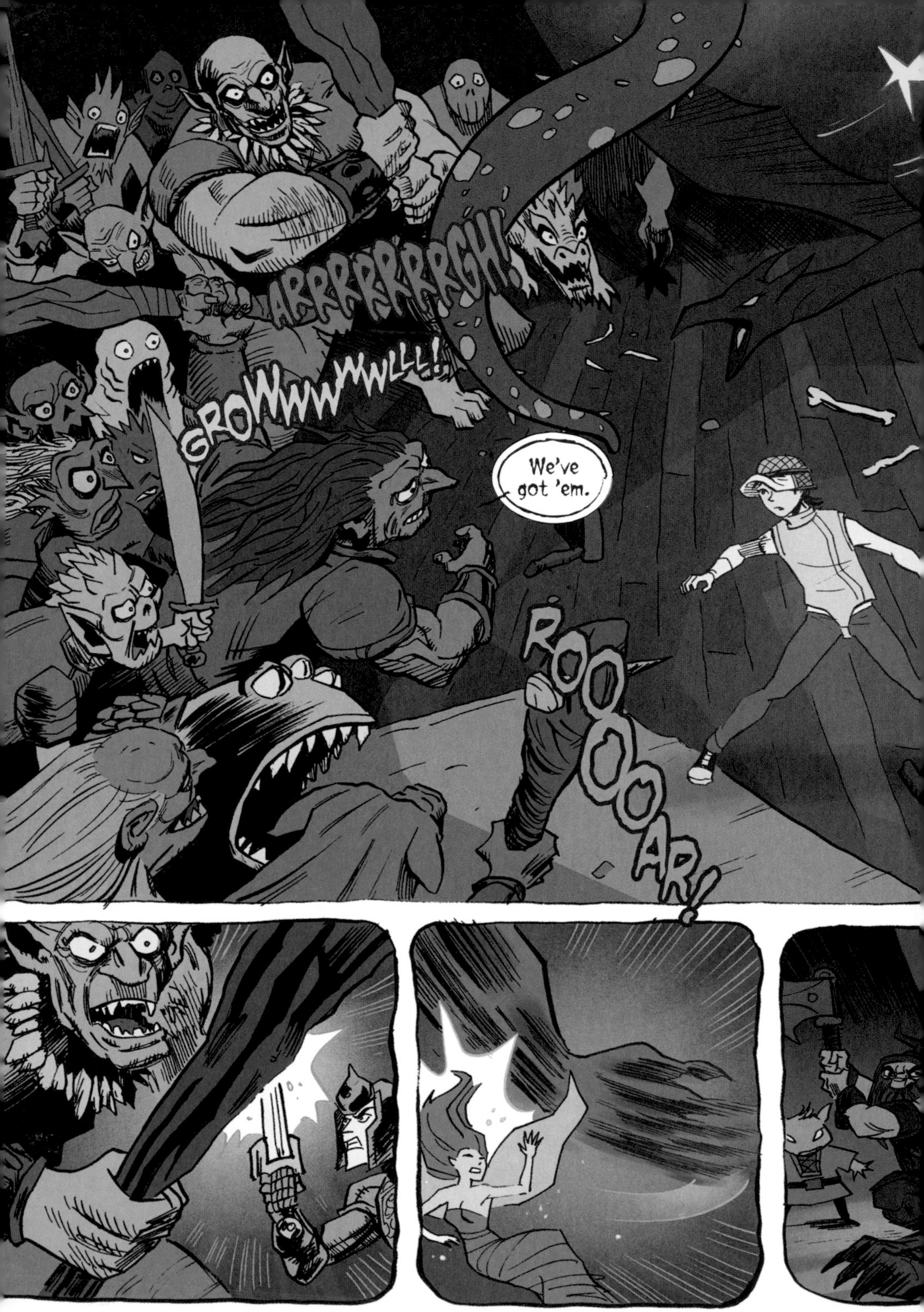
ARRRRRRRGH!
GROWWWWWLLL!
We've got 'em.
ROOOOOAR!

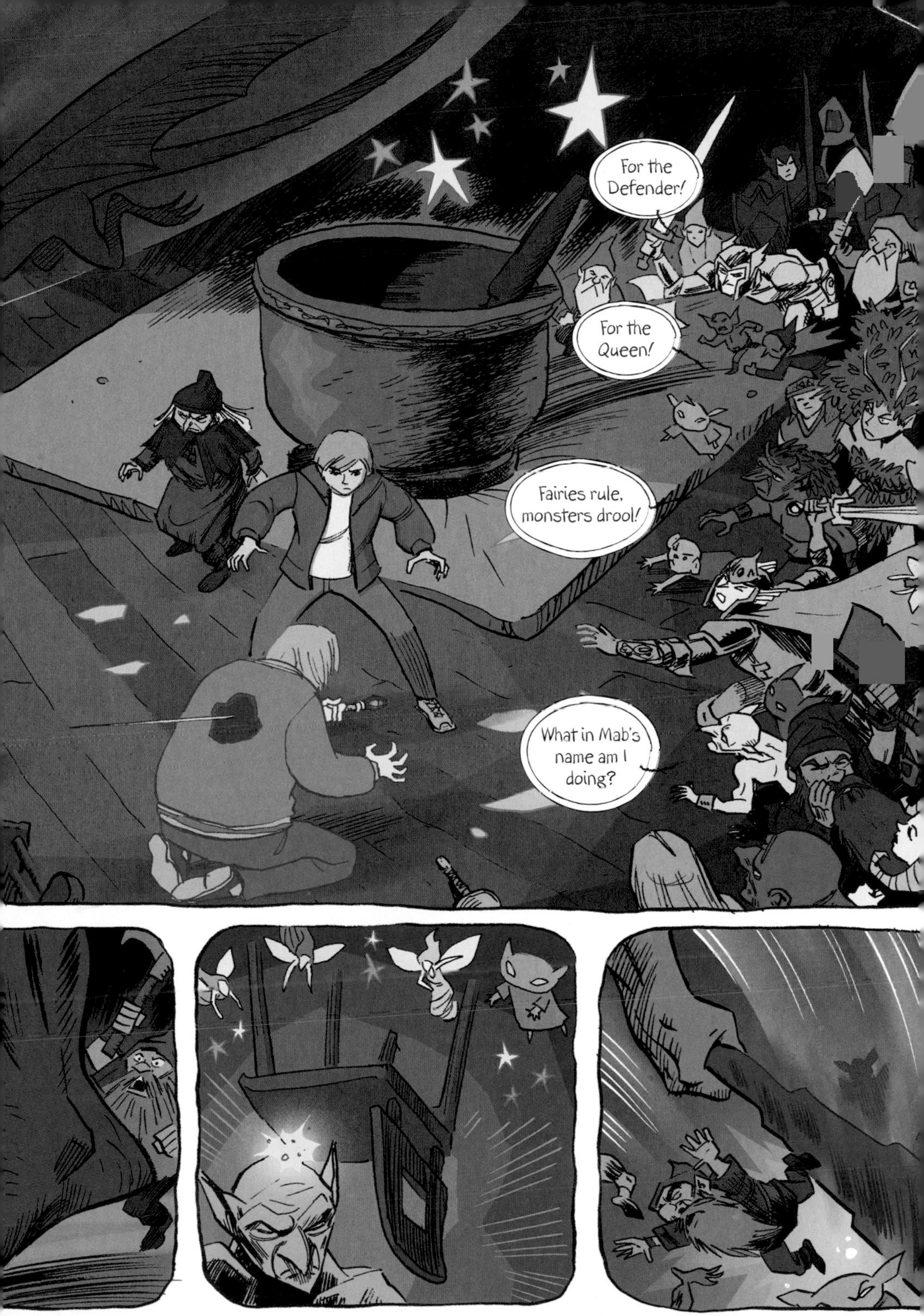
For the Defender!
For the Queen!
Fairies rule, monsters drool!
What in Mab's name am I doing?

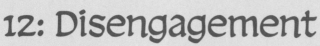

12: Disengagement

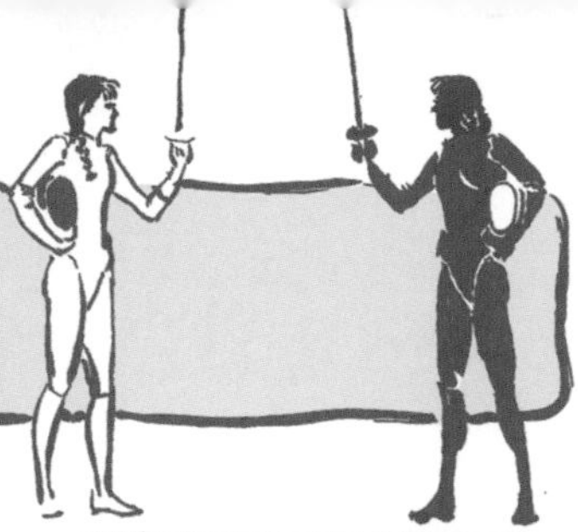

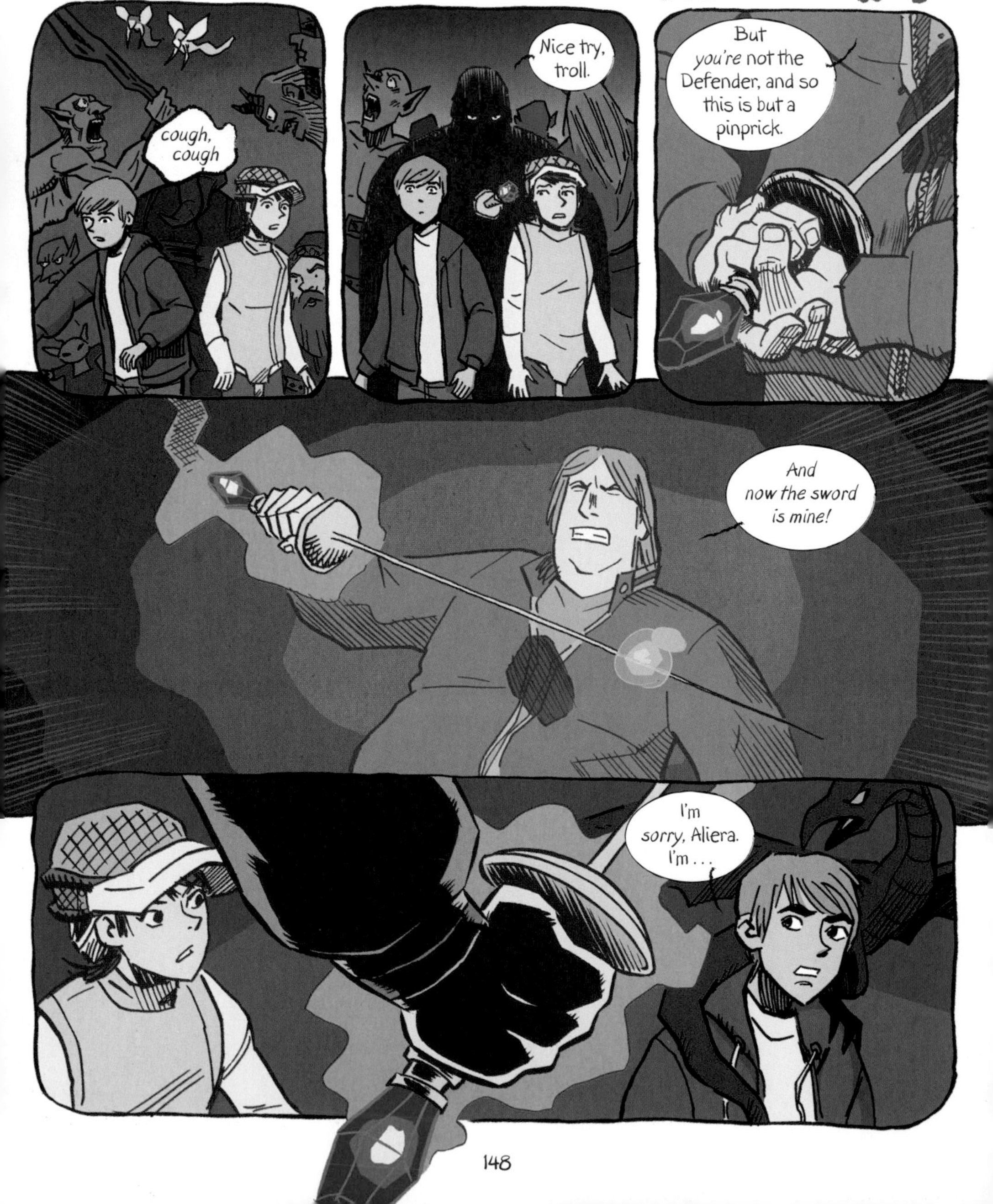
cough, cough
Nice try, troll.
But *you're* not the Defender, and so this is but a pinprick.
And now the sword is mine!
I'm *sorry*, Aliera. I'm . . .

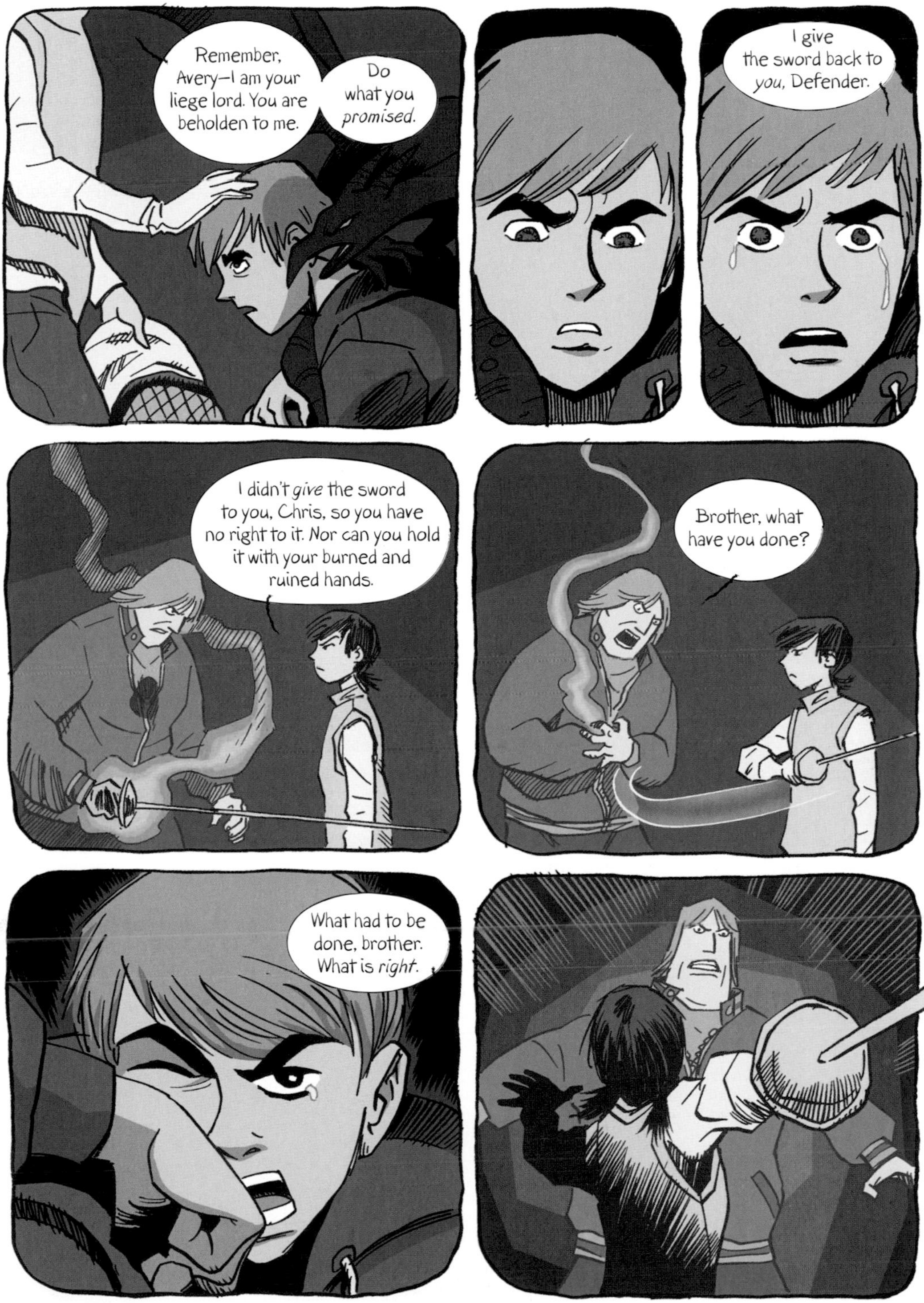
Remember, Avery—I am your liege lord. You are beholden to me.
Do what you *promised*.
I give the sword back to *you*, Defender.
I didn't *give* the sword to you, Chris, so you have no right to it. Nor can you hold it with your burned and ruined hands.
Brother, what have you done?
What had to be done, brother. What is *right*.

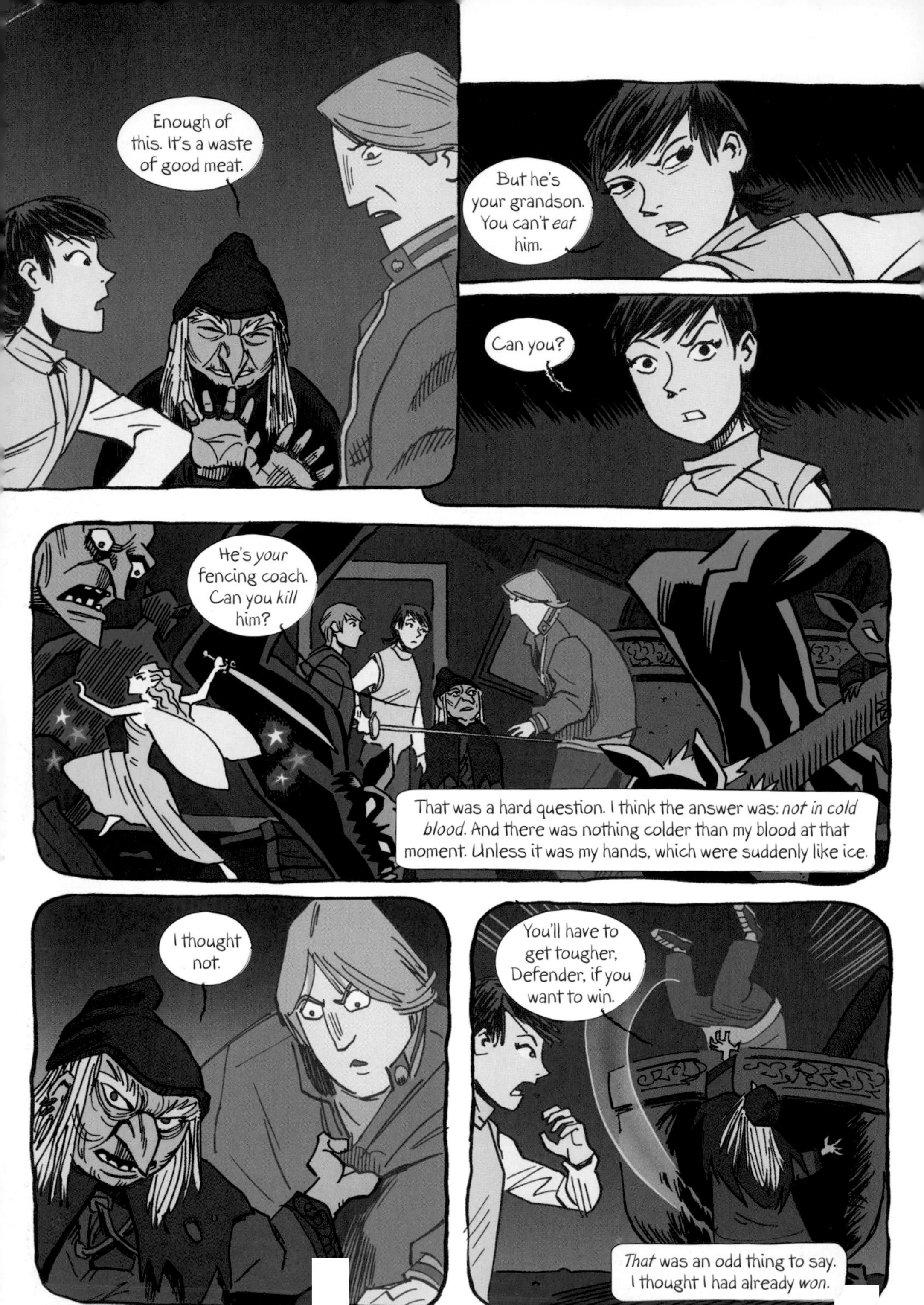
Enough of this. It's a waste of good meat.
But he's your grandson. You can't *eat* him.
Can you?
He's *your* fencing coach. Can you *kill* him?
That was a hard question. I think the answer was: *not in cold blood*. And there was nothing colder than my blood at that moment. Unless it was my hands, which were suddenly like ice.
I thought not.
You'll have to get tougher, Defender, if you want to win.
That was an odd thing to say. I thought I had already *won*.

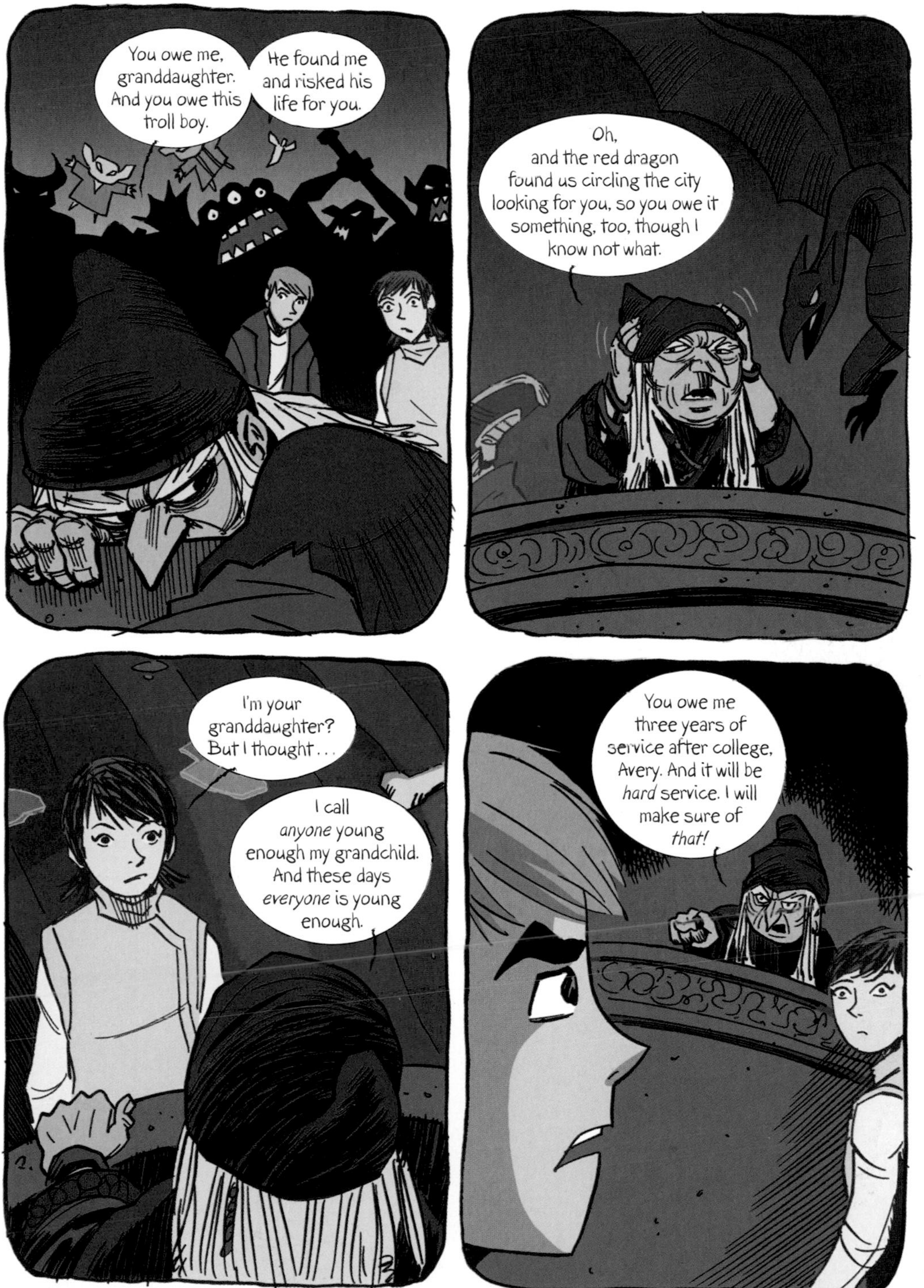
You owe me, granddaughter. And you owe this troll boy.
He found me and risked his life for you.
Oh, and the red dragon found us circling the city looking for you, so you owe it something, too, though I know not what.
I'm your granddaughter? But I thought . . .
I call *anyone* young enough my grandchild. And these days *everyone* is young enough.
You owe me three years of service after college, Avery. And it will be *hard* service. I will make sure of *that!*

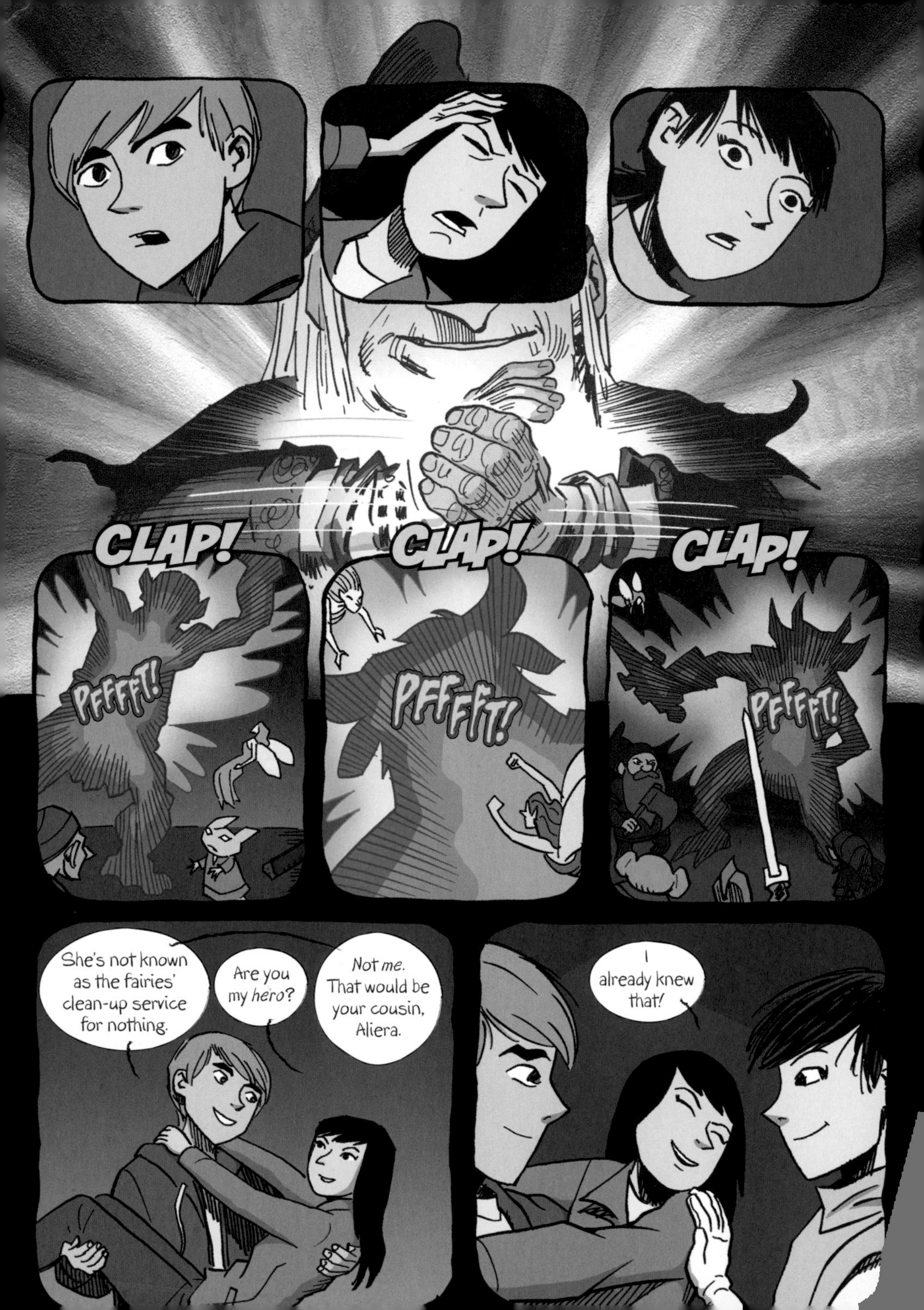
CLAP!
CLAP!
CLAP!
PFFFFT!
PFFFFT!
PFFFFT!
She's not known as the fairies' clean-up service for nothing.
Are you my *hero*?
Not *me*. That would be your cousin, Aliera.
I already knew that!

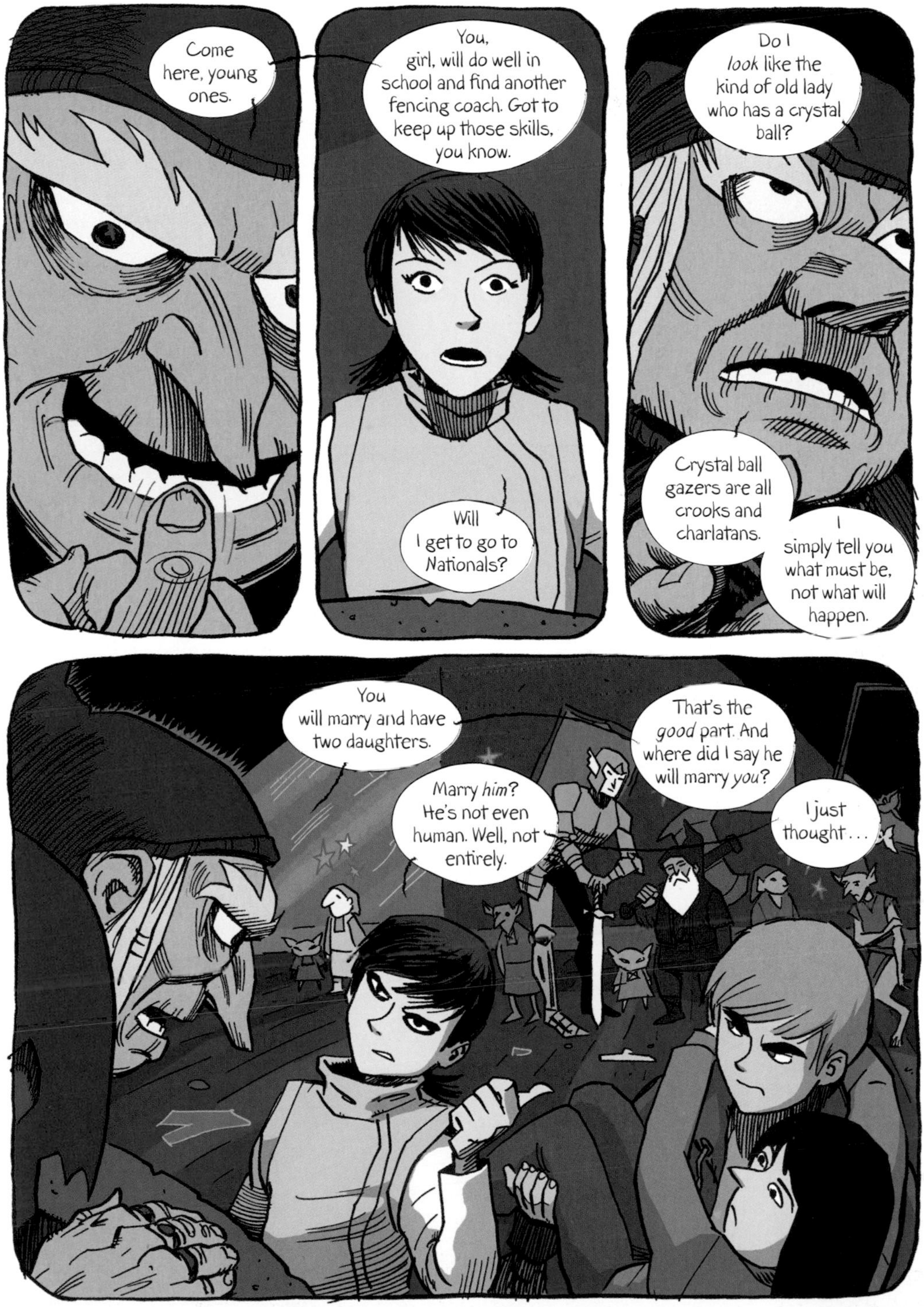
Come here, young ones.
You, girl, will do well in school and find another fencing coach. Got to keep up those skills, you know.
Will I get to go to Nationals?
Do I *look* like the kind of old lady who has a crystal ball?
Crystal ball gazers are all crooks and charlatans.
I simply tell you what must be, not what will happen.
You will marry and have two daughters.
Marry *him*? He's not even human. Well, not entirely.
That's the *good* part. And where did I say he will marry *you*?
I just thought . . .

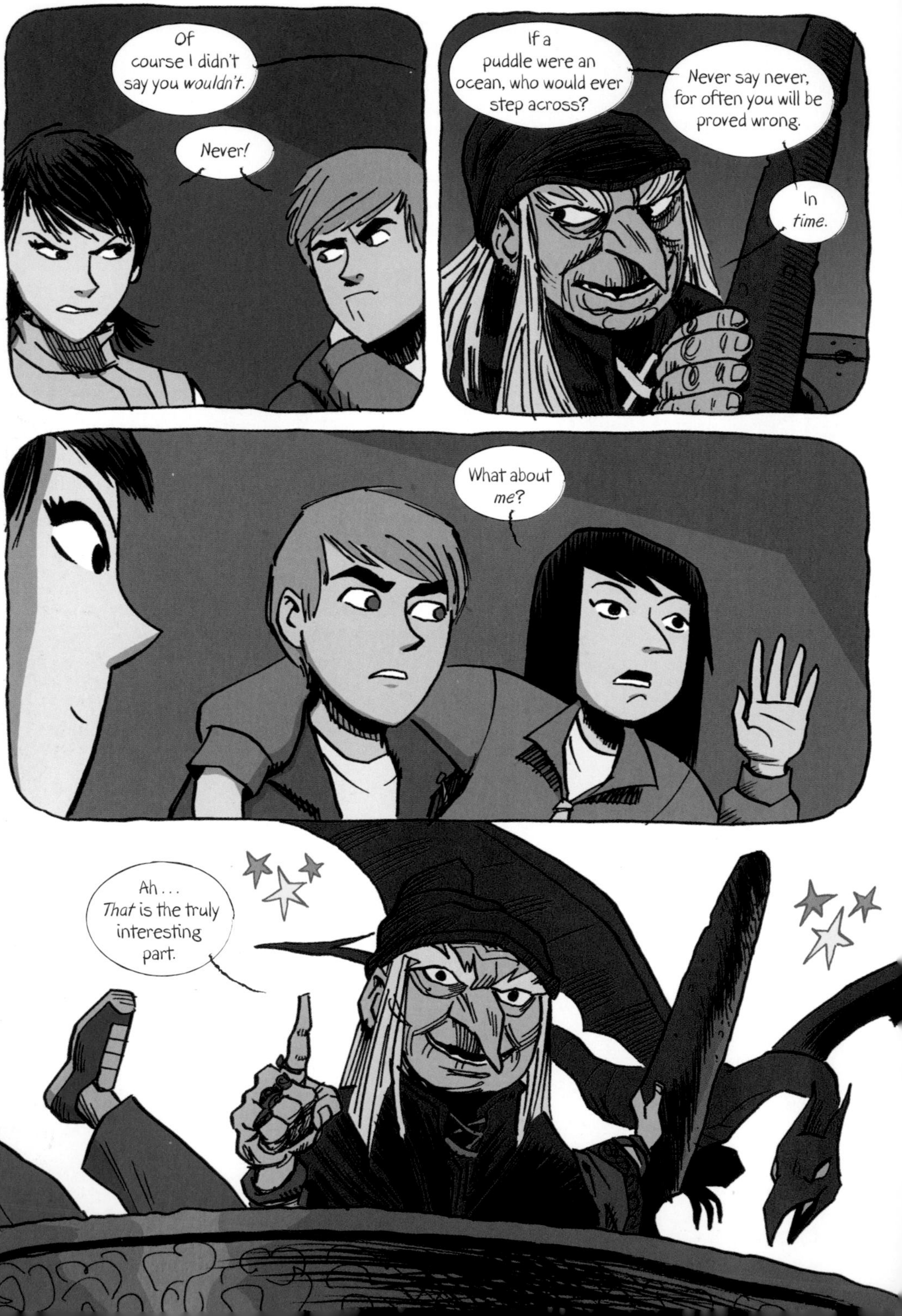

Of course I didn't say you *wouldn't*.
Never!
If a puddle were an ocean, who would ever step across?
Never say never, for often you will be proved wrong.
In *time*.
What about *me*?
Ah . . . *That* is the truly interesting part.

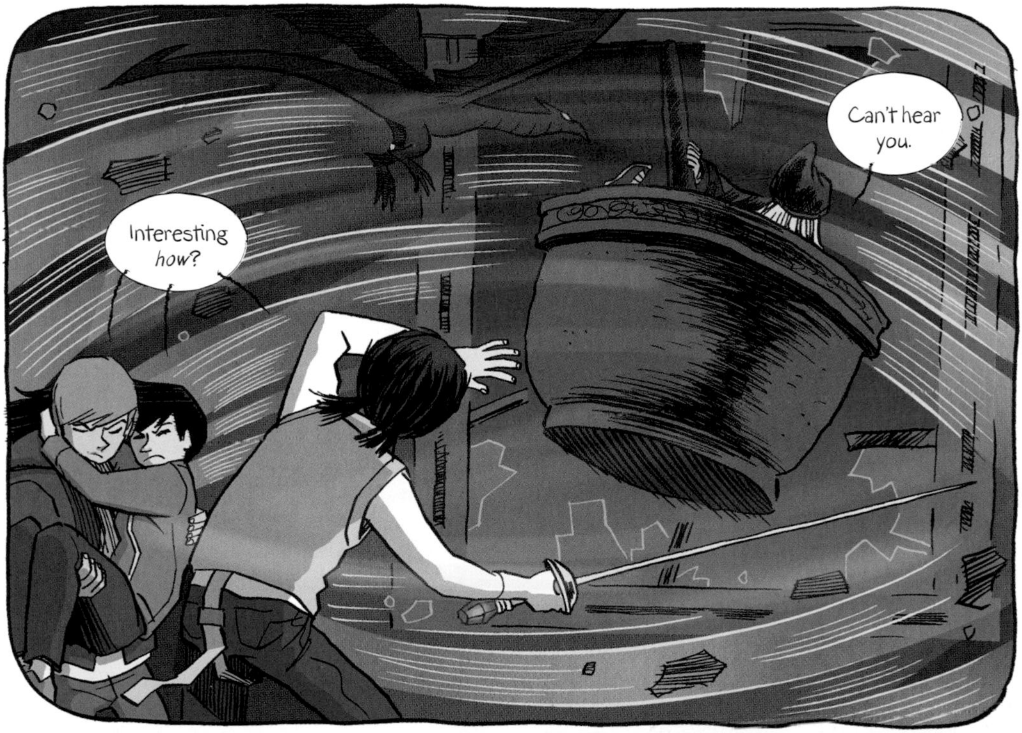
Interesting *how?*
Can't hear you.

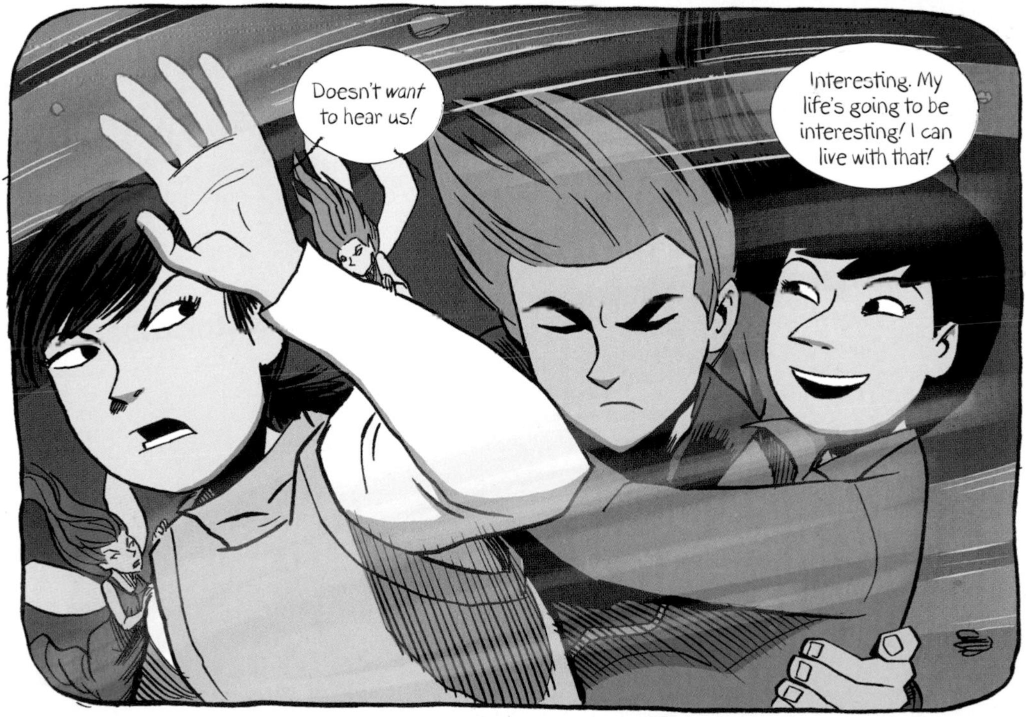
Doesn't *want* to hear us!
Interesting. My life's going to be interesting! I can live with that!

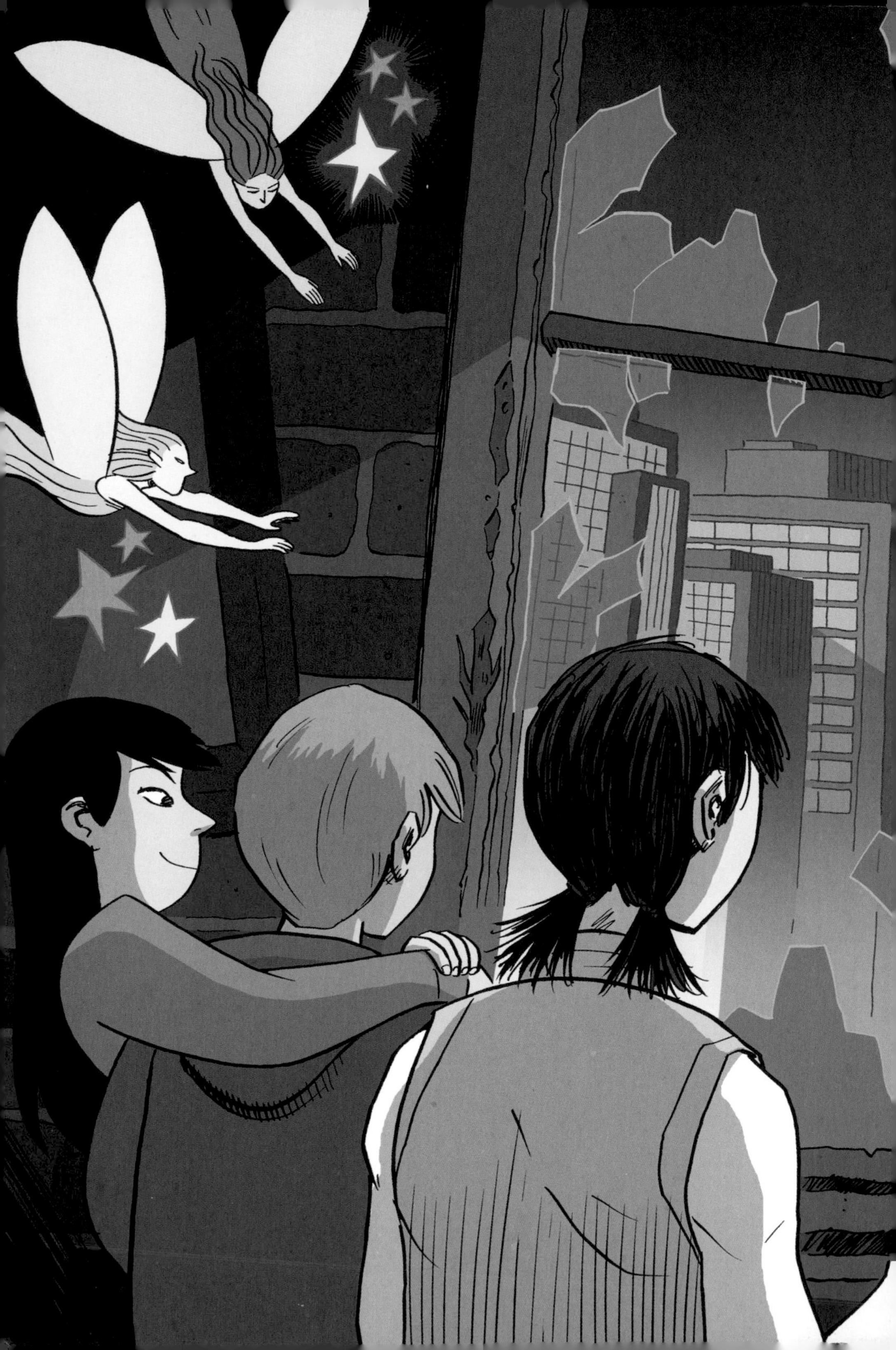

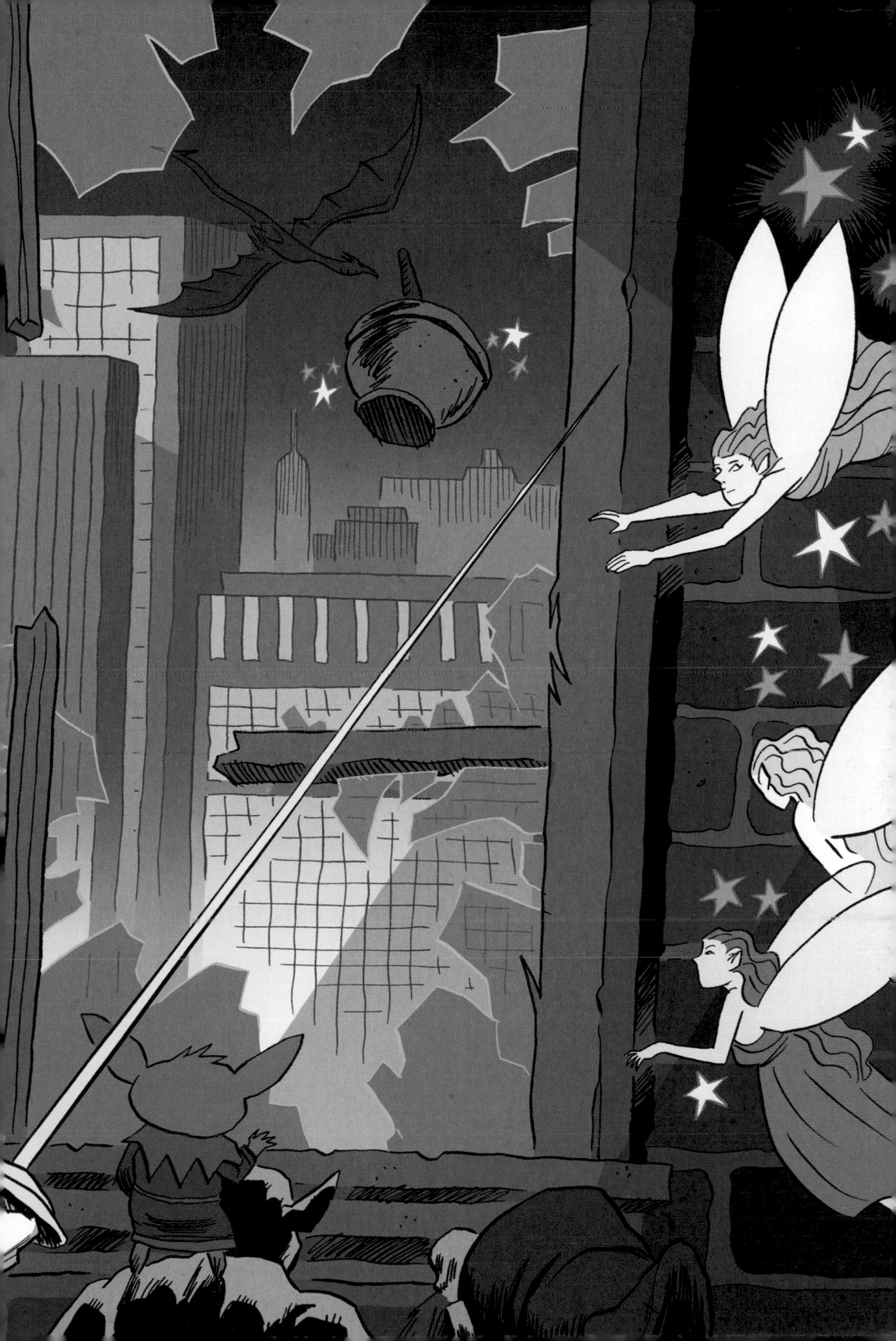

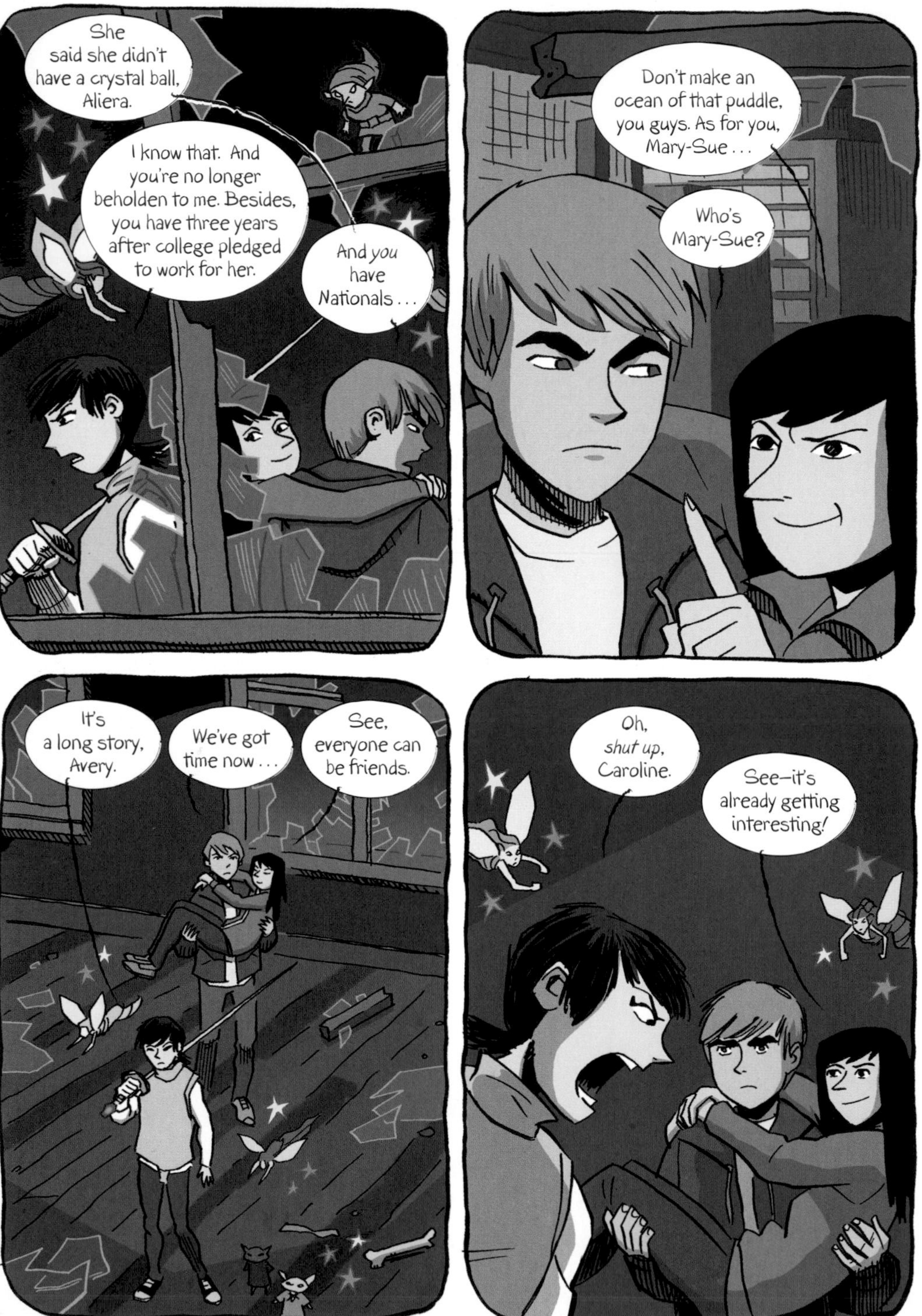
She said she didn't have a crystal ball, Aliera.
I know that. And you're no longer beholden to me. Besides, you have three years after college pledged to work for her.
And *you* have Nationals . . .
Don't make an ocean of that puddle, you guys. As for you, Mary-Sue . . .
Who's Mary-Sue?
It's a long story, Avery.
We've got time now . . .
See, everyone can be friends.
Oh, *shut up*, Caroline.
See—it's already getting interesting!

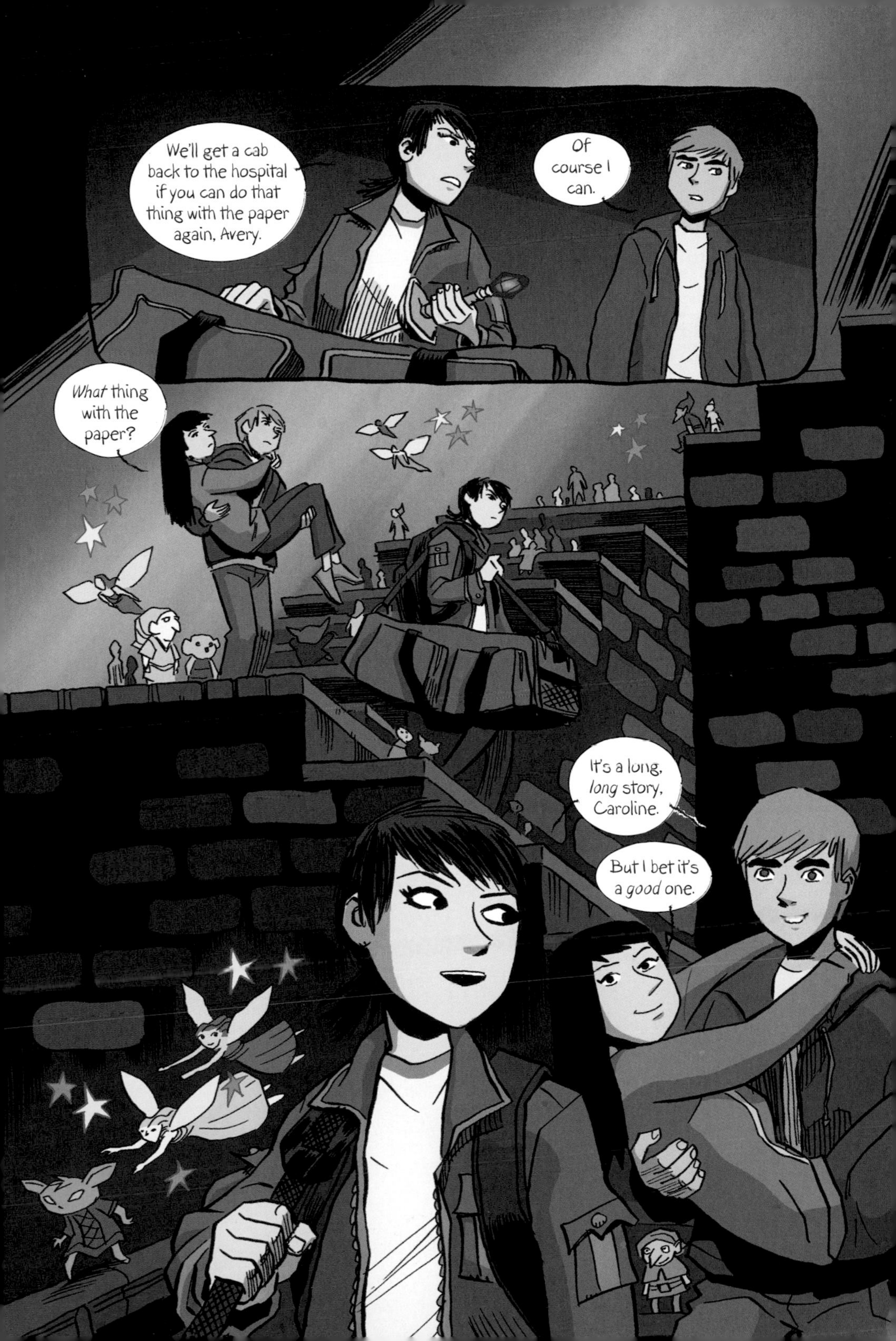
We'll get a cab back to the hospital if you can do that thing with the paper again, Avery.
Of course I can.
What thing with the paper?
It's a long, *long* story, Caroline.
But I bet it's a *good* one.

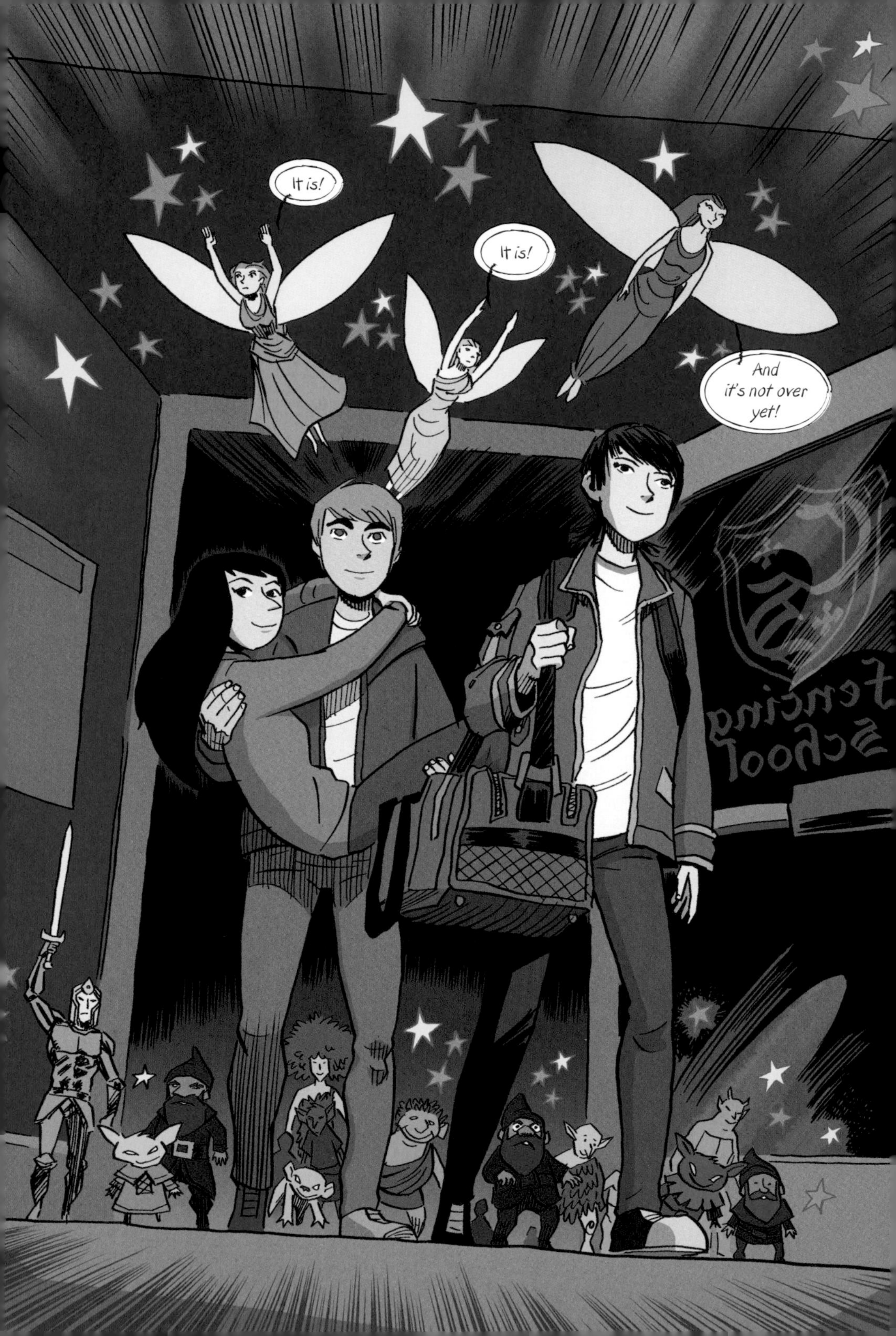
It is!
It is!
And it's not over yet!
Fencing School

FOR MADDISON JANE STEMPLE-PIATT, ONCE A FENCER, NOW A BALLET
DANCER, AND ALISON ISABELLE STEMPLE, WHO DOES MARTIAL ARTS.

FOR HEIDI STEMPLE, WHO ALWAYS GIVES GREAT ADVICE ON BOOKS,
FENCING, AND THE WHOLE WIDE WORLD.

FOR DEBORAH TURNER HARRIS FOR DINNERS AND PLOTTING SESSIONS.

AND FOR TANYA MCKINNON, THE BEST OF EDITORS, WHO ASKS QUESTIONS,
QUESTIONS, QUESTIONS, SOME OF WHICH I CAN ACTUALLY ANSWER.

−JANE YOLEN

TO MY PARENTS, FRANCESCO AND GEORGIA CAVALLARO, WITH
SPECIAL THANKS TO LISA NATOLI AND JOE MONTI.

−MIKE CAVALLARO

First Second

NEW YORK

TEXT COPYRIGHT © 2013 BY JANE YOLEN
ILLUSTRATIONS COPYRIGHT © 2013 BY MIKE CAVALLARO

PUBLISHED BY FIRST SECOND.

ALL RIGHTS RESERVED.

FIRST SECOND BOOKS ARE AVAILABLE FOR SPECIAL PROMOTIONS AND PREMIUMS. FOR DETAILS, CONTACT: DIRECTOR OF SPECIAL MARKETS, HOLTZBRINK PUBLISHERS.

COLORS BY GRACE LU

CHAPTER HEADING ILLUSTRATIONS COPYRIGHT © 2013 BY CHRIS SPENCER

FIRST EDITION 2013

FIRST

EDITION

ISBN: 978-1-59643-619-0

1 3 5 7 9 10 8 6 4 2

FIRST SECOND IS AN IMPRINT OF ROARING BROOK PRESS, A DIVISION OF HOLTZBRINCK PUBLISHING HOLDINGS LIMITED PARTNERSHIP 175 FIFTH AVENUE, NEW YORK, NY 10010

CATALOGING-IN-PUBLICATION DATA IS ON FILE AT THE LIBRARY OF CONGRESS.

PRINTED IN CHINA BY SOUTH CHINA PRINTING CO. LTD., DONGGUAN CITY, GUANGDONG PROVINCE

BY ART WE LIVE